J. D. WILLIAMS

Blessed by Song

First published by J. D. Williams Publishing 2026

First edition

ISBN: 979-8-9948859-0-1

This book was professionally typeset on Reedsy.
Find out more at reedsy.com

Contents

Blessed by Song

J.D. WILLIAMS

About Blessed by Song

The third book in the Julia Tate Song Series finds Julia floundering in a life-threatening crisis, while her young daughter Aria navigates a new school, and tries to maintain her cool around Luke, a guitar player who has her spinning. Julia's faithful husband Raine must manage their musical mix of a life as he battles the uncontrollable sea of change swirling around them all.

Julia Tate Song Series

Bound by Song leads Book 2, *Born by Song,* and Book 3, *Blessed by Song,* through the popular music industry as Julia Tate becomes a beloved singer-songwriter against all the odds, inspiring millions of fans. Julia strikes a powerful chord as she encourages women to follow their own dreams of career, motherhood, and love. The background world of music is positively intertwined throughout the books, adding to the allure of celebrity, while giving real insight into the challenging world of a popular recording artist.

Series: *Bound by Song, Born by Song* and *Blessed by Song.*

For more information, go to www.jdwilliamsbooks.com

Cover design: Author Services Australia, designer Britt Wilson.

First edition March 2026

Author's Note

First, I must apologize to my readers of Books 1 and 2 who have been waiting for Book 3. As characters Julia and Raine would do, I'll shoot you straight. In March of 2024, I was diagnosed with scleroderma, which was quite a surprise. I know everyone is dealing with something, so I won't dwell on it, but I've learned that I don't quite have the stamina I used to. Writing and editing take me a bit longer now, which is why it took more than two years to finish Book 3, *Blessed by Song*.

Second, Julia's story line in this book was difficult to write. Without spilling too many beans, if you read the epilogue of Book 2, you know Julia faces a breast cancer diagnosis. This disease is complex from both a diagnostic and treatment standpoint, and I hope I captured it accurately (see the Resources section). Like many of you, I've seen its impact up close—on family and friends. As I was finishing this book, my cousin Kim passed away from triple-negative breast cancer, a heartbreaking loss for everyone who knew and loved her.

To anyone affected or walking through this disease now, please know that my heart is with you and that I am listening. If there is anything you think I need to change in this book, you can email me at **info@jdwilliamsbooks.com**.

Finally, although I have two wonderful editors, we are a small team. If you happen to spot any editing or other errors, feel free to let me know at the same email address above.

Acknowledgments

Thank you to my family, friends, and followers for your support. To every person who has read pages, downloaded a digital book, ordered a paperback, given a rating and/or a review, or streamed a song, thank you isn't enough. Every review, like, comment, and share are greatly appreciated.

Thanks again to two wonderful editors (K and B). I truly value your feedback, expertise, and guidance. Working with you is an absolute delight.

Special thanks to Jill, Gary, Sydney, Levi, Sharon, Carol, Julie W., David Bradley (and The David Bradley Show podcast for the inspiration), Sharon (from Australia), Diane M., Joyce, Ken, Ron, Don, Roxann, Pamela, and Emlynn, for your support. I know I've probably missed a few people, but I see the likes and comments! Thanks to my dad for being the kind, wonderful person you are. Finally, thanks to Chris for supporting all my hours at the keyboard—I couldn't do this without you.

Lastly, as introduced in the epilogue in Book 2, *Born by Song,* and mentioned in the Author's Note, Julia faces a breast cancer diagnosis. Breast cancer has likely touched everyone in some way. I tried to take care with this disease, and those directly impacted. I referred to many resources in the development in this book, and those breast cancer and emotional health support resources are listed at the end of this book.

Dedication

I'd like to dedicate this book to my grandmother Marie, who was a wonderfully kind and very special person. She also made the most amazing cinnamon rolls and chocolate chip cookies. Her children, grandchildren, and great-grandchildren all miss her.

I'm also dedicating this book to Benji Kushner, who co-wrote the song "Free to Roam" with me. Benji was an *amazing* guitar player.

Chapter 1 – Julia

I'm standing on the side of the stage, anxiously waiting for my sixteen-year-old daughter to perform. I absentmindedly run my hand to my right breast and over the slight lump just as Raine saunters up, putting his arm around my side. I quickly drop my hand and grab his hand. I haven't been able to tell him about the spot because I don't want to worry him. He thinks my doctor's appointment tomorrow is just a regular appointment. He knows nothing about my previous scans, and I've been able to keep the biopsy from him. He looks down into my eyes, giving me a warm smile. The gray around his face and deepening wrinkles around his bright, bold green eyes make him appear distinguished and, to me, more handsome than ever. I lean into his frame as his arm grips me tighter, my head leaning into his chest.

"Was she nervous before she walked out there?" he asks.

I laugh as I look up at him and respond, "Are you kidding? She's my daughter. She about threw up over there on the side of the stage." And we both smile as Raine chuckles. Aria clearly inherited my stage fright. I continue, "I got her calmed down and focused. I think she's okay now."

"Good. She also has my confidence and she'll be fabulous."

"I have no doubt," I say, leaning back to give Raine a sideways glance as he leans down to kiss my cheek.

Just then, the band starts up and Aria's guitar strums through the speakers. Here we go! Aria's first real gig here in Nashville. I'm terrified for my baby girl, but in my heart, I know she'll pull through like I do and be great.

We stand backstage listening to Aria's short set of three songs. Aria had been asked by our good friend, and one of the artists Raine works with, Wayne Carson, to come out and sing a few songs at our local county fair. Several thousand people fill the outdoor covered bleachers, and even though they have no idea who she is, when they announced her full name, Aria Wagner, it sparked some recognition in the crowd that she's our daughter, and they gave her a slightly raucous welcome. Aria's performing a couple of covers, and then she'll sing a song that I wrote years ago, so some more people may recognize her then. But Aria specifically wants us to keep a low profile, and I totally get it. Even though our names open doors for her, there's a whole lot of pressure too.

As I listen to our girl belt out a few strong high notes, my mind drifts to my doctor's appointment. Several times when I tried saying something to Raine about it, I couldn't get the words out. I can't believe he hasn't noticed that something has been off with me, but Aria's show has been a good distraction, I guess. I also can't bear to see his look of helpless fear, just like the night when I miscarried our baby boy Jonah. It's the same look I had this morning after my shower, when the mist was still on the mirror. I took a swipe down the middle and was greeted by sheer, desperate terror.

My thoughts go to back to my doctor's appointment, and I say a quiet prayer to myself. *God, they need me. Please make this okay. It has to be okay.*

Chapter 2 – Julia

Dr. Henley catches me staring at her certificates and diplomas hanging on the back wall of her office. She's been my gynecologist, and obstetrician, and after all this time, I consider her a good friend. When she looks into my eyes, I instantly know. This isn't good news. Instantly the room grows colder, and I rub my upper arms. I should have worn a warmer sweater.

Dr. Henley takes her seat behind her desk as I walk over and sink into a chair in front of her.

I lead, "How bad is it?"

Dr. Henley tries to keep her voice light, but she always cuts to the chase, and I like this about her. "It's stage three, Julia. Could be better but could be worse. I've got you scheduled with an oncologist to discuss next steps and a treatment plan."

I'm nodding along but the numbness is starting to set in and there's a light buzzing in my ears, like I'm going to faint. This whole scene doesn't seem real. Now I'm really regretting not having Raine with me. I'm not catching every word as my mind is going down a million curved paths all at once. How am I going to tell Raine? What about Aria's schoolwork and what about the house, the animals and all of it?

Dr. Henley has been speaking the entire time, "My assistant out front has already arranged your appointment with an oncologist, Dr. Hunter, so we can get started on the right treatment right away. Julia, did you get that? Do you want me to call Raine?"

At the sound of his name, I snap back to awareness, "No … no, I'll call him. I'll handle this."

Dr. Henley asks, "I kind of thought Raine would've been with you today?"

I make a face like "are you kidding, you do remember my husband, right?" A slight smile flickers across her lips.

She continues, "Well, I've got some materials at the front desk for you that explain some of the next steps from chemotherapy to surgery and other targeted treatments. It will explain some of your options before you meet with the specialist. And if you need me to help explain anything to Raine, I can do that."

I nod and then instantly stand because now my face is growing hot and all I want to do is run from this room as the walls close in. Dr. Henley walks from behind her desk and takes me into her arms for an embrace. I hug her back, but everything seems distant and hollow, like I'm not really here.

I pull back and give her a nod and head to the front desk, where I talk to the assistant, get the materials, and confirm my next appointment for the following Monday.

As I drive away, still in a daze, my mind travels over the road I've been on for the past seventeen years, from winning the reality music show *Next Real Star;* to my second chance marrying the love of my life, Raine; losing Jonah, our first baby, which almost destroyed me and our marriage; finding the courage to continue on; and then having our daughter, Aria, and all the love, joy, struggles, and triumphs she brings to our lives. With Raine as stubborn and arrogant as he is, we still have our moments, but our marriage has survived a tough music industry that continues to challenge us.

After Aria was born, I took several years off and then I focused on songwriting. Thank God my writing is still in demand. I perform now and then, but for the most part, Raine's producing career has sustained us. So, I made sure our baby girl had the best life possible. Now, at fifty-seven, I'm facing the fight of my life.

How in the world am I ever going to tell Raine that it's cancer? *Fuck cancer.*

Chapter 3 – Aria

I pull my truck up to the front of the high school and peer up at the now empty building. I'll start my classes at this school, the Nashville School for Performing Arts, on Monday. I drove over here to see what all the fuss was about. Dad insists that I attend this school, and when he makes up his mind, I don't have a choice. I let out the huge sigh I'm always holding. Dad wants me to change to a public school right before my senior year, and even though I understand it's to help Mom, it really makes zero sense. I've been in a home-school pod all my life and I'll be more than a year ahead of everyone here. This will set me back and I'll have to postpone everything I'd planned for my music career.

As I pull away from the curb, I catch a young guy with longer dark brown hair, watching me. His hair hangs down a bit, and I can't get a good look at his face, but he's obviously staring at me. I give him a slight smile before he spins away, his long legs rushing him quickly out of my sight. Definite potential, I think as a sly smile crosses my lips. I gun the gas pedal and squeal out of the lot, catching my face in the rearview, and for just a moment, I see my mother staring back, and my chest tightens. Although my eyes are green, speckled with gold—not like her bright, bold sapphire blue—they're shaped like hers. I shake my hair down to cover my reminder. Although I purposefully try to look messy to catch people off guard, I've heard the words "you're striking" more than once.

I'm heading home and straight to Dad's studio. I know I'll find him there. He never stops working now. He's got to keep busy and that's a good thing. Dad can't be alone with his thoughts for too long. He's apt to crumble and go down a dangerous, addictive path, so I do everything I can to keep his mind straight. My stomach tightens at the thought that I could lose him. I have to do everything in my power to prevent that.

My mom, the beloved world-famous singer-songwriter Julia Tate, is in the fight of her life. Mom's been battling stage three-A breast cancer for a year now. They found a tumor near her breastbone and some cells in nearby lymph nodes. Mom had a round of chemo followed by a full mastectomy. All that treatment left her scary thin and tired all the time. At first, she tried continuing with everything as normally as possible, but eventually the fatigue took its toll. The hardest was losing her hair. I gaze at my reflection and my full head of hair. Yes, it's a superficial thing, but losing all your hair is devastating for women, I don't care what anyone says. It's a big part of a woman's identity. Mom tried to act like it was no big deal, but I knew better. I noticed her red, swollen eyes as she covered her head. In a messed-up way, I think she thought my dad would love her less. As if that would ever happen. My dad thinks she walks on water, but for some strange reason, with her illness and changes, I don't think she could see it anymore.

A heavy sigh escapes my throat when I think about my dad. We're so much alike. Stubborn with addictive personalities. Luckily, I've stayed away from any type of alcohol or drugs. I don't need to add that to my mix, but sometimes having something to ease my mind, even if temporary, seems like it would help. But I've decided to turn my focus on music and writing.

I pull up the drive to our house, park, and walk in. My dad, Raine Wagner, is one of the most successful producers and songwriters in Nashville. He's worked with country icon Bret Savage for years. Wayne Carson, the major country artist I got to open for last year, is another of his country superstar successes, among other acts in rock and other genres. Right now, Dad's working on a new project with Wayne, which I'm sure will be spectacular.

I walk through Dad's studio door and catch my father with his back to me, sitting at the control board, his favorite spot. At fifty-eight years old, his dark hair is thinning a bit on top, but he still has a lot of hair, with its signature spiky look on top. Dad's chair spins around. I guess you would call my dad handsome with his rugged, striking features. His bold green eyes come alive from when he's surrounded by the work he loves, but now there's always an undercurrent of sadness hanging over him. The same sadness we've both been lugging around for a year now.

"Wow … it's not even noon and you're up," he says, giving me a mischievous grin.

He gestures for me to sit down next to him, and I start to plant myself in a chair, but first he pulls me into a quick embrace as his lips graze the side of my head. My parents have always been affectionate with me. I chalk it up to having me at an older age. Both were over forty when I was born. Now that Mom's sick, I think these displays of affection are even more important to him.

"Funny. You told me to go over and check out the new school, so I did."

"And?" He spins his chair to look at me fully and raises up a bit expectantly, almost proud that I did something he asked.

I casually mess with some charts on his mixing board and avoid his eyes. "I'm sure it'll be cool. Noticed a cute boy outside of the building," I say with a glance from the corner of my eye. This will irk him. Dad will never handle me dating any boy … ever.

A dark look crosses his eyes. It worked. "And he'd better stay the heck away from you, young lady."

I roll my eyes, "Dad, I'm seventeen. Boys will happen one day. You'll have to face it."

"Not in my lifetime." I spot a brief flicker of terror cross his face. This happens every now and then, like he's thinking he'll have to manage all my crap by himself for the rest of my life. Instantly my heart plummets because I sometimes have these same thoughts. Dad quickly spins back around to his mixing board, hiding his face from me.

I change the subject, "It's cool, Dad. I'm sure I'll like the school." I can't stand seeing him upset and it happens a lot lately. "Wayne coming in today?"

"No, just comping vocals and finishing up a couple of mixes. You want to help me by cutting background vocals?" He looks back at me, a spark of life entering his eyes.

"I don't know … maybe. I'm supposed to meet Savannah at the mall in a couple of hours. I need new shoes for school."

My dad instantly reaches for his wallet, pulling out a wad of hundred-dollar bills.

I put out my hand in protest, "No, Dad, I'm good. I'll pay for them."

His shoulders slump. I should give him this. This is one thing he can do for me. In a small way it makes him feel better, so I change my mind. "Okay, a little bit will help." He smiles and forks over a couple hundred-dollar bills. More than enough.

My parents' relationship has always been complicated. They both have relayed their versions of how they tried to make it work, lost each other, and then "finally got it right." They've been together for eighteen years. Before Mom got sick, they rarely spent a night apart, and even during Mom's last stint at the hospital here in Nashville, Dad was at Mom's side every night. They have a rare love. It's more than true love; they're basically one person.

Dad asks excitedly, "You want to hear what we've got so far on Mom's song?"

I shuffle uncomfortably in my seat. It's one of the last songs my mom wrote before she got sick. Every time I hear it, it's hard to stay in control, and I'm big into control right now. If Dad plays it for me, I'll lose my shit in his studio.

"I think I'm going to go ahead and head to the mall. Maybe later?"

"Oh ... okay. No problem." He goes back to the console, and I can't see his face, but the disappointment is evident in his tone. Working on anything that has to do with Mom helps him.

Dad hits a button on the console and music instantly blares from the small speakers mounted in front of us. We're done talking. He'll play Mom's song over and over again. He talked Wayne Carson into recording it, and Wayne was lucky to get it. It's one of the best song's Mom's ever written.

"See ya, later, Dad." He waves his hand in the air but doesn't look back at me as he continues to mess with the dials on the recording console.

I find Savannah's number in my phone, and she picks up as I'm climbing into my truck. Dad insisted on getting me a new black Ford F-150. Another gift. He thinks these things will make up for all our fears.

"Hey girl," I say.

"How'd it go this time?" Savannah asks. She's very aware of what's going on right now.

"About as well as I thought it would. I'll meet you in by the cosmetic counters."

I climb into my truck and silently pray, asking God to watch over my father. With Mom gone, I constantly worry that something will take him over the edge.

My parents have always been open with me about everything that's happened during their lives together. I know all about their struggles and addictions. Mom told me about their ten-year love drama and how my dad is the love of her life, it just took him forever to figure that out. As I think about it, I can't help but smile. My dad is one stubborn S.O.B. One day, I hope to find a love like theirs. But that will be *years* from now. I need my own music career first. My parents want me to pursue music, but I want it more than they do. I want to be as good a writer, if not better than my mom. And I want to end up producing like my dad; that's my ultimate goal. It's not easy being the kid of famous parents. Everyone has expectations, but it's nothing like the expectations I put on myself. It's not just following in their footsteps; I have more to prove. I must be brilliant on top of being their kid. One thing's for sure; this new music school is serious business. I'll have to up my game.

I ease my truck down our driveway, hitting a button on my phone, and it goes to my favs, randomly selecting an old Tears for Fears song. I need something distracting right now.

I sing along, my dark, thick alto voice taking over the space in the cab of my truck. My voice is different than my mother's. She has a light, angelic, soprano voice—very pretty and easy listening. I'm like a truck barreling down the highway, loud and boisterous. It's like they put my dad's voice in my body. I have more of his frame, too. I'm feminine looking, but I'm taller and thicker than my mom. I stand a good five inches over her. I sing along as I head down the road to meet my friend.

Going to the mall and getting new shoes is an excuse. While I do need new shoes for school, it's more that I need to keep myself busy. Another loud, heavy sigh escapes me. I wonder what Mom is doing right now? I haven't talked to her this week. I should call her, but she always sounds so tired, and every time I get on the phone with her is a bit terrifying. I'd give anything to go back to normal when she was here, bugging the crap out of me to finish my schoolwork, or to clean out the horses' stalls. God, how I miss her.

Chapter 4 – Raine

My back is toward the console, and I focus on taking deep breaths as tears form on my lashes. It seems like I'm constantly holding them back and failing miserably. The sound of Aria crinkling her things and putting them in her bag reaches me. She says goodbye and I awkwardly put my hand up in return, but I don't dare look at her. I can't. Aria's worried about me; everyone is. And they should be. I'm worried too.

I hit "play" on the console. The soft sound of a piano drifts through the room, followed by strings, a cello, and violin. Julia loves stringed instruments, especially the cello. Wayne came in the day before and cut a vocal on the song, and although it's a powerful performance, it's not quite right. The song needs more emotion. Julia's song is about rising through loss, and it's amazing and incredibly unique. Wayne used the word "authentic." I agree. Julia wrote the first verse about her dad and how he took care of six kids all alone. The second verse is about a man staying by the side of his wife while she's sick, and it's obvious where she got much of that. And the third verse. Well, that verse is something else entirely and it's about our Savior dying on the cross. I haven't asked Julia about that verse yet. I figure she'll tell me about it when she wants to.

My eyes keep darting to a family picture on top of the console. It captures one of the best days of our lives, when Aria was born. After suffering through so many difficult days, it seems like yesterday. Julia's face is glowing with excitement because they had just put tiny Aria on her chest, and I leaned down next to Julia's face for the photo.

My phone rings, starling me. It's Julia's twin sister Jody. She checks on me every couple of days.

"Hey Jod."

"Did I catch you at a bad time?"

"Just working on a new song. I've got time."

"I checked on flights. We can visit next week before everyone goes back to school. Will that work?"

"Does for me, but I need to check with Aria," I reply. "She's the one with the busy schedule. You know … teenagers." A light laughter escapes me, but it seems hollow and out of body.

Jody and her family live in Montana. She and Julia are incredibly close, and being around Jody and her family will be comforting right now.

"Well, we'll plan on heading down there next week and if something changes, we'll move the flights. Sound good?"

"Sounds great. Looking forward to it. I'll get back to you tomorrow to confirm."

Having Jody here will do us good. Through this entire nightmare, just having Jody nearby has helped keep my head on straight when so many times it seemed like it was about to pop off. I hit a button again on my console and the sound of strings blares from my front speakers. God, I wish Julia were here to hear this. I can control this; my work in the studio is the only thing I can manage right now, which is why I'm even more determined to make this song the biggest of Julia's career. This song has Song of the Year written all over it. I've got to make it perfect.

Chapter 5 – Julia

I'm sitting in my hospital room waiting for my third doctor to come and do their thing. It's a regular occurrence; they come in and do their regular blood pressure, pulse, and other checks, and then they walk through what they are going to do today. Some days it's a transfusion of my therapy drugs, or I meet with a physical therapist to keep my body and energy up, but most days I'm stuck in this room bored out of my mind.

I've got too much time on my hands and way too much time to think, which often leads me to look in the mirror at how much my face and body have changed. Usually I gasp at the bloated, short-haired, tired image looking back at me. Not the road I like to go down. At least I can take walks in the garden area when I feel up to it. In an odd way it keeps me sane to have this regular routine after so many months of uncertainty with this disease.

I've been down at this Texas cancer center off and on for the past several months. I've got a counselor here too and she's walked me through what I'm going through and feeling. It's a lot like the grief I went through when I lost Jonah. I'm well past denial and I accept what I'm going through, but I don't think I'll ever accept this weird grayish short hair that's slowing growing in.

Almost one year ago, I sat Raine down and gave him the news that I had stage three breast cancer. That was all I knew at the time. I didn't know the details of what kind of tumor cells I had, or what the treatment would entail. Just that gory bit of information. Then I had to tell Aria, and that's one memory, specifically the stunned look of shock, that I'd like to remove my from mind.

I found out my tumor cells were HER2 positive and that the cells had spread to my lymph nodes on my right side. For breast cancer, only about 20 percent of people have this kind. It's aggressive. They started me on a targeted form of chemotherapy right away. Not fun. Before, I was struggling to lose weight, but chemo wasn't the answer I was looking for … and then I started to lose my hair. I know people tell you it will grow back, wigs look normal, all that bull crap, but when my hair started falling out into clumps, the tears fell. A daily stream of tears.

That's when the real terror appeared on Raine's face, and I hated seeing that. Since then, I've seen that look too often. Raine doesn't do well with blood or hospitals since we lost our baby boy Jonah so many years ago. I pause as those memories flood in. Cancer doesn't seem like anything compared to losing Jonah.

The doctors started me on the chemo to try and kill any cells that may have traveled outside of my breast and lymph nodes. Then came the surgery. A double mastectomy followed by reconstruction. The mastectomy wasn't that bad. Sure, there was pain and my breasts were just gone. But one week later they went in to rebuild both breasts, taking flesh from my stomach and a bit from my thighs. That was something I wouldn't wish on anyone, not even my worst enemy. One month of not being able to pick up anything over my head or really do anything. I don't do helpless well … not at all. Luckily, my best friend and personal assistant Tracy was there to help, and my sister Jody flew in from Montana. Without them, our household "car" would have crashed. No one would have eaten, made their appointments, or anything. That's when I realized how much Raine and Aria depend on me for everything in our day-to-day lives. That's also when the real soul-crushing panic took a hold of my heart. It has been lodged there every day.

Months of overwhelming nausea, and being too tired to get out of bed but I tried to act like everything was normal when it wasn't. It wasn't at all. I couldn't ride my horses or even brush them. Then after Dr. Hunter walked me through the targeted treatments down here in Texas, I've been preparing my mind for anything that might come next.

Of course, I read everything I can and have been asking my doctors a zillion questions. I have the kind of breast cancer that can spread to other parts of my body. That's why they wanted me to come down to Texas for this treatment. Today I'll find out if they think I'm done and can finally head back home.

I look out the window of my room and think back on those months in Nashville when I was going through chemo and surgery, and although they were the toughest weeks I've ever had in my life, they were also some of the sweetest moments ever. I was surrounded by all the people I love more than air. I would do anything right now to see their faces. My phone buzzes. It's Raine with his daily check-in.

Chapter 6 – Raine

I'm finally closing down the studio for the day. Earlier, Wayne dropped by the studio to put down a new vocal on Julia's song. I still think we can make it better, but it's remarkably close to the unattainable sound that's playing non-stop in my head. We'll get there and I'll know when it's right. Wayne also recorded background tracks, and the song is really coming to life.

Julia is probably finishing up her daily set of tests down in Texas, so I hit the button to call her.

"I was hoping you'd try me today," Julia's out of breath response always catches me off guard.

"Is this a good time?"

"Waiting on the doctors for my third round of fun. You know the routine."

I grimace but try to keep my voice light, "We had a good day today, babe. I can't wait to play your song for you. God, I miss you." As I talk, my hand instinctively goes to my chest, trying to steady my breath. I have this never-ending dull ache as I think about what the love of my life is going through. I'd be right there with her, but I've got to keep working. Physically trying to calm myself is one of the ways I keep myself from my liquor cabinet. After all these years of being clean, I'm still an alcoholic, and every minute is a struggle. I quit my beloved bourbon, but I can still taste it, especially when my stress is high.

"I'm sure it's great, Raine, and I can't wait to hear it, especially with Wayne singing on it. But you know all I care about is you and Aria. Are you eating? Is our girl okay?"

I can't help but smile as I casually tell our daily little white lie, "I'm good, kid, and Aria is doing great. She went and checked out her new school today. I think she'll like it once she gives it a chance."

Her sigh echoes over the phone.

"Jules? What's up ...really?"

"Sweetheart, I'm okay. I just miss you two, you know that."

"Did the doctors say if next week is a go? Do you get to come home?" My voice drops at the end. I can't help it.

"They'll confirm it when they come in, but should be a go. I'm planning on leaving in a couple of days."

"I wish you'd let me fly out and travel with you. What if something happens and you need help?"

Exasperation fills her independent voice. "Raine, I'll be fine. I've been getting stronger. We don't need to spend any money that we don't have to."

"I don't care about the money. All I care about is you, you know that."

"I do know that, but there is no need. I'll be fine."

I'm getting pissed 'cause she won't let me help, so I change the subject. "Jody and the family are coming in next week too. They want to see you."

"Good. It'll be good to see them." There's an uncomfortable pause, like we both don't know what to say. "Well, hon, doc just came to the door. I'd better go. I'll text you later if there's a change."

I frown at the thought of more doctors coming in for their usual pokes and prods. Julia's a champ, but it would try every nerve in my being. "Alright, I'll call you tomorrow around this time."

"Sounds good, babe. And Raine ... I'll be fine, I promise. Love you."

I can't help but smile at her clearly exasperated but motherly tone. "Yes, dear. Love you, too."

I press "end" and absentmindedly my hand runs up my face and through my hair. For the past several months, if not a year, all I am is tired. I'm tired of all this crap.

As I leave my studio and start to walk around our big empty house, I swear I smell her perfume. Julia put so much love into this house, and I smile every time I think about all the spots where we've made love, when Aria wasn't at home, of course.

I go out the front door and look down the massive drive, remembering the day we moved in. Julia was like a little kid, excitedly traipsing through every room and taking in the view out back. Now we have the horses that we take care of. It was always Julia's dream to provide a sanctuary for animals. We have five horses, two dogs, and a few barn cats roaming around. Since she's been sick, it's my responsibility to feed all the animals and make sure they're taken care of. Before, Julia took care of them and she loved it. She loves taking care of all of us.

I walk back inside toward the kitchen and head for the refrigerator knowing that when I open it, I'll just stare at the contents. I never want to eat, but I make myself. I'm always anxious now, like I'm coming out of my skin. I need to be doing something, anything. Anything to keep my mind off the fact that I'm here alone and she's down in Texas.

I wonder if Aria is still up. Her truck was parked in the garage when I walked outside. I walk back to the main foyer, passing walls lined with gold and platinum records, awards, and pictures of our life. I don't want to look closely at these walls. Too many reminders of happier, easier times when all three of us were together. Aria fills most of the pictures and I'm okay with those pictures, just not the ones with Julia.

I make it to the top of the stairs and look down at the hall toward Aria's room. Her light's out, so I head down to my bedroom and the part of the house that currently haunts me. I picture Julia everywhere and the smell of her lingers on all her clothes. I pause at the doorway of the closet I built for her after we lost Jonah. I flick the light on. Her perfectly lined up shoes and clothes match her obsessively punctual personality. I smile as I run my hand down her dresses, pausing on one gown. It's the one she wore when I won my first music award with Bret Savage.

That night at the country music awards, Julia told me we'd win as our SUV pulled up to the red carpet. She grabbed my hand and made me look at her. She'd said these words with an all-knowing confidence that made me stop cold.

"You will win tonight," she said as her eyes danced with excitement.

"Baby, either way, I've won," I replied.

"No." She moved her hand up to my face and made me look at her. "You will win, and you'd better be ready with your speech." She looked straight into my eyes with such seriousness that it took my breath.

She was right. Not only did we win Album of the Year, but we also won the award for Song of the Year. After celebrating for hours that night, all I wanted to do was get her back to our room. I'm quite sure we conceived Aria that night. I smile as I think about that wonderful memory.

Julia has always had a sixth sense. She knows when something is up and can sense when something is wrong. I'm convinced she knew she had breast cancer months before her mammogram. She'd already started planning. Of course, I didn't realize it then but looking back, she'd known. She started preparing the house and her affairs even before she had her tests back.

I walk over and collapse on our bed, letting the softness of the mattress engulf me. As I stare up at the ceiling, my mind drifts to changes we need to make to Julia's song. When it comes to music, especially her song, my mind never rests.

I close my eyes for a moment as I picture Julia lying next to me, laughing at something I said. God … I miss her, but it's more than that. I don't work right when she's not here. I hold the memory in my mind for as long as I can before it fades, like these memories always do. A single tear rolls down the side of my face, and I let it hit the pillow. Then I silently pray, as I do most nights, that God will bring her back home healed and that this chapter of our lives is over. I'll get the love of my life back home where she belongs.

This night, I dream about Julia. It's a recurring dream that I've had while she's been away. I'm in the hospital, and I'm searching and searching, but I can't find her room. I'm running down empty corridors and calling out for her. I pass nurses who walk by me in silence, but no one looks at me. I stop at room after room, running down hallways that never end.

I wake up with a start, sweat soaking through my T-shirt and boxers. Realizing it was my same, tired dream, I pull off my clothes and walk to the bathroom for a towel to dry out my soaked hair. I glance at the alarm clock.

It's almost six. I slept three hours longer than usual.

I fall back against the pillows and run my hands over Julia's side of the bed trying to picture her there next to me. Just a few days, that's all I have to wait until she's home. These past few weeks were eerily similar to when she left our home and went to Montana after Jonah died. It's been more than difficult not to fall back into my old habits. Having Aria here helps keep me from doing anything stupid, that and the fact that my good friend Bret will tear me in two if I step out of line.

One of the best parts of my morning is that I have time to remember Julia's touch. I can picture her here with me and I hold on to these memories for as long as I can before I pull the covers back to start my day.

Chapter 7 – Aria

I'm lying in bed listening to songs on my iPad when I do an internet search on my new school. Of course, I'm curious about the new guy who was hanging out in front, and I want to see if I can find him. Soon, I'm not disappointed. The third item on the home page is about a concert held the previous spring. I scroll down the page and there he is. Not like he's a Greek god or anything like that, but with his olive-colored skin and those dreamy long locks, he comes close. It's hard not to stare at his image.

There's his name: Luke Greyson. My new crush. I've had a few, but never one that's lasted very long. As soon as someone gets too close, I end it. And I know why. I don't want to get too close or get hurt, not after dealing with Mom. It's all about control and I'm big into control right now. I know this about myself. But man alive, Luke's more than hot. Based on the article with his photo, he was one of the lead guitar players in last spring's show. Figures. I'm just like my mother. We both have a thing for guitar players, I think with a smile and a familiar pang hits my chest as my mind wanders to my mom. I shake my head to get back to the task at hand. Of course, my father never knows about any of my crushes. My mom knows a little bit 'cause we've talked about it. Mom's not naïve, but at seventeen, of course, I'm a virgin and Mom knows. I sigh thinking about the most uncomfortable conversations I've ever had, and a smirk takes over my lips remembering our condom talk. Mom gave me condoms not knowing I didn't need them.

I think Mom's proud that I'm still a virgin. We often talked about how important respect is in any relationship. Mom told me how she'd made many mistakes with men. But once she fell in love with Dad, he was the only man she ever truly wanted.

I continue perusing the school's website and find Luke's bio. It's impressive. He's had leads in the school's musicals, and other performances in and out of the school. He's done local theater, but there's a national commercial on the list. It also says he was a lead guitarist on other songs throughout his time there. There it is, more icing, I mull as my eyes continue scanning his gorgeous features on the screen.

The students at my new school are serious musicians. Some are already working professionally. I've worked as a background singer for my parents, and I've performed live with my own band a couple of times, but with parents like mine, those experiences were handed to me.

I silently worry that I won't live up to expectations. Do I really have what it takes? I log out of my iPad and stand, staring into my full-length mirror. I tug at my oversized shirt, trying to cover my hips. I'm a full-figured girl. Not heavy, but I have curves. Thank God I have long legs; they're the one part of my body I actually like. I cock my head to one side studying myself hard. Am I pretty? I'm not sure. My long, dark hair, like my mother's, is thick, but not very trendy. I rarely take time to fix it up properly. What's the point? But for the first time, I wonder if I should care to look hip. I pick up my cell phone and dial my hairstylist.

"Yeah, I'd like to make an appointment on Saturday. Noon is fine. A long pause ... a cut and, you know, highlights or some color. And a mini-facial too ... could you connect me with the spa?"

I end up booking a pedicure and manicure too. I contemplate a massage but decide against it. Although I have money at my disposal, I'm still conscious of spending too much of my parents' fortune. They both worked hard for it, and I don't want to be reckless.

I hang up the phone and smile. Luke, huh ... now I have a reason to be excited about this school. At least it gets my mind off everything else.

Chapter 8 – Aria

The following morning, I stare up at the ceiling, replaying a fight I had with Mom a few days before she left for her treatment in Texas. I regret that day more than anything, and a familiar lump forms in my throat as my words drum along in my mind.

"Promise me you'll help him," Mom said, her voice raspy, probably from her own worry, and from the tears she's holding back.

"Mom, of course, he'll be fine. He's too stubborn to want my help, but of course."

Mom rubbed a hand across her brow as she absentmindedly rolled her clearly tense neck. "Aria … I need you to take this seriously. You're the only person to get him through this. I don't want to put this pressure on you, but he'll dwell on this … my not being here will get in his head. You've got talk to him. Keep him busy, things like that."

I picked up my phone and started scrolling, anything to not look at her. "I'll do what I can, Mom. But I can't talk about this anymore. I just can't. You'll be fine and back here before you know it."

And there it was. I deflected and put her off 'cause I couldn't handle it. Mom reached over to squeeze my hand, but she didn't say another word. She didn't have to. I'd disappointed her and that's the last thing I wanted to do.

I stagger out of bed and walk to a full-length mirror catching a quick glance, grimacing at my slovenly reflection. I shower and then head down to the kitchen. It's Saturday and Dad beat me there, a cup of steaming coffee in his hand, with music charts stretched out before him on the counter.

"Hey, baby girl. Sleep okay?"

"Sure," I lie. "You?"

"Of course, like a baby," Dad replies dryly.

An awkward glance passes between us. We're both lying and trying to convince each other to buy it, which is really getting old. I walk past him to the cupboard and grab my own mug and fill it to the brim. I open the fridge and pass on anything before planting my butt down hard at a bar seat at the counter.

"What are your plans today? The mall?" Dad asks.

"Jeez. No. I do more than go to the mall, Dad." He laughs as a disgusted look crosses my face. "I'm going to the salon and then the library."

Dad's eyebrows go up with some surprise before he continues, "How about we make dinner tonight, kid?"

"You've got it, but I'll cook. I'm better than you." Sarcasm drips from my lips. This I get from my dad.

He laughs out loud but nods in agreement. He starts to walk out of the kitchen, charts in hand, obviously heading toward his studio.

"Bye, baby girl. I'll call you later," he calls out. He gives me a glance, and I nod back as I drink my coffee, giving him a thumbs-up.

When I reach the library, I pull into a stall and cut the engine. Then I take a good look in the rearview. I love my new trim and hair color, and the facial gave my tired and drab skin a good, healthy glow. I jump out, grabbing my purse. The library is one of my favorite places, but again, I'm reminded of my mom. We spent countless hours here. We both love books and would trade the same romance novels back and forth.

As I walk through the front door, I do a quick double take and then quickly duck down taking cover. Luke, *that* Luke, the one guy I was practically cyber stalking, walks through the metal detector in front of me heading toward a tall stack of non-fiction books. I'm instantly wiping at the puddle of sweat across my brow. Great. That'll be attractive. I want to meet this guy, but not now. Even though I'm all done up from the salon, I didn't envision this kind of meet and greet.

I stand from my crouched position, hesitating slightly, hoping it will give him time to move on. Then I slowly follow through the detectors toward the tall stacks of fiction books, and where I hope is safety. I swivel my head, casually peering around for him, and then I cautiously sneak toward the "R" section. Why do boys have this effect on me? Yeah, I talk a big game, but when it comes down to it and a guy tries to talk to me, I'm a big pile of mush. The superstars in Dad's studio don't bother me. Maybe it's 'cause I grew up around them. But if there's a cute guy standing in front of me, I'm a total doofus. I round a tall row of books and slam right into Luke, my purse scattering to the floor and everything tumbling out of it.

"Oh! … I'm so sorry," I stammer, instantly dropping to my knees on the floor, trying to gather all my belongings with one hand while rubbing my head with the other. But I don't dare look at him. If he sees my face right now, the bead of sweat rolling down my forehead will reveal everything.

Luke drops to the ground next to me and his knee casually rubs against mine. It's a good thing I'm wearing jeans, because a spark shoots up my spine. When we hit heads, his books scattered too, and his long arms stretch out to grab them. I peek at the titles, "Guitar for Exceptional Players" and there's another on chord progressions. Obviously, he's not a slacker guitar player.

His calm, serene voice soothes my senses. "You sure are quiet on your feet. I didn't hear a sound before we collided," Luke says, straightening his long legs while organizing his books back under his arm. He puts his hand out to help me up, scoring several points.

I take his hand, and for the first time, I gaze into the most gorgeous, deep brown eyes that, at present, sear into my soul. I slowly come to a standing position, dumbfounded. I haven't said anything back because any chance I'll form any semblance of a word is lost. All I do is stare at him. Not only will he think I'm a klutz, but dumb, too.

Finally, I discover words again, "I'm stealthy … I mean good like that. "And, you know, this is a library. Just trying to be a quiet." I snatch my now burning hand back from his touch, just in time to catch the bead of sweat before it makes it all the way down my face.

One corner of his lustrous mouth rises slightly and his eyes dance. "I'm Luke," he says boldly, his eyes staying locked with mine.

I mutter back, "Aria."

"Yes, I know," he says, reaching his hand back out toward me.

I don't think I can touch him again, but I slowly put my hand back out, take his grip in mine and it's glorious. A tingle rolls up my arm. I just hope it doesn't show up on my face. "How do you know my name?" I ask.

"Your parents aren't exactly unknown," he says with a slight laugh. "And I was at a concert when you sang back-up." There's a slight pause. "Not bad. I might add."

He's of course referring to my singing, but, in my mind, I wish he were referring to something else about me. I can't read anything in his eyes about that.

His words strike me. "Not bad?" I reply with slight ironic disgust, my arms folding across my chest. "Who do you consider 'good'?" For a moment, an image of my mom flashes before me. She'd say these words; they aren't something I'd typically say, and it makes me stand a bit taller. I'm glad this part of her has rubbed off on me.

"Aretha Franklin, Adele, Whitney, when she was in her prime."

"I have something to aspire to then," I say with obvious sarcasm. "All artists with a supernatural talent that's almost impossible to reach."

Luke looks directly into my eyes and just smiles. My breath catches. I hope I don't appear as obviously taken on the outside as I am on the inside—but my body is totally betraying me right now.

My hand goes through my newly coiffed hair. I can't seem to stop moving. Luke, on the other hand, is standing still and he seems so calm, like he doesn't have a care in the world. I change the subject. "I've never noticed you at this branch. Do you come here often?"

Luke chuckles, at me or my cliché, I'm not really sure. "Only on my off days. I had to pick up a few more guitar books. Can't stop learning, you know." He gestures at the books in his hands with his words.

I nod. Again, I'm silent. Words still escape me. Finally, a sentence squeaks out. "What do you mean, only on off days?"

His eyes continue to hold mine, "I work part-time at the guitar shop on Broadway. You know, the one on the corner? I give lessons there."

"Oh." I look down at my feet during our pause.

"Well, I guess I'll leave you to the fiction section," he says, nodding toward the books lined up in the stacks.

Again, all I can do is nod. Luke semi-laughs before he leaves. I stand there like a dope, watching as he glances back, giving me a slight wave as he casually saunters away. My limp hand goes up in reply. I slide away and quickly run around a stack of books.

As I duck behind the stack, I slap myself on the forehead as I silently berate myself. *Idiot! You are a complete IDIOT! Jeez, was that the first time you talked to a boy?*

Obviously, it wasn't, but never has any guy, especially one that handsome with the eyes the color of coffee with a hint of cream, left me so defenseless. I sway slightly and then lean heavily against the stack, trying to gain any sense of composure. Then, I smile. Well, it's a start. I met him. After several moments, I spin around and search for a familiar author hoping a good book will calm my nerves.

I finish gathering my stack of romantic fiction and then walk over to the non-fiction music section, curious about Luke's guitar books. I play a bit of guitar, but just chords. I wonder if I should challenge myself. I also play a little piano, thanks to my parents making me take lessons. I pick up a book on guitar technique when I notice a biography about my mom sitting on a nearby shelf. It's written by someone who was a friend of my parents at one time. This low life wrote the book based on their private conversations and other innuendo. It's not an authorized autobiography.

I seethe as I stare at it. I hate this type of smut. Although it praises my mom for her work, it portrays her as weak with a bad taste in men. It portrays my father as a selfish, arrogant addict ... far from the truth. True, my dad has a strong personality, but he's more than his addiction. I absolutely loathe this book. I wonder if Luke noticed it. For the first time I'm worried about one person in particular reading this crap, and it stops me.

I'm tempted to grab the book from the shelves, take it home and destroy it, but I pause and look through the pages. My heart drops when I get to a family picture in the middle of the book. Mom's healthy, with her long, dark hair, well before she got sick. We all have big, genuine smiles. That seems like ages ago.

Screw this writer. One day I'll turn the tables and write one about him. We'll see how he likes that. I keep the guitar book in my hand and head to the check-out. I have a new goal. I'm going to learn how to play guitar better, not just rhythm, and surprise everyone. Including myself.

Chapter 9 – Luke

I finally have time after work to run by the library. After picking up the guitar books I wanted in the non-fiction stacks, I remember a book in fiction I wanted. That's when I see her. Aria Wagner. She moves quickly toward the fiction section, ducking down and moving like she's running from a fire. I'd secretly hoped I would get the chance to meet her before school started and now, here I am. I couldn't miss her checking out our school the other day, and one of the school's administrators confirmed that she'll be joining us.

I head straight in her direction, absentmindedly straightening my shirt, and I shake my mop of hair hoping it lands in any sort of order. I pray I don't have anything in my teeth.

She's walking so fast that I think I've lost her. I stop in the "S" section and then turn toward "R," hoping to catch her trail when, BAM … I run smack dab into her.

After our brief and very disconcerting encounter, a huge grin fills my face. She seemed more nervous than I was, and I instantly liked her. There's a sadness about her, but you can't deny there's also a fierceness there, and I love it.

During our brief interaction, I've already gathered she'll be a worthy adversary in class, and I love a good challenge. Her sadness, or maybe it's more like wariness, intrigues me. She tries to hide it, but it's there in her eyes, and man, those eyes. I got tangled up in those bold green eyes. Her other parts are equally appealing, as I picture the image of her figure in my mind. She's in great shape, that's easy to see. She's not too thin like so many girls these days. In jeans and a simple shirt, she's voluptuous in the right places.

I boldly walk toward the library check-out, quickly scan my books, and then stride toward my old blue truck, oblivious to the beautiful brunette peering out of an upper story window watching my every step.

Chapter 10 – Julia

"They've done everything they can do here, Trace. So, thank God, I get to fly home on Wednesday." It's my weekly call with my best friend, confidant, and personal assistant. We've known each other for more than thirty years and she's been through so much with me. I don't hide anything from her.

"Well, it's about time. What are they saying? Do they think it's all gone?"

"The doctor's said it's looking good, but I'll find out for sure when I get home. They'll follow up with Dr. Henley back in Nashville, but the scans here are showing no signs of cancer." My voice catches at the end. It don't know if I believe it myself, not after the chemo, losing my hair, these treatments and the nausea, diarrhea, all of it. And the entire time being consumed with an overwhelming fatigue. I've even developed this weird rash out of nowhere. Somehow I hope that goes away before I go home. I make a mental note to ask my doctor about it.

Tracy's voice is soothing, "Thank, God, Jules. I'm sure Raine is relieved."

"Trace, Raine worries how the sun is going to come up. I can tell him that things look good, but you know him, he worries and worries, and worries some more. He won't believe anything until he sees me."

She laughs because she also knows him too well. "Raine said Jody is coming in too … do you think he'll plan a big party or something?"

"Oh, good night, I hope not. I need things to quiet down for a while. It's okay if you and my family are there, but no more than that. Make sure he doesn't go overboard, okay?" I practically plead with my good friend.

"I'm on it," she says with all seriousness.

"I can always count on you, my wing man," I say with a chortle.

Tracy adds, "If people only knew."

And for the first time in a while, we both laugh from shared memories.

I'm brought back to reality when we hang up. Yes, doctors here are hopeful, and the scans look good, but no one will say for sure if I'm totally in the clear. No one wants to go that far ... yet. And I'm frustrated. I want a clear-cut answer, but I try to remember that in life, there's whole lot of gray. Not easy for someone who wants everything in black and white. It doesn't keep me from continuing to ask a ton of questions though. I know I'm totally driving them crazy.

I do know one thing: I can't wait to leave these sterile white rooms and get back to the color of my Tennessee home. If I never see another white wall, I'll be happy. In fact, I'm thinking we need to add color to our house. I don't ever want to see a white wall again. Not ever.

I've already started pulling my things out of the closet and drawers and putting them in my bags. Luckily, I've had my own room the entire time I've been down here. One of the perks of having a comfortable life is that we can afford it, and I don't take that for granted. So many don't have this luxury or health care at all, and I'm grateful that we planned well.

I've set up an appointment with Dr. Henley to go over the results when I'm back in Nashville, and any next steps. I pray to God that we finally get some answers, that I'll soon start aftercare and can get on with my life. I'm tired of being a burden on my family. I don't want them to have to deal with any of this crap. I look down at my arm that's got this red streak running down it. And God help me; they've got to give me something to help with this awful rash.

Chapter 11 – Raine

I'm at my console when Wayne walks in the studio door at the house. Although it's a Sunday, weekends don't mean anything to musicians, artists, and producers.

"Raine, man, this sounds great!" Wayne exclaims as he nods along to the latest version of Julia's song. "I love what you've done."

I'd been obsessing over a new mix all morning and I've added a new upright bass track, which adds warmth to the tone of the song. "Thanks, man. Been working hard on this one. You up to cutting another vocal today?"

Wayne gives me a generous smile, "That's why I'm here. I've got a good one in me today."

I nod, gesturing toward the vocal booth. "It's ready to go."

Wayne smiles as he grabs a bottle of water and the lyric sheet before heading off to the soundproof booth that adjoins my main room. When he's ready to roll, I play the new mix so he can get a feel for the changes. A relaxed smile crossing my face, I nod to my recording engineer, Max, that we're ready to start. I can feel this one in my bones. Today is the day we're going to record vocals on the next Song of the Year. I just know it.

I'm leaning back in my chair hours later when I know we've got it. I say, "Great work, Wayne."

"Thanks, buddy. Julia will be so proud when she hears this."

I nod at him as a large lump fills my throat. Luckily, my sound engineer Max interrupts. "Wayne, do you want a copy to take with you?"

"That'd be great."

I raise my hands back over my head for a good long stretch. Sitting for six hours straight is never a good thing, and my back is killing me. This is when I really want a glass of bourbon—to help ease my back pain. Coupled with missing Julia, this is when it gets hard for me.

"Thanks again for giving me this song," Wayne says, grabbing his copy, and giving me a good friendly goodbye clap on my back.

"You bet. You're the only one who could sing it the way that Julia would want."

"It feels good to finish that one," I say to Max after Wayne walks out the door.

"It's the best song you've ever done, man. I'm not kidding." He gives me an appreciative nod.

"I hope you're right, Max. To win Song of the Year, it has to be."

Later, as I'm listening to the song alone, tears stream down my face. It's absolutely beautiful, and Jules will love it.

I eventually get myself together and head down the hallway toward the kitchen. Aria's noisily clanging pans in the kitchen. She gives me a sly grin when I enter the room.

"I've got everything prepped; we just need to get these babies on the grill," she says, gesturing to two huge steaks sitting all seasoned and ready to go. "You up for it?"

"Shit ... I mean shoot. Who do you think you are talking to?" I say, taking a little bow and she laughs.

I He-Man pick up the steaks and stride toward the back screen door and out onto our back patio. Aria follows along as I assume my power stance in front of the grill. We have a small fridge outside, and I grab a bottle of water, humming as I do. I take the two slabs of meat and gingerly place them on the hot grill.

Aria grabs a soda from the fridge and slides into a patio chair, staring out at our back pasture. Two horses are out of the barn, casually grazing in a nearby field. It's a serene moment and one I'll treasure; I just wish Julia were here with us. Thank God she'll be home soon.

Reezie brings me back to earth. "So, how'd it go with Wayne? Did you finish the song?"

"We did. It's magical. I can't wait to play it for you both Wednesday night when your mom gets home."

There's a sigh from Aria and I'm not sure if she's aware she did it.

I pause for a moment before continuing, "I really want you to sing back-up on the song though. It'd give it that little special something."

Her eyes light up, "How about when Mom gets back, we sing on it together?"

"She'd love that," I say with a smile, while I casually flip our steaks that are sizzling nicely on the grill as an amazing aroma drifts into the air.

"I'm physically drooling, dad. I haven't been this hungry in months," Aria adds.

"Well. It looks like we're almost there. What else are we having with these? Not just steak, I hope?"

Aria rolls her eyes. "Already taken care of, hoss, I mean DAD. I made a salad and picked up some of that potato salad you like from the deli. Should have all your favorite food groups covered."

"Wow. I am impressed, but I'm still trying to figure out what the occasion is. Anything you need to tell me?" A sudden flash of fear hits me. What if something is up?

"Nope, just trying to take care of my old man for once. You need it, Dad."

"I'm fine," I slightly growl as my eyes focus on the sizzling steaks.

Aria stiffens in defense, "I didn't mean anything by it, Dad. I wanted to do something nice for you. You've had a lot on your plate lately."

Instantly my shoulders sag. I hurt her feelings.

Aria says softly, "Those look about done."

"Yep, they are. Let's sit in the dining room. I want to sit at a table for this."

"I'm on it," Aria says, escaping to set the table.

I sear both steaks and dump them on the platter before I head in, chastising myself as I do. Aria is trying to do something nice, and I've been a jerk. As I walk in, Aria's humming Julia's song ... she has been paying attention. A slight smile crosses my lips as I head toward the dining room.

Aria stops singing when I enter, but it's too late. "Don't stop on my account. Sounds good." A long pause ensues. "I've never heard you sing Mom's song."

"Just on my mind. I miss her."

"I know you do. I miss her, too."

Aria takes her seat as I put the steaks down on the table and slowly slide into a seat, as if I'm eighty. I put my elbows on the table, and I look at her.

"We're both doing the best we can, and I think we're doing exceptionally well, all things considered."

Aria leans over and grabs my hand, giving it a slight squeeze, but she won't look at me. Julia is finally coming home, and I know we're both clinging to having her here but not knowing what it will be like. We sit in silence for a moment, staring down at our meal until I take a steak knife and hold it straight up in the air like a crazed man, and then I angle it downward, stabbing into one of the huge steaks before throwing it on my plate.

Aria chuckles as her green eyes dance, "I think you got it, Dad."

I smile as I reach for a nearby bowl filled with salad, scooping a huge helping on my plate.

On this night, we keep the conversation light, something we haven't done in months, because of the overwhelming fear that's consumed our lives. There's an unspoken emptiness in the room that's been there for weeks, but for the first time in a long time, hope is returning to us both.

Chapter 12 – Julia

I fly back to Nashville tomorrow. Today, I'm headed to one last session with my therapist here in Texas. We're on a first-name basis; it's been that way with many of the doctors, nurses, and others here.

As I casually walk into her small office, suddenly I'm struck by an overwhelming sense of loss, like I'm leaving a good friend.

"Whoa, Jules, you look like you've seen a ghost." Samantha gestures for me to take my regular seat and I flop down heavily, my head thrown back against the comfortable cushions. I've spent many hours in this room, going over my woe-is-mes, but mainly we talk a lot about food. I have a problem with food. Even with cancer and the nausea of treatment, I still have a problem with food.

"Maybe I have." I pause, trying to collect the rapid-fire thoughts that are going off in succession in my brain. "You know I'm leaving tomorrow. For good this time," I add for emphasis.

"Yes, I'm very well aware," she replies as the corners of her mouth turn up. Samantha shoots me straight and it's kept my head from swiveling off down here.

"You remember when I said, when I first got diagnosed, I went out to a diner and ate mashed potatoes, you know, my comfort food."

"I do ... and?"

I pause, looking out the window at the bright sunny Texas sky. "Even though food is far from what I want most of the time ... I really want some mashed potatoes, right now."

"And why do you think that is? Why do you crave your comfort food when you are about to go home?"

Samantha always makes me answer my own questions. She won't let me off the hook. I give her my best, "Really, you're gonna make me work for this" look, and then I reply, "Probably, cause I'm terrified that they'll have to take care of me again. Did I get it right?" I ask her for confirmation. I know this is part of it but there's more to it and she'll drag it out of me.

"That sounds logical. Anything else?"

I push my back against the pillows like I'm hoping they'll swallow me up as she gives me a shit-eating grin.

"Well, I guess ... it's because I'm worried what Raine will think." She nods, so I reluctantly continue. "I know he saw me at my worst through the chemo and surgery, I mean c'mon, I lost my breasts. But I don't look any better ... worse, in fact. I can see it. How is he going to stand this? I ask, gesturing down the front of me, grimacing.

Samantha has been sitting across from me, smiling her knowing smile and listening. She gets it, I know she does, but she's going to keep pushing me.

Samantha chimes in, "We've talked about this for a while. Has Raine ever rejected you once during this entire process? Through the surgery, treatment, any of it? Has he ever looked at you in any disgusting way or not wanted to hold you or give you affection?"

"No. Of course not."

"There's your answer, Julia."

I nod at her. My brain knows she's right, but my eyes look at my pudgy, pillowy body every day.

We continue to talk through the rest of my session about my upcoming results and how to manage stress, uncertainty, and everything that could come up when I'm back home. Maybe I'm having this reaction because I'll really miss Samantha. She's been a crutch while I've been here, and I can talk to her about things that no one else would understand unless you've been around cancer patients talking about the same things day after day.

As I walk out to leave, she hands me a few articles to help with my aftercare and gives me this wonderful, tight embrace.

"You can always reach out to me down here. Just because you leave, doesn't mean we can't continue to help."

I have no idea why, but my chin starts to tremble. "Thanks … for … everything, Samantha," I finally manage to squeak out. I'm being such a pansy-ass, which makes me shake my head in disgust.

Samantha hugs me again, and as I turn to leave, she gives me such a big thumbs-up and wide-eyed grin that I bust out in laughter through my tears. This is one of the reasons why I'll miss her.

Chapter 13 – Raine

I send a text to my good friend Bret asking to meet me for breakfast at one of our favorite diners. Bret's a country music icon, and one of my oldest friends. Bret surprised us all by settling down shortly after I married Julia. He and his wife bought a huge spread near our house and now that he's semi-retired, we meet up for our golf games and occasional meals.

Bret's engrossed in his phone as I roll up and park. He indicates I'm late with a glance down at his watch.

"Really, man? Five minutes tops."

"It's still five minutes of my life I can't get back," Bret says, with insincere exasperation. He grips my neck for a quick hug while he reaches out and slaps my thinning stomach. "Finally start that exercise routine?"

I roll my eyes at him. "Nope, just a general lack of food."

Bret grimaces as I continue. "Let's get in here, I had a huge dinner with Reezie last night, and now I'm starving."

We stride into the diner. We're regulars and although Bret usually turns some heads 'cause he's famous, people don't pay us any mind here.

We settle into a booth, and a waitress comes by and we both order coffee. Bret doesn't waste any time peppering me with questions about when Julia is coming back and what the doctors are saying. I tell him everything I know before the conversation gets to why I really need to talk to Bret.

"The doctors are telling her it looks good, but we won't know for a while." My voice catches. I don't do uncertainty well, and Bret knows it.

Bret's been nodding along, "One day at a time, Raine. That's all you can do. But there's something else. You should be happy that she's coming back, and I can tell something's hanging over you."

Bret knows me well. I stare out the window studying the busy street in front of the diner, trying to find the right words. I don't want this to come out wrong. My gaze comes back to Bret. "You know when Julia first got sick, her whole body changed ... she didn't feel like herself and it really cut into how she was with me." I pause because this is really uncomfortable.

"Well, she had major surgery, and she lost all her hair, Raine. I don't think she really felt all that attractive. And?"

The waitress comes back with our coffee, and I let her know we need a bit more time before we order food. Then I drop my tone down to a whisper. I don't need any ears other than Bret's. "She'd hardly come near me, Bret. She didn't want me to see her and stayed covered up all the time. With the stress, her hormones were all over the place."

Bret shakes his head with understanding, but he leans in, keeping his voice low, "I get hormones, Raine. I live with all girls, remember? You and Julia talk about everything; have you talked about this? Jules doesn't shy away from anything with you. Not the Julia I know."

I lean in toward him with my forearms resting on the table. "She hasn't been herself, Bret. We haven't been intimate for months, and of course, not while she's been in Texas. I don't know what to do. She doesn't want me to come near her in that way. I hug and kiss her, but she's not attracted to me anymore." Although this is awkward, it feels good to get this off my chest. It's been weighing on me.

Bret leans back and waves his hand with a flourish, "That's bullshit. It's probably because she thinks you'll reject the way she looks now, Raine. That's it. You've seen her physically after the surgery, right?"

I lean back and give him a huge smile. "Yes ... they did an amazing job. She looks great. And I don't give a damn about her hair, or how much she weighs now or ever. She says she's puffy from the treatments. I don't give a shit about that. I just want her."

Bret shakes his head at me like I'm daft, "Why am I always saying this to you? Then you have to tell her that, Raine. You've got to show her. It's not rocket science, man. Figure out how to tell her she's beautiful to you, no matter what she thinks."

"Easier said than done," I mutter.

Bret rolls his eyes at me. "I heard that. Nothing worth having is easy. Put your big boy pants on and show her that you desire her. That's all I got." Bret picks up his menu and scowls as I chuckle.

He continues. "Now, can we finally order and not talk about you? I live with my wife and three young daughters ... there's not a whole lot of sympathy coming from me."

He looks across at me with a shit-eating grin, but there is no way I'm feeling sorry for him. That will never happen. Bret's a multi-millionaire with people helping him do everything. Nothing is hard for him. Believe me. I grab my menu, shaking my head with a smile.

He's right, I know he is, but how do I convince Julia that she looks good when she can hardly look in a mirror? I get it. But she's beautiful to me and always will be.

Chapter 14 – Aria

I bought the necessities I'll need for school and comfortable, flat shoes at the mall. I needed something practical for walking all around the campus.

Dad isn't home when I pull up the drive. I'm glad he got out of the house. I grab my acoustic guitar from my room and head out to the back patio to sit by the pool. I haven't picked up my guitar in weeks, and I need to make time to play if I'm going to get any better. I open one of my new library books to study some new chords.

Later I'm watching Dad ferociously clean out the pool. So far, he's mowed the front lawn, washed every car in the garage, done four loads of laundry, and now he's cleaning the pool and outside patio area. We do have people who help with these tasks, and these two people, Amanda, our housekeeper, and Jacob, who helps around the grounds, are standing with me on our deck, watching Dad with amusement

Jacob looks my way, his brow furrowed with frustration. "Aria, I did offer to help, I swear."

"I have no doubt," I say, giving him an apologetic smile. I know Dad's working out his demons in his own way. He personally must ensure everything is perfect before Mom comes home.

Amanda chimes in, "I tried to help him freshen up the clothes in her closet … but he won't let me near her things."

I give her a sympathetic glance. "I'm so sorry," is all that I can say. Dad clearly doesn't know what to do, so he thinks he has to do everything. I continue, shaking my head with a laugh, "Jacob, you'll probably have to go back over the cars."

Jacob rolls his eyes as we all walk back into the house. There's nothing we can do when he gets like this. I guess we should be grateful that he can find things to keep him busy. I'm sure it helps him with all the uncertainty that's been swirling around us.

I look back at Dad as he works on the pool and wonder if I should go and help him, but I think twice. He needs to do this alone.

Chapter 15 – Luke

I'm finishing up the chords on a new song. This one seems so good that I have goosebumps as I play. That rarely happens. My mom's in the living room and I want to play what I have for her if she's up to it.

Mom's sitting in a chair in front of our TV with a blanket draped over her lap. She's awake but gives me tired eyes when I enter the room. She looks much older than her forty-five years, and her grayish blonde hair could use a good brushing, something that doesn't come as easy to her now.

"Mom … you want to hear a new song?"

An easy smile crosses her lips, "Of course, pumpkin, I always want to hear what you've written."

I'm not a fan of being called pumpkin, but I give her some grace. I'll always be her five-year-old son. "It's not perfect yet, but I think it's a good one. It's called "Coming Home."

I sit on the couch next to her and pull my guitar onto my lap, making sure I'm in tune. Once satisfied with the sound, I start to play and sing. Mom closes her eyes as she listens. When I'm finished, I look at her and it's then that I see she's dabbing at obvious tears.

I reach out and touch her arm, "Mom, you okay?"

She's quiet for several seconds. "That was amazing, Luke. I think it's one of the best you've ever written. Where'd you get the idea?"

I pause. I'm not sure I want her to know my true inspiration, but then I decide it's safe to tell her. The truth would never get back to Aria.

I lean back, giving her my most casual of looks, hoping it will hide my feelings. "Remember I told you about that new girl, Aria, who's transferring into school?" She nods. I continue, hoping I won't reveal my crush. "I was at the library yesterday and ran into her. I mean I literally smashed right into her. I had just left the biography section and noticed a book about her mother, Julia Tate, she's a famous songwriter in town, and then there she was. And she looked so sad, Mom. The tabloids all say Aria's mom has cancer, so part of the song is about that ... like finding your way through all that.

"It's beautiful. Maybe one day you could play it for her?" Mom says with an obvious, lighthearted smirk. My mom's a smart lady; she figured it out.

"Oh ... I don't know about that." I look down, fidgeting with my guitar, and nervously play a mini guitar solo. My nervous tick.

Mom continues, "Well, you'll have to play it next year during your creative songwriting contest at school. I think you'd win."

I nod at her as my mind drifts. I wonder if it's good enough to win the elusive end of year prize. Every school year, the best original song gets a demo session with some of the best area players and an award-winning producer. Then the song is pitched to up-and-coming artists, and even big-name icons. It's a once in a lifetime opportunity. Last year, I thought I had a good song, but I only made it to the top ten. I think my new song has a shot.

But right now, I have got to change the subject and get our minds off my Aria infatuation. "You hungry? I'm thinking about making hamburgers?"

Mom nods. It's rare getting her to eat anything other than soup, so this is a good sign. She replies, "Sounds great and I'm happy to help."

She makes a move to stand, and I move my guitar as I jump up to help her. Once she's up, we slowly make our way into the kitchen. Mom moves like she's eighty and inside, I silently sigh.

She glances over at me, "How about you help with the table. I can make dinner on my own tonight."

"You got it," I say, scurrying to the dining room. As I prepare the table, I silently pray to God this song is something special. Then I'll be able to get Mom the care she needs and take better care of her.

Chapter 16 – Julia

I can't get to the plane fast enough. On the way to the terminal, I had to stop a couple of times to catch my breath, but now I'm at the gate and boarding. Tracy arranged for me to sit in first class, so I'm one of the first on the plane. This helps because I'm not waiting around for so long. I hope no one recognizes me; not that they would. With my short, grayish hair and baggy sweats, I'd be shocked if anyone notices me. I'm so used to being an anonymous patient at the hospital, I've forgotten what it's like to be out in the real world, and how amazing it is to wear real clothes and not hospital garb.

I grab my seat and send Raine a quick text letting him know I'm on the plane. He sends me a message right away.

"We can't wait for you to be home, and by we, I mean me. LOL."

I laugh but my chest tightens. I should have worn something nicer than stretchy, soothing cotton. I can't even fathom wearing anything revealing or putting on makeup right now. I know he gets and loves "sick me." He's had to deal with it back in Nashville for months, but maybe I should try a little harder.

Right now, I'm overwhelmed by "what-ifs." My head falls back against the headrest, and I close my eyes. I can't imagine trying to be sexy for him or even for me anymore. I just don't care. Not with this body. I'm tired, bloated, and ugly. There is no way he'll want me. Not like this.

A flight attendant comes by offering me a drink, and for the first time in a long time, I order a glass of wine. Ever since Raine went public with his struggle with alcoholism, and since my diagnosis, I rarely drink except for a glass of wine now and then. But my overwrought nerves could use one. This saddens me even more. I should be strong enough to get home without a crutch. This thought is playing over and over again in my mind. What will Raine think when he sees me? I haven't let on how grueling these past few weeks have been. Even though the treatment helped, it did a total number on my body and, I'm reluctant to admit, my mind.

I must remember that my goal was to return home to the people that I love, and I'm doing that. My heart overflows when I think about seeing the only two people who I'll walk through fire for, but physically, I'm beat. How am I ever going to deal with Raine wanting me physically? I do *want* him, that hasn't changed. But I don't want him to see or feel my body right now. I glance down at the lower part of my body. I look gross.

Sitting at the gate, I pull out my makeup mirror, trying to make sense of my mousy, gray hair and lack of makeup. I release a heavy sigh. I know beauty doesn't last. I came to grips about my age a while ago, but Raine didn't sign up for all this. I put my things away and prepare to depart. It's time to buck up, buttercup. In just moments I'll be back in Raine's arms, where I belong.

When I walk out to greet him, the weight of it all hits me and it almost makes me crumble right in front of him, but somehow I stay steady. Although I only spent a few months in Texas, I sometimes wondered if I'd ever get to the final day. Raine visited once for a week; that was all the time he had. Since Raine can't stand hospitals, he spent much of his time at a nearby hotel and only visited me at night.

My long-time Nashville physician, Dr. Henley, and my specialist, Dr. Hunter, recommended the Texas facility for the newer treatments and holistic medicine they could provide. With my kind of cancer and the risk that it can move to other organs, everyone thought it would be best. I really hope the treatments helped because the time away from my family has been pure hell.

Raine's glowing face is a little slice of heaven, but I can see his worry lines for miles. The entire time of my treatment, he's had this look like he's expecting me to break apart, like I'm glass or something. That's why I have to be strong right now, no matter how I'm feeling.

On the way home, Raine takes my hand in a vise-like grip. At one point, I hold up my hand with an obvious grimace and he laughs. God, I missed that laugh. I lean over, giving him a big kiss on the cheek. He responds by throwing his arm across my shoulder, pulling me as close as he can to his body with these dang seat belts. The closeness is always there between us, but there's a gnawing in the pit of my stomach when I think about getting home and facing him alone in our bedroom. I don't want him to see my body like this.

Chapter 17 – Raine

I wipe my sweat-soaked hands down on my jeans. As I look over at the purple tulips sitting on the seat next to me, I'm second guessing them. Is this too much? I had no idea how big of a deal to make this. In my mind, Julia coming home warrants her own street parade, but now I'm overthinking. She never likes a fuss being made over her. The few times I showered her with jewelry or other gifts, while I know she loves and treasures them, she'd rather have had time with me and Aria. This I know. She does love purple tulips, though, so I think I'm safe with this one gesture.

She finally walks off the escalator and toward our waiting SUV. Today, I hired security and a driver. I never know if the paparazzi have discovered she's traveling and will be waiting at the airport. With Julia's illness, we've been in the tabloids a lot lately and today I don't want anyone bothering us. She also asked me not to meet her inside 'cause she didn't want a scene.

I jump out of the car as she boldly strides out, strong and in control. That's my Jules. I want to run to her, but I let her walk up to us, pulling her carry-on behind. She didn't need a whole lot of clothes at the hospital, so she only has the one bag. I take a large step toward her, pulling her up in my arms, and she melts against me and sighs. She presses her head against my chest as I kiss the top of her head before she looks up at me. Then I finally get to give her the kiss I've been longing to give her these past few months. She's okay with these displays of affection. That's never been a problem, it's our private intimacy she's been avoiding.

I pull back and run my hand down her face. She blushes slightly before saying, "We probably should get inside the car."

I smile as I get her loaded inside. Our driver has already taken care of her bag. We strap ourselves into our seats, then I lean in and grasp her face in my hands, giving her another kiss. Julia just smiles. She does look a little tired but not too bad. To me she looks amazing and all I want to do is be near her. I take her hand in mine as the car starts up and we're finally headed home.

Chapter 18 – Aria

Dad made me decorate the house with cheesy balloons, but at least we picked up flowers to give the house some class. I selected white balloons so they wouldn't look too crappy. I'm finishing up when the car pulls up the drive. My heart is flying now that Mom's finally home. I'm trying to focus on the joy, hoping it counters the overwhelming sense of doom that's been hanging over me.

The car stops and the back door opens. Dad runs around and gingerly helps Mom out of the car, which I'm sure she hates. She doesn't like helpless. My first take is that she looks good, but gaunt. A strong sense of bile starts rising in my throat.

We ordered dinner so we wouldn't be bothered with cooking. A chef's in the kitchen making sure our dinner is good and hot. Dad wanted Mom's favorite foods but knowing that she's been nauseous, he made sure everything is on the milder side.

My eager inner six-year-old runs to the front door to greet them. As soon as the door opens, Mom's face fills my field of vision and in seconds I'm in her arms. I can't remember the last time I've hugged her this hard.

"Whoa! I … can't … breathe," she laughs, engulfed in my arms.

I manage to laugh with her as I step back, and then she leans in and tenderly kisses my cheek. I watch Dad as he brings her bag in; he's got a spring in his step that's been missing, and a broad grin fills his face. Finally, our house doesn't feel so empty.

"Of course, you both know I'm thrilled to be home," Mom says, looking between the two of us. "It feels like forever." She glances around the foyer as if everything looks new. "Look at those flowers ... oh my goodness!"

"I think I bought every tulip in Nashville," I add with a self-conscious smile. Dad gives me a wink. I know he's pleased with how everything looks.

He pulls Mom in close and looks down at her, "Are you hungry? We have dinner ready just in case."

"I am actually and a good meal with the two people I love most would be wonderful." Mom reaches out and takes my face in her hands. Dad leans in and hugs us both. The whole moment seems unreal to me, like part of me can't believe it's really happening.

Sure, it may seem sappy, but we've always been an incredibly close family, and this is a moment I won't ever forget. Ever.

Chapter 19 – Raine

It's surreal having Julia back in the house. We share a lighthearted dinner, and then the moment I've been waiting for. I casually mention playing Julia's song later as Aria, her head resting in her hands, looks on expectantly.

"Yeah, Mom, do you want to hear it?" Aria exclaims with delight. "Dad wants us to sing back-up on it, too, and I thought we could do that tomorrow?"

"I'd love to." There's a pause as Mom's trying to keep her composure before adding, "And I'd love to sing on it with you, Reez."

I jump up. "Let's go down to the studio. I have it ready to go."

Once we're all settled in my studio, I look back at Jules, and she's sitting on the couch behind me, and Aria's sitting next to her, holding her hand.

I mention, "I think it's the best song you've written, love," then I hit "play" on the console.

The strings start in with the intro, and then Wayne's booming timbre blares through my speakers as he sings the first few lines. I glance back at Jules and her head is down, listening. Aria is looking at me, smiling. When it gets to the first chorus, Julia looks up at me and smiles with tears in her eyes. I knew she'd love it. I let it play through the entire song, and when it gets to the bridge and the strings come up, it quiets down to the last verse and Wayne comes in almost solo. Julia's hand comes up to her mouth. When the song finishes, she's silent.

Aria can't control herself, practically squealing, "Well? What do you think? It's amazing, isn't it?"

Julia looks at Aria and then at me, with tears on her face. She nods yes, and a sweet smile takes over her lips. I stand, pulling her up in my arms.

She whispers in my ear, "I love it, Raine … wow … I absolutely love it."

"I love you, Julia Tate. Don't you ever forget it." And I lean down, giving her a huge, glorious kiss on her lips.

Aria breaks up our moment, "Um … I'm right here, you two."

Julia pulls away from me, and we laugh before I add, "Get used to it, kid."

Earlier, Jules mentioned she wanted to go to the barn to see the horses. So, I pull our golf cart up to the front door and we take a leisurely evening drive around the property. I don't know if she wanted to try and walk it, but I didn't take any chances.

Before she left for Texas, anything physical would tire her out, so I became accustomed to driving her around the property in our cart. Years ago, we bought the adjoining land near our house, so at present, we have close to thirty acres.

Right now, we have five horses in the barn. When we started getting horses, Jules would be up early, with Aria in tow, taking care of them. As Aria grew, they would take rides together. That completely stopped this past year, but Aria helps me manage their care, along with Jacob, and she's done an amazing job. We also have two Shepherds, Lute and Lyre. They freely roam around the property, and on many nights they've been my only companions.

Julia's changed into sweats and a ball cap, and as she climbs into the cart, the dogs come running up to join us. She reaches out to pet each one tenderly. Lute whines his reply. We slowly drive up the hill to the stable as the dogs run alongside.

I place my hand on her knee. "How does it feel to be back?"

She places her hand on mine, "Oh hon, you have no idea. You know I missed you, and Reezie, but I missed everything about this place. The smells, the scenery, everything." She sighs, pulling her cap down and settling down in her seat, looking out around her. To me, she's never looked more beautiful. In the early August heat, the sun's still up, but it's starting to set, giving the pastureland a warm glow.

When we get to the barn, Julia takes her time greeting each horse and giving each one a thorough inspection. She even takes the time to brush a few before we start back to the house. It's now dark, but the property lights automatically come on, so I can easily see my way around. She's fidgeting in her seat now, so different than when we started our drive up the hill and I'm certain of why.

I break the silence between us. "You tired? It's been a long day."

"I am. Could really go for a long, hot bath. You know me," she says, with a slightly nervous laugh.

My stomach's in my throat. I never want Julia uneasy in our home, and my goal is to make her comfortable, so I take Bret's advice. I slow the cart to a stop, resting my arms on the steering wheel, looking directly at her.

"Jules, I want you to feel as stress free as possible. There's no pressure about anything with me … between us. You know I love you, more than anything on this earth, other than Aria. You do what you need to do to feel comfortable. Nothing else matters to me."

Her face relaxes as she gets my meaning. She reaches out and takes my hand in hers.

"I love you too, both of you, more than you know. And I never want to disappoint you. I know what you're saying … I just need some time."

With that I nod, and we continue our peaceful drive to the front of the house.

Chapter 20 – Julia

The next few days are a blur as I get back to my regular routine and prepare for Jody and her family to arrive. Aria and I record our background parts on my song, "He'll Stay." I can't remember the last time I had so much fun in the studio. We drove Raine nuts between takes, but eventually we settled down and added the parts he wanted. When Raine played everything back, what we added took the song to another level. The enormous grin on Raine's face told me he agreed.

Years ago, we built a guest house on the other side of our pool, close to the pasture. Today, I'm getting the house aired out and ready for our guests. I can't wait to spend some much-needed girl time with Jody. After my diagnosis, I often confided in Jody and Tracy about all the crap I was going through. They kept me sane when I lost my breasts, and then when I got even larger boobs. They were also there when I lost my hair. Now that my hair is growing back, I'm getting more and more used to this new me—although I'm still shocked when I look in the mirror.

Right now, I'm in the main suite of the guest house and making up the bed. Amanda, who joined us shortly after Aria was born, has prepped the house, but I told her I'd finish up. Even though I'm not quite up to par, I need to do normal things. For so many years, I had Aria to care for. That and running our mini ranch. Now that Reezie's older, and for the first time going to school away from home, I have no idea what I'm going to do all day. I still write songs, and many artists have cut them over the years, but I haven't stepped foot on stage or performed solo for years.

After making the bed, I pause, looking down on it. The overwhelming guilt these past few nights with Raine—hell, the last few months—floods through my mind. Since I've been home, he's given me a wide berth, like he said he would. He hasn't pressed me for anything physical. Of course, he hugs and kisses me, taking every ounce of my breath, and I do want more, but he hasn't made one move for sex. Most nights, I'm in bed asleep before he even comes in. I never know he's there until the next morning.

I catch my image in a nearby mirror. Of course, the oversized, comfortable sweats don't do a damn thing for me, but other than that, how could Raine be attracted to flabby, puffy me? At least most of my rash is gone and I'm getting over some of the fatigue. But I don't have an ounce of muscle tone, just flesh hanging from my bones. If I tried a push-up right now, I'd fall flat on my face. I try a quick test and flop to the ground, then try to push myself up in a girl-style push-up with my knees still on the floor. It's not pretty, but I manage to do two in a row before collapsing down on my arms. Well, it's a start. An ugly start, but it is one.

When Jody gets here, I'm going to drag her out on a ride with me. The horses need it and so does my ass. I get up off the ground and finish cleaning the room with this goal in mind. I'm going to build muscles back on my frame. That's the only way I'm ever going to let Raine see me naked again.

Chapter 21 – Aria

Watching Mom with her sister Jody makes my heart explode. Jody, her husband, and their daughter Sarah arrived yesterday, and today I helped Mom saddle up a couple of horses so she and Jody could take a short ride around the grounds. Mom told me they'd take it easy. They'd better, because lately we haven't ridden our horses, except my favorite gelding, Charlie. Mom saddled up her old mare, Butter. Jody's on another, more docile, mare, Cinnamon, so they should be fine. I tried to help them with their saddles and bridles, but Mom was hell-bent on doing everything herself. She's been that way the last few days—all piss and vinegar, but in a good way. Dad stood at the barn door and watched the whole scene with a pleased grin on his face.

When they get back, we're gonna have a cook-out. I'm running to the store to pick up a few items, and my cousin Sarah, who's much older than me, is riding shotgun. Sarah was in high school when I was born, so she's more like an aunt than a cousin.

"You start classes at the end of next week? Looking forward to that?" Sarah says as her eyebrows rise.

"It'll be different. I did have other kids around with homeschooling, along with all the people Dad had at the studio, so I think I'll be okay. But this *will* be different," I reply, masking my already churning stomach. I've been trying not to think about my new school a whole lot. Other than running into Luke at the library, I won't know a single soul and that makes my head hurt.

"Reez, you'll be great. You're beautiful, funny as heck, and you can make conversation with a brick wall. You won't have any problems making new friends. It'll be good to get away from the same people you meet around your parents. You know, all those rock stars," Sarah says with a sarcastic smirk.

"Yeah ... maybe," I reply laughing. But I'm not convinced. What if I turn out to be one big, classic dork around my new classmates? Sure, I'm good around Mom and Dad's studio people, and I have made good friends through other home-schooled families, but this will be hundreds of kids in a performance-based school, and I'll be competing against them. I've watched *Mean Girls*, and I know how girls can get. I hope I'm above all that, and that it won't be so dire. Oh, I have my petty moments, but my parents raised me not to judge people, and they can't stand any kind of bullying. In fact, Mom hates any form of disrespect. In Mom's world, there are three things that show you have integrity: You put your shopping cart back, take care of animals, and tip well. She doesn't tolerate anything less.

We get to the store, grab the items we need, and head back to the house, but my conversation with Sarah rings through my already scattered brain. Amid my preoccupation with Mom and getting our lives back to normal, I've put school on the back burner. But it's there, looming, and then the bile starts to rise. I'm so much like my mom.

Chapter 22 – Julia

It's wonderful to be back on Butter going for a leisurely ride. I'm sure my legs and ass will regret this tomorrow, but for now, the steady thump of the horse's hooves striking the ground is soothing.

Jody breaks my reverie. "So, now that we're away from everyone. How are you really doing, Jules?" She gives me a look that I grew up with, letting me know I can't bullshit her.

"I'm slowly starting to get back to normal." I pause and she lets me finish. "But there's that little voice in the back of my head telling me to worry. I can't help it."

Jody nods, "Are the side effects going away?"

"Most, but I still want to take a good nap, like all the time. At least my stomach is starting to even out and I'm not running to the bathroom every hour. That really sucked."

Jody chuckles and replies, cutting to the chase, "I bet it did. When will you know if the treatment worked?"

"We have an appointment coming up with Dr. Henley to go over my latest scans. My doctors down in Texas thought everything looked good, so I'm hanging on to that ... and I've prayed more in the last year than ever before." I look at Jody and give her a big smile.

Jody nods with a slight laugh. "I was talking to Jay about everything, and I mentioned how strong you've been. You really have been, Jules. I don't know how I would have done with something like this, but you've been handling this, while still taking care of Raine and Aria."

"They're my world, Jod, you know that. I worry that I won't be here for them … that's kept me up so many nights. If I'm not here, what will happen to Raine? That's terrifying to me."

Jody doesn't say a word, and we ride for several moments, both lost in what that reality could mean for Raine.

Finally, Jody speaks, "Raine is stronger than we think. I'm sure, heaven forbid, losing you would destroy him, but he has Aria to think about."

Her words hit me hard. He does have Aria, and that reason alone instantly calms me. No matter what happens, Raine will be okay because he must be for her.

We ride along making small talk until my butt can't take it any longer, so we head back to the barn. But Jody's words continue to ring in my mind. I hope I'm past this whole nightmare, but we won't know for weeks, months, or even years if I'm finally free of cancer.

Chapter 23 – Raine

Having Julia back home is like a dream. I'm doing everything I can to make her feel safe and comfortable, and with Jody and her family here, it's like we're back to normal. There may be a gray cloud hanging over us, but I'm doing my best to ignore it.

As I stand in front of my grill next to Jay, we're doing our best not to scorch the burgers. Everyone requested hamburgers, but of course I wanted steaks. They wanted something simpler, which was probably a good idea.

I scan the back patio scene, and a sigh of contentment escapes me. Overlooking the scenery of our back pasture with the sun going down, I watch the people I love and cherish causally enjoying this night. A lighthearted sound of conversation and laughter fills the air, and it's perfect. I take a drink of my soda as I flip a burger. Jay's holding a koozie-covered beer looking as relaxed as I am. Now that I've been sober for so many years, it doesn't bother me for others to drink beer around me. We don't keep liquor in the house though. That'd be dangerous. Julia drinks wine on occasion, but she doesn't drink around me, and that's another reason why I love her.

As I watch my Julia, sitting there casually talking with those she loves the most, it hits me that I love her more than ever. I just wish she weren't so hard on herself and let us be as close as we should be. She looks amazing and somehow, I've got to make her feel that way. I know the chemo and treatments took a toll on her. She covers herself up in loose-fitting clothes to hide her figure, but every time I catch a glimpse of her, I think she looks glorious. I've told her many times that she could weigh three hundred pounds, and I wouldn't care. Somehow I've got to get her to accept her new figure and love herself. Then maybe she'll let me physically love her. The ache I have for her is unbearable. At night, I hide out in my studio until she's asleep because all I want to do is gather her up tight and make love to the one woman I need more than life.

I focus back on the grill right as Jay warns me that everything looks done.

"Shit … I could have burned these." I grab my tongs and quickly start pulling the meat off the grill. "Glad you said something," I add with a laugh.

Jay catches my gaze. "Jules looks good, Raine," he says with a wink.

My face turns scarlet, but I have a huge smile. "Yep," and then I pause for a moment. "You know, you and Jody could help me. Jules doesn't think she looks that good. She's too hard on herself, and after everything she's been through, she needs a little encouragement."

"I get what you're saying," Jay says, giving me a knowing nod. "I'll say something to Jody tonight." Jay grabs a platter, "Now let's scoop the rest up before they all burn and we ruin dinner." I laugh as we finish our task.

Chapter 24 – Julia

I love having my family here to visit, but after a few days of over-the-top compliments from everyone, I finally corner Jody in the kitchen and ask her what's up. They're too obvious.

Jody looks down sheepishly, "Raine may have mentioned that you don't think you look so great, so we're trying to give you some encouragement. It's too much, isn't it?"

Both my hands come to my hips. "Jeez ... yes, not subtle at all. Coming from Raine and even a couple of comments from you, and I wouldn't thought much about it, but from Jay? Jay has, in the thirty years I've known him, never said one word about the way I look. He could care less about that sort of thing. Didn't you think I'd notice?" I ask, my voice rising with frustration.

Jody gives me an apologetic smile. "Raine's trying to make you feel better, Jules."

For the first time in a long time, this makes me pause. I drop my arms dramatically. "Okay, well, if that's what it's gonna take, grab Sarah and us girls are going on a shopping spree. I've got to get out of my sloppy sweatpants, so let's go to the mall and have a girls' day out." I gesture toward the door impatiently. Jody pauses for a moment and then scurries out of the room.

We spend a good part of the afternoon going from store to store as we all try on outfits and shoes. Jody, Sarah, and Aria easily find things they like, but nothing looks right on me. I'm sure it's in my mind, but I can't find anything suitable. I'm about to give up when finally, I try on a simple wraparound dress that covers me in the right spots, giving me the waist I need. It also accents my new full-figured chest. I'm not used to my full C-cup breasts when I used to be a decent-sized B. I'm still not sure about my boob decision.

I walk out of the fitting room to get a second opinion.

Sarah chimes in first. "It's perfect! Raine will love it!" she squeals, looking at Aria who nods in agreement, but she looks more bored than anything.

Jody adds with a warm smile, "It looks great on you, Jules. And damn ... wish I had those," she says, gesturing to my overflowing bosom.

I roll my eyes and I'm sure my face is flushed. "The doctors went a little overboard. I did tell them I wanted them bigger, and that's what I got!" I say with a laugh as they join in.

"Raine won't be able to keep his hands off you," Jody adds. I nod and give a slight smile but my stomach flip flops. Is that what I want? Do I want him to touch me and all my added flesh? My dreaded obsession with my weight is rearing its ugly head. Right now, I'm totally out of control. Cancer has left me helpless when it comes to my body and there doesn't seem to be much I can do about it.

After several more days of fun and relaxation, Jody and her family travel back to Montana. Aria starts her classes at the new school in a few days. Soon, I'll be at home with nothing to do.

I'm hitting our workout room every day to try and work off the extra pounds, but all I feel is sore, and not in a good way. Raine's keeping his distance. I'm grateful he's giving me space, but there's this painful awkwardness between us. I miss him physically. I'm thinking about this as I sit in our kitchen nook, a hot cup of coffee in my hand, watching Raine and our ranch hand Jacob work on a fence post. Even at fifty-eight, and with extra pounds around his middle, Raine cuts an impressive figure. Every time he lifts a pole and puts it in place, the fabric of his sweat-soaked T-shirt stretches across the muscles of his upper arms. My insides stir in a way they haven't in some time. Tonight, I need to find the courage to wear my new dress for him. But this thought fades quickly when I think about my squishy arms and thighs, and I don't even want to think about my stomach. My mind doesn't want him to touch me, but other parts of my body really do. My phone rings. It's Tracy.

"Hey, Jules. You have a moment?"

"Sure. What's up?"

"Got a call from Trent Austin yesterday, you know, your old writing buddy from *Next Real Star*."

"Of course I remember Trent. What does he want?"

"He's gonna be in Nashville working on a project with Aria's new school. He wants to know if you want to write together."

"Hmm … maybe? I'll need to check with Raine about it first. He might be weird about me working with Trent." I pause and add lightly, "You know him."

I can almost hear her smile on the other end. "Yeah, I do know him. Okay, let me know. Trent said he'll be in town soon." There's a slight pause. "Everything getting back to normal?"

"Sort of. I look like shit, and I don't want Raine to touch me, but other than that, it's a typical day," I say, chuckling.

"Jules, you're beautiful, and you know Raine thinks so. We're all older, with everything that comes with that. You *know* he understands, plus you've been battling flippin' cancer … what do you expect? That'd you'd be marathon ready? He doesn't expect that!"

I'm sure my heavy sigh of exasperation is noticeable. "I know … I know. I hear you. We'll work it out. We always do."

"Alright, girl. Let's have lunch next week and we can talk more about this Trent thing. He still gets major cuts, Jules, and it would be good for your career."

"You got it."

I hang up and my gaze goes back to Raine and Jacob as they continue working on the fence. I take a deep breath and decide that tonight is dress night, and I'll even suggest we go out to dinner. That will shock the heck out of Raine, I think with a smile as I head toward the stable to saddle my horse, Butter. In the meantime, I'm gonna work on my ass.

Chapter 25 – Raine

When I finish working on projects around the property, I go inside and find a note from Julia on the kitchen counter. She went to the nail salon and will be back later this afternoon. She tells me that she's made a reservation for us for dinner and expects me to be in something a little nicer than jeans. I take a step back and set the note down on the counter in surprise. Julia hasn't wanted to go anywhere other than running errands since she came back from Texas. The fact that she wants to go out in public and expects me to dress up is a big step and gives me reason to hope. But I take a deep breath and try to remain calm. Maybe she just wants to get out of the house. We already know Aria is going to Savannah's house and then to a movie, so it's just us tonight. I shouldn't get my hopes up that this could be a date night, but it does sound promising.

I practically spring up the stairs to our bedroom and hit the shower, contemplating what I'll wear. I haven't worn anything other than jeans or shorts for months. I don't know if anything will fit.

Since her whole illness started, I haven't taken care of myself, and I know I look squishy. Jules doesn't feel good about the way she looks, but maybe she doesn't think I look that great? I pull off my shirt, staring in the bathroom mirror at my disheveled dark hair with gray streaks, and I shake my head in disgust. I've totally let myself go. I'll have to wear a black shirt and pants to hide the roll around my stomach.

I've finished my shower and I'm trying to make some sort of peace with my hair when Julia knocks on the bathroom door. She pokes her head in, catching me in nothing but a towel. I instantly suck in my stomach.

"I see you got my note," she says with a sweet smile.

I continue focusing on my hair but take a quick glance at her through the mirror. "I did and I must say, I'm surprised." She quietly looks at the ground. I don't want her to feel uncomfortable, so I jump back in. "And incredibly pleased. Where are we going?"

"You know that newer, upscale Japanese restaurant close to here? I've heard good things. It's not too fancy and we can get sushi or something kind of healthy." Her voice drifts off at the end.

"Sounds perfect," I quickly reply. I bravely look at her but still try to suck in my gut, knowing it's no use. "What time are we supposed to be there?"

"Six-thirty. I'll have just enough time to shower and change."

"I'll be out of your way in a few minutes," I reply awkwardly.

Before she got sick, we'd think nothing of getting ready at the same time. But now Julia wants her space, so I always make sure she gets it.

She nods and backs out of the room, and then I frantically finish my hair and give myself a good shave. When I step into our room, she's gone, so I grab my black slacks and shirt and quickly dress. Everything is a little tight, but it will have to do. I finish with a pair of black boots. Just as I'm done, she walks back in, so I stand to leave.

"Bathroom is all yours," I say. As I walk by her, I give her a quick kiss on the cheek, my hand lightly touching her face. She stops my hand for a moment and holds it there, leaning against it.

"Thanks, love. I'll be down shortly."

I walk out, my heart lighter than it's been in months. Baby steps. That was one of the most intimate moments we've had in a long time. There's a chance.

Chapter 26 – Julia

After I finally get my earrings in, I stare at my necklace in my hands and realize it's hopeless. My hands are shaking so hard that there's no way on God's green earth that I'm ever going to get the clasp together. Should I take it downstairs and ask Raine to help me? That would be embarrassing ... or would it? It might be an icebreaker.

I slide on my strappy three-inch heels and take one final look at my reflection while standing in the humongous closet Raine built for me. I've been able to fill it with my clothes and shoes, but I've been good about giving a lot of stuff away, so it hasn't become too cluttered. Now back to my reflection that I've been trying to avoid. This dress suits me, and with my shorter hair, it makes my neck appear longer, which is why I need a necklace to cover the empty space.

I gaze down at the amethyst necklace in my hands. It's Jonah's birthstone and Raine gave it to me after we lost him. I only wear it on special occasions and tonight would be a good night to bring it out. I close my eyes and take a deep breath, gathering my wits, and then I twirl out of the room, necklace in hand. What am I, seventeen? I can do this!

As I hit the landing at the top of the stairs, Raine's back is to me. He quickly swirls around, startled, just as my still shaky hand grips the top rail. He looks like he's going to run up the stairs toward me but holds himself back and watches me take step after laborious step down the stairs. It's like I'm walking in sand, but my steps get easier as his bright green eyes never leave mine and he has a slight grin that instantly brings me peace.

I hit the bottom step. He takes one long stride and he's right in front of me.

"Wow ... that dress is amazing," he says, reaching out to take my left hand. I'm still clutching the necklace, and he feels it in my hand. "What's this?"

I open my hand up, "I need help getting it on ... I'm struggling with the clasp."

Raine gives me a broad grin as he takes the necklace from my hand and with his other hand moves me around so he can tenderly drape the necklace around my neck. Now I can smell his cologne; it's one that I bought him last year and my head starts to spin.

"This clasp is so tiny ... but I think I've got it. Hang on, let me put my readers on." I laugh as he pulls them out of his pocket and then continues. "There ... now I've got this bugger ... they really need to make these things bigger," he says, laughing. He finishes, and I can feel the stone pressed against my heart, right where it should be. His lips lightly graze the back of my neck, and my knees instantly go wobbly.

Raine pulls me lightly back against his frame, holding me there against him. "Really, Jules, you look wonderful. I was stunned for a moment."

I lean back against him hard, loving the feel of his strong arms against me. I'm in the safest place ever, and for the first time in more than a year, the weight lifts off my shoulders.

"Thanks, sweetheart. Well, we could stand here all night, but I'm hungry and we're about to be late," I say, chuckling.

Raine spins me back around to face him, smiling down at me as he runs a hand up to my face and places the gentlest kiss on my lips. Again, my knees fail me, but luckily, he has one arm around my waist gripping me tight and holding me upright.

"Your wish is my command, darling. Let's go, because if we keep this up, I won't be able to let you go."

He keeps his hand in mine and leads me out the door to our waiting Jaguar, which somehow is washed, waxed, and ready to go. Jacob's standing there ready to open the door for me.

"Nice touch," I say to Raine as he tucks me inside. I smile at Jacob giving him a thumbs-up. When we're both settled in, Raine gives me another surprise. He pulls a bouquet of purple tulips from off the back seat and hands them to me.

"What are these for?" I ask, my eyes wide with surprise.

"We haven't been out on a so-called 'date' in forever. I want you to have your favorite flowers."

"They're beautiful." I lay the flowers across my lap as he puts the car in drive, and we head out to the restaurant. We're both quiet, lost in all that's happened and what could be.

Although I had made the reservation, Raine must have called ahead because as soon as we arrive at the valet stand, they take the utmost care of us. We're led to a quiet corner. Sometimes people still ask for autographs and pictures, and a few people pause when we enter the room, but we make it to our seats without any fuss.

I order a club soda with cranberry and Raine gets his usual soda. I've heard wonderful things about the sushi at this restaurant, and they deliver. We both order different kinds, and we share until we're spent. It's a relaxing night away for us; something we haven't done in so many months that it almost seems new. I catch Raine staring at me a couple of times, and it makes me squirm in my seat. Sensing my dismay, he takes my hand and then leans in and kisses my cheek. His face has a tender glow that's been missing, and the worry lines I'm so used to seeing are almost non-existent.

As we make our way home, Raine takes the long way, like he's delaying our arrival. As we get closer to the driveway, I sense his tension build, so I put his mind at ease.

"Hey hon, how about you drop me off at the front and then go put the car away, while I head up for a quick bath and then we meet up in our bedroom?"

I can't miss Raine's nervous exhale of breath.

"Are you sure, Jules? Tonight was wonderful. I don't want you to feel any pressure."

"Raine ... I love you and I want you to know how much. I'm okay."

He takes my left hand and squeezes it hard, never taking his eyes off the road. There's excitement in the air mixed with an electric energy coming from both of us. Raine's eyes are big and bright, and every nerve in my body seems alive. Raine pulls up, and I get out, grabbing my flowers as I do. I give him a glance back as I say, "Give me time to put these in water and get ready. But I'm expecting you stark naked in our bed, pronto, buddy."

Raine grins from ear to ear as he gives me a salute. I shut the door and laugh as he squeals the tires up toward the garage. I shake my head and run up the front steps. Once inside the door, I take care of the flowers and then get up the stairs as fast as possible. For a moment, I have second thoughts. Raine's going to see and feel what my body is like underneath this dress after all the stretchy latex is gone. I groan out load. There's no time to be a pansy. Time to put my big girl pants on. But I should stay away from mirrors, I think as a trickle of doubt crosses my mind.

Chapter 27 – Raine

It took all my strength not to run up the stairs and ravish Julia when she appeared on the upper landing. I had to force myself to play it cool. I didn't want to scare her, but DAMN. She looked stunning and the dress showed off her curves, including her enhanced bosom, flawlessly. It's been a long time since we both made ourselves presentable to the outside world, and I must admit, we still clean up well. When she asked me to help her with her necklace and she pressed close to me, all I could smell was her perfume. I wanted to swoop her up right then and head back up the stairs, but I held back, and I'm glad I did. My only worry now as I'm closing the garage is being able to last. We haven't been together for months. I feel like an eighteen-year-old kid with hormones flowing through me that I can't control.

When I get inside the house, I check all the doors and make sure we're locked up for the night. Aria's car was in its usual spot, so that's one less thing to worry about. I stop in one of the guest bedrooms that's always stocked and take the time to brush my teeth and check my hair. When I enter our bedroom, I hear water running and the faint sound of Julia humming. That's a good sign. She's likely not regretting her decision to tell me to join her in our bed.

I go to our closet and strip down nude as ordered and then climb under the covers. There's continued movement in our bathroom and then finally the light goes out. It's several more moments before she steps out, wearing a cream-colored negligee that hits her mid-thigh. It's sexy, but not over the top. There's barely any light on in the room, but I can see Julia making her way to the side of the bed and she silently slides in. In the darkened room, I can hear her breathing and sense her unease. She used to walk around semi-nude all the time, but not anymore, and I get it.

She slowly rolls over toward me, and I move ever so slightly toward her, putting my hand on her hip. Julia raises herself up, putting her head up on her hand and she looks at me.

"Okay … now what?"

I can't help but laugh out loud. Thank God she broke the ice. In one swift movement I pull her tight against me and lay a big kiss on those lips that I adore. Julia responds in kind, her hand going to my hip, pulling me tight against her. A groan escapes from deep within her. Her body is warm against me in all the right places and already I think I'll explode. It's been too long.

You would never know that it's been months since we've been together like this. I look down at her slightly flushed face, and never in my life have I laid eyes on anything more beautiful. Her hands are gripping my upper arms, and she looks deep into my eyes. I lean down to the side of her face to whisper in her ear.

"I love you so much, my beautiful wife." Although I never, ever, want us to be apart again, this was worth the wait. I kiss her long and deep, and then I proceed to make love to my wife until the sun comes up.

Chapter 28 – Julia

I stumble into the kitchen the next morning still groggy from last night's escapade. I smile slyly to myself and then my face instantly flushes. What am I, a schoolgirl? I chide myself silently before grasping the much-needed coffee from the freezer to make a pot, or two.

I'm still slightly mortified that I let Raine see me in all my pudgy glory, but he didn't seem to mind. I'm sure he noticed each time I flinched as his hands grazed my stomach, or when he gripped my upper arms, but I tried to let it go and focus on the wonderful things he was doing. And damn, it was glorious. I've been a fool to have kept us apart for so long, and I won't let it happen again.

When I looked down at him in our bed, he looked so peaceful, like a little boy and more relaxed than he's been in months. There's a noise behind me as Aria shuffles in, wearing her usual long, comfy robe and slippers. I quickly focus back on the coffee machine.

"I heard you two come in late last night. Do anything fun?" Aria's right eyebrow rises slightly as she speaks.

I spin around, giving her my full attention. "Now, now, young lady, your parents are allowed to have a date night," I reply in a mock stern tone, but my face must give me away because a smile spreads across her lips.

She laughs as she gently squeezes by me to get to the fridge. "Well, I'm glad you both had a fun time. I noticed you even took the big kids' car and not dad's truck, so I figured you went to like a real restaurant and didn't just grab take-out." She grabs a yogurt and some fruit, and then she saunters toward the kitchen nook. My gaze follows her.

I lean casually against the counter, trying not to give Raine and me away, "Yes, we had a "big kids" meal with servers and everything. We would have invited you, but we knew you had other plans." I add, "It was good for us to get out of the house. Been a long time since we did anything normal like that."

Aria is dumping blueberries into her yogurt, and she stops. "Yes, it has been a long time since we did a whole lot of normal things." She continues to mix up her yogurt as she talks, "You know, Mom, I wish we could have taken a vacation before I started school. We can plan something for winter break? I'd love to go somewhere ... just the three of us?"

"I'm sure that can be arranged," I say as I hit "start" on the coffee maker.

"What can be arranged?" Raine asks, making a beeline straight for me. He grabs me and plants a kiss on my lips. Aria groans out loud.

"Dad ... please ... I'm trying to eat over here!" Aria's clearly disgusted but giggling at the same time.

When Raine lets me up for air, my hands instantly go to my hair to try and fix it, and I embarrassingly struggle with the robe I threw on. I'm a hot fricken mess. Raine grins broadly as he grabs me by the waist and pulls me tight to him, whispering against my hair, "You keep that up and I'm taking you back upstairs."

I'm squirming in Raine's arms and Aria again exclaims, waving her spoon dramatically, "Jeez, can you two stop, please! I'm losing my appetite!"

I don't know why she's carrying on like this. We've always been affectionate in front of her, but it's been a while since Raine's been like this. I make a funny face her way and Raine laughs.

Raine pulls away from me and asks, "How long on that coffee? I'm dying over here."

I smile, grab us both cups, and stop the machine midstream to get some. We make our way to the table with Aria.

"Well, kiddo, the big school day is almost here. Are you ready?" Raine asks teasingly, but I'm sure he's serious. We're anxious for our girl.

Aria doesn't miss a beat. "Dad, you know I'm ready for anything, but are they ready for me?" she jokes and I have to smile. Raine gives her an "atta-girl" smile and a high-five. This conversation makes me remember that I need to ask Raine about Trent Austin.

"That reminds me, Raine. Tracy said Trent Austin will be in town in the next couple of weeks, he's got something going on at Aria's new school. He wants to get together and write. What do you think?"

Aria knows who Trent is because everyone in the music business knows his name, and she knows I wrote and sang with him during *Next Real Star*, but she has no idea that Raine had misplaced jealousy about him and all that hullabaloo. Maybe I should have waited until we were alone to mention it, but Raine doesn't miss a beat.

"That would be fantastic. You know what I think about Trent's writing, and it'd be wonderful for you to start working again." He leans in and kisses the side of my head, then he casually takes a sip of coffee, like he doesn't have a care in the world.

"Okay …" I say with some hesitation, not because of Trent, but because I just put it out there that I'll get back to work. I don't know if I'm ready and maybe I shouldn't have said anything. "I guess I'll let Tracy know it's a go." Raine senses my hesitation because he puts his cup down and grabs my hand, giving it a big squeeze.

"It'll be great, Jules. Just like riding a bike." And then he gives me a huge grin and a dramatic wink, and I almost spit my coffee out at the table. Aria was glued to her phone and missed the last part that passed between us. Thank goodness. I give him a light kick under the table as he stifles a laugh. Aria looks up.

"What?" she asks.

"Nothing," Raine replies.

"Do I need to separate you two?" Aria asks, trying to be all tough and serious.

"We'll tone it down, sweetheart, just for you." I give Raine a self-conscious grin as I squeeze his hand in mine. Although I've agreed to start writing again, and my stomach is now tied up in knots, I've got to jump on that horse sometime.

But right now, as I look at my two loves, I don't want to be any place else on earth. What a glorious start to my day.

Chapter 29 – Aria

When Dad mentioned my new school, I played it cool, like sure, I'm completely ready. I've bought some new clothes, the supplies I'll need, and the required books. But deep in my heart, the fear is overwhelming. I figure it's the pressure I'm putting on myself because I must be successful. Going to this new school will help my mom, so I've got to be ready. But what if I don't fit in? I've never been around so many people before except for when I'm on stage and singing.

My truck takes its final turn into the school parking lot, and I find the nearest spot to the entrance. I don't care that it's rows away from the front door. I need several minutes to compose myself. I cut the ignition and as I pull the keys out, my right hand is noticeably shaking. I grab it with my other hand and close my eyes while taking a deep breath. *C'mon, chicken shit ... you've sang for thousands of people, what are a few hundred teenagers?* But the gnawing in the pit of my stomach won't stop.

I take a moment to check my look in the rearview before I open the door, clutch my purse and backpack, and finally close and lock the door. Today I'm wearing something I consider to be low key. I've got on simple jeans that are cut just above my ankle, short black boots, and a short-sleeved black sweater. I stayed away from anything high-end designer. I didn't want to scream money. Even though many of the students here come from wealthy families, a lot of the kids are on scholarships. I don't want to stick out—I just want to blend.

As I make my way to the front entrance, there are a couple of security guards situated outside. I get a couple of stares as I get in line to go through the metal detectors, which are one of the requirements of entering a public-school facility. I already have my new school badge, so when I get to the front, they scan me in, check my bags, and then I'm inside. The hustle of everything is thrilling. There's a sign that says "office," so I walk that way. This is where I'll get my new schedule.

I enter and join a small line until I'm finally in front of a stern-looking woman, with glasses at the end of her nose, who's taking each name and then rifling through a folder. She finds my schedule without lifting her head. As she pulls the document out and her eyes finally meet mine, she gasps loudly, stopping with my schedule just out of reach.

"Aria Wagner? As in *Julia Tate's* daughter?" she asks with enlarged, starstruck eyes. Her voice has gone up several decibels, and several people in line lift their faces from their phones to stare at me. I can't miss a couple of looks going up and down my frame. Not all the looks are friendly.

My eyes dart down to the floor and then back to hers. "Yes ... yes, that's me."

Her eyes get even bigger. "Wow ... I had no idea YOU'D be at our school." Her voice continues to rise. I just want it to stop. "Here you go," she says, finally placing my schedule on the counter so I can read it. "Your first class is English Lit, on the second floor. This is your locker number, also on the second floor, and here is the code, written on this form. Welcome to the Nashville School of Performing Arts," she ends loudly with a flourish of her perfectly manicured hand.

By now, every person in line has stopped what they were doing to stare at me. I grab the document from the counter with a quick, "Thanks." Then I spin around, keeping my head down, and walk straight out the door. There are a few whispers as I leave. That is not the way I wanted to start my first day. Sure, I thought someone might recognize me, but I'm not the famous one in our family. I hoped when people heard my name, they wouldn't necessarily put two and two together, but I was wrong.

I scurry toward the nearest stairway to find my locker. Then I can rid myself of all the book weight I'm carrying. When I was home schooled, I never had to haul so much crap around with me, but here I am, out in the real world. After dumping my things, I check my schedule and grab what I'll need for the first couple of classes. With my books pressed tight against my chest, I make my way to my English class, praying I won't get any more unwanted attention. I want to be a regular student, just like everyone else.

I have just settled into a seat at the back when the only person I know at this entire school walks in. Him. Just what I need. I do my best not to make eye contact. Out of the corner of my eye, Luke scans the room as he enters and says hi to a few other people. He then pauses. I take a glance his way, and our eyes meet. He gives me the biggest smile. Instantly my stomach plummets … or my heart stops beating, I'm not sure what has happened, but something seems really off when his eyes meet mine. There's an empty seat right next to me. *Please God, no, don't let him sit next to me.* But God is not on my side today as Luke saunters over and slides into the seat on my right.

"Well, hello, Ms. Wagner," Luke says boldly as his eyes bore into mine, his right upper lip curled ever so slightly.

My mind stumbles for a witty response back, but I got nothing. "Luke. Good to see you again." Instantly I'm chafing myself … *"Good to see you again?" What am I, forty?*

Luke continues, leaning toward me slightly, his self-assured nature coming through in full force, "So, I see you found your way around this big ol' school. What do you think so far?"

My eyes dart away and then back to his as I manage to squeak out, "Different. Definitely different." I don't want him to think I'm not open to change, so I continue, "But I don't mind a challenge, so I'm sure I'll get the hang of everything."

He jumps back in. "Our instructor for this class, Mr. Wheeler, is a stickler for APA style. Just a heads up."

"Good to know," I say nodding, but I have no idea what APA means.

We're cut short by the brisk entrance of a short man who barely says hello and asks someone to pass out the syllabus, and then it's off to the races. My first day of class has begun.

Chapter 30 – Julia

I got my baby girl off to school, and Raine went to his studio, so I might as well follow up directly with Trent. Tracy sent me his number, and I'm surprised to learn it hasn't changed in all these years. I think about texting him but it's stronger to call. He picks up right away.

"Julia Tate … well, all be!" His strong Texas drawl is as pronounced as ever. He cuts to the chase, which has always been Trent's way. "Tracy talked to you about writing together?"

"Hi, Trent. Yes, she did," I reply, hoping my voice remains calm and casual. For some odd reason, and even though I'm happily married, Trent has a way of making me act like a flustered schoolgirl. I cut to the chase as well, "I'm interested."

"Good! I'll be in Nashville next week to meet with administrators at the Nashville School of Performing Arts. I'll be in the area for quite a while, and I'd like to keep busy while I'm in town."

"Can you say what you'll be doing with the school? My daughter just started her senior year there."

"I can't yet … but she'll find out about it soon enough. How about we plan something for next Thursday or Friday? I can arrange a studio space?"

"Either day would work, and we can work here at the house. We have a studio or we can work in my office." I pause, trying to steady my frazzled nerves. "I'm looking forward to this, Trent."

"Me too, Julia. Will be good to see you."

"Likewise."

After the call ends, I'm dying to know what he'll be doing with the school, but I'll have to impatiently wait and find out from Aria.

I haven't heard from Trent in all these years. After *Next Real Star*, Trent continued to have amazing success as a writer, as I have, but we didn't keep in touch, other than a few run-ins at award shows and public appearances. We're always cordial though. I never considered writing with him, likely because of the awkwardness of Trent's well-known crush and Raine's obvious jealousy, I think with a smile. Raine continues to be protective of me, but after all these years of marriage, and our ups and downs, he's calmed down considerably. I wasn't too surprised by Raine's reaction to me writing with Trent. I've written with all kinds of people. And I can't wait to pry about what Trent's doing at Reezie's new school.

But right now, I've got the rest of the day free, and that's not good. We have an appointment with my doctor tomorrow. I'm doing my best not to think about it, like today and every day is just a normal day, but it's not. Every sense in my body is alive and I'm so edgy, like I'm gonna snap. My counselor in Texas, Sarah, explained that cortisol levels will go up due to stress of the unknown, but it's hard to explain to someone who doesn't know what it's like to feel like you're coming out of your skin.

I try to stay present in the moment, but it's easier said than done. I've been consistent with my exercise, so I'll hit our workout room, and then I'll run up to the stables and saddle up Butter for a ride. After finally breaking the ice with Raine in the bedroom, we haven't been able to keep our hands off each other. Although I struggle with my squishy body, I've relished the last few nights with Raine's strong arms around me. I love that we're intimate again.

As I change into my workout clothes, the ache in my muscles is a good reminder of my nightly escapades with Raine. I grab a bottle of water and steel my mind to strengthen my body so I can keep up with Raine. If only I can get my roller coaster mind to stop racing.

Chapter 31 – Raine

I'm finishing up the final mix on Julia's song, "He'll Stay," so we can get it to radio and launch it on streaming platforms. Wayne Carson's itching to get it out there. We'll also have time to submit it for big-time song awards. Even though I'm listed as the producer, this is Julia's masterpiece.

Aria and Julia recorded amazing background vocals. There is nothing like family harmony, and the timbres of their voices blend perfectly. Adding their voices to the mix makes the song even more angelic.

I finish selecting the best parts of the song until I have what I want, and then I send the files out for the final mix. They should have the final version sent back to me by the end of the week.

My mind wanders to how so much has changed in the past few weeks. Thank God we're growing closer after what we've all been through this year. Aria started her new school today, which is exciting for her, but I can't sit still because we're letting her out of our sight. We've protected Reezie, too much. Yes, she's been around all kinds of people, but she's sheltered, and we know it.

I glance out my studio window as Julia makes the long walk up our hill toward the horse barn. I smile watching her climb the fence to join her horse, Butter, and then she grabs the reins and leads the horse to the barn. For a moment, I think about joining her, but Jacob approaches. He'll get her whatever she needs, and maybe she wants to be alone.

I've known about her doctors' appointment for several days now. I've been trying to push it out of my mind by staying busy in my studio. This is the first chance we'll have to go over Julia's final tests and discuss next steps in her treatment. I silently pray that this entire nightmare will be over, or at least we'll have a clear next step. I glance up as Julia leads Butter out of the barn with a saddle. She climbs up, heading down one of her favorite trails.

With all my heart, I hope this is how she gets to spend the rest of our days, doing whatever the hell she wants, and that we'll never have to see doctors or hospitals, or go through any of this bull crap ever again.

Chapter 32 – Aria

Overwhelmed is an understatement. After my first homeroom class/Luke distraction, I manage to make it through all my morning classes, including a Guitar 101 class, which may end up better than I hoped. I sit by a couple of other girls and make small talk. No one acknowledges my famous parents, so I'll take that as a good sign.

I take a humongous breath as I enter the cafeteria. I imagine I'm eating alone, which is fine, or at least that's what I try to convince my fluttering heart.

The room is half filled. I gather up the healthiest items I can find including a banana and a bottle of water, and head to an open table at the back of the room. Only moments later, Luke strides in with a few friends and they head to a nearby table. I put my head down 'cause I don't want him to see me, but within minutes, I feel the presence of someone standing next to my chair. My eyes dart up.

There he is, calmly standing by my chair. "Find all your classes on time?" he asks while those deep brown eyes glow with sincere kindness that's entirely too disconcerting.

I slide up from my slouch. "So far so good," is my too quick reply, before I add with all the smart ass I can muster, "But the day is young."

He smirks. "I'm sure you'll be fine. Wanna join our table?" He gestures toward the table full of guys, but I shake my head.

I don't think my nerves can handle sitting with a bunch of guys I don't know.

"I'm good here … just getting my bearings. Thanks, though."

"Sure ... see ya around." He gives me a subtle wave bye.

I nod as he spins around, heading back to his table as his buddies watch. My attention immediately goes back to my plate, and then I pick up my phone, but I can't miss the guys chiding Luke at his table. Great. My fingers frantically type a text to my best friend Savannah. She'll be busy with her own homeschooling work, but she may have a minute.

She instantly replies, "How's it going in the real world? I'm bored out of my mind. Calculus."

I send a laughing emoji back, "Lunch ... and Luke. He's in my homeroom and just invited me to join his lunch table. I think I'm in trouble. LOL."

And I am in trouble. Savannah sends a question mark, and I promise to fill her in later. I grab my schedule so I can study the rest of my day. After lunch I'll meet with my voice coach, who's also my advisor, and then I have music theory followed by a dance class. I'm glad my dance class is last. I'd rather be a sweaty mess at the end of the day.

I let out a heavy sigh, slouching back down in my seat and focusing on the food in front of me while pretending my phone is fascinating. I'm glad for some solace during lunch, but I've never been more noticeably alone. I know everyone isn't staring at the sad new girl, but with every look I get, I can't help but wonder.

When I step up to the office of my advisor, Dr. Antonia Grace, the most wonderful sound of a female operatic voice resonates from the room. I give a knock and then a striking, exotic brunette greets me at the door. She gives me a wide smile and steps to the side, gesturing for me to come inside.

I'm quite taken by the room, and by Dr. Grace. There's a rich, gorgeous maroon rug covering the floor, comfortable chairs, and the pictures on the wall look like they were all taken in Italy. The room is decorated tastefully, like I've stepped inside an Italian opera house. There are pictures of her center stage dressed in long gowns. Dr. Grace, who looks to be close to my mom's age, is wearing a long pencil skirt, flowing blouse, and three-inch heels. She's professionally coiffed with her long dark hair pulled back on the sides of her head, but the rest cascades down to the middle of her back in long, luscious curls. Her makeup is flawless and dramatizes her deep brown eyes perfectly.

Dr. Grace runs to her record player. Yes, it's an actual old-fashioned record player, and she lifts the needle off the album. "Sorry, was just enjoying a moment during lunch to listen to one of my favorites." She gestures for me to sit, and I grab a nearby chair, putting my bag of books down by my side. "Do you like opera, Aria? It fits with your name?"

I sit up straight and respond, "I haven't heard much of it to be honest," I reply.

Dr. Grace gives me breathtaking smile, "Well, you are about to be introduced to it." Dr. Grace sits in a large leather chair in front of her desk, not behind it, directly across from me. This has a more friendly feeling than having her take a seat behind the desk. She leans forward as she continues, "Tell me, why are you at this school? I know a little bit about you, and about your parents, but what do you want to achieve while you're here?"

I pause uncomfortably, glancing down at the rug. That is a good question. Why am I here, other than my parents said I had to come here? How do I answer this? Honesty is the best policy.

I look directly at her. "Well, initially, I enrolled here because my parents wanted me to come here. You see, I've always been home schooled, or in a home school pod, but my mom's been sick, so they wanted to make things easier for her. But I've been a performer all my life and this seems like a good step for me … to, you know, get better at my craft. I've had some training in playing instruments, but that's from my parents or what their friends have taught me, or what I've picked up on my own. This seems like a good step in what I hope will be my career." And that is the truth. Even though this wasn't my idea, I do think this school will help me.

Dr. Grace has been listening intently and nodding along. "What is your focus then, do you want to write, perform, both? What is the ultimate goal for you?"

This is the first time I've said these words out loud. "I want to be as good as, if not a better performer and writer than my mom … and produce someday like my dad," I say with all seriousness. I don't mention my goal of learning to play lead guitar; that's my secret.

Dr. Grace doesn't miss a beat, "Those are fantastic goals, and quite attainable, especially with what you'll learn here. To help you reach those goals, we'll start with some vocal exercises and strengthen up your instrument. As for writing, I read your schedule, and music theory and guitar will help with that, and I'm sure you've already started working on your writing. There is an annual writing contest open to all students. You'll learn more about that in your music theory class. Your dance classes will help with stage presence and performance. Next semester, we'll make sure we get you enrolled in our initial production classes, but first, let's focus on voice and performance."

She quickly stands and gestures for me to do the same. She walks over to a cassette recorder and hits "record." Then Dr. Grace leads me through vocal exercises and scales. She sings a phrase and then I follow as she sings along. I'm familiar with scales as I've played them on guitar, but the tongue twister phrases she has me do, going up and down in key, are new. I laugh a few times as I mess up and her eyes twinkle, but she pushes me to continue. She takes a few breaks to walk through correct stance and breathing, and when it's time for our class to end, she stops, walks over, and cuts the tape off. She pulls the cassette out and hands it to me.

"I know cassettes are old-school, but find a cassette player and run through these exercises every day if you can. Next class, we'll pick out a couple of songs for you to learn to prepare for juries. Juries are what you'll perform for your final voice grade." I nod along like I know what she's talking about.

The bell rings, so I pick up my book bag as she watches with a smile. "It was good to meet you, Aria. I look forward to working with you," Dr. Grace says, her deep brown eyes smiling with her entire face. I can't help but smile back. I've found my favorite teacher.

Chapter 33 – Luke

At school, I wait in my truck a little longer than usual hoping to catch Aria walk in, and I get my wish. As she makes a beeline for the entrance, I grab all my gear and follow, careful to stay several feet back. I don't want Aria to think I'm like a stalker or anything like that. I'm just curious about our new, famous student.

My friends try to stop me as I head in, and I make small talk with my buddies as we walk along. Aria goes straight to the office, likely to get her schedule as a brand-new student. Because I preregistered over the summer, I received my schedule at home. Inside the front entrance, off to the side of the office, I casually continue my conversation with one of my friends, hoping I'll catch her when she walks out. Many minutes pass and then Aria scampers out of the office with her head down, heading straight up the stairs. I continue talking to my friend, but my eyes follow her as she bolts up the stairs.

As I casually make my way up the stairs, I can't help but smile. We'll both have lockers on the second floor. That's not hard to figure out, so I'm sure to run into her. As I head to my first class, English Lit, it's a great start to my day.

Having Aria in my English Lit class is a wonderful surprise, but seeing her at lunch is even better. I know my friends will give me a tough time about asking her to join us, but I don't care. I figure she won't, but it's worth a try.

As I make my way to my music theory class, I get another shocker when Aria enters the same room I'm headed to. She doesn't see me, so I hang back and let her take a seat before I casually walk in to find mine. In this class, we have assigned seats in alphabetical order. As my last name is Greyson, I'm in the middle of the room and she's in the back. She catches my eyes for a moment, and then quickly looks down. I should have expected we'd have more than one class together. This isn't a huge school, we're in the same grade level, and studying the same program.

Music theory is not my forte. I wasn't really looking forward to this class, but now it's looking up. I peek behind me and Aria's thumbing through her book. A class assistant hands out the syllabus and soon Dr. Alicia Smith graces us with her presence. And when I say grace, I mean it. I've heard some not-so-great things about Dr. Smith. She's tough and grades on a bell curve, which ends up with very few students doing well. There is no other option when taking this class. This is the only music theory class offered, and you must pass it, so here I am.

Dr. Smith is tall, stern looking, and I don't think anyone has ever seen her smile. She gives a brief, no-nonsense introduction and then she calls on each person in the room. We have to state what we hope to get from this class. I should have been prepared for this, but I'm not, even when she starts at the front of the room, which gives me time to think.

Other students give the standard responses like "I want to improve my songwriting," or "to better understand music." I need something original that doesn't sound dumb, but I'm struggling.

Then Dr. Smith looks down at her seating chart and asks in her nearly monotone voice, "Luke Greyson?"

"Yes ... I have to say as a guitar player, I'm hopeful this class will take my knowledge of my instrument to another level."

Dr. Smith pauses and then nods. I didn't think it was that bad ... it wasn't that original, but it didn't stink. I don't dare look back at Aria. By the time we get to the back of the room, we've heard every reason imaginable. Aria's second to last.

Dr. Smith introduces her with some flourishing remarks. "Well, class, it seems we have music royalty in the room." I catch a hint of a sneer on Dr. Smith's face as she gives her comments, but Aria doesn't seem fazed as she sits there listening intently with a bright smile on her lips. Our instructor continues, "Aria Wagner, what do you hope to gain from this class?" All heads swivel to Aria as she speaks.

"Thank you, Dr. Smith. Happy to be here. I'm familiar with the Nashville number system when songwriting and working in the studio, so in this class, I'm hopeful to get a better understanding of the basis of theory behind that system."

It's a different answer than anything else we've heard, and Dr. Smith seems taken aback.

"Yes ... yes, I am familiar with the Nashville number system," Dr. Smith responds harshly as her nose goes up in the air. "We won't be using any of THAT in my class," she retorts with obvious disdain. Dr. Smith moves on to the last student, and my eyes flash to Aria's face. I can see the instructor's comments didn't visibly touch her 'cause there's a slight smirk of satisfaction on her lips.

I've read about the Nashville number system, and I have some understanding. It's the main way Nashville area musicians work because it allows them to chart chords using numbers, so they can quickly transpose any song into any key. Aria gives me a slight hint of a wink as the corners of that gorgeous mouth turn up just a touch. I blush before I spin around in my seat and our attention goes to the front of the room. This may be my favorite class.

Dr. Smith relays information about this year's songwriting contest. Each spring, students can submit their best original song for a panel of instructors, and they whittle them down to the top ten songs. These songs are performed at the end of the year all-school show. Typically, the winning song is recorded with area musicians and a producer. Dr. Smith alludes to a twist this year, letting us know we'll find out more during our all-school assembly next week.

She proceeds to walk through the syllabus and class expectations. When our class is finally over, I pause to catch Aria, and we stroll out at about the same time.

I lean in, whispering to her, "Is music theory all you expected and more?"

A quiet snicker escapes with my words.

Dr. Smith lingers near the doorway. When we're finally out of earshot, Aria replies, "Definitely more than I expected." She gives me a full-on gorgeous grin, and all I can do is stare. She adds, with a flip of her head back toward the classroom, "I'm used to some hostility, comes with the territory." With that she gives a hearty laugh. "Got to run, Luke. Good seeing you again."

My heart about thumps out of my chest, but I respond as casually as possible, "Good seeing you, too, Aria."

Chapter 34 – Julia

I'm pacing around my kitchen. I'm sure Aria is fine, but with her gone all day at school, I'm coming unglued. Raine's footsteps bellow down the hall, and as he appears in our kitchen, his eyes catch mine. His furrowed brow tells me he's worried about our girl.

"She's fine, Raine. Our girl's got this," I say, and then I walk up and wrap my arms around him as he engulfs me against his body with a hearty laugh.

His face is against my head, and he says against my hair, "I know. I'm sure she's doing great. But it's hard to let her go." He pulls back to look down at me, "When you were here helping her with schoolwork, we knew who she was with every moment of the day. Now, we'll have no idea. I haven't heard anything from her. Not a text, emoji, nothing. It's killing me."

I pull him tight against my frame before moving away, but I keep his hand in mine as I tease him. "You know, we could have spent this day doing something a lot more fun ... in this completely and totally empty house."

In one swift motion, Raine sweeps me up in his arms and runs toward the stairs. I gasp out loud, "Raine! We don't have time!" I squeal, but he doesn't pay me any mind, taking the stairs two at a time. It's a struggle for him though because when we reach the top floor, his face is red, and a slight sweat breaks out over his face. Of course, Raine acts like it's nothing.

"We ... have ... plenty ... of time," he stammers, trying to catch his breath before continuing. "I plan on making sure you enjoy yourself over and over."

My head goes back in a hearty laugh. We make it to the bedroom and once inside, Raine closes the door with this foot, still carrying me in his arms. Once we get inside, the thought is ringing in my mind about how gross and sweaty I am after my ride.

"Hon, we could take a shower first?"

Raine, whose lips found their way to my neck, pauses. "I don't care that you were out riding. I don't care."

With that, Raine proceeds to rid me of my clothes, and we make the most of the time that we have before Aria gets home.

Later, as I'm lying next to Raine, he says, "We made it in plenty of time. We could go for another round?" A mischievous grin fills his face.

I smile lingeringly back at him, "Baby, I'd love to, and I'm sure our girl is quite aware that we're a happily married couple, but I don't want to flaunt it that on her first day of school, we acted like we don't have a care in the world. She'll think we dumped her off so we can spend all day in bed."

Raine gives a hearty laugh. "It would be good to spend all day in bed though," he says listlessly.

I laugh as I lean up to kiss this wonderful man who makes me happier than I ever dreamed possible. God, I love my life. "I take first dibs on the shower though," I say, jumping up and running toward the bathroom.

"Sweetheart, I could watch you do that all day. You're beautiful."

As I reach the bathroom door, I stop and roll my eyes at him, shutting the door as I yell out, "If she gets home before I'm out, meet her at the door."

He yells back, "Anything for you, love."

Chapter 35 – Aria

After a long, but good first day, I start up my truck and call Savannah. She'll want the details.

"Tell me all about it ... I've been waiting all day to live vicariously through you," Savannah replies with her girlish, high-pitched laugh.

"Two classes with Luke." That's all I say. Savannah gasps.

"NO! Well, you did want to get to know him. How was that? Awkward? Tell me everything!"

"It was good, actually." I'm grinning, although she can't see it. "I can't help it, Van, I really like him. It's not just because he's breathtakingly beautiful with eyes that melt you like butter, but he's got this niceness about him ... he's sincere, and boy, can I tell fake. And I've been around *a lot* of fake with Mom and Dad."

"I bet," Savannah replies knowingly.

I continue rattling on, "I have my first class with him, English, which should be good. I've always done well in that subject, but we also have music theory, and I don't know much about theory at all. My training has mostly been by ear or what they use in the studio, and the teacher clearly let me know that's not what she teaches in *her* classroom." My mind goes back to that class. I know I'll butt heads with Dr. Smith because I'm too stubborn.

"Oh Reez, you'll be fine. You were by far one of the best students growing up. You'll do great. Just give it some time to feel your way around. Now tell me more about Mr. Gorgeous," Savannah squeals. So, I dive in, telling her everything about him, from what he was wearing to the way he lingered around for me after music theory. I think there's mutual attraction there, but I can't bring myself to say it. Savannah does it for me.

"He's got the hots for you, and you know it. And why wouldn't he? You're smart, beautiful, and as we all know, amazingly talented. He'd be a fool."

"Yeah, maybe." My mind can't help but wonder why. Is it more about my family and less about me? That's been the case before. And do I really want or need this right now? There's a gnawing in the pit of my stomach when I think about some guy tearing my heart out. I really don't want any part of that. Nope. No way.

I end my call as I pull up our drive. Both my parents' cars are parked out front. When I enter the house, this amazing smell comes from the kitchen, which typically means Dad's cooking something special.

I drop my book bag near the bottom of the stairs and head toward the wonderful aroma. I'm really hungry 'cause I didn't eat much during lunch. When I round the corner, Dad's standing at the stove, tossing seasoning on some vegetables before he places them back into the oven next to a baking pan. It's chicken carbonara, one of my favorites. I smile as I reach him.

Dad gives me his full attention and a quick side hug. "There's our girl!" he says with a huge smile, his eyes crinkling up. He leans down and whispers in my ear. "Don't tell your mother that I said anything, but she's been worried sick … you know her. This was your first day away from us, like ever, and she's not handling it very well. Take it easy on her tonight, okay?"

I take a step back and give him a sly smile. It's not just my mother. He wouldn't be making one of my favorite dishes if it were just Mom. "Sure, Dad. I get it," I say with a smirk. Dad nods and then his attention goes back to our meal. I ask, "Want me to set the table, or do you want to eat outside? It's still nice out."

He replies, "Sure, that'd be great."

I grab everything we need and then set our patio table outside. Soon, Mom joins me, fresh out of the shower with wet hair.

"Took a ride today and needed to freshen up," she says. "Let me help you with that … so, how did it go today?" Her voice is a little shaky and it rises at the end. Dad was right. They both have been freaked out. I don't want to say anything about Luke, at least not yet, but I want to put her mind at ease.

"You know, it wasn't that bad. The classes are interesting, and I think I'll come away from the whole experience with tools to help my career."

Mom stops placing a dish down to listen and nods as I finish, a smile curling her lips. It must have been the right thing to say.

"That's wonderful, honey. You know, your dad and I just want you to be happy. We know you'll do great, no matter what you decide to do ... and I can't thank you enough for taking this step to help not only me, but it might end up being good for you professionally."

Slight tears form in my mom's eyes as she says this, so I stop what I'm doing and step toward her, putting an arm around her shoulders for a quick hug. Mom accepts it as our heads rest against each other for a moment.

Finally, Mom breaks away. "Okay, let's finish setting the table before your dad runs out here with dinner. Better be soon, 'cause I'm famished."

"Me too. Let's prod him along. Sometimes he needs it."

A knowing smile passes between us as we run back inside to hurry Dad up with dinner.

Later, when I'm back in my room and alone, I think back on my day and what my mom, dad, and Savannah all said. They all think I'll thrive at this new school. I hope they're right.

Now, with Luke, who knows what happens there. I don't want to put much hope into that whole scenario, and I shouldn't. I don't need anything more on my plate. But I realize I'm already wondering what he'll think about everything, like my songwriting, and even my choice in clothes. He's definitely someone I want to get to know better, but I'm putting the cart before the horse. I don't know him, and I need to focus on what I want. I don't need to get bogged down like some love-struck schoolgirl. But damn, I love that he towers over me. And those eyes ... I lose myself in those two deep brown pools. I shake my head, grab my music theory book, and crack open the spine. Nothing like a little music theory to bring me back to reality.

Chapter 36 – Raine

Last night, we decided to get a good night's sleep after I gave Julia a much-needed massage. Her shoulders were so tight, it felt like I was rubbing a brick and not her back. I chalked it up to today's appointment with her gynecologist, Dr. Henley. Julia hasn't said much about it, but I can tell it's weighing on her.

We load up into my truck with carafes of coffee in hand. I give Jules a soft, encouraging grin as we ease out of the garage. We're quiet as we speed down the Interstate. We both know what's at stake. We'll find out if the treatments were successful and the next steps, if any. It's a big day.

When it's our turn, we're ushered into Dr. Henley's private office. We've been in this room before, and it's not one of my favorites. I'm fidgeting in an uncomfortable chair watching minutes on a clock tick away like years. Julia's sweaty left hand is in mine. I give her my best "we've got this" smile just as Dr. Henley sweeps into the room with rushed elegance, a brown file in her hand. She's much older now than when Julia was pregnant with our first baby, Jonah. She's let her hair go completely gray, and I take comfort with that. Dr. Henley takes her seat in front of us, instantly giving us a huge smile. Julia exhales loudly, but it could have been my breath, I'm not sure.

Dr. Henley speaks right away, "It's all good news. The latest PET scan shows no signs of cancer, Julia. The targeted therapy seems to have worked, and they're not finding any trace of tumor in any organs."

I squeeze Julia's hand as she looks my way. I take a mental picture, so I won't ever forget her face at this exact moment. It's a mix of relief, shock, and happiness.

Julia's gaze goes back to Dr. Henley. "So, what's next?"

"Regular checkups and scans to make sure we don't see any tumors or changes in any part of your body. Every three months to start." She pauses and gives us both a big smile, "At this point, it looks really good, Julia. Really good."

Julia looks at me with tears in her eyes and it's all I can do to hold my own back. Dr. Henley stands and we follow. She walks around her desk and wraps Julia up in a huge hug as I look on, grinning like a child. They've been friends for a long time through good and bad, and it's a wonderful, tender moment for them both.

"Now get out of here, you two. I'm sure you have more fun things to do than hanging out in my office. I've told the front desk to schedule a follow-up in three months, and they'll make sure you get another scan before that appointment."

I shake Dr. Henley's hand before we leave. We stop at the front desk as ordered and as we go out the front door, I grab Julia in a hug and hold her tight against me, her arms wrapping tight around my side.

"Nothing but good news here, kid. We need to celebrate."

"What do you have in mind?" Julia asks laughing, tilting her head up to look at me.

"We have a completely empty house until about five ... what do you think I have in mind?" I say, looking down at her in all seriousness, pulling her in tighter.

"I'm game," Julia says, giving me a sweet smirk. "But I have one request first."

"Name it."

"I've either been nauseated or eating healthy for more than a year now. Could we please stop and get a loaded hamburger from the diner? Even a strawberry shake, too? I could really go for one of those."

I laugh as I give her a good squeeze. "You've got it. That sounds perfect."

I unwrap my arms and take her hand, and we race toward the truck, both of us laughing like little kids. Today is a wonderful day.

Chapter 37 – Julia

The next few days pass quickly. We told Aria the good news, and I can see the weight lift from her shoulders. I told my sister Jody, and I had a good, long talk with Tracy, too. Raine's walking on air and I'm relishing the lightness we all feel. But something is up with Aria. She doesn't say much about school. We get the usual school is good, I like my classes, yada, yada, yada, but something is weighing on her. Not in a bad way, but she's preoccupied.

Right now, I'm trying to get our house presentable for Trent, who'll arrive shortly. I haven't written at home in some time. As I restlessly touch up each room, I've been doing a cheer leading session in my brain, while also trying to keep my breakfast from coming up. Raine offered to let us use his studio, but I'll be more comfortable in my office. I have my guitar, and years ago, we put a decent piano in the room, so Trent will have something to play. Since I haven't kept in touch with Trent, this could be awkward, which is another reason why I'm a complete mess.

Our loud doorbell goes off in our foyer, and I rush to meet Trent. As I pull the heavy wooden door open, he's standing there with his back to me, surveying the view of our drive. He spins around and it takes my breath away. Trent looks the same as he did twenty years ago. He's as handsome as ever with just a touch of gray at the temples of his sandy brown hair. His bright blue eyes light up and slight wrinkles crinkle at his eyes with his smile, highlighting a few more lines, which makes him look more distinguished. Trent wears his years well.

I'm greeted by his familiar drawl. "Well, Julia Tate! You're as beautiful as the first day I met you."

He steps toward me and gives me a hug. I return his embrace. I've always liked Trent. Even with what happened during the show and how he almost disclosed my relationship with Raine, he was genuinely a nice guy and always sweet to me.

"Trent … wow," I say taking a step back away from him while gesturing for him to come inside. "You look exactly the same as you did years ago. You haven't changed a bit!"

He smiles at me and then takes a moment to look around the entryway of our home. "I must say, you and Raine have done well. Your home and the grounds are quite impressive."

"Thanks, Trent. We're blessed that Raine has been busy all these years," I reply with a kind smile. "And I've been lucky to have many songs cut."

"What is it now?' Trent asks. "You've had at least thirty songs on the country charts and many more cuts?"

"Something like that," I respond, shyly. "I'm just lucky I've been able to do something that I absolutely love for a living."

As I lead Trent down the hallway toward my office, I point out the kitchen and a close bathroom. When we enter the room, Trent takes in his surroundings and immediately goes to my desk full of pictures of my life with Raine and Aria.

"These are beautiful, Julia. I'm so glad everything worked out for you and Raine," he says, with a huge smile. He's being sincere, I can tell.

"Thanks, Trent. As I said, we've been blessed." I gesture to a small table near our piano, asking if Trent needs anything to drink, and he asks for water. I grab two as he takes a seat near the couch. He's carrying a satchel, and he takes out an iPad and logs in.

Trent looks up at me expectantly, "So, tell me, anything you feel like writing about, and do you want to focus on guitar or piano?"

Maybe it's because I've worked with Trent before, but instantly my racing heart starts to slow down. I look directly at him, "We've had great luck writing on piano, so how about we start there?"

He nods, "Wonderful. Any titles you have in mind?"

"You know ... I just got wonderful news, and I can't stop thinking about instances in life that spark tears. What if we write a song around that, and about big instances, good and bad, where tears happen in our life?"

"I *love* it." Trent moves to take a seat at the baby grand piano and plunks out some chords. "Should we start with the chorus and then see where that leads us in the verses?"

"Let's go for it."

For the next two hours, I lose myself writing with a master songwriter doing something that I've really missed. We take a brief break, but Trent is so focused. Before I know it, we've got a good chorus and one good verse down with ideas for two more verses.

I'm waving goodbye to Trent just as Raine's truck pulls up the drive. He parks near Trent's car. Trent greets Raine, and they shake hands, exchanging a few words. I'm waiting inside the front entrance trying to catch their conversation. With what happened during *Next Real Star*, it always makes me a little anxious when the two meet. But they've shared a few words at the award shows, and it's been fine. I don't expect today to be any different, but I can't help but pause.

Raine enters and catches me standing there. I look down, busted.

He gives me a knowing grin. "Well, hello love, fancy meeting you at the front door, waiting for me." He tosses his keys on the credenza and swoops me up in his arms, planting a kiss on my neck as a loud groan escapes his throat. "Damn ... you smell good. Should I be worried?" he says, putting me on the floor and peering into my eyes.

I shake my head and laugh, "Really? No, you shouldn't." Then I dive right in, "So what did Trent say to you?"

"Nothing really. A quick 'love the house, and thanks for letting us write here.' He said it went well."

I nod and smile at him, "It did, and *man*, it felt great to write again. I've missed it."

Raine smiles broadly, "Good, I'm glad. Will you write with him again?"

There might be a hint of trepidation, but it could be in my head. "We didn't finish the song we're working on, so yes, we'll need to write again.

Plus, it sounds like he'll be here for a while working with the school. He wouldn't tell me the details, although I did try," I say with a laugh. "Trent said that the students will find out about it next week."

Raine looks thoughtful, "That's interesting. If Trent's coordinating something with the school, it's a big deal. He doesn't do anything small."

I nod as Raine grasps my hand in his. "I'm starving ... didn't have time for lunch."

"Right there with you. We didn't take a break for lunch either."

Raine pulls me toward the kitchen. "I'll whip us up something, unless you have other plans?" He has a sly smirk on his face.

I shake my head at him, knowing his mind lately is usually in our bedroom, "How about we get some lunch, and then I'm going for a ride. It'd be good to clear my head a bit."

"Got it. But you wanna meet up later for a secret, you know, rendezvous?" Raine gives me a not-so-subtle wink, which makes me laugh. I reach out and give him a light smack on the ass with my own wink as we head to the kitchen.

"Maybe."

"There's still a chance," Raine says, leaning down to give me a big kiss before he goes to the fridge. As I watch him, I thank God for how lucky I am.

Chapter 38 – Aria

I've had several days of doing the same thing. Go to the same classes, take notes, make small talk with a few people, including Luke, even though my time with him is slightly different, then I go to lunch by myself and scroll through my phone. Then it's off to more classes. I do think I'm making a few new acquaintances, but this is harder than I thought. It's more cliquish and I'm an obvious outsider. It's finally Friday and I'll get a break from all this.

At lunch, I grab my usual items and head over to my table in the back, far away from everyone, and take out my phone. I'm starting to send a message to Savannah when suddenly Luke's standing next to me, a lunch tray in his hands.

"Can I join you?" he asks, a hint of hesitation in his usually secure voice. I'm caught for a moment in shock. As I move to put my phone down, I sit up straight in my chair. "Sure … be my guest," I say, gesturing to one of the many empty chairs around the table.

Luke drops his tray down and then settles into the chair next to me, giving me his gorgeous sly grin as he picks up a bottle of water. He glances down at his tray and sighs before turning his attention my way. "I admit, not very appetizing." Luke picks up one corner of his slice of pizza before letting it plop back on the plate. I can't help but chuckle.

"Yeah, I tend to stick with bananas and yogurt, and away from anything processed. But the toppings might be okay?" My nose turns up in obvious disgust. "Would you like my yogurt?" I ask as I pick the cup up, extending it to him.

Luke laughs. "I'll take my chances with this mystery meat." He pauses for a moment before cautiously asking, "So, your first week here ... what do you think? Do you think you'll like it?"

I reflect for a moment before answering. "So far, so good, other than a little sparring with Dr. Smith. I like the classes, and even though I don't know anyone yet, I think I'll enjoy it here."

Luke leans back in his chair, placing his hands behind his head, seemingly relieved. "I'm glad," he says openly. Then his attention goes back to his lunch tray, and he picks the pizza back up, "Well, I better try this before it's too cold and really gross.

We continue our lunch, just the two of us, exchanging small talk between bites, and for the first time this week, I feel like a real student at this school.

Chapter 39 – Luke

My interactions with Aria are going better than I expected. She's a breath of fresh air in an environment that's become entirely too boring and stale. I always enjoy seeing her in our mutual classes, but today when I asked her to join her table, it went better than I hoped. I guess I shouldn't be so surprised. She clearly was raised to be polite, but I didn't expect her kindness and wit. That's icing.

By the end of the day, I can't wait to get home so I can work on new music, but first, I've got to stop by the market and pick up a few things for Mom. She can't drive anymore, and she relies on me to get what we need. I grab our groceries and as I'm checking out, I glance at a magazine in a nearby rack. There's one with several photos of Aria's mom as she's leaving the airport with her head down. She's trying to avoid the photographer, but you can see that she looks pale and her short brown hair is mixed with gray. The headline's terrible and paints Julia Tate as still suffering from cancer and barely hanging on. I frown and my stomach churns when I think about Aria. She seems so strong. I know the media is often less than honest, and I wonder how hard this is on her. Because I take care of my own mom with her illness, I know how difficult it is to manage things you never thought you'd have to.

When I get home, I call out as I open the front door. Mom yells back from her bedroom. I carry the bags into the kitchen and put everything away. Then I head to Mom's room to check on her. She's in bed as usual, where she's likely been most of the day. Mom's been on disability for about four years now. With her disability pay and my dad's life insurance, we're doing okay, but money's tight. I wish I could hire someone to take care of her during the day.

I lean against the doorframe. "I picked up everything on your list. Do you feel like having supper? I can whip up eggs or some soup?"

"Thanks, Luke. Soup sounds great. I made a sandwich for lunch, but soup would be nice … I can help." She tries lifting herself off the pillows but falls back. Today is one of her tough days.

I put my hand up, like it's taken care of, "I got it, Mom. I'll bring something back here for you."

She smiles at me and then asks for the TV remote. I grab it off her dresser and hand to her. "Must be time for me to pick some letters," she says with a smile.

I laugh as she turns on her favorite show. "I'll be back shortly," and I whip around toward the kitchen. I close my eyes and try not to sigh out loud. I wish things were easier. I'd give anything to help her.

I walk to the cupboard and grab a decent, organic can of soup that's one of her favorites. I heat it up in the microwave, while I cut up vegetables and take out some crackers to go with it. I wish this were better, but it's the best we can do, plus it's something she'll eat. Her stomach gets upset so easily that we keep her meals mild and easy.

I carry the bowl on a tray down to her room. When I enter the doorway, it looks like she's asleep, but she stirs, so I take the tray and put it down by her bedside.

"Smells good," she says with a smile. I put the tray close to the side of her bed so she can reach it. She'll eat as much as she wants, so I'll leave her alone. I head out the door and look back to see her reach out for the spoon and napkin as she prepares to eat. Good. She's hungry today.

I head back to the kitchen and open the freezer. I grab a frozen pizza, which is fine by me. I preheat the oven and while I wait, I check my phone and notice a message from one of my good friends, Matt. I wouldn't call him a best friend, but he's been a friend since grade school.

"Dude, what was with you at lunch today? Who is she?"

I'm quick to respond, "You don't know who she is?" I'm surprised. I thought that everyone would recognize Aria. I jump back in. "Aria Wagner ... daughter of Julia Tate and Raine Wagner. You know, Nashville country music royalty."

Matt texts me back right away. "I had no idea! You rarely step away from us for anyone, but today, you ghosted us. I get it. She's GORGE, dude!"

I pause for a minute. I have to respond carefully. I really like this girl, and I don't want Matt or any of my other friends to treat her casually, but I don't want them to know how much I like her. "She is very pretty, Matt. I ran into her at the library and we struck up a convo. Just trying to make the new girl feel welcome."

"Right ... she's hot. LOL. See you tomorrow."

I don't address anything further. "See ya."

But Matt is right. Aria's more than hot. She's my ideal and I've known it from the first moment I met her. It's not just her physical characteristics, or her smile, it's everything about her.

I think about the new song I've been working on, "Coming Home." After dinner and checking up on Mom, I'm gonna get back to it. I've never been more inspired to write the best song I could ever write.

Chapter 40 – Raine

I've been on cloud nine ever since we came home from Julia's doctor's appointment. I'm relishing the fact that Julia is cancer free, our intimate life is getting back on track, and we're both working again. But I know things can change on a dime. My hand goes to my chest, and I pause for a moment. I don't know why I can't let myself stop and enjoy the roses, or in Julia's world, tulips, but there's always a lingering doubt that the bottom will drop out.

I check my phone. I'm expecting an email from Wayne's people about Julia's song, "He'll Stay." They think they'll drop it at the end of next week. We've been putting these wheels in motion for a while now and creating initial promo teasers. I'm like a kid at Christmas, and I can't wait to share the promo with Julia. I need to come up with a special way to let her know about this, but I don't think I can hold this news.

My phone dings and the email hits my inbox. They're featuring "He'll Stay" as the single dropping first out of ten songs on his new project. Julia's name is on all the promo materials as the featured writer. Now we've got a reason to celebrate.

Julia's up at the barn, so I hop in the golf cart and race toward her with Lute and Lyre running alongside. I pull up to the barn, hop out of the cart, and when I enter the barn, Julia's with another of her favorite geldings, Snickers. He's tethered and she's tenderly brushing out his mane while she talks to him. Each animal on our mini ranch is like a pet to her, and she babies them all. Julia finally sees me standing at the corner of the barn door, or maybe it's because our two dogs are creating a ruckus at the barn door.

She pauses and smiles, "Hey there ... what's up? You don't usually come up here during your workday."

I stride her way as the dogs follow behind cautiously. They're friendly with all our horses, but they know their limits. I'm practically yelling before I reach her, "I have big news, young lady, and I had to share it right away."

"Better be good," she says with a sarcastic smile.

I can hardly control my enthusiasm as I bellow out, "Wayne is dropping 'He'll Stay' next week as his first single, and you're listed as a featured writer. They feel the same way I do about this song, Jules."

She stops brushing Snickers, puts the brush down, and gives him a good pat before walking across the large room to meet me.

Of all the clothes I've seen her in, when she wears her tight riding jeans and boots with her hat, it's my favorite. As she walks toward me now, it stops me in my tracks. Being back home, surrounded by everything she loves and back in the sun riding every day, even though she still looks a little tired, Julia's never looked better. I rush to her and take her up in my arms, swinging her around. She laughs at my exuberance.

"Well, hello, cowboy," she says against my lips as they join hers. I think about rushing us both to the golf cart, but we'd have a horse to untether and put back out in the field. There's no way she'd let me be that irresponsible.

I unlock my lips. "I had to tell you right away, I told you this song is special, Jules. I can feel it."

She nods, resting her head against mine before I slowly let her drop back down to the ground.

"Let me take care of this horse and I'll meet you back down at the house. I do need to run to the feed store today, and I also want to check out some new paint for the house. Care to join me?"

"I can't think of anything I'd rather do," I reply with a look of mock enthusiasm.

Julia laughs, then smacks me on the butt as she goes back to Snickers, but not before crouching down to love on the dogs, who happily follow me back to the cart and down the driveway.

Maybe I'm too excited about the song, I don't know, but it feels like a good sign for where we are, and Jules deserves some good news in her life. The song is special and Wayne agrees. Now we'll find out what the world thinks.

Chapter 41 – Aria

After an incredibly boring weekend hanging out with Savannah and helping Mom in the stables, I'm facing my second week at school. It seems a bit more normal now. During English, my first class with Luke, they announce we'll have a special school-wide assembly in the auditorium right after class. I give a quick glance at Luke as my eyebrows raise, and he shrugs his shoulders back at me.

As we walk out of class, Luke saunters along next to me making small talk. He mentions that having us all meet for an announcement is unusual. We pass a few of his friends, and he gives a fist bump here and there, but he continues walking with me toward the large auditorium at the center of the school. You can't miss the oversized triple set of two-story double doors. We're on the right side of the auditorium, so we walk in and make our way down the side about ten rows from the front. I try not to put too much into the fact that Luke stayed with me so I wouldn't have to sit alone. We take our seats as other students stream in, a steady chatter echoing throughout the room. The stage is bare except for four chairs to the left of a center-stage podium.

"Well, this really is odd," Luke says, giving me a side-eye and a slight grin. Chills race down my back.

I glance back at him, trying to avoid getting swept up in his eyes. "Any idea what this is about?"

"Nope. Maybe we're all in trouble," he says mischievously.

By this time, the room is full, and the lights dim. The room starts to quiet down. Luke nudges me as the principal of the school, Principal Fieldstone, walks out from the left toward the podium. I've never seen this man in person, only online, but his gray hair and wispy beard instantly give him away.

He makes it to the podium and does his own quick mic check, tapping the top to make sure it's on.

Principal Fieldstone jumps right in, "Students, faculty, and guests. I'm sure you're all wondering why we called this mandatory assembly." He loudly clears his throat and continues, "Each spring we have a song contest open to all students and the ten top songs, as voted on by our faculty, are performed at the end of year show. The student with the winning song can record his or her song with Nashville area musicians. This year, our school's been invited to participate in an even bigger project. Mainstream Studios contacted us with a request to write their title track for their upcoming major motion picture, 'Love Struck.'"

My eyes meet Luke's, and his brows rise in surprise as his pleasant smile broadens.

Principal Fieldstone continues, "So, for this year's contest, we'll pick the top ten songs, then narrow that down to the top three and each of these songs will be performed in the early spring. Based on that performance, judges will select one of the songs as the title track for the movie. Students who wish to compete can view select excerpts from the screenplay, and you'll have the chance to meet with the director and executive producer. We'll also have an award-winning L.A. songwriter here to help the top three contestants with their final performances, and our own Dr. Smith, as part of her music theory curriculum, will be a consultant on the project. I'd like to bring the team out for you to meet."

Our principal stops and directs the audience to the right as one by one he introduces the people who will fill the empty seats on stage. My mouth went dry when he mentioned Dr. Smith's role in the contest. Not a good sign for me. My attention goes to the stage as each person walks out. Principal Fieldstone introduces the director and producer, both names I've heard of. Then Principal Fieldstone calls out the name I knew I'd hear. When he says Trent Austin, out walks a handsome older man with grayish brown hair. He's slender and not as tall as I imagined, but he oozes confidence. Trent takes long strides across the stage while raising his hand to the welcoming cheers from the crowd. Trent stops center stage to shake Principal Fieldstone's hand before taking his seat. Finally, our own Dr. Smith stalks across the stage, barely acknowledging anyone before finding her seat.

A steady murmur buzzes across the room as three people with microphones make their way down the aisles. Microphones are also handed to the show's judges on stage.

Principal Fieldstone puts his hands up and all quickly quiet down. "I thought there would be questions. You can come down to the front of each aisle to ask them."

There's a nervous silence as students decide if they dare ask anything. I'm surprised when Luke jumps up, making his way to the front.

The first question is about the timeline and deadlines and that's easily answered. We're in the month of August and contestants will perform for the first time in December. They'll cut the list down to the top ten, and then in March, the top three songs are performed for a larger audience. We'll have plenty of time to work on songs.

Luke courageously steps to the microphone. "Yes, thank you, Principal Fieldstone and distinguished guests." I giggle. That was over the top, but I admit, it was a nice touch. "Can we have multiple songwriters on our songs if we want?"

It's a decent question. In prior years, the school's contest was always a solo songwriting contest. I don't think this has come up before.

Principal Fieldstone looks back at his panel, and the other judges confer with Trent. When finished, Trent speaks. "That's a good question. Often, songwriters co-write with others. In fact, that's usually how it works in the real world. For that reason, I don't see why you couldn't work with another student, or students, if you want to."

As Luke makes his way back to his seat, his eyes catch mine and he gives me a huge wink. As he slides into his seat he whispers, "Well, this will be an interesting year." Our attention goes back to the speakers and the remaining questions.

Wow. This *will* be an interesting year. I look at Luke from the corner of my eye and he's listening with rapt attention. Why did he ask about co-writers? Should I ask him about that? Would he want to work on a song with me? That would be amazing and the more I think about it, it's a wonderful idea.

Chapter 42 – Raine

We hit the feed store and I load up the truck for Julia, and now I'm faithfully trailing behind her in the paint department. Not that I mind following her, but this isn't our usual hang. Ever since she's been home, she's mentioned changing up the house from our white, black, and gray tones and giving the house some color. I'm not against this at all, but I have no idea what she's thinking. I'm along for the ride and I'm thrilled she's excited about something. If she chooses hot pink or something like that, I'll just have to go with it.

She's pulled at least a hundred color swatches from the selections available when finally, she stops and exclaims, "That's it!"

Finally she's landed on something, but I keep this to myself.

Julia swivels her gorgeous frame to me with a swatch of five colors on one strip and points to a deep reddish burgundy in the middle. She's still in her riding jeans, and she's swapped her riding hat for a ball cap, but she manages to take my breath.

"This is what I was looking for. Just the right color to add a splash of life to the kitchen."

I nod to her. I wish I cared more about this. I've always left home design and decor to her, except for the studio, and when I had her closet renovated after we lost Jonah. My chest tightens at the thought of him. That loss never goes away.

"What are you thinking? Coloring one of the walls or something?" I ask, following Julia up to the paint counter.

"Yeah, probably. We can try it out and see if we like it, but maybe we paint one of the side walls in the breakfast nook, and then also use this color as a basis for items we put in the room, like a vase, and new pictures and stuff?"

"I like that," I say, nodding. I stand to the side as she gets a small sample from the staff, and then we saunter around the store. We grab a few more house plants for her office and other items for the guest house. In the many years we've been married, we haven't spent many days like this, but now that Julia doesn't have to prepare assignments for Aria, we'll get plenty more of them, and I'm all for it. This makes me wonder about her songwriting with Trent.

"Have you heard again from Trent about writing?"

"No, not yet. He said he'll be here for a while, so I'll get my chance. I'm gonna call Tracy tomorrow and check about working with a few more people. You said Wayne is dropping promo next week for 'He'll Stay.' Do I need to do anything to help?"

"I have no idea, but I'll find out. Are you up for it?" I ask as my voice rises questioningly. Since she's been sick, Julia has avoided the public eye, so I'm more than surprised.

"I think I am. Not that Wayne would need me for anything, but it could be fun?" Her tone is strong, but there's a look on her face that doesn't quite match her words.

A slight smirk crosses my lips, and I grab her hand as we head back out to my truck.

"You're gonna need help from Jacob to unload all that feed … we really didn't think this through, 'cause don't look at me," Julia says with a snort.

As we reach her side of the truck, I push her up with a friendly tap on that gorgeous butt.

"I've got this feed, young lady. I'm not that old."

She's laughing as she looks down at me. I close the door and boldly stride to the other side. A grin spreads across my face. When we get back, my first call will be to Wayne. She gave me the green light, and we've got Julia's song release promo to arrange.

Chapter 43 – Julia

As soon as we get home, Raine and Jacob unload the truck while I gather the few items we bought for the guest house. As I make myself busy, my mind won't stop. I didn't really think through my offer. Am I ready for the public eye? I still don't look that great, as I glance down at the soft layer I'm carrying round my middle, and my jeans are way too tight. Not to mention my hair. Other than a wig, there's no way to hide my short hair, so I'll have to embrace it. I consider calling a salon to see if they could work their magic or add extensions, but I can't expect miracles.

I finish with the guest house and then carry my new sample into the kitchen. I'll paint a large swath on the tester and then hold it up on the wall. I'm standing in the center of the kitchen staring aimlessly when a voice comes up right behind me.

"Is there a bug on the wall?"

Aria startles me out of my trance and I spin around with a gasp, then keel over in laughter as my daughter stands with her arms askew on her hips, staring at the wall like she's ready to go and kill a spider. I hate spiders.

I take a seat to try and calm down. "Oh … my … gosh!" You scared the crap out of me! No! No bugs or spiders. We bought a sample of paint and I'm picturing it on the wall."

"Oh, cool. What color?"

"It's a reddish color … your father thinks it's too much, but I think we should go for it," I say with an insecure chuckle. I point with my words, "What do you think about this back wall in the breakfast nook, and then we'll add picture frames and a vase or something to match? I won't do the back splash or anything like that, just a bit of color to bring this room to life."

Aria replies, her eyes dancing, "I like it! And who cares what Dad thinks … he's clueless about this sort of thing anyway. Where is he? I have some news from school."

"He went straight to his studio when we got back. I agreed to do some promo with Wayne. He's a little overexcited about it." My voice drops at the end.

"That sounds like fun!" Aria exclaims.

Speaking of her father, he walks in and catches us mid-stream.

"What sounds like fun?" he asks, giving Aria a side hug.

Aria chimes in before I can stop her, "Mom doing some promo."

Raine nods with a smile and instantly my stomach drops. "Wayne's booked on the Daryl Bradshaw podcast next week, and he wants you to join him. It includes video. It's a live taping, probably at least an hour … maybe longer." Raine stops, raising his eyebrows expectantly as he waits for my reply.

My hands are tightly clasped together and I'm sure my pasted-on smile is giving me away. "Hmm … video … okay, I guess so. I have no idea what we'll talk about for an hour, but I guess that works." I quickly change the subject, remembering Aria has news. "Reez, what did you want to tell us?"

Aria excitedly fills us in on her impromptu school assembly. I'm completely intrigued as we listen to all the details about the song contest and potential opportunities for her and the other students. No wonder Trent couldn't say anything.

Raine leans against the kitchen counter and asks, "I'm sure you're going to enter a song?"

"Yeah, I think so, Dad … they'll let us co-write too, so I'm thinking about that."

I finally get a word in, "Well, this is wonderful and a great opportunity for you to showcase your talent."

Aria nods along, but I can tell by the look on her face that she's not so sure. Raine senses it too because he offers his own words of encouragement, and then he brings us back to the sample of paint sitting on the counter.

"Did Mom tell you about her new project?" he asks, pointing teasingly toward the back wall.

"Yes, and I love it. In fact, we should start right away," Aria says as she reaches for the sample and heads toward the wall. "How about we just slap some of this on here and see how it looks?"

I'm smiling back at her, nodding in agreement. Raine shrugs his shoulders, so Aria and I grab a couple of brushes and actually slap some of the bold new color on our now gray wall.

"Well, then I'm going to order us a semi-celebratory dinner because I don't feel like cooking," Raine says, opening his phone. "Any suggestions?"

Aria yells out, "Pizza!"

He looks at me questioningly, like really. Pizza? I nod yes, and he places an order of our typical favorites, a thin crust meat lovers, a spinach and mushroom for me, and I'm sure he'll order a salad.

My attention goes back to the wall. We use up the entire sample in the middle of it, and then we take a step back. We're lucky we don't have red paint all over us, but I did manage to get some on my hands, and Aria has a smudge on her face.

Raine comes over and takes a picture of us both, as I give him "a look" like, seriously?

"Don't even think about using that against me later," I tease.

"Oh, don't worry about it … I will," Raine says laughing as he walks out of the room back to his studio. He calls out, "I've got to call Wayne back and confirm your podcast appearance."

My stomach acid instantly rises. Back in the public eye. I'm not ready.

After a good long, hot shower later that night, I'm standing in my massive closet, staring at my wardrobe, wondering what I'm going to wear for next week's podcast. I'm wrapped up in my own insecure thoughts, and when Raine comes up behind me and puts his arms around my waist, I jump, startled.

"Sorry, love, didn't mean to scare you," he whispers against my hair.

My insides burn with desire as he grips me a bit tighter.

"I loved what you were wearing today. Nothing like seeing you in your riding jeans, all sweaty after a ride. I'll take that every day."

"Well, that's good," I respond quietly, leaning against him as he runs his lips down my neck. "Because that's what I plan on wearing every day for the rest of my life." Except for next week, I think uncomfortably, and I tense up.

"What's wrong?"

"Honestly … next week. I shouldn't have agreed to do the interview, Raine," I say, slowly spinning around to face him.

Raine reaches out and takes my face in his hand. "You look fantastic and this will be a piece of cake, Jules. Just talk about the song … and if you want, talk about what's been going on. We've always been straight with fans and there's no reason to stop now."

He stops talking and moves his lips to mine. My breath catches as his other hand grips me tight around the waist. After a moment and in one giant swoop, I'm in his arms as he makes his way into our bedroom and sets me on the floor. The room is already dark; he shut off the lights when he came in. The only light comes from the closet, and we can still see each other. I'm wearing a thin robe over a long negligee. Raine's still in his work clothes. He proceeds to slide my robe off my shoulders, and my hands work on the button of his jeans. We're silent and we go through motions we've made hundreds of times, removing our clothes until we're both naked in front of each other, wanting and waiting.

"Have I told you today how beautiful you are?" Raine whispers out before taking me into his arms, placing me on the bed, his body covering mine as we lose ourselves in each other.

We're lying in bed, wrapped up in each other's arms. My head nestled against his shoulder as Raine gently strokes my hair. I relish where we are right now, so different from a year ago.

Raine quietly asks, "What is it, Jules. What is going on in that gorgeous head of yours?"

I lean up on my arm, looking him in the eyes. "I was thinking about how blessed we are ... and I was comparing this moment to a year ago, when I was so sick. We were at the hospital and things were so very different."

I press my head down against his shoulder as Raine pulls me tightly against him. He doesn't say anything. We haven't talked much about my health since we left Dr. Henley's office with our good news. I don't want to jinx anything. Although I still get tired easily, I've focused on keeping myself as physically and mentally strong as possible. But I wonder if we should do more. We've lost our spiritual life, and we need to do more normal things.

"What about going back to that church we used to go to before life got busy with Aria? Would you be okay with that?"

There is a slight pause, but then I'm surprised by Raine's answer, "I'd love that, Jules. That'd be good for us. Honestly, with the stress of everything, it'd be good for us to get into a rhythm of a location. They might have an AA group I could join."

I raise up on my arm so I can see his face. "Have you wanted to drink these past few months?" Raine hasn't mentioned AA or drinking to me in so long. I really don't know how to take this other than he has been hurting much more than he's been letting on. One of my biggest fears.

Raine smiles sheepishly and chuckles, "Of course, but you and Bret would've kicked my ass."

I laugh as he lays me down on my back, resting on his forearms, looking down into my eyes. "Seriously, Jules, this past year was rough, you know that, but having Aria here was a saving grace, and of course there was my work." He pauses and looks down before continuing, "But I almost slipped a couple of times. AA might help, and going to church with you is something we could share."

My arms wrap up around his neck, "Every day I don't think I can love you any more than I do, but then you surprise me."

Raine leans down and gives me the sweetest kiss as our bodies instantly and naturally react and again we blend as one.

Chapter 44 – Luke

As I'm walking into school the next day, I'm trying to figure out how to ask Aria if she wants to write a song with me. But how can I do it without sounding desperate or stupid? Coming from a seasoned songwriting family, what will Aria think of some no-name high school dude asking to write with her? I'm not in her league. I've got to seem competent and professional, like I've done this sort of thing before. I'm running phrases through my mind and not paying attention to my surroundings when suddenly, Aria's right in front of me, like she's been waiting for me. My shoes make noise 'cause I stop so suddenly.

"Hey, Luke." A slight smile is playing on her lips.

And with those two words, my face turns a color of scarlet that matches the stripes on the American flag.

"Hey, Aria."

We both continue walking together toward the building. Luckily, the silence is brief as Aria jumps right in.

"I'm glad I caught you before class ... I realize you haven't had much time to think about it, but when you asked about songwriting with other people for the contest, it made me think you'd be open to it. I wanted to see if you'd like to work on a song together. Since you're known for being such a great guitar player, I thought we'd work well together. I know it's quite an ask, but what do you think?"

Keep your composure ... keep your composure, my brain practically screams. I look at her and manage to say, while trying to hide my gargantuan smile, "Well, sure, Aria, that'd be great. I'd love to write with you." I want to say something more about her strengths. "Coming from such a famous songwriting family, I'm honored that you want to write with me."

I've embarrassed her because she grows quiet, watching the ground as we enter the school and proceed up the stairs toward our lockers. The guitar strapped to my back slows me down a bit and Aria waits for me as I maneuver through the people.

We reach the top of the floor, and she speaks. "Okay, so do you wanna schedule something then? We could write at my house?"

I didn't get this far in my mind. I never thought about the where or when. "Sure, that'd be great. How about this weekend? Would that work?"

"Sure ... that should work. I'll need to check with my parents first though."

Now things grow awkward between us. We have an actual writing appointment ... and I already need to tell my brain, "It's not a date, it's not a date."

I reply, "Okay, I'll see you in class."

With my words, Aria whips around, speeding off toward her locker, and I get a few minutes to clear my head. She asked ME to write. There is a God.

Chapter 45 – Aria

It's Saturday, the day I'm writing with Luke. I tried to sound casual when I let my parents know that we'd be writing at our house. I did everything possible to not let any emotion flow through my voice or show on my face. I'm not sure they're convinced. I've never invited a "boy" over before for anything. I caught a grimace flash across Dad's face, and I swear the corner of Mom's lips curled into a slight smile. Great. They think this is something other than a writing appointment, which, in the back of my mind, I think it could be. Right now, and maybe for the first time ever, I hope it is. But I can't let that remotely get to my heart. Not yet, at least.

My entire week poured like molasses. I spent three days trying to figure out which room we'd write in. I don't want this to be too formal, and I want Luke to feel relaxed. Of course, Mom offered her office, saying it has always brought her luck. I spent another evening trying to figure out what I was going to wear, and I landed on casual jeans. Finally, last night, with Mom's help, we baked some cookies, and I have drinks ready. Now I'm arranging and rearranging everything from the placement of the chairs to the pillows on her sofa. I've never been this hyped up—about anything.

We're starting at one, and I'm sweating bullets by twelve thirty. Of course, Mom and Dad decide today is the day they're painting the kitchen wall, so a big plastic tarp covers the kitchen floor, and the furniture is spread all around with some streaming out into the hallway. They're painting it themselves, and right now, there's loud music and peals of laughter coming from the kitchen. They're going to totally embarrass me; I just know it.

Luke's truck pulls up through the open gates a few minutes early. I knew he'd be punctual. I peek out from behind a front curtain. He pulls up out front and I watch him grab his guitar and backpack. When he steps out and closes the door, he casually looks up at the house and around the grounds. As I see him make his way to the door, I move that way. Loud noises are coming from my parents in the kitchen, and a groan escapes me. We'll have to walk by that doorway. He won't be able to miss them.

The doorbell peals just as I make it to the door. The laughter in the kitchen stops. Not good, I think before I swing the door open wide. Luke gives me a toothy grin. He's in a milky brown shirt that matches his eyes, along with black jeans and boots. Be. Still. My. Heart. I don't know if this is going to work.

"You found us," I manage to squeak out, gesturing for him to come inside.

"I did … and I'm sure you've heard this before, but wow. Quite a spread."

"Yeah," I say, looking down with an uncomfortable pause, which is quickly filled with the laughter and banter of my too loud parents.

Luke's eyebrows rise over his too gorgeous eyes. I quickly look away before I'm lost in them.

"My parents are painting a wall in the kitchen. That's why the music is on so loud." There's an awkward pause. "Would you like to meet them?" My voice rises; the trepidation is apparent.

"I'd love to meet them," Luke says, giving me that huge smile. He seems very calm, which makes one of us. I really hope my parents don't act a fool, but I know that's a long shot.

I lead him down the hall toward Mom's office and we pause at the kitchen door. Both Mom and Dad have stopped painting and they're standing there, just staring at the door like they're expecting us. At least they turned the music down. Mom gestures for us to come into the doorway. Both she and Dad have dabs of red paint on their faces and all over their clothes. I don't know how any paint made it onto the wall, but somehow there is a coat fully covering it.

"And here he is, this must be Luke," Mom says, with a goofy wave and a huge grin, her eyes twinkling. "I'd shake your hand, but I'm a mess." I give my dad a glance and he's slightly glaring at Luke. Dad just nods our way, his hand tightly gripping a paint-covered brush. His grip is so tight that his fingers are the color of the paint.

"Very nice to meet you both, Mr. and Mrs. Wagner. Thanks for letting us work here today. You have an amazing home," Luke says directly to Mom. Mom's face gleams. My dad stands there stoically, his eyes never leaving Luke, staring at him like he's gonna take him up behind the barn.

"Thank you, Luke. You caught us trying to spice this room up a bit. Aria told us about the contest. That's so exciting!"

"Yes, it is, and I'm honored to get to write with Aria."

My dad continues to just stand there, staring at Luke, gripping the paint brush in his hand. It's starting to get uncomfortable. Mom gives Dad a slight scowl. It must work because he finally speaks.

"We don't want to keep you two from getting your *work* done. Nice to meet you, Luke." The edge in Dad's voice is undeniable, and I see Mom's eyes slant ever so slightly with this words. She's not pleased. And now that I've been completely and totally humiliated by my parents, I just want to get out of here pronto.

"Yeah, Dad ... we need to get to *work*," I say, putting the same emphasis on "work" that he did. I continue, "I'll see you both later."

I give Luke an apologetic smile and lead him out of the room as Mom's trailing words follow us, "Have fun, you two, and let me know if you need anything." Then there's muffled voices. I'm sure Mom is giving Dad a piece of her mind. Yep, they totally blew it.

"Sorry about that ... sometimes they're a lot to take."

"I thought they were great," Luke replies. "Your mom is as nice as I imagined, and your dad is exactly what I thought he'd be. Protective."

I roll my eyes at him. As we reach the office and enter the room, I give him a nod and smile, "Yes, Dad's always been a bit, um ... much, I guess you could say."

"That may be something we could write about; you know, a girl who goes kind of wild due to her protective dad?" Luke offers.

"That's not a bad idea."

Luke finds a spot on the couch, unpacks his things, and then grabs a bottle of water from the table. I stand there watching nervously until I'm sure he's got everything he needs. Then I take my seat. When we're both finally settled, he looks at me.

"So, in addition to your dad not liking any guy you're around, have you had any other ideas that you want to write about?"

"I did jot some thoughts and potential titles down. Mom taught me that's how she starts a song, and then she adds in life experiences, inspiration from movies and books, things like that. How about you?"

"The same. I have a list of some ideas I've been working on. We could start there or come up with something entirely new?"

From that moment on, the creative juices flow. We toss a few ideas back and forth before finally landing on one idea we both like. It's a theme of a girl telling her guy to shove it and letting him go. The song's called "Free to Roam." I wrote the title down a year or so ago while watching our horses run in the pasture, after a recent crush had hurt my feelings. Luke loves the title and so we're writing our first, I guess you could call it, up-tempo, cowboy song.

With Luke's guitar talents, we come up with a driving chord structure in a short time. But with my own knowledge of the Nashville number system, and learning some new guitar licks, I'm carrying my own weight. I offer a few chord suggestions that Luke seems to like. The lyrics flow easily between us. It's not long before we finish the first two verses, the chorus, and a bridge. By now it's easy to see we're both a little fried and need a break.

I put my guitar down by my side, "How about some fresh air … we could walk up to the barn, and you could meet our horses?"

Luke lets his guitar slide down with a slight sense of relief. "I'd love that," he says, his eyes gleaming. "I also noticed the two Shepherds up near the barn when I pulled up. They were watching me as I got out of the truck. I wasn't sure if I'd have to run for it?" Luke says with a lighthearted, but semi-terrified chuckle.

"That's Lute and Lyre, Mom's other babies," I say with a grin. "They're docile, plus Jacob, our ranch hand, is up at the barn working. The dogs like to be where the action is, so you were safe. Let's go meet them, too."

I lead him out back toward the kitchen, which to my relief is now empty, and out toward the sliding glass doors, onto the patio. I stop and swirl around, wondering if he wants anything from the fridge. I guess Luke's entranced by the bright maroon wall because when I spin around, he slams right into me, my face pressed firmly into his chest. It's a reflexive moment for us both as Luke's hands instinctively come up and grip both of my arms around my biceps as if he's catching me. This brief moment with my face in his chest gives me a good whiff of his cologne and my head swirls.

I jump back like I've touched fire. Luke's face is priceless. His sly smile mixed with those smoldering eyes make my already weak knees sway. He reaches out his arm to catch me again but then pulls it back as I regain my footing.

"Well, aren't I the most graceless person ever," I say, staring at him as I inch farther away. One side of his mouth turns up ever so slightly. He's laughing at me ... I know he is. "That's the second time I've ran right into you."

"Again, completely my fault," he says, but the timbre of his voice has dropped. "I was taken by your parents' masterpiece," he adds, his eyes gesturing toward the bright wall.

"Well, that is a lot of red," I say, nodding as we stare at the wall uncomfortably. I add, pointing toward the fridge, "I stopped 'cause I thought you might want something else to eat or drink while we're here?"

"I'd love a soda."

Finally, the distraction I need to move completely away from him. I scamper to the fridge, grabbing us a couple of drinks, along with a couple of carrots. As I hand him a drink, our fingers graze and a bolt shoots down my arm. My eyes dart to Luke's and he's casually opening his drink like it's nothing. It's just me then, I think. Damn. Why am I so weak around him!

I break the silence, "Okay, let's go. We should find a golf cart outside, and we can drive up the hill."

"Cool."

We walk out. Sure enough, a cart is close by, and so are the dogs, who come up to Luke for a good sniff. He greets them both like a seasoned pro. He's not scared, and it's only moments before Lyre is on his back asking for belly rubs.

"Well, that didn't take long," I say laughing. I'm rubbing Lute's head as I add, "Couple of great guard dogs you both make."

It's a typical fall day. The sun's out, but it's not too hot or cold. We load into the cart, and I drive us up the hill to the barn as the dogs follow. There's a nice breeze, and the leaves are just starting to turn. I figure Mom's out riding. When we reach the barn, I'm relieved that there's no one here. I should have checked the garage for their cars to be sure. I really don't want an audience, or for Luke to be uncomfortable.

We walk into the barn, and I see out the back door that all our horses are grazing in a nearby field. Well, at least I know Mom's not riding. We head toward the closed gate, and I lean my forearms on it as Luke does the same. I'm pointing out each horse by name when Charlie, my favorite horse, starts walking our way. When he reaches us, I take the carrots out of my back pocket and hand one to Luke.

"I didn't think these were for us," he says with a chuckle.

I give him a look. "I would have at least cleaned them first," I reply sarcastically.

Charlie makes his way to me and nudges my arm. He figures we have something for him. I hand him my carrot, and he takes it in one giant bite, munching it as I scratch him between the ears.

"Charlie here is a gelding, and the horse I usually ride. We've had him for years."

Charlie, figuring Luke also has food, makes his way to Luke, who gives him a carrot. Luke softly pets his mane, talking gently as he does, "You are a beautiful horse, and so friendly." Charlie stands between us allowing this pampering for a few more minutes.

My heart sings. Luke's good with animals, too. Big points.

Luke asks, "How long have you all lived here?"

"Since I was little. I grew up here. We didn't have all the land around the house though. Dad's bought about thirty acres around the house over the years." I point at another horse in the field. "Mom bought Butter first, and then over the last ten years or so we've added the barn and the other horses. I think Mom would like goats and all kinds of animals, but she hasn't had the time, until now." My voice drops at the end of my sentence.

Luke's quiet for a few moments before he replies, "You said 'now.' I'd be lying if I said I didn't know your mom was sick, Aria. She looks well now though?"

I sense that I can talk to him, maybe because he's never asked about it. "She is doing better, Luke, and we're all hopeful about it. And what I meant was she used to manage a lot with my homeschooling and this ranch, but now she has more free time."

Luke's listening intently, and he looks back out at the field as Charlie rejoins the rest of our small herd. "Well, I hope y'all get goats. I *love* goats." He gives me the widest grin, and I can't help but laugh.

"Yeah, I love goats, too."

"Should we go back and try to finish this song, or are you done for the day?" he asks.

"I think I'm fried … we recorded what we have. How about we sit with the song and then work on it again next weekend?"

I push away from the fence and Luke follows, "Works for me. We could write at my house? You could meet my mother."

The way that he mentions his mom is endearing and intriguing at the same time.

I give him a big smile, "Sure, I'd like that."

"Of course, my house is nothing like this," he says, gesturing to the surroundings.

"All this," I say, looking around the grounds, "has nothing to do with anything I've done."

"Well, I can't wait to have a house like this one day."

We're back at the cart now and as we get in, I look right at him, "And I'm sure you will, Luke. I have no doubt."

He smiles and leans back against the seat, crossing his arms as we drive down the hill toward the house. I notice Dad's truck is gone. Good. At least

I don't have to worry about him lurking around.

Chapter 46 – Julia

I think I'm going to be sick. Why in the heck did I agree to this? Cause I'm a masochistic fool, that's why. Today is the Daryl Bradshaw podcast live taping. I've got to be there in an hour, and I'm not ready. I don't think I'm going to make it. I've almost thrown up twice. Raine has checked on me several times, and I swear I hear him coming up the stairs again.

I yell out to stop him, "I'm working on it. Will be down as soon as I can!" His footsteps stop and go back down the stairs.

On Saturday, I politely ordered Raine to the mall so we could get out of Aria's hair, and I'd hoped to find something decent to wear for the podcast. But as I am standing here, trying to work some magic, I realize it may be hopeless. I had the salon give me some new highlights, and that looks okay, but I can't get my fake eyelashes on my eyes, and trying to get eyeliner on straight is hopeless. My hands won't quit shaking. Aria's already left for school, so I have no one to help. This is a disaster.

I try one last time with the lashes and I finally get them on, but now I'm a sweaty mess. Good thing I haven't changed yet. After getting some semblance of my face on, I put on my outfit—it's all black, but my jacket has some nice brown, suede fringe. It'll have to do.

Finally, I quietly walk down the steps toward where Raine's waiting by the door with a guitar case at his feet. He's staring at his phone.

"Ready as I'll ever be." I must startle him, 'cause he almost drops his phone. I'm about three steps from the bottom when Raine looks up at me and smiles.

"You've never looked better," he says with a tender smile. It does make me relax a tiny bit.

"Why did I let you talk me into this?" I ask with a chastising tone as we make our way out the door.

"If I remember correctly, you offered," he says with a lighthearted chuckle.

"Oh yeah, that's right," I reply dryly. "Well, remind me to talk me out of it next time.

He nods at me, "You got it, darlin'."

As we make our way to the interview location, I'm taking short, shallow breaths. Raine reaches over and takes my hand.

When we arrive, I get out on leaden legs as we walk into the small studio, where we're greeted by Daryl's assistant, Janna. Wayne's already here, and he greets me with an embrace and then leans back, admiring my look.

"I love the hair, Jules. You look great." The terrified look on my face makes him add, "This will be a piece of cake. Just a conversation amongst friends."

The host, Daryl, walks in and greets us warmly. He's an older man, with a lot of gray and a full beard. I like him instantly. He suggests that we join him in the studio and chat for a while before we tape. We settle around a casual table. Wayne and I are set up in front of our own microphones and given headphones. Raine is behind me tuning his guitar, but he settles onto a couch out of camera view.

Daryl sits across from us dressed very casually in a shirt bearing the name of his show. He's the first to break the ice, a strong country accent slicing through the uncomfortable silence. "Well, first off, thank you both for being here. It's not every day that I get such big-name stars in my little studio," he says with a huge grin.

Wayne is the first to reply, "We're both happy for the opportunity to be on your show, Daryl." Wayne gives me a glance as he continues, "I've done a couple of these before. How about you, Julia?"

"Nope, first time," I squeak out. At least it sounds like a squeak to me, but the guys don't seem to notice. I catch Raine out of the corner of my eye and he seems perfectly calm, watching the scene unfold with his acoustic guitar resting against his leg, his arms crossed in front of him. I do catch the slightest of winks my way and this gives me a tiny bit of courage.

I add, "I'm sure I'll figure it out."

Daryl nods, replying, "I usually like to shoot the crap a bit before we begin taping so you have a chance to wind down. Makes for a better interview. Also, I won't ask the usual questions. I want my audience to really get to know you, so we'll talk about anything really.

Wayne jumps in, "Sounds good to me."

Daryl adds, "I know about the new song, Wayne, and that Julia wrote it. So that will be the focus at the end. I got a chance to listen to it thanks to your team, and I must say ... wow, gonna be a hit. And I'm not just saying that."

I'm positive my face is glowing beet red. I don't know why I get so embarrassed when people talk about my work in this way, but I just do.

Luckily, Wayne chimes in, taking the focus away from me. "Thanks, man. I knew it was a hit the moment I heard it, and I'm glad Julia gave it to me."

They both look at me, so I smile. "I couldn't think of anyone else I'd want to sing it."

Daryl nods, "Well, I'll mention the song at the beginning, then we'll talk about other things and then come back to it at the end. Then I'll have you sing a bit of it. Sound good, Wayne?"

"Perfect. That's why Raine's here," Wayne jokes as all heads spin to Raine, who nods with a smile.

Daryl then asks, "Are there any topics off limits?"

This is my opportunity to say I don't want to talk about my illness. I look over at Raine, and he gives me an encouraging smile. I look back at Daryl shaking my head no.

We continue to chat for about thirty minutes before we get ready to record. By now, everyone is more at ease, and you don't really notice the cameras. The only thing reminding me that I'm about to tape an hour-long interview is that I have to purposefully lean into the microphone. But since I have Wayne here next to me, this shouldn't be too bad.

When the little red taping lights go on, a rush of adrenaline flows through my veins, but it fades as we have a conversation. We talk about the music business and songwriting, and Wayne discusses being on the road. Daryl brings up my illness and dealing with the paparazzi, and I relay what the last year has been like from my treatment, being away from home, and the fact that currently, everything looks good. Everyone responds with thankfulness. It doesn't seem stressful talking about it. In fact, it's a relief getting it off my chest.

When we're an hour into the show, Daryl brings us back to why we're here and that's the song, "He'll Stay."

"So, Julia, tell us why you wrote this song?"

I smile as I describe the lyrics to the song. "Well, I started it as a tribute to my father. My dad was the primary caregiver for me and my sister from a young age, so the first verse and chorus are about him. The second verse is about a man staying by his partner's side through illness, and the last verse ... well, I don't like to explain that verse. I don't think I wrote it, but that it came through me." I shrug my shoulders, "That's the only way I can explain it."

"Now I'm intrigued!" Daryl replies. "We have Raine here and he's going to play for Wayne to sing it. Sound good?"

Wayne responds, "You got it ... but only if Julia joins me on harmony."

I laugh and nod as I respond, looking at Wayne, "Do I have a choice?"

Raine does a quick tune of his guitar, and then he starts the opening chords.

Then it all comes back naturally. Wayne starts to sing and I join on the harmony parts. Everyone in the room is listening intently. Wayne gets to the third verse, and he sings it solo with Raine playing quietly along. I join Wayne on the last chorus to the end.

When we're done, there is a spattering of applause from Daryl's small staff, and I look over at Wayne and smile.

"I tell you what ... that is going to the top of the charts!" Daryl adds. "Where can everyone find this song, Wayne?"

"It will be out this Friday at midnight, on all the usual channels," Wayne replies. He mentions his website and that people can preorder it.

Daryl brings his focus back to me, "And Julia, you've never sounded better.

Do you have more songs planned, and when will you get back on stage?"

"I am writing some new songs … maybe one day I'll get back out on stage. Who knows?" I don't dare look over at Raine's shocked face. I've never mentioned performing again to him, but I have been thinking about it.

"Well, I can't tell you how much fun this has been." Daryl turns directly to one of the cameras. "You heard it here first folks, Julia Tate may be getting back out there to perform, and you know where to find Wayne Carson's new song, 'He'll Stay,' starting this Friday. Go save it, download it, all the things." He turns back to both of us. "Thank you both for visiting with me today. It's been a hoot."

Wayne and I both echo our thanks, and then Daryl officially signs off.

When the cameras go dark, my tense shoulders instantly slouch. Then I reluctantly look at Raine, whose face gleams. Oh no. What have I done?

Daryl confirms he's going to air the show tonight at six, so we all plan to coordinate our social media channels with promo posts. His team coordinates the links with me as Raine packs up his guitar. I'm more than ready to go. This has been a long morning. I give Wayne a quick hug, and we all say our goodbyes as we wave to the staff, making our way out the door toward Raine's truck.

Raine's quiet. He doesn't say anything until we're about to pull out on to the street.

"So … you're thinking about performing again?" he asks, giving me a sly smile.

"I said maybe. Just maybe, Raine." My cautious tone is serious. I don't want him running off to the races.

"Didn't sound like a maybe to me and now it's permanently on record," he teases excitedly like a kid ready to bolt out of school.

My exasperated sigh makes him laugh. All I want to do is change the subject. "Can we stop and get coffee and something to eat? I'm starving."

"Sure, darlin'. Whatever you want," he says sweetly before adding, "But I'm not going to let this go."

My arms cross my chest, "I didn't think so."

Raine gives a huge guffaw as we head toward our favorite local coffee shop.

Chapter 47 – Raine

The wheels in my head are spinning the entire way home. Julia, of course, has been silent, only giving me a few worrying looks. She knows what I'm thinking. I can't get over the fact that she wants to perform again. She hasn't wanted to perform in so long that I was shocked when she said it to the world. In my mind, I've already picked out her band members, set list, tour schedule, and, of course, ways to incorporate me and Aria. Our own little family band.

We stop and get our food, but I only get a few words during our drive. She's texting, so I ask her about it.

"I'm looping Tracy in on the podcast and asking her to post everywhere that it's airing tonight."

"So, you *do* want people to hear the podcast?" I tease, and she gives me a glare that could melt my face off. I should drop it, but I can't stop myself.

"What are you thinking ... putting a band together, playing a few shows solo? What about scheduling a few shows here in Nashville? We can easily make that happen."

Julia stops texting, giving me her full attention. "I haven't gotten that far, Raine. Honestly, the words just came out. Yes, I have been thinking about singing in public again, but I just started writing again. It's more about getting some songs out there."

My focus goes back to the road as I contemplate her words. "So, like doing some songwriting nights, or something like that?" I'm sure my disappointed tone is obvious. Julia needs to be back out there on the road on a real stage, performing full-time, opening for other acts. That would be amazing. She could easily fill seats.

She replies, in her best "I'm over this" voice, "Maybe something like a songwriters show. I haven't thought about the details, I just want to perform my own songs again. Now, can we drop it? We need to focus on helping Wayne get the song out. That's what we should be thinking about."

"Agreed." I've stirred up a hornet's nest, and I don't want to make her nerves any more strained. In the back of my mind, I know it's not good for her health.

I add, "I bet Aria would post something on her socials, too. She's much better at it and since she's started performing, she has some followers. She could help us get the word out."

"I'm sure she would. That would help since I haven't posted much lately."

By the time we're pulling up the drive, and although it's still early fall, the sun is beating down on top of us. The dogs run down from the barn and joyfully meet my truck at the garage. Julia climbs out, greets both dogs, and heads toward the house.

"I'm gonna take a shower," Julia says, walking away without looking at me.

There is an edginess to her voice. I'm sure I've pushed her too far. "Okay. I'll be in the studio if you need anything."

I watch her walk to the house as the dogs follow. They'll go anywhere with her. I see Jacob up at the barn. I'll check to see if he needs anything before I follow up with Wayne on any other promo. Plus, this will give me some time to figure out how to tell Julia I'm sorry.

Chapter 48 – Julia

Why in the Sam Hill did I mention anything about performing? I instantly regretted the words the second they flew out of my mouth. Me and my big mouth. I strip naked and decide that a long bath should help ease the tension from my neck and back.

When I'm finished and dressed, I send Tracy another text asking her about writing with Trent again. If I'm going to bite this bullet, I'll need more material.

Tracy responds. "Trent sent me a message last week. He went back to L.A., but he'll be back next month and wants to get together soon."

"Good. Follow up on a few dates." Then I let her know about my big mistake. "Well, I stepped in it and mentioned performing again during the podcast. Raine is ALL OVER IT." I add a sad face emoji for emphasis.

"OMG! This is great! I've already been contacted about having you and Raine on the country music awards show. Could I mention it?"

"Oh, my gosh, HECK no! Nothing like that. Just a few live shows. Not national TV Trace! Get serious."

"LOL. I had to try. They want you to present an award again. How about that?"

"Maybe. I'll check with Raine. For now, let's focus on songwriting. Could you line up a few more writing sessions?"

"On it."

And with that, my stomach's doing somersaults. Even though I just showered, I consider throwing on some old jeans and going for a ride, but I land on going up to the barn to see if Jacob needs any help.

I head up the hill with the dogs and when I reach the barn, both Lyre and Lyft find places to lie down on the cool barn floor. Jacob has already fed the horses, and they all are out in the adjoining pasture, so I walk over to the gate. My horse Butter comes up to greet me.

"How are you, old girl?" I say as Butter puts her head in my hands. I reach up to scratch her favorite spot behind her ears. I'm glad I came up here to clear my mind. Although, yes, I've been trying to move forward and I'm writing again, did I just agree to more than I'm ready for? What if I'm doing too much, too soon? Raine has got to realize, and so do I, that I can't put myself out there the way I used to. Today's show was a lot of stress. Is this really what I should be doing?

I should go and tell Raine to cancel any more promos, and message Tracy to cancel any shows, but I don't want to disappoint them … or, in a way, myself.

Butter's had enough and she leaves to join the rest of the herd. I put my hands on the railing and rest my head there, watching all the horses peacefully graze in the pasture. What have I done? I may have really blown it this time.

Chapter 49 – Aria

I'm walking out of school, reading Mom's text about helping with her podcast promo, when I walk right into my truck's side mirror. I spin around to see if anyone is watching, and there's Luke, standing next to his own truck fifty feet away, holding his sides, doubled over with laughter.

It takes everything I have not to flip him the bird. But instead, I smile and give him a sweet, casual wave, like I totally meant to do that. Then I hit the clicker, open the door, and climb in with as much grace as I can muster. Luckily, my book bag didn't slide off my shoulder, making me look even more foolish. I don't dare look back at him. But I can't help but smile knowing he's watching me. It's not in a stalkerish kind of way. Other kids are getting into their cars all over the parking lot. It was kind of sweet. Except for the part where I once again looked like a complete and utter dork.

I finish texting Mom, letting her know Savannah will help too. Mom tells me when the show will air and where. I'm kind of freaked out. She hasn't wanted to be public about anything in years, so this is a good thing ... I think.

After sending the details to Savannah, I get up the nerve to look up, and Luke's truck is gone. I figured it would be, but I wanted to make sure he left before I did. I'm sure he'll tease me about my gracefulness when I meet with him on Saturday. Thinking about writing again with Luke makes my insides flutter. That boy, or should I say young man, is too much for me. I've got to remember that we're writing partners. That's it. We're just writing together.

By the time I pull up our drive, it's getting dark, and the house is full of light. All the cars are in the garage. When I get out, I'm hit with the full aroma of steaks on the grill. Dad's cooking, so either he did something wrong or we're celebrating. Either way, dinner's going to be fabulous.

I head toward the back patio area and there Dad is with a set of tongs in hand. He's out here alone, which is good. I'll have a few minutes to really find out how the podcast taping went.

Dad's back is to me and he's staring at the flames coming from the grill. "Smells amazing," is all I get out when he visibly jumps.

"Gosh dang it! You scared the bejeeezus out of me!" he says, twirling around with the tongs in one hand and a soda in the other.

I shouldn't laugh due to my face-first truck mirror incident, but I can't help it. "Oops ... didn't you hear my truck?" I reply in defense, my shoulders raising questioningly.

"Yes, but you usually go in the *front* door." He snarls, with a semi-smile, while turning his attention back to our food.

"So, what's up? Steaks on Wednesday. What happened?"

His gaze goes back to the grill and he blurts out, "Your mom mentioned she wants to sing again, and I pushed."

I'm shocked for several moments as we both stare at the flames. "Really? In public ... like in front of people?" I'm obviously not in control of the words coming out of my mouth. I can't believe Mom wants to sing solo again ... live. Especially after being sick this past year.

"That's usually how it's done, sweetheart, yes," Dad replies sarcastically, giving me a look.

"Whoa ... when?"

"I don't know." Dad stops and pulls the steaks off the grill before continuing. "She wants to do a few songwriting venues or something like that, but yes, live, and for an actual audience, not just us."

Our conversation stops when Mom steps out onto the patio to join us.

"Those smell amazing," she says, before adding, "and I just walked right into your conversation that awkwardly ended."

Dad's not afraid, looking right at her. "We were talking about you wanting to perform live and how much of a surprise that is to us both, honey." He gives me a glance and a wink. Dad typically just blurts it all out. I admire that about him.

"Yes, I suppose it is," Mom replies, her voice dropping at the end. She does not sound enthused at all.

"I think it's awesome, Mom. Other than a few guest appearances for other artists, and your *Next Real Star* recordings, I've never seen you do your own thing." During that show, Mom and Dad seemed to live in a different world. Mom was such a strong performer. Now it's hard to imagine her that way.

"Well, don't expect lights and dancers or anything like that," she says, laughing. "Before we even got home, your dad had me with a full band and tour. I'm not ready for that."

Dad grabs the steaks, and we follow him inside as he replies, "What can I say, I see the potential. Always have, Jules."

She chides him, "Sure you did. That's why I never got your top score."

Dad stops and sets the steaks on the counter before he grabs Mom up in a fierce embrace and plants a big kiss on her lips. "I'll forever have to make up for my damn scores," he says with a slight smack on her ass.

My head goes down in embarrassment. They act like this every day, but still, the newlywed bit is a bit much. Sensing my dismay, they focus back on dinner.

Mom's already set the table in the nook so we can watch the sun go down. It's one of her favorite ways to eat a casual dinner. She has everything else ready. We make small talk and Mom finally asks how my writing session went with Luke. Dad gets quiet. I let them both know we're going to write again this Saturday to finish the song we started and work on another. I can tell Mom wants to quiz me about it, but I do my best to quash it. Mainly because of the look on Dad's face when I mentioned I was going over to Luke's house. Dad is too much, and I'm going to have to say something to Mom later.

When we're finished with dinner, Dad pushes his plate back and reminds us that the podcast is about to air. I've been aware 'cause my phone's been buzzing nonstop with social media notifications.

I pick up my phone and confirm. "Savannah and I set our posts to go out about an hour ago, and a reminder will post again on all my socials right before it goes live."

"Good," Mom chimes in. "I'll repost whatever you have, and whatever Wayne's team puts out."

"Are you going to listen to it?" I ask.

Mom shakes her head as she says, laughing, "I was there. But I'll be ready for any comments, good and bad. I'm not afraid of those."

Dad joins in. "I was there, too," he says, grabbing Mom's hand. "I don't think we'll have any bad press, or comments from this, honey."

Mom reaches up and tugs at the ends of her hair with her words, "I'm sure people will mention how I look … that's a given." She sighs.

I chime in, "Your new look is fabulous, and I bet others will think so too. Who cares about the haters and bullies."

Mom gives me a nod, but her eyes seem wary. "True. I never have, but still, I'm sure I'll get comments about that—maybe even about my voice, too." Her voice edges up slightly, "But, you know what, who knows … and who cares."

"That's the spirit!" Dad replies with gusto. "Anyone want dessert? I picked up some key lime pie at the store."

Mom nods yes, but I shake my head and give the excuse that I'm going to run up and watch my social media accounts. It's almost six and I don't want to mess this up. They're both playing this off like it's not a big deal, but I know being on the podcast stretched Mom's nerves. The tension from this one show and revealing herself to the public is etched all over her face.

I pick up my plate, clean it, and put it in the sink, before running up to the sanctuary of my room. I call Savannah on the way up.

"Everything set?" I ask. "This has to go well."

Savannah replies, "Yep. So far, the first post has generated thousands of views and clicks. I thought I'd need to turn the comments off because I can't get to them all, but it seems to have calmed down."

"Same here. I haven't said a word to Mom or Dad about the interest. I didn't want to freak Mom out. She's been so private that this is getting a lot of attention."

We agree to check the posts that go out in minutes, and then I go to Daryl's podcast link to listen to the show.

When the podcast starts, I'm pacing around my room, terrified for both my mom and my dad, but when I watch and hear Mom's voice, she seems completely calm and collected. She looks great. Yes, she's older and it shows on her face, but her shorter dark hair with light brown highlights is very hip. It works well with the black and brown suede jacket she's wearing. I check my computer and it's blowing up. I try to keep up with the comments while listening and it's no use. So, I go back to watching the show. I'll get back to the comments later.

My throat tightens when they get to the live song part. But when Dad starts to play and they get through the first chorus, I don't know why I was so worked up; Mom sounds great singing harmony with Wayne. Daryl is right when he says this song is a hit.

When the podcast ends, I go to my computer and on one social media platform alone, the show has close to fifty thousand views. Not bad for a country music podcast. Most comments are positive. Mom's right though; there are a few haters, but those comments are quashed by other people, so I don't make time for those.

I get back to people's comments, thanking them for watching and reminding them where they can preorder Wayne's song. I check Mom's social pages, and she's reposted my posts. All posts are generating considerable traction, and Mom's responding to people too. On her social pages, people are more kind and there aren't many snarky comments.

I think about texting Mom to see how she thinks it went, but I let it go. It'll seem like I'm hovering. I'm sure Dad has that covered for both of us. I'll touch base with Savannah in the morning to get numbers for Dad. He'll ask about that first thing.

I take a quick shower, throw on comfy PJ's, and stretch out under the covers. I pull out my phone, checking the comments one more time, and my heart swells for Mom. After this tough last year, she needs something good to happen.

Chapter 50 – Luke

Okay, now I'm borderline stalking her. I read on one of Aria's social media pages that her mom and Wayne Carson are on Daryl Bradshaw's podcast. For the past hour, I've been watching the show on my computer and reading the comments on Aria's page on my phone.

It's a great podcast. Really fun and entertaining and they both look like such stars. Then when they sing that song together … wow. I hope I can write a hit like that someday. But some of the comments on Aria's page are downright cruel, and they all have to do with how Julia looks. What's up with that? I want to reply, but I hold my tongue. Aria's responding to a few of the nice comments, and it's cool to watch her talk to people like this.

But is this too much? I've met her mom and her dad, but I really don't know them. And then after she caught me watching her today, she's going to think I'm weird or something. I watch the rest of the podcast and then shut my computer down.

I need to focus on practicing, plus we have a song to finish on Saturday and more to write. THAT is what I should be doing. Not watching Aria's family. But man, are they talented. Maybe I'm jealous 'cause I don't have that. I didn't know my dad. He was in the military and died when I was young. For several years after he died, we'd always go to the cemetery on Memorial Day, but since Mom got sick, we haven't made it there. I can't remember the last time I visited his grave.

I walk over to my small desk by the window. I pull open the top center drawer and take out one of the only pictures I have of my mom and dad together. It was their wedding day. Of course, Mom's beautiful in a remarkably simple white gown, and Dad is in full military dress. He's incredibly serious while towering over Mom. Mom's smiling and my dad has this semi-smirk on his face; I guess you could call it a grin. Maybe he was happy, but boy, he seems like he didn't take shit from anyone. Mom says I got his looks, and I guess I can see it. We both have dark hair and an olive complexion, but I don't think I look that serious, at least I hope not.

I remember seeing all the pictures of Aria and her family lining the hallway on the way to Aria's mom's office and my stomach tightens. I would love to have something like that one day.

I grab my notebook, opening it up to the page with the lyrics to my song "Coming Home," and I grab my guitar. Tonight, I'm going to finish it. I need to finish it.

Chapter 51 – Julia

The day has finally ended and I'm lying in bed waiting for Raine to join me. Raine's humming in the shower and it makes me laugh. He can carry a tune, but he doesn't sing much anymore. He finally steps out, towel drying his hair with another towel wrapped around his waist, and my chest tightens. After all these years, I still want this man.

Raine looks down at me. I'm under the covers, like I'm trying to hide away from the day. He looks at me tenderly. He stops what he's doing and drops both towels on the floor to quickly slide in next to me, grabbing me by my waist with one hand and pulling me hard against his frame.

He looks into my eyes, and I instantly relax against him.

"I thought the day went well," he says, peering into my soul, the way that only he can.

My eyes dart down, but he takes my chin in his free hand and pulls my eyes back up to his, making me look at him.

"It did, Jules, and you should see the numbers Aria was getting on her social pages, the fans *love it*."

"They hate my hair, Raine. I mean it, they don't like this look."

"That's bull crap. There were one or two idiots. Most people said they love your look, and they understand why your hair is shorter. Jeez, what's up with people and your hair? I don't get that," Raine says with obvious frustration.

"It's change. People like familiar."

He continues to try and reassure me, and I must admit, it's working. "Seriously, Jules, the podcast looked and sounded great, the song was spectacular. Wayne says the preorder numbers are great, and Daryl said his podcast numbers are the best he's had in months. I'll call that success."

"If you say so ... Tracy did text that I'm getting offers for other shows, so there's that."

"See! If it sucked, we'd hear crickets. Let's get to Friday and see how the song release goes." Raine snakes down lower under the covers and grips me tightly against him as I rest my head against his chest.

I think about pursuing things with him tonight. I always want to make love to him, but I'm tired. He can tell.

"I love you, sweetheart," he whispers. "I've always said, I love you more than anything else on this earth."

"I love you too, honey," I say, snuggling against him and letting out a heavy sigh along with all the tension I've been carrying all day. "I forgot to say thanks for dinner."

"Uh-huh," is all I get as he's snoring next to me. The side of my lip upturns. That's the last thing I remember.

The next morning, I wake up to the lightest kisses running down my neck and the slight tingling of Raine's fingertips running down my side. Now, this is the way I like to wake up.

Many moments later we're lying in bed, tangled up in our sheets, resting after making love, when Raine finally speaks. "That's my kind of morning."

After giving him a light kiss on his nose, I reply, "Maybe I should do a podcast every day?"

Raine laughs out loud and springs up to his forearms to look at me.

"I would *love* that. If I get this every day, we can make that happen."

I smile, reaching up to run my fingers through his hair as he stares down at me with the clear love and devotion I've counted on all these years. I'm the luckiest woman alive.

He breaks our spell, bringing us back to reality. "Speaking of the podcast, I'm going to call Wayne and see if there's any other promo we can do. Maybe there's a radio interview or something we could pull together."

A sigh escapes me, "You know I was kidding, right? I didn't really mean I wanted to do more. I think I'm done for a while."

"I know, darlin', but this song ... you and I both know it's special. We need to do all we can to get it out there."

I pause before I reply, "I get it, Raine. I'll do whatever you need, but please, nothing on camera. No more hair talk."

"You got it!" He springs from our bed, and I watch his gorgeous ass dart into our bathroom, and soon there's water running.

I grab my phone from the nightstand and run through the social pages one more time. There are even more comments, and I quickly turn them off. I don't need to see those. I send a text to Tracy letting her know I'm up for brief radio spots if they come up in the next few days but nothing that shows my face. When she asks why, I give her the skinny. Tracy totally gets it. I don't know if they can put anything together in such a short time, and I'd be good if they don't.

I glance at my watch. Aria will be on her way to school, so I send her a quick text, thanking her and Savannah for their help. We wouldn't have had that response without them. Then I stare up at the ceiling. My body feels even more tired today. I figure it's all this added stress, but my mind flashes to something my doctor said about fatigue as a warning. I won't let myself go down that road right now. I clamor out of bed and throw on a robe to get these thoughts out of my mind. I'll get a shower later. But first, coffee. I won't get anywhere without it.

Chapter 52 – Raine

Wayne has had calls for additional shows, so we're working on some appearances around town. Even if we could get radio spots, they'd at least want photos. I'll have to break this to Julia. We can line up a couple shows for tomorrow, the day the song goes live.

As I reminisce on our morning, there's an instant tightness in the center of my pants. Damn, that woman, I chuckle out loud. I still can't get enough, even after eighteen years together. Julia's feet pad down the hall, and I move to greet her as she brings me a steaming cup of coffee. God bless this woman.

"Thanks, love. Wayne has lined up two radio interviews tomorrow and he wants you to join him, if you're up for it? Both with video." Julia's face falls, so I keep going, trying to convince her. "Most shows air live video, Jules. It's how it's done now." I'm sure my last words aren't what she wants to hear, but she surprises me.

Julia replies boldly, "Screw 'em, Raine. I like my new hair. I'm gonna line up a pro to get me ready though. I don't need the added stress of trying to do my own hair and makeup."

"Perfect! Wayne said the first is at nine in the morning and the next around noon. You think you can find someone to get here early?"

"On it."

She twirls around with a mission. That's my Julia. Not afraid of anything.

I text Wayne letting him know we'll be at both. Wayne confirms that they'll have to sing again like on the podcast, and he needs me to play. This is turning out to be fun. If only we could get Aria involved and my family band dream would come true, I think with a smile.

The next day comes with a vengeance. It's an early call for hair and makeup for Julia. Even though it was at the last minute, Tracy was able to line someone up. It's Stella, someone Julia's used before, which is good. She's comfortable having her work on her face and hair, which is a bigger deal than I could ever imagine.

We've almost talked Reezie into taking a day off to go with us, but she said she can't miss school. She sure is taking her schoolwork seriously. I'm glad, of course, but I would've let her out of class for one day. Julia wasn't so thrilled with the idea of Aria missing any school, but I planted a seed that Reez could also sing harmony and it swayed her. Alas, my family band is not yet materializing.

We're already on the road to the first station. I'm driving with Jules in the front seat, while Tracy and the makeup artist Stella are tagging along in back. Julia likes having her own small entourage. I think it gives her courage a boost. She seems much more at ease today as she chats with her girls.

We get to the station and Wayne shows up a few minutes later. He has his own small group, and we fill the small station up. After our meet-and-greets, we set up in their main room.

We make small talk with the show's host, Tommy Jones. We've known Tommy for years, and he's had this show for as long as I can remember. Luckily for Jules, they said this spot will only be about fifteen minutes long. Jules and Wayne are sitting in plush seats to the side of the console and I'm sitting away from them, off camera for now, tuned up and ready to go.

I glance at Jules as they count us down. She's got a cup of coffee in her hands, and she looks like she's gonna have a conversation among friends. Stella did wonders and she looks amazing. Julia is more confident than ever. I give Tracy a huge grin. She replies with a thumbs-up. Then we're off.

Tommy opens by introducing them both and then goes to Wayne, asking general questions about what he's been up to and then bringing the conversation around to the song, which leads to why Julia is also on the show. Julia gives a similar explanation about the song "He'll Stay" as she did on the podcast, which leads Tommy to wanting us to immediately play it. So, I'm on. I strum the opening chords and then Wayne and Julia come in as before. This acoustic, stripped-down version is so different than my fully produced version, but the song doesn't need much, which is the mark of a good song.

When we're finished, the small group standing outside of our sound booth claps and cheers as Tommy takes a moment to acknowledge their response.

"That's a great song, Wayne and Julia. Wow. I sense a number one, but who am I, just a music lover who's been doing this for years," Tommy jokes.

Wayne laughs, "That means a lot coming from you, Tommy, seriously. You know every country artist, and you've heard it all. You know you've got to have a good song." Wayne says, gesturing to Julia, who smiles her reply.

"So, what's next for you both?" Tommy asks. "Wayne, I read this song is out tonight and available for preorder now. Will you tour?"

"Yep. We have tour dates up on my website now."

Tommy continues, "And what about you, Julia? You mentioned performing live on another show I will not name," Tommy says with a slight chuckle.

Julia gives a grin and replies, "Yes, those words did escape my lips, and I'm thinking about it. I'll be working on some new songs, and I want to get them out there."

Wayne jumps in. "I get first dibs, Jules."

"You got it!" Julia quickly replies.

Tommy adds toward the camera, "It's all settled, folks. Wayne's releasing an album now, but will be working on more Julia Tate tunes soon," which makes Wayne laugh.

Julia shakes her head and rolls her eyes as she gives a big smile. They close the show repeating where they can preorder the new song, social media channels, and then we're out.

Julia's shoulders visibly relax when the little red light goes dark. I give her a huge encouraging grin.

We gather our things, say our goodbyes, and as we're leaving, I pull Julia up against me and whisper in her ear, "That was great, darlin'. I think you're getting the hang of this."

Julia gives me a sarcastic smile, but whispers back, "You'll get a spanking later if you keep saying crap like that," the smile never leaving her face.

My head goes back in laughter. "I can't wait. I just can't wait."

Then we're off for a quick bite before we head to the next station, located in downtown Nashville. Just like this first show, it goes off without a hitch. The format is different, and we open with the song, followed by a brief interview with Wayne and Julia.

When we finally head back home, I glance over at Julia, who's watching the scenery pass. I grab her hand and give it a slight squeeze, and she looks my way. Her eyes are bright and glowing from a productive, exciting day, but there's a weariness there. Tracy and Stella are chattering in the back seat, and they bring Julia into their conversation until we get back to our home. I silently listen to their conversation the rest of the way home, but there's a pang in my gut when Julia's eyes met mine. I'm trying my best to ignore it.

Chapter 53 – Aria

Mom's song finally dropped last night. As Mom, Dad, and I are finishing up breakfast, Dad gets a text on the initial sales numbers.

"Song's doing well, love. Charted at number one on at least two streaming country charts. This is good news," Dad says, with his head buried in his phone.

Mom nods and gives him a smile, looking out at the pasture as she continues drinking her coffee. She doesn't say anything, and I can't read her face.

Dad continues, his head still in his phone, "I need to run and give Wayne's people a call. Can you take care of the dishes, love?"

Mom gives her attention to Dad. "What do you think?" Mom says as Dad dashes out of the room, pausing to give her a quick peck on the cheek.

"This is great, Mom ... a hit single!" I say, trying to gauge her true feelings.

Mom gives me a forced smile. "It is exciting, honey, but I'll be damned if I'm doing any more on-air podcasts or interviews. Not now at least," she says before lifting her cup of coffee and taking a slow, casual drink.

Her response is so calm and direct, it catches me off guard. I can't help but shake my head with laughter. "Oh, I totally get it," I say between laughs. "And I want to be here when you tell Dad, '*No more*.'"

Mom doesn't say a word but gives me a big smile. I gather up my plate and juice glass heading toward the sink as Mom finally asks.

"Are you writing with Luke again today?"

Damn. She went there. I need to play this cool. I turn on the water and casually start cleaning my dishes, "Yeah. I'm heading over to his house after lunch." I'm trying to control any quiver in my voice.

"Hmm … I think that's great. He seems like a nice guy. What can you tell me about him?"

I pause in mid-wipe and look out the kitchen window, then I carefully place the dish in the sink.

"Don't worry about those dishes. I'll get them." Mom adds, "Why don't you come back over here and tell me about Luke?"

I glance over at my mom as she's holding her coffee cup in front of her with both hands, watching me intently. I can see her eyes dance from where I'm standing. There's no use. She knows I like him. I've been too obvious.

I drag my body back over to the table and slump down in a seat. "There isn't much to tell, Mom. I really don't know much about him," I say, shrugging my shoulders as I try to sell my words.

Mom looks at me sternly and puts her coffee cup down. "Aria Marie Wagner, I carried you for nine months, and I've been around you for more than seventeen years. I've heard you and Savannah talk about a cute boy before, but you've never been like this. It's all over your face, even if you think you're hiding it. You like Luke … you like him a lot, that's easy to see, and I'm sure your father sees it, too, which is why he acted like a complete ass when Luke was here the other day. So, what can you tell me about him?"

A sigh escapes my lips as my hand rubs across my brow. The details I know fly out of my mouth. "He's a great guitar player, and he lives with his mom closer to Nashville. I first met him right before school started when we ran into each other at the library." I tell her a little bit about that story, including the part where we smacked right into each other, and the side of Mom's mouth curls up as she listens. "Other than that, I really don't know much. We have a couple of classes together … one class is music theory, so I know he's smart, and he's incredibly talented, I can see that. The song we've started is good, Mom, very good. And his eyes … wow, those eyes." I stop and roll my eyes before I get my control back. "That's it. That's all I know."

Mom's been nodding along, listening intently before she asks, "And do you know how he feels about you?"

"I have no idea."

Mom leans back in her seat. "He likes you, sweetheart, that's obvious."

"Why do you think that?"

"I have eyes, Aria, it's the way he looks at you. A mother can sense these things. He's smitten and it's another reason your dad acted like an ignoramus around him."

Her words swirl around in my head as my heart swells. Could he really feel something for me, too?

Mom breaks me out of my little daydream by placing her hand on mine. "Let's keep our discussion between the two of us, okay. No reason to get your dad even more riled up or he'll forbid you to write with Luke, and I see no reason why that should stop."

Mom and I have always been close, and we've been able to talk about anything. I don't think I've ever loved her any more than I do right now.

By the time I'm heading to Luke's house, Mom's words have been playing over in my head for hours. Now I'm a nervous wreck. I changed my outfit a dozen times before landing on a deep green long-sleeved blouse, simple jeans, and some regular black cowboy boots. The blouse is a flimsy material, and it flatters my figure, but it's not too revealing. The color sets off my eyes though, at least that's what Mom said. I took her advice on that one. I hope I'm coming across as casual and put together, but not over the top. I pulled my hair back in a simple ponytail, so it won't get in the way of my guitar playing. I slipped out of the house before Dad noticed. I think he'd be okay with what I'm wearing, but you never really know. He'd want me to wear a long-sleeved burlap sack and no makeup.

I pull up in front of the address Luke sent me and park at the curb. I cut the engine and peer up a slight hill to a smaller, older red brick home. In front there is a good-sized lawn, and well-kept shrubs fill up the space in front of the house. Parked in the drive is Luke's blue truck, and in front of his vehicle is an older gray four-door car, which looks like it hasn't been driven in months.

I grab my guitar and purse and walk up the gray cement steps to the door.

The front door is open and just as I'm about to ring the bell, Luke magically appears, opening the screen door. Every time he appears it nearly stops me in my tracks.

"I heard you pull up," he says as he takes a step back, holding the door open, gesturing for me to come inside. As I take a few steps past him into what you'd call their foyer, I get a whiff of his cologne. It's dark but subtle, and it's perfect for him. I should have held my breath when I walked by.

When I'm inside, we're both standing there awkwardly before he gestures around the room. "Welcome to our humble little house," he says, sheepishly. "I told you it was nothing like your house."

The small foyer leads to a small living room area with a huge picture window that faces the street. There's a short hallway and what looks like the dining room. Each room is spotless, and although I wouldn't call anything modern, it's tastefully decorated without a lot of clutter. I like the feel of the house. It's very homey.

I was nervous when he came to my house and I can only imagine he must feel the same. I instantly want to make him feel at ease. I smile with my words, "I love it, Luke. And I love the fact that the street is so quiet. Not a lot of traffic and noise. It's perfect."

His shoulders go down and he gives me a subtle smile. "I thought we'd write here in the living room area. It's the most open part of the house and I really don't have any other space that will work."

"This is great." I take a step toward a couch to unload my things and it's then that I notice he already set up his guitar, notebook, and phone by a comfortable chair across from the couch. There's a small coffee table between us with water and a few snacks. He has everything ready to go. I give him a look as if I'm making sure my spot is good, and he nods with a smile. I unpack my things and notice Luke's still standing by the door.

"Would you mind if you came back to my mom's room to meet her? She doesn't come out of her room very often, and when I told her you were coming, she made sure to fix herself up. She really wants to meet you."

A huge smile fills my face, "Of course! I'd love to meet her."

Luke has never said much about his mother. We make our way down the hall to the back of the house, past a bathroom door, and as we pass that room, Luke points it out to me. It's a feminine-looking room and I smile. Then we go past a closed door on the left, which I assume is his room, to the last door on the right. The door is halfway open, and Luke pauses to knock.

A light-sounding voice replies, "Yes, yes, come in."

I have no idea what will greet us. Luke opens the door and steps in, and I make my way to the entrance, peering inside and then I follow. Luke's mom is lying on top of the covers. She has grayish white hair, and her head is resting against the pillows. On her thin, frail frame she wears a simple blue shirt and pants, and a light quilt covers the lower part of her body. Her eyes grip me. They're Luke's eyes gazing back at me.

His mom speaks first. "So, this is the gorgeous Aria Luke has talked so much about." Luke groans and out of the corner of my eye, his hand goes to his brow.

"Mom ... please, you promised you wouldn't embarrass me," he says in a teasing tone.

"Of course, dear. I'm Janet," she says, reaching out her hand from across the room. I'm drawn to her like a magnet just like I'm drawn to her son. I step past Luke and I'm quickly at the side of her bed, taking her icy hand in mine. Janet pats the bed next to her, and I follow orders, sitting down at her side. Luke steps up a bit closer behind me.

"Now I can see you better. You are gorgeous. Wow ... you look so much like your mother and your father. Luke says you are quite the songwriter, too. I'm expecting you two to win this contest, you know." The same deep brown eyes that have mesmerized me for weeks dance in front of me.

I'm still holding her hand, which is gripped tightly in both of hers. "We are hopeful, ma'am," I reply.

"Please. None of the ma'am stuff. I'm Janet. I don't have time for formalities. Well, Luke has played his songs for me over the years, and you both have more going for you than hope."

Luke groans again before he joins in, "Mom, of course you're a little biased, but we'll do our best. We do want to win."

I chime in to put Luke's mind at ease, "Your son is amazingly talented, Janet, and I'm honored that he's writing with me, especially since I'm so new to the school. He's taking a real chance on someone." I glance back and catch Luke's surprised reaction.

"Well, Aria, you're being modest, but I can't wait to hear what you both write. I'm sure it will be great. I listened to the podcast your mom was on the other night. I'm sure that apple doesn't fall far from the tree. Her new song is amazing."

I'm caught off guard. That means Luke knew about the podcast. Luke cuts the conversation off before his mom can say anything else, divulging all his secrets. Knowing they both listened to my mom's podcast makes me think that Mom was right. Luke does like me.

Luke clearly wants to get us out of here. "Okay … okay, Mom. That's enough. We need to get to work."

I rise from the bed; his mom's hand is still in mine.

"It was so nice to meet you, honey. I look forward to seeing you again," Janet says before dropping my hand. Her smile is broad, and I can't help but smile back in return. She's easy to like.

"Mom, can I get you anything from the kitchen before we get started?" Luke's concern is obvious. As I make my way to the doorframe, I notice Janet's cane in the corner, slightly hidden from view.

"I'm good for right now, and I'll get it if I need anything. I'll do my best not to bother you two. Have fun."

Luke ushers me out and then stops, glancing back at his mom. I can't tell what he does, but Janet gives a slight laugh as he closes the door halfway and then swirls around to me, a sheepish grin covering his face.

He leads me back down to the living room before he says, "Sorry about that … we don't get many visitors, and when I went to write with you last week, she wanted to hear all about it."

"You have nothing to worry about. She's wonderful."

There's an awkward pause. I'm wondering what's wrong with Luke's mom. I don't want to be rude and ask, but it seems like he's reading my mind.

"Mom has an autoimmune disease," he replies. "Most of the time, she's too tired to get up and around much anymore."

I nod, considering his words, and then I jump right in. I'm just like my dad. "So, do you take care of her, and everything around here? You haven't mentioned your dad?"

Luke looks down and then gives me those eyes, filled with a determination I've seen several times from my own family, "Yeah, I take care of Mom, but I'm glad to do it. My dad died years ago. He was in the military, so it's just us." A fierceness enters his voice, "We do okay though, you know? We're doing just fine."

I pause before I quietly answer, "I can totally see that, Luke. Your mom's great and seems to be doing well, and this house is very well taken care of," I say, gesturing around the room. "I even noticed how well the yard looks, and that must be you, too. You're doing a good job, Luke. You should be proud."

Luke gives me a toothy grin before he says, "So why are we standing around? You heard the lady; we have a contest to win."

With that, we take our seats and get down to writing the best songs we can, because now I have an even bigger reason. Luke must win this contest so he can help his mother, and I'm going to help him do it.

Chapter 54 – Julia

I'm standing in our foyer, waiting on Trent. We've had many writing sessions now and have finished several songs. For several months, I've had sessions with other songwriters, and I'm up to a good twenty new songs to add to my repertoire. With the success of Wayne's performance of "He'll Stay," Raine's been bugging me daily about a live show. Even though I have the songs, I'm not sure I'm ready. I know it's the right time for me to get out there, but every time he brings it up, my throat tightens and I start to sweat. What if I won't have the voice and then I'll disappoint the audience. I'm just thinking about it now and I have to wipe my hands down on my jeans. UGH.

I shake my head to erase my thoughts. One of the reasons I'm glad I'm writing with Trent today is that I'm hoping he'll divulge details about Aria's song contest. She won't tell me anything except they get to perform their original songs for all the judges this week, and they'll narrow it down to the top ten. That's all I know. She hasn't told us anything else, but she has this look on her face that comes from me, and she's terrified. My momma bear's kicking in, so I need Trent to tell me more. I've made a ton of home-cooked baked goods. Maybe that will help, I think with a smile.

Right on time, Trent's car pulls up and his driver whips around the car to let him out. Trent always has a driver now. He says it's 'cause he's so busy. Every songwriter in Nashville wants to write with him. Three of our songs are already on hold with major country stars. As soon as we finish a song, someone instantly wants it.

I swing the door open wide and he greets me with a smile, but he looks tired.

"Hey Trent. You know where to go, do you want something to drink? A cup of coffee, maybe?"

"You're readin' my mind, Julia, or maybe it's just the dark circles under my eyes," he says with a laugh as I sympathetically nod.

"How many sessions do you have today?" I ask, shutting the door behind us, then he follows me into the kitchen. He stands in the doorway, watching me make him a cup of coffee.

"Four. But this is the only one that matters. Don't get me wrong, the other writers are good, but whatever we write today is the one that counts."

I can't help but look at him with a shocked expression, but Trent gives me a nod.

There's a pause and I decide to take the leap. "You know, I mentioned my daughter Aria attends the Nashville School of the Arts. She's performing this week, but she won't tell me anything about it."

Trent's apologetic drawl kicks in, "And I'm bound to secrecy, too, darlin'. Wish I could tell you more about it, but I can't say anything."

I look at him, nodding, "I didn't think so, but I'm a worried mother, Trent."

He gives me one of his gorgeous grins that fills up his face and makes his eyes crinkle up. I can't help but wonder how Trent has managed to stay single all these years. He was rumored to be dating an actress for many years, but nothing ever came of it.

As I hand him his coffee I ask, "Can I ask you a personal question?" And before he has time to respond, I jump, "Why are you still single? Why aren't you with someone or married by now?"

He takes the cup of coffee from my outstretched hand, and a slight smirk fills his face. "Julia, I've always liked that you say what's on your mind," he says with a grin, leans against the doorframe, and then continues. "I've dated through the years and at one point, I thought I found 'the one,' but it didn't work out. We both were always traveling and hardly ever together. It wasn't real. I'd love to have what you and Raine have, I really would, which is why I write about it all the time. I haven't met the one person who can tolerate what I do."

I nod along. "You said real … you need to find someone not in the public eye, Trent. That might work." In the back of my mind, my wheels are turning. I've never been a matchmaker, but Trent needs someone to help him navigate life, then maybe he wouldn't be working all the time. Not that there's anything wrong with it, but having cancer has really made me realize even more what's important in life.

Trent brings us back to the task at hand. "Enough about me … let's finish that song we were working on last time. It's a hit and I want to finish it.

"You got it."

It's well past noon by the time we finish our session, and then Trent rushes out to his next appointment. He did let on that his entire week is like this, except for Thursday. That gave me a hint that's probably the day Aria and her classmates will perform their songs.

After he leaves, I phone Tracy.

"Just finished with Trent. We may have another song to put out there soon. I'm sure Raine can help us with the demo."

"You guys are on a roll!" Tracy exclaims. She loves the fact that both Raine and I are keeping her busy. "Did he tell you anything about Reezie's contest?"

"No, of course not," I say, clearly frustrated. "There's a chance it's this Thursday, but that's not confirmed." I pause with a sigh as I wonder how to bring this up. "Trace, I want to ask something, and you may think it's odd. Please don't mention this to Raine. He'll get some weird idea in his head."

"O-kay," she says with trepidation. "Spit it out."

"Trent needs to find a girlfriend, wife material. Someone normal. Got any ideas?"

"Wow. That is an odd ask," Tracy says with a guffaw. "Why are you concerned about Trent's love life?"

"He seems sad, and tired. He needs someone to take his mind off working 24-7. He needs a life."

"It's nice of you to care, Jules, and I certainly won't let on to Raine that you're trying to help Trent's love life. Let me think about it. Since he's stuck here in Nashville, it makes sense to find someone who lives here for him to date."

There's a slight pause, and then Tracy chimes in on my ongoing pressure. "While I have you on the phone, what about scheduling your songwriter show? I could get you booked into a venue as early as next month. Ever since you did that podcast interview, I've been getting calls about it."

My sigh is long and loud before I answer, "I'm sure. Raine's been bugging me several times a day." There's another silent pause from me as my mind races with all that this show would entail and all the stress it will cause.

"Jules ... you still there?"

I cave. "I am ... okay ... go ahead and see what you can book, but pick someplace small and not famous. I'd like to start out subtle and see how it goes."

"Yah hoo!" Trace yells, and I have to pull the phone away from my ear. My regret is instant.

Tracy asks, "Do you want to tell Raine, or do you want me to do it?"

"I'll do it. I'll tell him tonight. Let me control this and when you find a venue, let me decide on it."

"You got it! I am *so* excited!"

"Really? I couldn't tell," I respond dryly as she laughs.

"Don't forget you have another songwriting session tomorrow. I'll text you the details.

After I hang up, it's all I can do not to run to the bathroom and throw up. I've got to get my mind off what I just agreed to do. It's a chilly fifty degrees today, so I throw on a coat and my work boots, and head outside to help Jacob in the barn. I'm sure he'll have something for me to do. My mind races as I ponder that I'll have to let Raine run with this, and that I'll also have to start practicing for a live acoustic show.

For the past several months, I purposefully have been avoiding any type of added stress like this, and I think it's been helping. I've been exercising and making sure I'm eating right. I've even managed to lose ten pounds. But still, what if I'm not ready, and is this really a good idea? I get to the barn and let Jacob know I'll muck out some stalls. Anything to still my racing mind.

Raine's been downtown recording with a new artist today and he's late getting home. Aria's a little late today, too, so I ordered dinner. As we finish up, I drop my performance bomb.

Their stunned stares make me feel like I have egg or something on my face.

"Seriously?" Raine asks, jumping up to grab me from my chair in a bear hug, practically taking all the air from my lungs.

"Yes …" I gasp. "Raine, please, I can hardly breathe," I manage to squeak out as he gently places me on the ground, his hands gripping my arms. The look on his face should be for something as wonderful as winning the lottery, not a simple songwriters show. "Really, this is *not* that big of a deal."

Aria laughs from the dinner table, and I watch as she gathers up her empty plate and says, walking to the kitchen sink, "Mom, are you serious? Hell just froze over." She walks away laughing.

My eyes go back to Raine's face and he's nodding in agreement, which makes me shake my head in amusement.

"Oh, my word!" I reply as he gathers me up and my arms go up around his neck. "If I'm doing an acoustic show, there is only one way I'm doing it, and that's if you are playing guitar for me. I'm not going to play and …"

"I'm hired," Raine quickly says before I can finish, laying a kiss on my neck.

I push back against his chest to look at him. "Really, Raine, let's please not make that big of a deal out of this. What if I'm terrible? I don't need a big crowd watching me go down in flames."

"You won't go down in flames … I promise," he says with sincerity as he again turns his attention to my neck, which makes me groan with pleasure, but also frustration.

"Pinky promise?" I say, jokingly.

"But of course," and he stops and holds out his hand, and we make our pinky promise.

"Now help me clean up our mess so I can go skulk upstairs in a bath."

Raine lets me go, but a huge grin fills his face, and he keeps looking at me like he did win the lottery, while the acid in my stomach rises in my throat. Right after my bath, I'm going to outline a schedule to get my voice in shape. I will not go down in flames. I won't.

Chapter 55 – Aria

I've plodded through the slowest week of my life. I'm standing backstage with the other performers waiting for Luke to show up, and in atypical fashion, he's late. They released the order of today's songwriting performances yesterday. Luke and I are performing near the end of the list. Luke is also listed as a solo performer; he didn't tell me about that. I don't know if I should be glad or worried.

The look on the prim face of Dr. Smith when she handed me a copy of the list was mostly disgust, with a slice of something I couldn't quite put my finger on. Her snarky smile is now burned on my brain. I'm barely squeaking by with a B minus in her class. Since she's coordinating the whole contest, I worry that somehow she'll influence our score. It's set my preoccupied brain aflutter.

Finally, Luke rushes in. My breath catches. He's in all black and he's even wearing a cowboy hat. I didn't think I could fall again, but it's happening. We're gonna look like twins. I'm in black, but I've got a couple of splashes of hot pink in my blouse. Mom says I need to wear color on stage, not all black. I left my hair down and straightened it, and it's hitting the middle of my back. I'm so used to wearing my hair back that it's driving me nuts. Luke's eyes meet mine. I lose everything else around me as we both pause for what seems like minutes, then he takes a step toward me.

"Dang … you clean up well," Luke says with obvious admiration.

I'm sure my face turned the same color of pink that's in my shirt, so I direct my attention back to him, "I can say the same about you. You look great, Luke, seriously … love the hat."

His olive complexion tinges a slight red. Good, it worked. Two can play this game. I'm gripping my guitar tightly at my side, hoping it will keep Luke from noticing my shaky hands. I really wish we were performing early. I don't do well with waiting.

"Sorry I'm late. I know you want to run through the song again, but I think we're good, Aria." I nod my head while he talks, but I'm not so sure I have the harmony part down right. I ask him about his solo performance.

"You're up first with your song. What song are you going to do?"

Luke looks down, unconsciously shuffling his feet, before he replies, "It's a song I started months ago called, 'Coming Home.'"

He doesn't want to say more, so I don't press any further as we both walk over to a couple of empty seats, and he starts to unpack his guitar.

Luke must notice my hands, because after he leans his guitar against his chair, and for the first time ever, he takes my hands between his hands. A warmth shoots through me that shocks my senses.

"You're shaking." That's all he says as I look down at our entwined hands.

My head nods. "Yeah, I've inherited my mom's stage fright."

"I never knew your mom had stage fright. She hides it well."

Our conversation, mixed with the warmth of his hands, soothes my nerves. "Mom says as soon as she steps on stage, it disappears, it's just while she's waiting to go on that's brutal. She almost gets sick," I add with a laugh. I think to myself how the same thing happens to me, and how I'm praying I don't have to run to the side of the stage to vomit. That would *not* be appealing. Luke's now looking at me with what seems like pity—I've got to change the subject.

"I think I'm better," I murmur, sliding my hands out from between his. A sliver of disappointment crosses his face, but there's a sly smile, too.

"Good, 'cause we're going to be great, and we're going to win this thing," he says with the same kind of confidence I'd get from my dad. It's infectious. I grin at his words.

I say, "Let's get these guitars tuned and maybe we could run through the chorus one more time to make sure I've got it." Luke nods, and we get to work.

It seems like minutes later they're calling his name to perform his solo song. He stands and grabs his guitar, but before he walks away, he glances down at me and gives me a smile that lights up his face. I'll never forget how his eyes are shining from excitement, maybe mixed with a bit of fear, but mainly I think it's because he's doing something he loves.

After he walks out, I set my things down and go to the side of the stage to peer out from behind a curtain. He's standing center stage as he plugs in his acoustic guitar. There are some words exchanged with people in the audience, but it's hard to tell with the lights glaring toward the stage. There's a long table set up in the middle of the auditorium and four or so figures sitting there. I can't see anyone else in the large room.

They finish talking and then there's strumming of Luke's guitar as clear as day. Then his words come, and man, are they powerful. He tells the story of a soldier coming home from war to a family that loves him, but he struggles to find his place and it's not exactly what he thought coming home would be. The chorus is simple and beautiful. Then the second verse is about a woman who's sick and comes home from the hospital to a family who loves her and expects life to return to normal, but nothing will ever be normal again. Again, it's not what she and they thought coming home would be. The last verse tells the story of an old man, dying and waiting to come home to heaven, but it's exactly like what he had pictured in his mind, and he finally was coming home. The song is beautifully written, with an amazing chord structure, and it's perfect. His song would be an epic title track for the movie we're all writing for.

When Luke finishes, I rush back to my chair. I don't want him to know I was spying, and I have to somehow wipe the disappointment off my face. His song is amazing, and I don't think our song will come close. I'm glad for him, but there's an ache in the pit of my stomach as I realize I want to win, not only for Luke, but for me, too.

Luke steps out from behind the stage curtain heading straight for me. I look up at him with a pasted-on smile, and I purposefully place a questioning look on my face.

"How'd it go?" I ask, making sure to raise my voice at the end.

He smiles, and replies humbly, "Pretty well, I think. I messed up a chord in the middle, and I could have sung one chorus a bit better, but it was the best I could do. That's all I can ask for."

I'm nodding along as the ache in my stomach gnaws at me, "I'm sure it was really good, Luke." My words feel false because I know the truth. His performance was stellar and no one else stands a chance, including, weirdly, us.

It's late in the day when they call our names and there are only a few other people left backstage. We've gone through our song a couple of times to try and stay fresh. I'm sure I have the harmony down, but my energy is low. Luke's doing everything he can to keep my spirits up by telling really corny jokes, which has helped. He must think it's my nerves, and part of it is. We've got to be perfect to have a chance at the top ten.

Finally, they call our names and we grab our guitars. My knees buckle slightly when I stand, but I'm able to mask it. Being the perfect gentleman, Luke lets me lead as we walk to the center of the stage, where there are two mics set up. I go to the far mic and plug in my acoustic guitar as Luke does the same on his side. Then we both face the front and wait.

A faceless voice announces from the table, "Now we have Luke Greyson and Aria Wagner, performing a song called 'Color of Love.'"

Another voice, a male voice I recognize as Trent Austin's, says, "Is there anything you'd like to tell us about your song before you begin?"

We decided we'd describe this song as a good track outlining the theme of emotional strife between the two main characters that's prevalent throughout the entire movie. Luke takes the lead and relays our explanation, while I add that we mutually worked on the lyrics and structure of the song.

There's nothing left to say, so I look at Luke, waiting for him to begin playing, then I'll chime in on guitar as planned. He's singing lead, thank God. As soon as he strums the opening chord and I jump in, any shakiness left in my arms and fingers, and throughout my entire body, magically disappears. When it's time for me to join in the harmony parts, my voice rings true right along with his, and it's at this moment that a wave of peace washes over me. Mom describes this as knowing you are in the right place, at the right time, doing exactly what you are meant to be doing.

By the time we get through the bridge to a small break, I look fully at Luke and he's having as much fun as I am. We get to the last chorus, and I stop playing as he takes over. I'll jump back in at the end. I stand there watching him sing and my heart swells. I've fallen head over heels for this dark-haired, gorgeous guitar player. Exactly the kind of guy my dad warned me about growing up. Luke's eyes meet mine as I join in and we sing the last two lines together in perfect harmony as his guitar strums the final chord. We finish to a near-empty room, with zero applause and no reaction, which is really weird.

Finally, the shrill voice of Dr. Smith breaks though the silence, "Thank you, Luke, and Aria. That will be all."

We unplug our guitars and walk to the side of the stage, where Luke pulls back the first curtain and waits for me. I meet him and as the curtain drops, we're caught between two curtains where no one can see us. Luke takes the plunge and grabs my free hand, pulling me against his frame, and plants a hard and fast kiss on my lips. I thought my knees were weak before. It's a drive-by kiss. As we hear the name of the next performer, Luke pulls away from me, dropping my hand like it's on fire, and then he pulls the second curtain back so I can walk through. I catch his eyes and they are burning, and he has this smile that is ingrained on my heart. That was perfect.

We walk back to our chairs in silence. We pack up our guitars and then head out the stage doors, toward an exit door. It's late afternoon now and regular classes have ended. As we walk to the front of the school toward our waiting trucks, they're two of the only vehicles left in the lot. Luke hasn't said anything. I glance down and I notice his free hand next to mine flex and release, like he wants to grab my hand, but he won't. I look at the ground and smile.

We instinctively head to my waiting truck. I realize I need my keys, so I fumble inside my purse. We get to my driver's side door just as I find them and I open the lock, then Luke takes my guitar and backpack and loads them up on the passenger side before coming back to me as I wait, watching him.

"We did well, Aria. I think we've got a shot," he says, standing a foot from me. I'm glad he's keeping his distance, because I can't control myself right now.

"I have to be honest, Luke. I heard your solo song, and it was amazing." As I'm saying this, Luke looks away, as if he's guilty of performing it. "I hope it wins; I truly do," I add.

"Well, thanks. That means a lot coming from you ..." He then gives me his full-on gaze, and everything stops. "I guess I should apologize for what happened ... you know, behind the curtain."

I start to laugh, but then I realize he's serious. "Apologize? No, no need to apologize. That was awesome," I blurt out. Luke chuckles as I realize I've completely opened myself up. He takes a step forward and grabs my hand in his.

"Behind the curtain, huh? Might be an interesting song title."

I give a light laugh, nodding my head as I'm lost in his eyes that have taken on a slightly darker hue, "Now, that's one I wouldn't want my dad to hear."

And then it's Luke's turn to laugh, but his face grows serious as if realizing he wouldn't want my dad to hear it either. "Yeah, your dad is truly scary, Aria. I didn't say anything at first because I didn't want to offend you, but wow. Just wow."

I smile at him, instinctively taking a step closer. He drops everything he's holding to wrap me up in his arms as I place my head against his shoulder, while one of his hands goes behind my hair against my neck. I've been in the arms of a guy and hugged before, but this is something different and much deeper. This feels like home. We hold each other like this for several moments.

I pull back and step away, "Speaking of my dad, I should get going. He'll start to wonder where I am."

Luke nods, but he doesn't let go of my hand and I don't want him to.

He finally lets it go, and as I'm getting in my truck, and he's standing at the door, he says, "Seriously, Aria, our performance was stellar. No matter what happens, we should ask your dad to record our song."

"Yeah, I agree. And we sound good together, that's for sure."

He closes my door and I start up the truck. We don't talk about anything more; no next steps or anything, and that's okay. Today was enough.

As I pull out of the lot, I look over at the teachers' parking lot, and there's Dr. Smith standing next to her car, clearly watching me drive away. I can see her scowl for miles. Was she watching us the entire time? Well, even if she was, so what? Students can date, but she gives me the creeps. I try to shake it off, but something about her just isn't right.

Chapter 56 – Julia

I've cleaned our upstairs bedroom and bathroom, mopped the kitchen, and now I'm out of things to clean. I always clean when I'm stressed out. As I drink my herbal tea, which is supposed to calm me down, my eyes flash to the clock on the microwave and a sigh escapes me. Aria's late and Raine's not here, so I have no one to vent to, and nothing left to do.

Today, Aria rushed out of here like a bat out of hell, carrying her guitar. She was dressed for the stage with a lot of color and everything, and her hair was done, not up in a hair clip or ponytail. She skipped breakfast and raced out the door without saying a word.

Finally, the front gates open and Raine's truck pulls up the drive toward the garage. I'm glad but disappointed. I wanted to talk to Aria before he got home. Raine knows something's up the minute he walks in.

"You're wearing the same clothes as when I left, and the whole house smells like bleach."

"Today was the day, Raine. I'm sure of it. Aria's not home yet."

"She's not home? It's almost six. Did you call her?" His voice rises with every syllable. My mind didn't even go there.

"I'm sure she's fine." But he's already dialing her number and puts it on speaker.

"Yes, Dad?"

Raine's tense face instantly relaxes.

"Where are you?"

"Pulling up the driveway," Aria replies with clear frustration, like she's wondering why her parents are bugging her.

"Oh . . . okay, see you in a few."

By the time she walks in the front door, we're standing in the foyer like a couple of dorks.

Aria gives us both a look, and I know we are actual dorks. "Oh my gosh! What? I'm home. Can't a girl get a break, already? Sometimes you two are too much."

"You're a little late, honey," I say, coming to our defense. Aria's still in what I would call "performance attire," so I take the plunge. "So, was today *the* day? Did you perform for the contest?"

Aria drops her things in the foyer in frustration. "What do you think, Mom? I'm sure you talked to Trent; you see him every week. And when do I wear this hot pink and black blouse? Only for stage. So, yes, we performed today."

I reply in my best motherly tone, "First, you need to pick up your things and put them where they belong, and second, Trent wouldn't tell me anything. He couldn't."

"Alright . . . just give me some space. Please!" Aria grabs her guitar case and backpack and huffs her way up the stairs as we watch in amusement.

I call out after her gleefully, "When you're done with your temper tantrum, I want to know how it went."

"Maybe I won't come down," Aria yells back sarcastically.

Raine replies, "You'll have to come down eventually or you'll starve."

When she's out of earshot, Raine asks, "What's up her craw? You just asked if she performed."

"I have no idea," I say, before adding, "Maybe it didn't go well?" But in the back of my mind, I'm thinking it's all about Luke. Something happened, so she's avoiding the subject entirely. I can't help but smile. She may tell me eventually.

Aria does come down when she smells the chicken Raine's cooking in the oven. We thought food would work. She's showered, and now she's fresh in sweats, with wet hair and no makeup. Maybe I can get something out of her once she's had a good dinner.

"Glad you could join us," I say, placing the last of the dinnerware on the table. "Could you grab the pitcher of iced tea from the fridge?"

Aria nods but doesn't say anything as she brings it to our kitchen nook. "How much longer, Dad? I'm starving."

"Didn't you get lunch today?" I ask.

She replies, without much emotion, "No time. I had a protein bar."

I sigh at her, "Well, that's something."

We get dinner on the table. I ask everyone to say grace before we dig in. Aria looks tired, so I won't press her, but then she asks Raine about studio time.

"Dad, what do you charge to produce a demo?"

"It depends, honey, on how complicated it is. Is there a full band, how long does someone want to spend on vocals, things like that. Why?"

Aria looks down at her plate and fiddles with her food. "Just wondered."

Raine gives me a side-eye, so I ask. "So, we know you performed for the contest today, were you happy with it?"

Aria responds, but her eyes stay focused on her plate. "Yes, Mom. It went well. But we won't know until after the holiday break what ten songs will make it to the next phase of the contest."

I try to get more out of her. "Okay. Do you want to record your song? Is that why you asked your dad about producing a demo?"

"Maybe ... Luke mentioned recording it." Aria's keeping her head down, focused on her food. Now I know there's something going on with Luke. But I take what she's saying as a good sign.

"Oh good," I reply. "Well, your dad wouldn't charge you to do that, Reez. He doesn't charge me for demos."

Aria looks up, clearly exasperated. "I'm not saying that's what we want to do. I was just asking."

"Got it." I give Raine a look, and he shrugs his shoulders. He's clearly missing the drama I'm getting from her vibe, and that's a good thing. I drop it. I got the info I wanted to know; their performance went well.

When we finish eating, Aria heads back upstairs for an early evening, while

Raine helps me clean up the kitchen. He asks about Aria's mood.

"It's probably nerves, Raine, you know how she gets. Just like me," I explain.

Raine shrugs his shoulders. "Yeah, maybe. She sure is acting odd, though. She knows I would never charge her for a demo."

"Maybe it's not for her, but for Luke?"

Raine grimaces, so I quickly change the subject, "Hey, there is something else. Next week I have a CT scan. Do you want to come along for all the fun of my follow-up visit with Dr. Henley?

"Sure, babe, tell me the day, and I'll clear my schedule."

Raine grows quiet as a familiar uncomfortable look I've been trying to avoid crosses his face, so I work to ease his mind. "Dr. Henley's office left a voicemail today. It's just a routine follow-up visit."

He stops and places the dish he was holding in the sink and twirls me around into his arms. "Nothing about you is routine or regular, darlin', and I wouldn't want it any other way."

It's a week after my CT scan, and I'm sitting with Raine in Dr. Henley's office waiting for her to walk in. I'm having a bit of déjà vu, and just as Raine grips my hand for reassurance, she joins us. Right away, I can tell something is up by her furrowed brow. Raine's grip tightens around my hand.

Dr. Henley sits down hard in her chair with a file in her hand, looking right at me and then at Raine. She's direct and I'm grateful for that.

"There's a small shadow on your right lung, Julia. It might not be anything, but we're not sure."

My lungs, now in question, deflate, letting out the enormous breath I was holding. Raine's grip on my hand lessens a bit, like the air left him too. I don't dare look at him.

I jump in, "Okay. So, how do we know for sure?"

Dr. Henley replies, "I'm going to send you in for an MRI, but you'll need to see a different specialist about a biopsy, as soon as possible."

I dare to peek at Raine. He's staring at the doctor with his hand still wrapped in mine, so I give it a squeeze to get his attention. When he glances at me, the shocked despair on his face is a look I'd hoped never to see again.

"Will it be a different surgeon than before?" For some reason I just need to keep talking.

"This will be Dr. North, who specializes in pulmonary. He's a friend of mine, Julia. I've already talked to him, and he'll meet with you on Monday, if that works?"

I again look at Raine, who replies, his voice low, "Sure, I'll clear my schedule."

"Good. My assistant has the details at her desk. We'll send you up for the MRI today if that works ... Julia, please try not to jump to conclusions. We won't know anything until we get the biopsy results back. This may not be anything. Everything else on your scan is clear."

Dr. Henley stands and moves around the table to pull me up into a hug, bringing the seriousness of the situation home. Raine stands stiffly and then leads me out to her assistant, his hand pressed against my back. He gets the address for Dr. North and our next steps as my numb body stands next to him in silence. Then we make our way up to the imaging center for my MRI.

When we're walking back to his truck, Raine sidles up next to me, putting his arm around my shoulders. That's when I lose it. Not in a loud way, but my shoulders hunch over, and the silent tears start to stream. I really thought we'd made it past this. Sure, I've been tired now and then, but we're doing everything right, from my diet and exercise to keeping the stress low, except for those stupid promo spots. And now I've got to do a singing gig in the middle of this. My mind whirls through all the steps I've taken since I've been home from the hospital until this point. What did I do wrong? Fuck. This.

Chapter 57 – Raine

When we get home, Julia goes upstairs to change and then she's heading up to the barn, which is surprising. She's acting much stronger than I am on the inside. I head to my studio to try and take my mind off our news, but it's no use. I sit down at my corner desk and notice a text from Tracy.

"I can get Julia booked at one of the biggest songwriting venues in Nashville next month. I know she said a small venue, but this would be AMAZING! Text me back when you get a chance. I want your opinion before I talk to her."

I have to call her back to set the stage. Tracy picks up right away.

"Gonna shoot you straight, Trace. Don't know if Jules will want to do the show now. So, talk to her before you set anything up."

"Why? Raine ... what's going on?" Concern ebbs from her voice. It's not like Jules to back out of a commitment.

"Just talk to her before you move forward with anything."

There's a pause. "Raine, are you okay?" Tracy asks the one question I always dread.

I'm completely honest. "No, Trace, I'm not. But don't worry, I'm calling Bret next. He'll help."

I can't miss Tracy's huge sigh on the other end. "I'll call Julia right away."

"She may not answer. She's headed up to the barn. You may need to give her a little time."

"Okay. Well ... you really shouldn't leave me hanging like this."

"I know." And it's my turn to sigh, but I just can't get myself to tell her the words that are ringing through my out-of-control brain, *Julia's cancer may be back*. "Send Jules a message to call you."

I should call Bret immediately, but I need a few moments to settle my overwhelming need for a large glass of bourbon. In times like this, it's always there, my devilish friend, waiting for me to fail.

I flip through some other messages and see one from Wayne. After I read it, I want to race to Julia and tell her the good news, but now is not the time. In January, Wayne's going to submit "He'll Stay" for Song of the Year. I'm not surprised; the song's still blowing up the charts and it's rare that when I turn on a station, I don't hear it in rotation. It's heartbreaking to have this wonderful news, and I want to run and tell Julia, but right now, I doubt she'd care. I can't imagine the fear and anguish that's running through her. And I'm not there for her. I was silent the entire drive home as she stared out her passenger side window.

I message Wayne back, thanking him for the good news. Then I send a message to Bret. He'll know what I need to do.

I pull up in front of Bret's house. It's unusually quiet for a house filled with kids, but it is the middle of the day, and they're all at school. Bret told me to meet him up at his garage in the back, which is quite a hike. By the time I reach the large double garage doors, I'm out of breath. Loud music blares from inside. Bret's working on one of his many cars. He must have six vehicles right now; all vintage and all rare and expensive.

"DUDE!" I yell out, but he doesn't hear me from the doorway, so I go in and stand in front of the older model Mustang he's working on to get his attention. He sees me and smiles, grabbing a device to turn down the drone of heavy metal coming from the speakers above our heads. Even though we're out in a garage with the doors open, it seems warm inside, and then I notice the large heaters sitting just inside the large doors.

"Why don't you shut the doors to keep it warmer in here?" I ask as Bret puts his tools down and walks over to a nearby fridge to grab us a couple of sodas.

"I like the fresh air and it's not that cool yet." Bret's in a heavy flannel shirt and boots. I dressed a bit warmer too, knowing he'd want us to talk out here in what I jokingly call his "mini-man mansion." It's his hideout when things get to be too much inside, although I've known at least one of his girls to be out here helping him with his cars. Next to golf, this is his favorite hobby.

Bret hands me my drink. "Are you ever going to finish this one?" I ask, gesturing toward his beloved muscle car. I've watched him tinker on this same car for years. He's given it a new coat of paint, new wheels, and tires, but he's been messing with the engine forever.

"She's almost ready," he says as he tenderly looks at this mint green beauty. The car even has a name, but of course I've forgotten it. I've helped him work on it a few times, but working on cars is not really my thing.

"Is Jessica out?" Bret's wife volunteers with many charity groups and foundations, so she's often gone during the day. Bret's semi-retired and he's often the only one at home.

"Yep, we have a good couple of hours until she's home. She'll pick up the girls and be here around four." There is a slight pause, but then Bret just blurts out what's on his mind. "Raine, you usually come over on a weekend when your girls are busy, not during the week, so I know something is up. What is it?"

I take a seat on a nearby stool. Bret's known me forever and the concern on his face is evident. There's no bullshitting around this one.

"We were at the doctor's office this morning. There's a shadow on Julia's lung." Bret stops what he's doing and takes a nearby seat, crossing his arms as I continue.

"We don't know any more than that. Julia has a follow-up with another specialist next week to arrange a biopsy."

Bret looks out the wide-open doors at his expanse of land, which includes a small pond right in the middle. We used to come out here when Aria was little and fish. I smile thinking about that memory.

After a few moments, Bret responds, "I'm sorry, man. I hate this for you all, you know I do." A few more moments pass before he continues, "As you said, you don't know anything more, so we have to pray that it's nothing. That's what we'll do tonight. We'll pray for all of you, Raine."

I nod and get a little teary because that's all any of us can do. I take a sip of my drink, trying to maintain my composure.

Bret adds with a smirk, "I'm sure this is not helping your urge to drink. Shit, I'd want a whiskey after hearing that."

I look at him nodding, "You have no idea. Too bad it's cold out or I'd make you go play a round of golf or something."

"I do have a pool table in the back, remember?"

"I haven't played pool since I almost punched out that young punk songwriter. What was his name? I honestly don't remember."

"I don't either," Bret says, and I can't help but laugh at those memories. Bret has been through so much crap with me and Julia. He even traveled up to Montana to write when I was trying to get Julia back after our baby Jonah died. He's been my best friend for years, and when I'm going through any major turmoil, he always has a way of bringing me around to what is real and right.

"You know, I should be angry with you," Bret says with a slight look of frustration.

"What the heck did I do now?" I ask as my shoulders rise questioningly.

"You gave Julia's hit song to Wayne. You could have helped me out, man! I haven't had a hit in years, and you give it to that guy. Seriously?" He takes a drink of his soda and then crosses his arms like he's pissed.

I laugh. "You know, Julia's been writing a bunch with Trent … I'll put in a good word on the next one, so you'll get first dibs."

"What a friend you are. Asshole," he teases.

I hold up a hand and gesture to our surroundings, "I think you're doing alright. You really don't need a 'Julia Tate' song."

Bret laughs, "True, but it couldn't hurt. She's hot right now, Raine. Everyone wants her songs."

"Wayne's nominating the song for music awards." I can't help it. I've got to tell someone and I can trust Bret.

"I'm not surprised. That song is probably, no, it is the best song Jules has ever written. I told Jess that the first time I heard it, and I almost called you right then to complain."

I smile at him and pause, looking out at the scenery in front of us. The leaves have all fallen from the trees and winter will be upon us soon.

"You know, Aria mentioned taking a family vacation and we need to do it. Maybe someplace warm during the winter break. Do you think you and Jess, and the kids, would want to come?"

Bret looks at me excitedly, "We would love that, and I'm sure I have the time. It's Jess's schedule we'd have to work around, but I think that's a great idea. You know, someone sent me information about a private Catamaran excursion you can take around the Bahamas. What about something like that? We could rent the boat for the week and not have to worry about anything or anyone."

I not at him in agreement, "That sounds perfect. No paparazzi to bother us. I'll have to convince Jules that we can leave the horses and dogs for that long, and Aria would have to break away from her phone, but that could be the best thing for all of us right now."

"I'll find the info and send it to you." Bret stands and look at me expectantly, "Now, while you're here, why don't you make yourself useful and help me with this green goddess so one day I can get her running."

I put my drink down and stand, giving him a look like "What are we waiting for?" as Bret laughs. He hands me a wrench, as though I have any idea what to do with it. Then he walks over to stand in front of the open hood and proceeds to walk me through what he's doing as I try to listen. At least it's getting my mind off the day, and now I have a vacation to plan.

Chapter 58 – Aria

For the next couple of weeks, Luke and I act like nothing much has happened. We go to our usual classes and chat, but there hasn't been anything like the big kiss, and I don't really know what to think about it. But at the end of each day, like clockwork, Luke waits for me outside of the front entrance, walks me to my truck, and gives me a huge hug before we go on our way. I want to ask him about what happened between us, but I've been a big ol' chicken. With everything going on with Mom right now, I have way too much streaming through my mind, and now I'm constantly wondering what is up with him. It's becoming too much and I need answers.

I may get my answer today though. Even though we finished the song for the contest, we're gonna continue working on new songs.

I'm standing in our foyer waiting for Luke to arrive. It's colder now, so I'm wearing a heavy green sweater, black jeans, and boots. I struggled with my hair all morning, but finally ended up in a ball cap.

There's a delightful smell of chili coming from our kitchen, so at least we'll have something to eat. I knew Mom would be home today, and Dad is planning on working in his studio, so there's a good chance for more parental awkwardness. Ever since we got Mom's news, everything's been weird, although we all try to act like everything is cool. The look on both my parents' faces is hard to hide, and now when I walk into a room, their hushed tones bother me the most.

Mom says she'll have her biopsy right before we go on winter break, and now Dad has planned some boat trip for us and Bret's family. He thinks it'll make all our worries disappear for a few days and maybe it will. It was my idea for a family trip, so I'm playing along that it's fine that I'll be trapped on a boat with my parents, Bret, and his girls.

But first, Mom's playing her songwriting show next week. She's looking forward to that like she's going to the dentist, and she *hates* the dentist. She asked me to sing with her, and it's the least I can do.

I glance out the window as Luke's truck pulls through our front gates. When I open the front door, I try to stifle my escaping laughter, but I can't stop myself. This guy could have walked right out of a jeans commercial or an old cigarette commercial … and I mean that in the best of ways. DAMN. Even in a winter coat and jeans, Luke's like magazine hot.

He steps through the doorframe suspiciously, looking down his front side, "Do I have something on me …is there something wrong?" he says with a gleam in his eye.

As I try to stifle my laughter, I come clean. "Luke, you look like you walked off the set of a commercial, seriously." I'm flirting with him—on purpose.

His head goes down in embarrassment, "It's just a winter coat and jeans, Aria. What do you expect? It's cold out today." He's sarcastic but teasing me.

He shakes his guitar off his shoulder as he mentions the aroma, "Dang, I smell something spicy."

"Mom made chili." I lean in like I'm telling him a secret, "Don't say anything, but it's one of the only things she knows how to make."

Luke nods with a look like my secret is safe. He gathers up his things, and we both start down the hall to Mom's office, but we stop at the kitchen door. Mom's back is to us as I call out, "When will the chili be done, Mom?"

She twirls around as she says, "Hey honey, an hour or so. Good to see you again, Luke." I notice how tired she looks; I'm sure Luke will notice it, too.

"Good to see you too, ma'am."

"Please, Luke, call me Julia."

"Yes, ma'am," and we all laugh as he continues, "I'll try to get that right next time.

We continue down the hall to the office, unpack our gear, and get to work for the next few hours finishing up two songs and rehearsing our contest song, but then I can't take it any longer.

"It's time to eat," I say, practically throwing my guitar to my side and standing.

Luke replies, "It's about time. I'm sure you heard my stomach growling over my guitar."

When we get to the kitchen, my parents are there eating at the bar. We grab our own bowls and drinks and join them. I'm seated next to my mom and Luke is on the end, which is good. He doesn't have to look directly at my dad.

Mom breaks the silence, "So, Luke, Aria tells us your performance for the contest went well, but she didn't say anything else. Care to enlighten us?" Mom stares down our way with an expectant smile. I see Dad leaning in too, waiting for his response. Dad seems a little less abrasive today, which is good for me.

"Our performance went very well ... in fact I bet we make the top ten, ma'am, I mean, Julia." My dad grunts.

"Aria also said you performed another song solo and that it was, in her words 'amazing.'"

I groan. Really, Mom? Can I ever have something that's private? I lean down and give her a look to match the thoughts in my head.

"Well, that's kind of her to say. Yes, I did perform another song, called 'Coming Home.' It's a simple song really. Not that big of a deal."

Now my dad's interested. Being a hit songwriter and known for finding new talent, dad chimes in. GGRREEATT.

Dad asks, "When did you start writing, Luke?"

"When I was about ten, sir. My mom bought me a second-hand guitar, and I started taking guitar lessons shortly after that. But I didn't get what I'd call serious about writing till I started going to our school." Luke pauses and gives me a smile. I give him a look like "I'm sorry about the inquisition."

"Uh-huh," Dad replies, clearly interested.

Here we go. I glance over my shoulder at Mom, and she smiles at me, like "It's okay."

Dad continues, “And how many songs have you written?”

But it’s Luke’s response that about makes me spit out my chili, “Oh, I’d say about two hundred or so songs, but there are only twenty that I’d consider any good.”

I slowly swivel my head toward Luke and he’s nodding at me like that’s completely normal. I don’t think I’ve even written twenty.

Dad won’t stop, “Have you recorded any of them … got any demos I could hear?”

“I’ve recorded a couple of songs, but I don’t think the demos are good enough, sir.”

“Well, how about after lunch, you grab your guitar and come down to the studio and play a couple for me. I’d love to hear them.”

And he did it. He went there. I have zero issues with my dad trying to find new talent, he does that all the time, but not the guy I’m interested in! I give Mom a “Is he serious!” look, and she shakes her head while shrugging her shoulders, like “You know your dad.”

“I’d like that, sir,” Luke says, giving me a gorgeous smile that lights up his face as he continues to finish his lunch like it’s no big deal to go and play songs for one of the biggest producers in town. This does not happen every day.

When we’re done eating, Luke grabs his guitar from the office as I apologize for the forwardness of my father, but Luke won’t have it.

“Oh my gosh, Aria. What an honor that he’ll take the time to listen.”

His face gleams with excitement, so I try to prepare him. “Just know that he’s really straightforward, Luke. I mean he does not soften his feedback … not at all.”

“I’m not worried. We both just performed for Trent Austin and that was great. I’ll be fine.” Then I see his look of determination, and he’s probably wondering how I could question his ability, which I’m not doing.

I try to soften it, “I didn’t mean you can’t handle it, but I know my dad, Luke. He can be a Grizzly.”

That makes Luke laugh, then he picks up his guitar like a gun. “I’ll be just fine, Aria.” I can’t help but laugh with him, but I’m not so sure.

We walk down the hall to the opposite side of the foyer and before I knock on the heavy wooden studio door, Luke stops me.

"Wish me luck," he says with the same gleam in his eyes he had when he stepped off the stage.

"Good luck," I whisper, then I knock loudly, and my dad's voice bellows for us to come in.

I leave Luke alone with the bear, wondering how it will turn out. I head back to the kitchen and catch my mom standing at the kitchen counter with a cup of tea in her hand. I roll my eyes at her.

"He's always working, Reez, you know that. It will be fine." I step closer to her, and she wraps me up with her free arm.

"How are you really, Mom. With everything?"

"I'll be fine, sweetie, but mainly, I'm worried about your father. But I'll be fine," she repeats. "Really wish I didn't have this upcoming performance though, but we'll get through it."

I know she's trying to be strong, but her words don't match her eyes, which won't look at me when she says this. Only the part about her show seems truly honest.

I hug her a little tighter as she continues, "I'm going to go upstairs to pull some clothes together for the charity auction we'll have at the show. Do you want to come and help me while the boys are busy?"

"Sure, why not. Dad hijacked my songwriting session, and I don't have anything else to do."

For the next two hours we tag clothes for the auction. By the time we're finished and walking back downstairs, Luke and Dad are walking out of the studio like a couple of old pals, and again I groan. Mom gives me a wink, but now I'm pissed. Luke is my guy, not Dad's new pet project.

Luke says his goodbyes, and Dad tells him he'll be in touch, so obviously it went well. I walk outside with him, not only to find out details, but I have to find out what's going on with us. I don't have time for uncertainty.

I'm casually standing there as he loads up his gear. He's like a kid rambling on about how cool it was to play songs for my dad, and "He had such great feedback" blah, blah, blah. I'm nodding along and saying "uh-huh" the entire time. Finally, I get a break as he leans against the door and looks at me, crossing his arms with a huge smile.

"So, you'll be working with my dad, now? Is that it?"

"I don't know if you'd call it that, Aria. Why? Is that not a good thing?"

"Well, it makes things complicated ... you know, between us ... and speaking of 'us,' what is this?" I ask, gesturing between the two of us. We're standing a couple of feet apart, which is a good representation of "us." Luke, obviously happy, and me standoffish because now Luke and my dad are best buds.

Luke's face looks perplexed, "I don't think it changes anything between us ... we're still really good friends, Aria."

And there it is, that word. "Okay, *friend.* I don't usually have 'friends' that kiss me after performances, but if that's what you want, then fine. My dad won't let me date any of his acts anyway."

I twirl around with a flourish, not looking back as I book it through our front door, slamming it behind me and running up the stairs to my room. A few minutes later, his vehicle starts up, and from the window in my room, I watch his truck slowly head down our drive and out onto the street.

I should have known Luke would do something like this. I've been such a fool! My dad was right, I should never trust guitar players. Hell, I should never trust men at all. You can't count on them. They all suck. Good riddance, friend.

Chapter 59 – Julia

The day of my "big songwriter show" is finally here. Tracy booked a smaller venue, and we've kept the promo at a minimum, but it sold out in a day. We arranged for a couple of my latest co-writers to open the show, and I think Trent and other industry folks will be in attendance. *Great.* For my first performance in years, I wanted this to be low key, but it'll be a much bigger deal than I'd hoped.

I know Aria and Luke's relationship is strained at best. Aria let me in on that little secret, but Raine doesn't have a clue that his "new project" has caused a rift with our daughter. Raine invited Luke and his mother to my show. I haven't had the guts to tell Aria that Luke will be there, and I really don't want to experience her fury when she finds out. Raine can be oblivious to Aria's love life 'cause he wants to be. In his mind, his little girl will forever be ten. Heaven help us when Aria gets serious about a guy one day. Raine will have a come apart.

I'm pacing around the dressing area of my infamous closet, trying on outfit after outfit, but I can't decide on anything. I'm sending photos over to Tracy for her opinion, and now I'm waiting for her reply about the latest option.

Of course, Tracy knows all about my latest scan. She's acting more terrified than I am about next week's biopsy. It's a simple procedure. They don't have to knock me out or anything. It's just a needle biopsy through my ribs. I've already had all the necessary tests I need before the procedure. After the biopsy, they'll take an X-ray to make sure everything looks okay with my lungs, and then I get to go home and take it easy for a few days.

We'll leave for our boat trip right after Aria finishes the last of her mid-year exams, so we'll have a nice long break. I should get the results while we're on our trip. That is if we can get good WiFi while out on the water. Raine assured me this is a posh boat, so that shouldn't be a problem. My phone buzzes with Tracy's verdict on my outfit.

"It's perfect, but I thought the last outfit was good. I don't know why you keep asking me?"

"Trace, they're both kind of revealing."

"Hate to break it to you, Jules, but you're in the music business. It needs to be a little revealing. Go with the one with the blue—it will look good with your eyes."

I send her a semi-smiley face back, but I'm not so sure. The front of the shirt cuts a bit low. My worry is about my new boobs. I stand in front of my mirror, holding the shirt in front of me. I have on the pants I'm going to wear, which are basic black and give me a lot of support. As I stare at my reflection, the dark circles under my eyes are so noticeable. There's nothing I can do about that, except use more concealer. I let out a heavy sigh and agree to go with the blue, light fabric blouse. I pull black boots with matching blue design down from the shelf. Stella is coming over in an hour to finish up and help with makeup 'cause I don't need that added stress.

Raine's heavy steps come up the stairs toward our door.

"What did you and Tracy decide on?" he says, entering my enormous closet. The room is so big that we could hold family meetings in here.

I hold up the blouse of choice, and he nods with a smile. "I love that one. It's perfect. What time is Tracy meeting you at the venue?"

"Six. I want to check my guitar and microphone before anyone gets there. Doors open at seven, right?"

"Yep. But you won't go on until close to nine. Is Aria riding with you?"

"I haven't asked her, but probably a good idea." I've got to fill him in on the drama with Luke. "You know she and Luke had a falling out, right?" He shakes his head no.

"The last time he was here to write with Aria, they had a little spat about you mentoring him. It broke up their arrangement."

Raine gives me a dumbfounded look. "What arrangement?"

Raine doesn't want to see it. "Raine ... Aria *likes* Luke in a romantic way... and I'm positive that he likes her, too. Since Luke is one of your new projects, that makes things weird. You always said Aria couldn't date any of your artists, remember?"

His shoulders rise as he asks, "She likes him?"

I roll my eyes. "Oh, my word. Yes! And now he's going to be at my show and Aria has no idea. I'll have to break it to her before we get there. Teenage drama before I have to sing. That's the last thing I need."

Raine leans against the doorframe, one hand under his chin, like he's thinking. "Aria's going to be your harmony singer most of the night, right?"

"That's the plan."

Raine's eyes light up. "How about we invite Luke up to play guitar on a song, too? That will break the ice between them."

"What about your rule with Aria and your artists?"

"Screw that," Raine says taking a step to me, removing the blouse from my hands, and setting it on my dressing table as he pulls me into his arms. "You dated a guitar player, and it turned out just fine. It's not like he's a signed artist or anything. I'm just helping the kid out."

My hands go to his chest, and I give him a sly smile, "Wow ... you are being very generous about someone who likes your one and only daughter, Raine. Who is this man I'm married to?" I ask, looking up at him questioningly.

He laughs as his lips find my neck and then they trace along my jawline up to my lips as he takes my breath away, his lips moving on mine insistently. His arms wrap me up tight, and for one moment I let myself enjoy the safety and warmth of his arms.

Raine groans as I pull away. "No time for that, not right now, mister. I have a show to freak out about, and my makeup artist will be here any minute now."

"Okay, but I want a rain check. And think about calling up Luke. Might take some of the sting out of their little spat."

Raine leans in and gives me one final lingering peck on my cheek, and then he walks out of the room. For most of our marriage, Raine's treated me like an egg; he never lets me break. But since we found out about the possible spot on my lungs and upcoming biopsy, he's been even more tender. He's joined me at every appointment, but we don't talk about the next steps or results or anything, and for that I'm grateful. I can't right now. It's there lingering in our minds, but I don't want to focus on it. We're trying to be present in the here and now, and that's all we can do.

The doorbell bellows, and I step into the hallway as Raine lets Stella in. I motion for her to come up to our room. Since she's been here before, she knows the drill. I grab my phone and send Aria a text letting her know she'll ride with me. That's when I'll lessen the blow about Luke. The more I think about it, the more I like the idea of having Luke join us on a song. I send Raine a text letting him know I agree with his plan. At least we can try and mend this broken fence.

Chapter 60 – Aria

I don't know why I agreed to ride along with my mom and Stella. At least Stella is driving, and not Mom 'cause she can't concentrate on anything right now. I thought I was bad. We drive up to the back entrance, and then I see the paparazzi, which surprises the heck out of me. Why are they at Mom's songwriting show? This is just a small out of the way venue. Then it hits me like it always does that my mom is, and always will be, a "star." I should have been prepared for this.

A security team is set up in the back. Stella mentions that she'll pull up so we can get out. Reporters line the short walkway into the back door, and as soon as the security guard opens the door, they start yelling at us. Mom exits the front as I step out of the back seat. She takes my hand, guiding me through the people. There are a few fans, too. Mom stops and greets the fans, then she waves and smiles as the reporters take her picture. She doesn't say a word to them, even when one yells out something hideous about her having cancer.

We make it inside and then we wait for Stella, who's parking the car, before we head into the main backstage greenroom. When we enter the room, I hear Mom gasp. Sitting on a center table is a huge bouquet of purple tulips. Mom covers her mouth and bends over with laughter.

"Your father is a piece of work," she exclaims, grabbing the card to read it and chuckling to herself.

"Let me read it," I tease.

"Not in a million," she says, looking at me with a smirk.

Stella managed to bring in Mom's makeup case and shirt, but other than having to change her top, Mom's dressed and ready. Stella heads out to the main room to find some coffee, and as Mom sets her things down, she lets out a heavy sigh as she gives me her full attention.

"There is something I need to tell you, Reez."

Oh no ... I don't like this tone. "What now?"

"Well, your father, let's be honest, is not quite as astute when it comes to your love life."

I'm nodding along as a pit starts to form in my stomach. I already know.

She continues, "Well, he of course invited Luke and his mother to join us here for the show."

I'm caught off guard. Not about Luke, I figured that she was going there, but about his mother. "His mother? She's going to come out of the house to come here?"

"Well, yes, I think so. That's what your dad said."

"She's not in the best of health, Mom. I can handle Luke, that's okay, but we'll need to find some place for his mom to sit. I know she has a cane. Not sure if she uses a wheelchair."

Mom smiles, patting my arm. "That's not a problem, honey. We'll make sure she has a seat next to the stage, so she'll be able to see the show. Let me run out now and see what we need to do."

I nod as Mom quickly walks away. Awesome. I should have known Dad would invite Luke, his shiny new toy, but having his mom here makes things awkward. I wonder if he's told her anything. A light sweat breaks out under my clothes. I dressed in all black with a hint of color, this time in the shade of blue to match Mom's shirt, but now I realize I'm not ready to perform in front of *him.* Especially because I'll be a sweaty mess.

By the time Mom makes it back, it's already six o'clock and a few more people are showing up backstage. Dad's booming voice greets me right before he enters the room. There's a slight scowl on my lips; I can't help it.

"There she is. Hi, sweetheart, all set to warm up?" he asks, a big smile across his face.

"I guess so." The snarky tone in my voice is obvious. "Where's Mom?"

"She's out front signing a few more items for the silent auction, but I think she's ready for a sound check. Should we go?" he asks, clearly excited about the night.

I nod, trudging out behind him. He's not catching on that I'm pissed at him.

As we make our way out the door, I scan the hallway for Luke and any sign of his mom, but I don't see them. The other songwriters who are performing have arrived and they're setting up in the greenroom across from us.

"Mom loved the flowers, Dad."

"Good. That's a tradition, sweetheart."

"Where's your guitar," I ask as we walk backstage, through the curtains and onto the main stage. This is a small venue, but it still seats a good three hundred people, and the room bustles with servers and staff as they prepare for the crowd they're expecting. Last I heard, it's standing room only in the back.

Dad stops to smile at me. "Already on the stage. I came over earlier today to make sure everything was ready."

I can see Mom through open doors in the back making small talk with a few people. She's joking with them like she doesn't have a care in the world. That's one of her specialties; she's great with fans and can talk with anyone. She sees us on the stage because she starts making her way toward us.

When she reaches us, she pauses long enough to lean in toward my dad for a quick kiss and a word in his ear, which I can't hear, but they both laugh. Mom will sit center stage with her guitar, and I'll be sitting to her right with Dad on her left. One big, happy family, except I'm still pissed at Dad for inviting Luke. Dad takes a minute to tune and then starts playing the new Wayne Carson hit, which we know like the back of our hands.

Mom begins to sing and then I join her on the harmony parts. I'm always less nervous on stage with my parents. It's comfortable on stage with the two of them. It's like we're playing in our living room just as we've done all my life. I can easily see the people in the room without the blinding stage lights shining in our faces. Everyone's stopped what they were doing and are listening intently. When we finish this first song, there's a splattering of enthusiastic applause. Someone jokingly yells out for another, which makes Mom laugh. We run through another more up-tempo song before Mom lets us know she's good.

When we walk through the back curtain and off the stage, there he is. Luke's watching us from the side of the stage with his mom. Janet's sitting in a wheelchair with her hand over her heart. I consider heading his way, but Mom beats me to it. Mom greets Luke, and then she leans down to give Janet a hug. Great. I'm sure they'll be instant friends.

I spin around, weaving through the curtains to the safety of Mom's greenroom. So, what if I seem rude? I don't have to be friendly with that man. Minutes later, Mom comes into the room acting like everything is hunky-dory. Then she goes there.

"Did you see Luke and his mother? Luke looks just like her."

"Yep," I say, grabbing a bottle of water from the service table. I really don't want to do this. Not now. Mom must sense this because she doesn't push. Dad walks in and he's another matter.

"I got Luke and his mom all set up, Jules. They're at a small table on the left-hand side, off the side of the stage. I asked a server to take good care of them."

"Thanks, honey. I appreciate that."

Stella, who's patiently sitting on a side couch reading her phone, lets Mom know it's time to freshen up. Mom hops into a chair in front of the mirrors and lets Stella work her magic. I should ask her to fix my face too, but why bother? Who am I trying to impress? Definitely not Luke.

Tracy finds us in what is now becoming a way too crowded room. I walk out to check if there's anyone in the audience I know. I invited my voice coach, Dr. Grace, and my best friend Savannah is supposed to show up with her family. I walk to the curtains and peek out. Of course, my eyes instantly go to Luke's table, where he and his mom are enjoying dinner. I see a couple of other classmates walk up to their table, along with Dr. Grace. Good, I'm glad she's here. Trent Austin's sitting at one of the center reserved tables, and my stomach does a little flip. Of course he'd be here; he co-wrote several of the songs Mom's going to sing. Trent's watching Dr.

Grace greet Luke with great interest. I would have thought they had met since she's one of our instructors, but I guess not.

I jump out of my skin when Dad's best friend and country star Bret Savage taps me on my shoulder.

Bret laughs heartily, "What's up, Reezie?"

"Hey, Bret."

"Where's your dad?"

I gesture toward the greenroom, and he walks away, tipping his cowboy hat. We'll have an intimidating crowd here, and a wave of nausea hits me, but I push it away. It's just like we're singing in our living room at home. I'll remind myself all night that's all this is.

After the other songwriters perform, and the stream of Nashville celebrities pop in to say hello to Mom and Dad, I'm positive I'm going to retch everywhere.

Now I know why Mom wanted a small, out-of-the-way show. This is not that. Not at all. This is a "who's who" of Nashville, and they're all sitting a few feet in front of me. Of course, I've performed with Mom in front of other celebrities before, but not with Luke, who'll be within vomit shot. I'm doomed.

Chapter 61 – Luke

When Raine invited me and Mom to the show, I figured it would be a little awkward. So far, I'm right on the money. I'm trying to shield Mom from any of the drama, but when Aria ignored us after they rehearsed, especially after the way her mom greeted us, it was noticeable. I explained that since Aria's dad is mentoring me, things are different. Mom's not buying it.

"You need to apologize, Luke. Whatever you did, just say you're sorry to Aria." Mom's pissed at me, and it's destroying our night.

"I'll try to talk to her after the show. I promise, Mom." But in my mind, things are much more complicated. Aria hates my guts because I went there. I said that she's a friend, when I know good and well I have more than friendly feelings for her. I fell in love with her that first day at the library.

When one of our instructors, Dr. Grace, came by the table, things got even more weird. Trent Austin came up at about the same time, and I had to introduce him to Dr. Grace. Talk about awkward. I had no idea they didn't know each other. Dr. Grace took it all in stride though. She really had no idea who Trent was, which was amusing to watch, as Trent explained, in his humblest way possible, how he's one of the biggest songwriters alive. Dr. Grace kindly listened as if it meant a big deal, but you could tell it didn't mean much to her. An amazing scene to watch unfold.

When the first of the songwriters started playing, the room was filled to capacity. I tried not to be starstruck when Bret Savage, Wayne Carson, and other country royalty took their reserved seats near our table. Mom, like Dr. Grace, isn't fazed by any of the famous faces in the crowd and is only interested in hearing Julia, Aria, and Raine again. I admit, I'm in agreement;

their pre-show rehearsal was amazing.

By the time nine o'clock rolls around, Mom's getting tired, but her eyes sparkle as the lights dim and Julia Tate walks out solo to thunderous applause, followed by Raine and then Aria. I try not to stare, but seeing Aria on stage like this is breathtaking. It's so clear to see parts of each of her parents in her face. They all take their seats on their respective stools, Raine and Julia pick up their guitars, and then the show starts. The next hour, I'm mesmerized, just like the audience of fans who have waited years for this moment. Before Julia performs each song, she tells a brief story about the origin of the song, and if the co-writers and the artist who performed the song are in the audience, she makes sure to acknowledge them. It's amazing to realize all the talent that is currently filling up this room.

As they near the end of the show and Julia's biggest hits, there is a pause. The stagehands bring another stool and guitar out on stage. Then Raine says they're going to invite someone from the audience to come up and join them. It takes a moment for me to comprehend that Raine is saying my name when a spotlight hits me across the face. I sit there dumbfounded. My mom nudges my shoulder, with the biggest smile across her face. I have no idea why Raine is calling me up to join them or what we're going to sing. This is a disaster.

I struggle to my feet and it's like I'm wading through quicksand as I make my way up the steps to the stage. I grab the acoustic guitar from the guitar tech's hands, then make my way to the chair on the other side of Raine. I'm glad I'm as far away from Aria as possible.

I give Raine a bewildered look, like "What the heck am I doing up here?" He smiles back like everything is cool and I'll be fine, but the sweat under my shirt starts to drip down my back.

Julia speaks into the microphone, "Luke's been co-writing with Aria, and Raine pestered him one day to play some of his songs. Luke's written hundreds of songs, and Raine says they are really good. As you all know, coming from my husband," she pauses, giving Raine a smirk, "that's saying a whole lot." The entire room laughs because everyone knows Raine is tough.

I lean down to get a peek at Aria and she's staring straightforward, looking as shocked as I am. She's obviously not pleased with what her parents are doing.

Julia continues, "So tonight, we've invited Luke up here to perform a song he's written with Aria called "Free to Roam." Raine will play along, but this will give me a much-needed break. Aria, why don't you move over here to my microphone?"

With that, Julia smiles and gets up and walks off the stage. Then it's just me, Raine, and Aria left to play. They couldn't pick the song we'd written for the contest because that would eliminate it, but they chose one I played for Raine that night in his studio. Many of the lyrics are Aria's, so this one is personal to her. I don't know how or if Raine's going to remember the song, but here goes.

The deafening silence in the room is overpowering. I'm still suffering from a bit of shock as Aria moves to the center mic, and then she looks at her dad, and then reluctantly glances at me, giving me slight nod. I instinctively start playing and Raine joins in flawlessly. Then Aria begins to sing the lyrics and it's perfect. It's much better than we've ever practiced in her mom's office. When it's my time to join in on harmony, I chime in, and from the corner of my eye, I see the slightest smile from Aria. At key spots in the song, Raine nods at me, and I add solo guitar licks, giving a bit of flourish to a previously unfinished-sounding song while he plays rhythm guitar along with me.

We get to the bridge where the song peaks on an extremely high note and Aria nails it. Her dad grins broadly, but he doesn't look at her or stop, and we continue to the end with Aria and me singing in harmony as the final notes of my guitar echo through the hall.

There's a moment of silence before the crowd responds, and then several people in the back get up out of their chairs. Trent Austin even stands up clapping. Julia walks back out as Aria finds her way to her seat, like it's just another day. Julia sits back down and addresses the audience.

"Now what did you think about that! Wow … am I a proud mama or what! Woo wee! That was amazing."

The crowd continues to clap, and by now I can tell Aria's embarrassed.

I'm still sitting there like a dunce, taking it all in, until it dawns on me that I need to leave. I get up, hand the guitar back to the tech, and make my way off the stage. I glance back to see the entire Wagner family, including Aria, smiling at me. Maybe this will make things better, I think as I head back to my seat. People walk up and slap me on the back after I get there.

Julia continues her set, performing her biggest hits from *Next Real Star*, and then she sings her biggest hit now out on country radio, but I really don't remember any of it. I just sang with Aria and Raine in front of most of Nashville country music royalty. Best night of my life.

Chapter 62 – Raine

Standing backstage, I run my hand across my face. Thank God this show is finally over. Putting it together and making sure everything went off without a hitch has been one of the most stressful events I've done in a while. It probably has more to do with what we're facing next week, but when you add it all up, from making sure all our friends and special guests were taken care of, to making sure the sound was right, the silent auction, and then the last-minute Aria and Luke drama, I'm fried. I can only imagine how Julia is feeling after this. And now we've got to get through next week's biopsy before we go and attempt to relax in the Bahamas. Thinking on it now, planning a trip right now wasn't the best of my ideas, but I had to do something.

Tracy walks up and hands me the keys to my truck. She's been a godsend managing many of the show's details. "Everything from the greenroom is in the SUV, including those humongous, gargantuan flowers. Did you really have to buy three dozen, Raine? She would have got the message with a dozen."

"Nothing but the best, Trace." I tease. "Now, where is that gorgeous wife of mine? It's time to go home."

"She's finishing up her matchmaking duties," Tracy replies, and my eyebrows go up questioningly.

"Oh, my word, what is she up to?"

"Raine, Julia wants everyone as happy as the two of you. But I think the situation took care of itself. You'll have to ask her. I'm not saying another word."

Aria walks up mid-conversation and must have caught some of what we were saying. "Oh, you mean Trent and my voice coach, Dr. Grace? Yeah, Trent has the hots for her. Mom's out there making sure it all goes according to plan."

I shake my head and change the subject, "Aria, where's Luke?"

"I have no idea," Aria says dryly before spinning on her heels and darting away like a rocket.

I head out to the front and there's Luke, still talking with Bret and Wayne, like they're all old friends. I smile. Good, those two would be good mentors for him. Luke's mother is waiting next to him, and she's clearly more than ready to go, so I'll go and help her out.

"Luke, my man," I say as I approach with my hand outstretched in a handshake, before continuing, "Sorry to surprise you like that, but you did well." The other guys nod in agreement.

Luke grasps my hand in a friendly shake, "Yes, sir. No apologies needed. That was amazing."

"How about we get your mom headed home," I say walking over to help her with her chair. She stops to grab my hand, holding it between her hands.

"Yes, thank you, Mr. Wagner, it was a wonderful show, but I'm all tuckered out and these guys will talk all night if I don't get Luke out of here."

"Luke, did you park in the back like I suggested?"

"Yes, sir."

"Well, let's get going then." I lead the small group up a small ramp that takes us out of the back entrance.

Janet looks back at me as I push her chair, "You know, this is motorized, I can make it." Her face is still gleaming from watching her only son have such a wonderful night.

"Yes, ma'am, I'm sure you could, but that wouldn't be very gentlemanly of me, now would it."

As I step outside, I'm glad to see the paparazzi have disappeared. Right after the show, they moved out front to catch the stars leaving, but they seem to have given up for the night.

I roll Janet's chair outside, and Luke runs to their car and pulls it up so we can get his mom into the passenger seat. She can walk the few steps, but I've got her by her arm and I get her situated as Luke takes the chair and puts it in the trunk. Wayne and Bret wait, and they say goodbye to Luke. You can clearly see that this kid is on cloud nine and it makes my heart happy.

"Again. Thanks for stepping up today, Luke. You did a great job."

"Yes, sir ... and sir, could you tell Aria that she sounded great? I didn't see her at all after the show."

"Sure, son, I'll tell her."

We watch Luke climb into the driver's seat and pull away. This is going to be much harder than I thought. Aria got her mother's stubbornness. I have no idea what's come between Aria and Luke, and frankly, I don't want to know. But it's clearly making them both miserable. I can't have my daughter or my new talent in a funk; that won't work. Although it may be inspiring and Luke will get new songs out of it, it's not good for our working relationship to have this kind of tension.

By the time we get out of the venue, it's after midnight and I'm famished. I'm following Julia in her car. Aria's riding with me, and Julia has Stella with her. At one point, I try to bring up Luke, but Aria's not biting; she does not want to talk about him, so I drop it.

We get home and after Stella's on her way, I suggest a late-night breakfast. Aria says she's not hungry, but Julia's in, so we make some eggs and bacon. Not the healthiest, but who cares.

"Glad you got that out of the way?" I ask her between bites as we sit along the kitchen counter. Julia changed into pajamas and her robe, but she still has her show makeup on. She's dressed up and dressed down and it's adorable. I still need a good shower.

She gives me a tired smile and a nod between bites. "What do you think, darlin'? I'm glad we did it. It went better than I'd hoped, and we raised about fifty grand for charity, so that makes it worth it."

"That's amazing. We had a lot of deep pockets in the room."

There's a pause and then I remember Tracy and Aria talking about Trent and her matchmaking. I give her a questioning look. "So, what's this about you setting up Trent with someone?"

She looks down sheepishly. "Oh, you know me … I mentioned to Tracy that Trent seems lonely and that we should find him someone, you know, normal, but I think it may have taken care of itself."

"It did, huh? How did that happen?" I ask, skeptically.

"From what Aria told me, Trent noticed her vocal coach from across the room. There was a spark … at least for him. Luke told me Dr. Antonia Grace has no idea who Trent is, which makes it perfect."

I give my beautiful wife a smile, shaking my head. I set down my fork before I turn the conversation to the topic we've been avoiding. "So … with next week and everything? Is there anything else I can do to help?"

Julia reaches a hand up to play with the ends of her hair. It's been a noticeable tic lately. "Raine, you help me every day. Everyone's walking on eggshells. I just want to get this biopsy over with, so we know one way or the other." Her voice drops at the end and she quickly looks away.

She picks up her dishes, grabbing mine as she walks to the kitchen sink. She rinses them off and puts them in the dishwasher silently before she walks back to me, taking my hand.

"There is something you could do, though?"

I'm surprised, but from my seated position, I pull her between my legs against my frame as she leans toward me with a tender smile. "Yes, my love, name it."

"How about we go up and take a shower because you and I were both hot and sweaty on stage, and then you proceed to give me a really good back rub because I finally went and did this show you begged me to do for months?"

I chuckle deep in my throat. It may sound like she's getting the good part of this deal, but I'll enjoy every moment of her offer.

"Your wish is my command." Then I proceed to pick up my wife and carry her up the stairs to our room to pamper her the way that she deserves. And for the rest of the night, we try not to think about anything else but being in the moment.

Chapter 63 – Julia

Part of me still can't believe I went up on that stage and sang through my collection of work for basically all of Nashville. Yes, I had Raine there to boost me up, and Aria too, but I did it. Now, when most people would be able to relax in the glow of that accomplishment and relish the success, I've got this storm cloud over my head, just waiting to rain down.

For days, I've been holding it all together the best that I can, but now images are flashing in front of me of what might happen if this biopsy doesn't go my way, and I can't seem to stop it. I went up to the barn early for some morning horse therapy and that helped some, but nothing can seem to ease the tightness in my chest and the thought that is replaying over and over again. What if it's back?

Somehow I get through the next few days. It's finally "the day." An air of dread permeates the house. I've caused everyone to walk around with this polite tone and energy, which makes me even more sick to my stomach. I just want this day to end.

We have to be at the hospital early, so we'll leave at about 5 a.m. I had another CT yesterday, so Dr. North is specific on the location. I'll just get a local anesthetic, and I'll be awake during the procedure. Then I'll stay at the hospital for a few hours to make sure everything is good. A simple one day, in-and-out procedure. At least, that's what I've been trying to convince myself, Raine, and Aria for the past few days.

I head down the stairs and Raine's already in the kitchen, a large cup of coffee in his hands. What I'd give for one of those, but I'll have to wait. He gives me a nod and walks toward me taking my hand as we head out to his waiting truck. He's already started it up, so it's nice and warm.

Raine woke up hours ago. I felt him stir much of the night and I don't think he slept much at all. Aria didn't get up. I told her not to, so she gave me an encouraging hug and even a kiss on my cheek last night before she ran up to her room. She's still not right after my show last week. We've got to figure out how to get her and Luke talking to each other again.

As we drive down the Interstate, Raine checks his rearview a few times, but I don't think much about it. He brought a thermos full of coffee, and the aroma is driving me mad.

"You know, you could have been kind and left that carafe back at the house. They have coffee there too," I reply dryly.

Raine turns up his nose. "I'm sorry, love, but I cannot do hospital coffee, not even for a day."

I must keep talking to calm my nerves, "So, are we all set for this big trip?"

Raine and Bret have the flights, the five-night stay on our very own Catamaran, and the excursions all planned. I'm genuinely looking forward to it. I like hanging out with Bret's wife Jessica, but I'm not so sure Aria is thrilled about having to spend several days with Bret's young daughters, although she's been agreeable about our trip.

"Everything's a go. The passports are ready, I've got everything I need, and I checked with Aria, and she says she's ready. You're the only one who hasn't packed yet." Raine gives me his look with a sweet, sarcastic smile, grabbing my hand and bringing it to his lips before our hands rest on the console.

I pause to look at our tightly enclosed fingers as I reply sarcastically, "I have been a little busy, you know, with that *show*. Plus, the thought of wearing a swimsuit is not high on my list now."

Raine shakes his head at me like I'm a knucklehead.

I continue, "If it makes you feel any better, I did order a few things, and they should arrive in the next day or so. We aren't leaving until Sunday, so let's get through this, Aria's last day before break, and then I'll pack. I have plenty of time."

"Uh-huh. You know we're limited to one bag each. That includes all your *shoes*."

I snort. "We'll be on a boat and on a beach? How many pairs will I need?"

He replies dryly, "Oh, I think you'll find a way."

I lean over and give him a friendly smack on his shoulder as I say, "I'll make one bag work, just you wait."

I'm glad he's been able to distract me, because before I realize it, we're here. Raine drops me off at the entrance inside the garage and then goes and parks.

He then meets me at the front entrance and takes my hand. His face has that ashen look I've seen before, and I'm reminded that Raine hates hospitals.

"We're not staying, Raine. Did you bring your coffee?"

He shows me his other hand with the huge mug as we walk through the entrance. Although right now I can hardly breathe, at least we're finally getting this over with.

Later that afternoon, I'm lying in bed at home, resting. It really wasn't that bad. I'm a bit sore, and I'm taking it easy just to be safe. I can't move around much for a few days, and I need to keep the wound clean. It's Wednesday, and Dr. North doesn't think he'll have the results by Friday, so we won't know anything until after we've left for our trip. But he'll call and send an email as soon as possible, so we should know something soon.

I haven't eaten much, other than a shake from the diner down the road. But thank God I got a bit of coffee, or else I'd also be battling a raging headache.

I hear Aria's feet race up the stairs when she gets home. Before she has a chance to knock, I tell her to come inside the bedroom. Her eager face is smiling, but she's looking at me like I'm breakable. Somehow, I've got to get these two to calm down.

"Everything went really well, sweetheart," I say before she has a chance to ask.

"When will we know something, Mom?"

Aria slides down next to me on the bed. "Probably not until early next week, but Dr. North will do his best to get in touch with us on our trip. Where is your father?"

"I didn't see him. Maybe he's in his studio?"

"And how was your day, anything new with Luke?"

"Nope, still hate him, Mom." She looks out the window like she doesn't care.

I can't help but sigh, but a smile cracks my lips. "Are you ever going to talk to him again?"

She gives a frustrated, dramatic sigh as she looks back at me. "Well, I'll have to if our song gets selected. I'm just his friend, Mom, plus Dad's mentoring him and he's talking to Bret and Wayne, too. It's now hopeless."

My daughter can be so over the top, and I wonder if she gets it from me. I give her an encouraging smile. "It's not hopeless, sweetheart. I bet Luke will come to his senses, just give it some time. Maybe it's the thought of being a celebrity. He'll figure out what's important soon enough."

"I doubt it," Aria replies with bitterness as her eyes grow dark. "But I don't really care, Mom. If he can't see what I mean to him, then he's not worth it."

I nod, taking her hand and giving it a squeeze as she looks out the window. I can tell she's fighting back a few tears, and we really don't need that.

"How about running down and getting me a cup of chamomile tea? I could really use one."

She must be glad for a task because she jumps up, keeping her face away from me. "On it."

I yell out after her as she bolts out of the room, "And tell that father of yours he had better have planned a good dinner 'cause I'm starving."

"Got it," Aria yells back.

I lean back against the pillows and sigh. I can't stand seeing my daughter filled with heartache, but there isn't anything I can do. Luke has to figure out what he's lost and if it's important enough to him. It's out of my hands. Which is a good reminder for me. I say a quick prayer, giving it all, including my results, to God.

Chapter 64 – Aria

Just two more dreaded days and I will finally get a break from Luke. I won't have to see him in class and act like everything is fine. No more fake smiles, no more missing our walks to my truck, no more feeling like I'm all alone again at this school. Sure, I have my new friend Charlotte, but we mostly talk about performing. Luckily, I can talk with Savannah every day, or my heart would explode from this, whatever this is. I thought my heart had been broken before, but never like this. And it's my own damn fault. I should never have let myself get close to him and won't again.

I'm heading to my advisory class with Dr. Grace. The bell has already rung and I'm a few minutes late. As I turn the corner, I see Trent Austin briskly walk out her door. I stop and jump behind some lockers so Trent doesn't see me. He checks the empty hall and briskly walks in the opposite direction. So, Trent and Dr. Grace, just like my mom wanted. At least someone is having luck in their love life.

I wait a few moments, walk to her doorframe, and give it a light knock. Her bright soprano voice rings out for me to come in.

"Sorry I'm late; got hung up in my last class," I fib.

"Oh Aria, you're fine. A few minutes won't hurt us."

Dr. Grace is calmly seated behind her desk, and she's never looked better. Her skin has a slight flush and her typically pulled back hair flows down in cascading dark curls.

"I can't tell you how much I enjoyed your mother's show the other night. Thank you for inviting me."

"Oh sure ..."

She cuts me off, "And your family is so talented. I knew your parents were famous, but I had no idea. And the other student, Luke, who played and sang with you. Why, he could be a member of your family the way he harmonized with you. Truly a special performance."

I've got to be careful here. I don't want my feelings to show. I give her a nod, "Um ... yeah, Luke is very talented."

"I've heard that you two performed together for the song contest, but that is all that I know."

Dr. Grace looks at me expectantly, like I've got to give her all the details, but that's the last thing I want to do.

"Yes, we did. We've written few songs together. Luke also performed a song of his own for the contest. I'm sure he'll do very well with that."

"Why do you say that?" Dr. Grace asks with all sincerity. Now I've done it. I've downplayed my own song to highlight Luke's solo song. I should be more careful.

"Luke's a good songwriter, Dr. Grace. That's it, and I think the song he wrote is exceptional."

"Do you want to win the contest with the song you wrote together?"

For a moment this stops me, because if we do win, then I'll really have to talk to him. But my true feelings emerge.

"Of course I want to win. I'm just saying that Luke is incredibly good."

"Well, I haven't heard the song the two of you wrote, but from what I watched of you both on stage the other night, there's magic there, Aria, and that's rare. The two of you together were perfect." It's the smile on her face that gives it away. She can tell I'm totally and completely in love with Luke Greyson. If she knows, then of course, everyone who watched us perform that night knows it too.

We finish the rest of my class running through my vocal instructions, but my day is ruined. I've got to get through one more day and then I can clear my head on this trip. This is so embarrassing.

I make it through Friday and as I'm walking out to my truck to finally leave, I hear Luke's voice yelling my name. I should just hop in my truck and tear out of the parking lot, but I pause, watching him run up to me.

"Your dad mentioned that you all are leaving for a trip this weekend?"

"Yep." I want this to be awkward for him.

He looks into my eyes, and I glare back. "Well … I hope you have a good time."

"Thanks." I swirl around and open my driver's side door.

"Hey Aria?"

I pause with one foot on the step of my truck, giving him a glance over my shoulder.

"Yes, Luke."

He looks at me with all sincerity, "Your dad mentioned what's going on with your mom … I'm really sorry about that. I had no idea. I hope everything turns out okay."

It's all I can do to keep my composure. I can't *wait* to speak with my dad later about how he told Luke our private family information.

I squeak out, barely looking at him, "Thanks." With that I throw my bag onto the passenger seat and hop into the truck faster than I ever have. In seconds I've started the truck, and I pull away without a glance as Luke stands in his spot, never moving, watching me drive away.

When I get home, I go straight to Dad's studio door. I can hear music, so I know he's in there. I don't care if anyone is in there with him. I open the door, and he spins around, his eyes slightly wide, then softening when he sees me in the doorframe.

"Hey Reez …"

But that is all I let him get out, "You told Luke about Mom!" I practically yell and it takes Dad aback. I don't yell at my dad, at least not if I want to live.

"Reezie," he replies in a stern tone, "we can trust Luke, and he figured out something was up, honey. He's not dumb."

My hands go to my hips. "What do you mean, he figured something was up?"

"Aria, you might think we're all good actors, but it's not hard to tell that something has been bothering us, every one of us. Luke asked me one day and I told him the truth. Truth is always a good place to start. Bret is also one of my artists and he knows the truth."

"So, Luke is one of your artists now?" My voice rises, filled with disdain.

Dad sighs. I can tell he's working hard to control his anger. "Kind of. We're all mentoring him in a way, honey, but it's nothing formal. I don't have a contract with him or anything. With the contest going on, it's best not to do that."

I won't back down. "Still don't think you should have told him. What if he tells someone? Then the rumors will start to fly."

Dad is not pleased. "I don't think he will."

"We shall see, won't we."

I spin out of the room and run down the hall. Mom yells at me from the kitchen, but I ignore her and run straight up the stairs. Sometimes these two really drive me nuts.

Chapter 65 – Raine

It's the day of our trip. I've finally wrangled everyone and their luggage in my truck and we're on our way to the airport. We're taking a small private plane down to Florida and then another chartered plane down to meet the boat in Nassau.

The air is so thick in my vehicle it's like paste. Aria's still mad at me. Julia got all her things into one bag, but you should see the size of her bag. I did remind her of the weight limit on the plane and now she's pissed at me too. I was talking about her bag, but she's still all riled up.

We meet up with Bret, Jessica, and their three girls, Amy, Amelia, and Andrea, who are now fourteen, ten, and five. Funny how all our kids' names start with the letter A. This may make the trip interesting. I'm grateful to Aria because even though there's an age difference between her and Bret's girls, she often takes on a big sister role, and they all absolutely adore her. Once we get on the plane, Aria immediately starts reading a story to their youngest girl, Andrea.

The sun is low on the horizon when we finally get to the dock to meet the captain of our private boat and his small staff. We have four cabins in total, so Aria will have her own room. Bret's girls get to share a room with bunk beds, and luckily, they're thrilled. We weren't sure how they would feel about their tight quarters. We knew Aria would need her own space.

We all get settled on board and set out for an evening sail, catching the final moments of the sun going down while enjoying an amazing seafood dinner. Since no one is drinking on board, we're relaxing with some creative mock tails prepared by the boat's chef. I already know Bret's vacation idea is a winner. There are zero distractions on our private boat, and we're away from everyone and everything.

I glance at my beautiful wife and for the first time in a month, even with the stress of waiting on her biopsy results, she looks peaceful. The next morning is Monday, so we should know something soon. Aria takes her leave early and heads to her cabin. Somehow, I'll have to figure out how to make up the whole Luke thing to her. The good thing is that we have clear WiFi on the boat, so Aria can stay attached to her damn phone.

As Julia and I are settling in our room, there's a strong, rapid knock on our cabin door. I open it up to find Aria, phone in hand, looking angrier than I've seen her in years.

"I told you telling Luke wasn't a good idea," she says, her phone in front of my face. I can see some kind of image, leading to a story posted by one of the trashy online news organizations.

I grab the phone. Julia appears at my shoulder reading along to an image of the two of us entering the hospital last week, and then an image of us leaving with Julia in a wheelchair as I load her into my truck. There's a corresponding story that Julia must be sick again with cancer. I give an audible groan.

"You don't know this was Luke," I say, coming to his defense. I look at Julia, "I thought there was someone tailing us that morning, but I didn't say anything 'cause I thought I lost them."

Mom looks at us both and shrugs, like she really doesn't care. "So what, Raine. They caught us going into a hospital and me coming back out looking like crap. Who cares?"

I chime in, looking right at Aria. "Exactly. Who cares."

Aria retorts, "I still think it was a bad idea to tell people we don't really know."

This time Julia jumps in, "Aria Marie Wagner! We *know* Luke, and I guarantee you this wasn't his fault. Reporters were at my show the other night. I bet you paparazzi have been staking out the house for days. It's no big deal."

Aria skulks out of the room, obviously frustrated that we aren't angry at Luke like she is. We have no reason to be mad at Luke.

Julia asks, "What are we going to do about that?" Her eyes dart to the door Aria just left.

"I don't think there is anything we can do. It'll have to work itself out." I let out a heavy sigh as I collapse onto our bed. "And it will ... eventually."

Both our phones begin to ping loudly, and I give mine a glance. It's Tracy, who's letting us know about the story.

"I've got this," I tell Julia.

"Good, cause I'm beat. Plus, I have to put all my shoes away," Julia says with a smirk while I grab my back in mock pain, heading out the door to the upper deck.

Bret is on the deck as well, smoking a cigar and enjoying the cooler night air. As I step up to him he says, "If I knew you were coming back out, I would have brought two cigars."

"I'm good." I hold up my phone. "I've got to follow up with Tracy. Some tabloid printed a story of us at the hospital last week. They never quit."

Bret nods in agreement, "Yeah, remember when Andrea was born and in the NICU? That was fun. I have never been so angry at seeing those pictures. Jessica was ready to throw punches when we finally left the hospital."

I nod at him. "I remember that well. Aria's furious. She thinks Luke leaked it to the media."

"No way. That kid has too much respect for you all."

"I know, but she hates him right now, so he can't do anything right."

"Well, you did make her boyfriend your new project, Raine. What do you expect?"

"I had no idea he was her boyfriend," I say, shrugging my shoulders in self-defense.

Bret shakes his head, smirking at me for being so clueless.

I follow up with Tracy and then scan my messages hoping that we've got an early email putting our minds at ease, but I got nothing.

I head back downstairs and when I get there, Julia's already asleep in bed. I don't blame her. Today was a long day with all the travel. As I watch her sleeping, I can't help but hope that this trip is worth it, for all of us.

The next morning, we're greeted by the wonderful smell of bacon and coffee. We drag ourselves up to the main deck to find Jessica and the girls already there. But there's no sign of Aria. We're sailing to a small nearby island today to see the large pigs they have there, and we can either just swim or we could go further out to sea and fish. All the girls want to swim and hang out on the beach, and their vote wins. Aria joins us later in the morning, but she walks out to a far deck with what looks like a journal in her hand, clearly wanting to be alone.

We spend the day swimming and enjoying a leisurely day at a beach with no other people. The water is sky blue and it's wonderful not to have to worry about anything. Tracy's bugged me a few times, but we've offered no comment on any article requests.

Later that day as we're cleaning up for dinner, Julia's phone rings. She's in the shower and doesn't hear it, but then her phone starts to buzz with messages. It's all I can do not to drag her out of the shower. When she steps out, I pick up her phone and rush to put it in front of her. This might be it.

She nods and goes to the voicemail message, which we listen to on speaker.

"Julia … Dr. North here, since I didn't get you, I'll send a text, too, but I wanted to get in touch with you as soon as I knew. Your biopsy is benign. We don't see any cancer cells at all, so this is really good news. I've sent this result to Dr. Henley and I'm sure she'll try to call you. I know you are on vacation, and I hope you get this message. You're welcome to call me back with any questions. But good news for you, Julia."

Julia collapses on the bed behind her, falling back against the covers. She's only wearing a towel and it's all I can do to not flop down next to her, but I give her this moment to take it in as I go and sit in a nearby chair. My head falls to my hands as an overwhelming feeling of relief pours out of my body. The weight of the last month falls off me like rain.

Julia speaks, her voice quiet but filled with the emotion she's been holding, "We need to tell Aria right away."

I don't say a word as I jump up to get our daughter who's in the cabin across from ours. I knock and then let myself in.

"Dad!" Aria says from her small bathroom. She's dressing and I totally barged in.

My hand points, directing her, "Aria, come into our cabin right now."

The whites of her eyes grow wide as she quickly throws on the rest of her clothes as I spin around, taking the two steps back inside our cabin.

I leave the door open as Aria follows me moments later. Her hair is wet and she looks terrified, standing by the doorframe, not moving a muscle.

Julia gives me a stern look, "You've scared the crap out of her, Raine!" And before I can defend myself, she continues, "It's good, Reezie. No cancer. It's all clear."

Aria runs over to her mother, and the two women I love more than anything else on this earth embrace as Aria starts to cry. Damn, this is going to be a great trip.

Chapter 66 – Julia

In more than a year, my heart has not been this light. I told Bret at least a hundred times that this trip was a wonderful idea. I know it could have gone another way, and we would've been okay, but once we got the news, we let ourselves go. Not in a totally crazy way, but we're having as much fun as humanly possible. Raine and Aria have been riding wave runners, and they've snorkeled and fished inside caves. We've laughed, loved, and lived. And I'm not taking one moment for granted.

It's early in the morning on the last day of our vacation. I got up earlier than everyone else to watch the sun come up. I'm up even before our small boat staff, so I make myself a cup of coffee and watch as the glorious light fills up the darkened sky in front of me. A sound startles me as Aria comes up the stairs, her journal in hand. She's writing a ton. She takes a seat next to me.

Aria quietly comments, "It really is gorgeous here, Mom. I'm going to miss this."

I lean my head against hers, "Me too, honey. This has been such a great trip. Thank you for wanting to do this and for being so great with Bret's girls. They adore you."

"It's been fun, Mom. Like having little sisters."

There's a pause as my mind flashes to Jonah, who's never far from the memories that could have been. Aria senses it.

Aria looks at me. "I know you miss him, Mom. Did you ever want to have any more kids after me?"

This question surprises me, or maybe it's because she never asked it. "You know, your dad and I talked about it a lot, but there were risks with having another baby. We thought about adoption, too, but then life with you got busy and everything was good. I guess it would have been better for you to have siblings, wouldn't it?"

I watch her closely as she looks down for a moment and then flicks at the cover of her journal. "Maybe ... but I think things turned out the way they were supposed to."

I smile at her words before I reply, "I do need to go see Jonah when we get back. Do you want to go with me?"

Aria pauses, looking out at the water before replying, "I'd like that, Mom."

"When you get back, you'll find out about the contest, too, right? Have you heard anything from Luke while you've been away?"

She shakes her head. "Nope, not a word. And yes, we'll find out who's in the top ten on the first day back. Then I'll know if I have to sing with him again."

I give her hand a reassuring pat. "Well, either way, you move on or you don't, it might be good to talk to Luke. You know, Aria, each day is such as gift. You never know what could happen. If there's something you need to say to Luke, I suggest you say it."

Aria nods and glances down at her journal. I know it's much easier said than done. It's obvious she's in love with him and she needs to tell him that.

Moments later, Raine joins us on the boat deck, a cup of coffee in his hand as he wiggles in beside me. I rest my head against his shoulder as we look out at the glorious scene in front of us. Aria moves to the front of the boat to sit by herself. Bret and all his girls join us. We'll tour the island today one last time and fish, then we'll enjoy our last dinner on the boat.

The next day, we all fly back together on one private plane. Aria quietly stares out the window of the plane, and I can't help but worry about her heart. Raine and Bret are carrying on and trying to decide which pictures Bret should post on his social media platforms. I'm glad I don't have to worry about such things, but I do wonder if I should attempt to put myself out there. And as I'd planned before this whole second cancer scare started,

I do want to perform live again. Against my better judgment, I plant that little seed in Raine's mind.

"So, my love," I say to Raine. "Now that I'm in the clear, how about calling Tracy and booking some more shows for me?"

Both Bret and Raine stop mid-sentence with blank stares before Raine jumps in excitedly, "Seriously? I thought you were done with all that?"

"Nope, I want to do it again." From the corner of my eye, Aria is listening intently. "And I want a full band this time."

Raine practically cuts me off, "Well, hot damn!" Bret laughs as Raine looks at his good friend, "I don't suppose I could get your retired ass to join in on the fun?"

Bret gives him a look like "maybe" and shrugs his shoulders, and then Raine grabs his phone and it's off to the races.

Aria exclaims loudly, "You have no idea what you have done, Mom. No idea."

I look across the aisle at Jessica, who is reading a story to her youngest daughter on her computer, and she rolls her eyes. Maybe I don't know what I've done. Raine will have me booked on a full-blown tour in no time.

With everything going on, we're behind on Christmas, which is next week, and now we have a ton of planning to do when we get home. I've already bought gifts for everyone, and they're hidden up at the barn, but we don't have anything decorated. Ever since we had a painful Christmas in Montana after losing Jonah, we make sure our holidays are filled with fun and we don't dwell on those memories, which isn't always easy. I also remember my promise to Aria. I always visit Jonah at this time of the year and when we get back, I want her to come with me.

When we land, Raine gets our SUV and pulls it up to the front entrance of the small private airport, and then I see them. A photographer sits in a car not too far from us, capturing our every move. Maybe it's 'cause of Bret, but I am so sick of this. As Raine loads the last piece of luggage into the back of the vehicle, I casually lean down close to his ear, letting him know about our little spy. A look I've seen a million times crosses his face. Then he smiles, closes the back gate, and saunters over to Bret. They exchange a few words, then the two of them boldly sprint toward the waiting vehicle. But before they get there, the car backs up haphazardly over a curb and races away. Raine gives them a wave.

"What were you going to do?" I ask, laughing, as he helps me into the SUV.

"I have no idea, but whatever it was, Bret was in."

I shake my head and smile. My husband, the protector.

This has been a glorious trip, and one paparazzo will not ruin our day. Yes, they may have taken a couple photos. But so what? They got us arriving with a bit of a tan, looking relaxed. Screw 'em. I just had the time of my life with the people I love and care about the most, and I got the most amazing news. Nothing will destroy our day.

Chapter 67 – Aria

I'm in the backseat as Dad maneuvers down the Interstate when my phone buzzes with a flood of text messages. All texts stopped during our flight and now they're pouring in, all from my friend Charlotte.

I open to the last message from her, and it just says, "Aria, I know you're gone right now, but PLEASE CALL ME WHEN YOU GET THIS."

My breath catches and I send her a quick text back that I'm in the car and can't talk. After several moments I get the message that practically stops my heart.

"Luke's mom fell and hit her head. She's in the hospital. I found out from one of his friends - I don't know anything more. Thought you'd want to know."

"Which hospital?!?"

"No idea."

Ice races through my veins. I have an overwhelming urge to get to him. I exclaim loudly, "Mom, Dad … Luke's mom is in the hospital. We need to get there."

Mom spins her head around to me, her eyes wide. "Oh no! What happened! Raine … we've got to get to him. He's all alone."

While driving, Dad goes to his phone, finds Luke's number, and hits "send" but it just rings before going into voicemail.

Dad asks, his voice urgent, "Aria, do you think he'll answer you?"

"I can try."

My hands are shaking, but I find Luke's number and send him a text telling him we know about the accident, and I ask where they're at. I stare at my phone for what seems like an eternity as we all hold our breath. Finally, my phone buzzes with his reply, and he tells me it's the hospital that's closest to his house, which makes sense.

I give this information to Dad, and our vehicle surges forward as he presses his foot on the gas and pulls into the fast lane.

"Raine, honey, get us there in one piece, please," Mom chastises him as she reaches her hand back to me. I take it. My palm is sweaty, but her tight grasp calms me some.

I swear we're going a hundred miles an hour and we're there in only minutes. Dad finds a place to park close to the front entrance, and we scurry inside. Luke let me know that his mom is in intensive care. So we stop at the desk to get directions.

I send Luke a text telling him that we're there. We stop at the nurses station on the ICU floor, but I see Luke from the corner of my eye walking out of a nearby room. He's wearing rumpled jeans, his hair's a mess, and it doesn't look like he's slept at all. We take cautious steps toward him, but then Mom rushes to him, gathering him up in her arms. Thank God for her. One of Luke's arms goes up re-actively to her back, but he seems numb. Mom takes a step back still gripping his arms.

Mom's rushed questions come out, "Luke, how is she, what can we do?"

Luke's tired eyes scan mine before they land back on Mom's. "When she fell, she hit her head and went unconscious. She still hasn't come out of it. There seems to be some swelling on the brain ... I think."

And then right in front of us, with the weight of what's happened, Luke starts to lose it, collapsing in tears. Mom instinctively grabs him by the shoulders, and I go to his other side as we walk him to a nearby waiting area couch. Dad swoops in to make sure we make it. We guide him to the couch and Mom takes off her coat, wrapping it around his shoulders.

Dad tries to be helpful, "Let me go and find some coffee and maybe some food." He rushes off.

Mom and I sit on either side of Luke. Mom adjusts her coat around his shoulders and then she wraps her arm around him as his head falls into his hands, and the tears continue to silently fall. It's awkward, but I sit close to him hoping he gets some comfort knowing that we're here.

Being the kind, motherly person my mom has always been, she instinctively continues to soothe Luke. It seems to work as his breath begins to settle. He leans back and sheepishly looks at me and then Mom.

"I'm ... so ... sorry about that."

Mom replies, "Hush, Luke, nothing to be sorry about. You're taking care of a lot right now."

Luke nods as he stares straight ahead. Our legs and shoulders are touching but that's it. I'm trying so hard not to take his hand or give him a hug, even though that's all I want to do. Luke takes his sleeve and wipes his face. This makes Mom search in her purse for a tissue.

A few moments later, Dad walks up with a tray of coffee cups and a couple of bags of chips.

Dad holds the tray out to us. "I couldn't find much on this floor."

I jump up to help him, taking two cups, and then I walk back to Luke, offering him one. He reaches up both hands and takes it from me. When our hands briefly touch, his fingers feel like ice. He uses the hot cup to warm them.

Dad sets the other coffees and chips on a small table next to us.

Mom continues with her questions, "Luke, have they said anything else about your mom's condition? What are they going to do?"

Luke's looking down at the ground as he responds, "Her main doctor should be coming to see me any minute now. I should know more then."

Mom continues, "Have you had anything to eat ... is there anything we can do for you?"

Luke glances up at my dad and then my mom, avoiding my eyes. "I'm just glad you're here. How'd you know?"

I quickly reply, "Charlotte let me know, Luke."

He nods. At this moment, we see several doctors start to enter his mom's room. Luke sees them too and jumps up, coffee in hand as he sprints toward the door. We all follow a few steps back.

Luke meets the doctors at the door, exchanging a few words with them, but I can't hear what they're saying. Luke lets us know with a hand gesture that he'll be back, as they all enter his mom's hospital room.

I look at my mom, and we all walk back to the couch. Dad, of course, with his nervous energy, grabs a cup of coffee and opens the lid to let it cool a bit. But he continues to stand.

"Raine, honey, why don't you sit down?"

"I can't, you know I can't sit, when I need to be doing something. We should call someone we know and get some other doctors here?"

Mom responds soothingly, "Let's see what Luke says … maybe we can talk to the doctor."

Twenty minutes pass as we all stare aimlessly at our coffee cups, our phones, and the clock on the wall. Mom smiles at me several times compassionately, like she's trying to give me strength. Finally, the door opens and Luke, along with the doctor, walk over to our little group. Luke introduces us to Janet's neurologist, Dr. Whitman.

Dr. Whitman speaks. "As I told Luke, his mom, Janet, is still unconscious, but the swelling in her brain is easing, so we shouldn't have to do any surgery. We'll have to wait and see what happens. I do expect that as the swelling continues to go down, she'll soon show signs of recovering, and then we'll take the next steps."

We nod along, and of course my dad chimes in, "Thank you, doctor. Anything that Janet needs, please make sure that it happens. I want her to have the best care."

Luke starts to protest, but one look from my dad and Luke understands he won't win this one.

"Yes, Mr. Wagner, of course." The doctor leaves and continues walking with his team as my dad walks with him. I can't hear what they're saying, but out of the corner of my eye, I see Dad exchange words with the doctor, and then a handshake. No doubt Dad is making sure no expense is spared.

Luke eyes the chips and Mom jumps up to give him a bag, which he takes graciously.

Mom says, "Luke, dear, you must be hungry." My dad has now joined us. "Raine, let's go find some real food for Luke and bring it back here. The cafeteria is around here someplace."

I give her a glance, like really, you're going to leave me here, but she just smiles back sweetly.

Dad takes Mom's hand, and they head to the nurses station to find some food.

Once they've gone, Luke, who has already demolished the bag of chips and has taken both the bag and coffee cup to the trash, comes back to me.

"I'm going to sit in Mom's room … do you want to come with me?"

"Oh … I don't know if that's allowed … is it?"

"It is if I want you to be there, and I want you there, Aria."

I do everything to hide my stunned face at his words. Luke wants me to be with him. Deep in my heart, I have doubts, and there's a thought that this is only happening because his mom is sick, but of course, I'll go with him. There is no way my heart will say no.

I nod, grabbing my purse. We head to the closed door of his mom's room. When he opens the door, it's difficult to hide my shock. Janet's head is wrapped up in a large white bandage and what I can see of her face is ashen. There's a tube coming out of her nose and she's hooked up to many machines. Luke goes to an empty chair along the wall and drags it next to the chair he was using. He takes a seat, gesturing for me to sit beside him. Without a word I walk over and settle into the uncomfortable brown chair. The thought crosses my mind that they must make hospital chairs without considering that people will be sitting in them for hours.

Luke gingerly takes his mom's hand and holds it in his. Neither of us say a word. He leans down and gives her hand a quick kiss and I see a tear roll down his face. Then his head goes down and he lays it on his mom's arm, resting it there.

I have to say something. "They did say she's getting better, Luke. That's really good news."

He nods. I can't help myself. My hand goes up and I lay it on his back. His body slightly relaxes at the feel of my touch. He doesn't say anything as we both sit like this for minutes, watching the machines monitoring her breathing.

Finally, Luke speaks in a whisper, but he doesn't look at me, "I forgot to ask about your mom and her test. It's okay if you don't want to talk about it."

I respond quietly, "We got good news, Luke. They didn't find any cancer."

Luke leans back, his tired eyes looking directly at me, "That's so great, Aria. I'm happy to hear that." A weak smile crosses his anguished face as he continues, "I'm glad you and your parents came here today, Aria … it means a lot to me." He pauses to look at Janet, "And to my mom. I don't think I realized how much it helps having you all here. Especially you, Aria." With those words, his free hand takes mine, holding it tight. My heart skips, but my mind is racing with all the emotions from the last few days. What does this mean? Is it just 'cause he's alone and needs someone to be here, or is this really about me?

Finally, I manage to squeak out, "I am glad I'm here too, Luke."

He gives me a pained smile as I glance down at our entwined hands. I'm thinking about my mom and how our family got such great news, compared to what he's going through with his mom. Life is so fragile. I've been so consumed with me and my mom that you never think that something like this could happen to someone else.

We sit there together, with our hands tightly clasped, holding on to the hope that Janet will soon wake up. I say a silent prayer for Janet and Luke. She has got to get better. She just has to.

Chapter 68 – Luke

When Aria and her family appeared, I realized how much I needed them. I've been trying to do everything on my own for so long that when they showed up, an overwhelming sense of love surrounded me. Then when Aria's mom hugged me, I lost it. They just left the hospital, and now as I sit in Mom's room watching her, the room is spinning again. I pick up my phone and text Aria. I can't stop myself.

"Aria - thanks again for coming here tonight and tell your parents that too. K?"

Within seconds, she replies, "Of course, like my mom said before we left, if you need anything - let us know. You KNOW she means it" with a smiley face at the end.

Just getting some words back is like a lifeline. I admit that I've missed my friend, and I've got to be honest with myself. I want Aria as more than a friend. I've been so blind. Blinded by the thought of stardom and what her father could give me and my so-called career that I almost lost one of the most amazing people I've ever met. She wouldn't have come to the hospital if she hated me. The realization that I've been a complete ass hits me hard. Ever since this happened, she is the one person I wanted to call but couldn't, and then she appeared. I don't deserve another chance, but I'll be damned if I'm going to blow it now.

As I sit leaning back in my chair thinking all these thoughts, there's a slight moan coming from my mom. Startled, I reach out, grabbing her hand.

"Mom ... Mom?" I say quietly, trying to illicit some kind of response while watching her face for any movement, and then I see it. Her eyes are flickering. I drop her hand and rush out of the room.

I yell out to the nurses station as they are the first people I see, "I think she's moving!" One of the nurses makes a call through a speaker system and I rush back inside just as Mom is trying to wake up, moaning loudly as she does. It's finally happening!

Doctors rush in and move me to the side as they surround her, flashing a light in her eyes. They can all see what I see as we watch my mom continue to struggle to move. Dr. Whitman walks in and goes to her bed as we watch her eyes completely open, and she groans. He gives me a glance and a smile.

Dr. Whitman steps to her bedside and orders some kind of medicine into her IV. I start to question him, but his words stop my anxious heart.

"This is good, Luke, we're giving her something for the pain. She's starting to wake up, and this won't stop that, but we need her to remain calm."

I nod as they continue checking her vitals. Her eyelids flick open wide and the first words from her lips start to form. It's not easy to tell what she's saying, but to me, the words are crystal clear.

"Wh ... Where's ... Lu?"

Tears form on my lashes as I reach her side, taking her hand, "I'm right here, Mom. I'm right here."

She visibly relaxes against the pillows at the sound of my words, or it could be what they put in her IV. There's some pressure on my hand and I look at the doctor and smile.

"She's squeezing my hand."

He replies, "That's good, Luke. That's very good."

Hours later, I'm sitting in a chair against the wall, watching Mom sleep. It's late now, well past midnight, but I want to send Aria a message letting her know what happened after they left, and I need to ask for a favor.

"Great news ... mom woke up after y'all left tonight. It was amazing! And she squeezed my hand. Still not sure if she'll have any long-term effects but GOOD NEWS! And I have a favor ... could you come by again tomorrow? I'd really like to see you."

I put my phone down; my heart is about to thump out of my chest. I'm sure I'll have to wait for Aria's response. I think she'll say yes. Then I can put my plans in motion. I can say I'm sorry and I need to do it the right way.

Chapter 69 – Aria

The first thing I do is check my phone. My heart rate starts to climb. First, because I'm so happy that Janet has woken up and that makes me instinctively jump out of bed to tell my parents, but then Luke's additional words stop me in my tracks. He wants to see me again … today. Of course, my heart is thumping like crazy, but my mind is telling me whoa, Nelly. Why does he want to see me? I can't put too much hope into it. No way. After the past few weeks of being his "friend," I can't let myself believe he wants more, and am I in the right place, especially after what has happened with Mom? Mom was okay, then she wasn't, and now she's okay again. I don't think my heart can take any more emotional drama. We're just friends. Friends who hold hands. That's it.

I race down the stairs knowing I'll find my parents in the kitchen enjoying their morning coffee, and I'm spot on.

"She woke up!" I blurt out, sliding across the kitchen floor, still in my PJ's and slippers.

"Oh, thank God," Mom exclaims. Both my parents look so relieved. "I knew in my heart she just needed some time. Do you know anything more?"

"Janet woke up and squeezed his hand, that's all Luke said," I say, omitting his ask to see me again. I still have to get back to Luke about that, and it must have crossed my face.

"Aria, is something wrong? Did Luke say something was wrong with Janet?" Mom asks, clearly fretting about the whole situation.

"No … no, it sounds really good, Mom."

Dad decides to chime in, "You know, I don't know what she'll need for rehab or whatever, but maybe we can help. She could stay here ... they both could for a while so she can get the help she needs?"

Mom joins in enthusiastically, "Oh, honey! That's a wonderful idea!"

My stomach tightens. Not so wonderful to have "my friend" around 24-7. "I don't know about that, Dad ... I'm sure they have insurance or something to help with that?"

Mom poo-poo's me, "Aria, we have a guest house. It's perfect for someone who needs everything on one level. Janet wouldn't have to deal with any stairs. And we could arrange someone to help her."

I'm going to totally lose this one. They're not going to give this up.

Dad continues with his plan, "Are you going to talk to Luke? Or do you want me to call him and talk about it?"

"I ... um, I think I'm going to talk to him later."

Mom's eyebrows go up with my words, but she doesn't say a word.

Dad follows up, "Good, then mention it to him and see what he says. I'll also call him later to talk about it."

I nod and twirl out of the room, heading back to the sanctuary of my room. I can feel Mom's eyes on my back. She knows something is up.

Back in my room, I get up the nerve to text Luke back, agreeing to see him knowing I'll have to bring up my parents' offer. How awkward. I get an immediate reply from him, and we agree to meet after his mom has her mid-day meal.

I put my phone down and rush to my closet. I'm already fretting as I stare at my clothes. What in the heck am I going to wear?

The morning drags until Luke lets me know now is a good time to head that way. I've been ready for more than two hours, so I rush out and check the foyer. The coast is clear—no parents. I race out the door to my truck.

I decided on simple black jeans, knee-high brown boots, and a sweater that matches my boots. I tried to keep my attire toned down—not like I was getting dressed up or anything—but I think I look good. I took the time to put in earrings and other pieces of gold jewelry. I usually don't wear much bling. Maybe I'm trying too hard, but I really don't care.

Luke's mom is still in the ICU, so I head up to that floor. When I step off the elevator and make my way to her room, I stop in my tracks. They've transformed the small waiting room area where we all gathered yesterday. There's a small table set up with two chairs, and a gorgeous bouquet of red roses rests on the table. Luke's standing by one chair, as if he's waiting for me. He's cleaned himself up. He's combed his hair and he's wearing black jeans and a button-down.

I pause, taking cautious steps toward him. Out of the corner of my eye, a couple of nurses peer over their desk counter watching the entire scene unfold. I've never been more self-conscious in my life.

As I get to the table, I ask quietly, "What's all this?" Luke gives me one of his gorgeous grins and I must say, it's glorious seeing him happy again.

"A bit of a surprise. I didn't know if you'd eaten lunch yet, but I wanted to do something special for you … for, you know, for being so kind to me … and my mom." He's sure to add Janet in at the end.

Luke takes the flowers and hands them to me. I grasp the big bundle in my hands and absentmindedly lean in to smell them. They're gorgeous.

I shuffle my feet. "Wow … well, this is really nice of you, Luke. You didn't need to do this. The eyes of our little audience bore into my backside, so I try to keep my voice low. "I … I mean we, we were more than happy to be of help, Luke, you know that." My fumbling words combined with the deep red flush of my face make Luke's grin grow wide. At this moment, I'm like a thirteen-year-old who's just discovered boys. *I. Am. Such. A. Dork.*

He tries to make me more comfortable. "This isn't the most ideal spot, but are you hungry?" He gestures to one of the seats at the table.

I nod, "Um … sure. I can eat." I don't want to let on that in my rush, I only managed a banana and I downed some coffee. If you look at my hands and the rustle of the flowers, the caffeine's not helping them right now.

"Great … let me take those roses back. I'll put them over here." Luke takes them from my hands and lays them on a nearby table, and then he helps me with my jacket and into my seat. To my surprise, someone who looks like a chef appears out of nowhere with two plates of food. It's nothing fancy: baked chicken, Au gratin potatoes, and some green beans, and he places the plates down in front of us. Another person rushes over with a couple of sodas. I sit there stupefied watching the scene unfold in front of me. Luke looks like a kid in a candy store who's just walked out with a bag full of the goods.

"How did you make all this happen?" I ask, wide-eyed.

"A little help from our audience over there." He gives a slight nod toward the nurses station. I don't have to look because I know who he's talking about. "I told them I wanted to have a nice lunch arranged for an incredibly special woman, and voila."

My face immediately goes down as I stare at my plate. I don't know what to say. Then Luke does something that makes me catch my breath. He reaches out and grabs my hand, holding it in his hand, across the table.

"I mean it, Aria. I can't thank you enough, and I wanted to do something for you. Not only because of Mom, but because I've realized something. I've missed you ... terribly. I didn't understood how much until I didn't have you to talk to, and then when Mom fell, you were the one person I wanted to call, and I couldn't. I don't ever want that to happen again."

As he's speaking, I raise my eyes to look into his, listening to every word. I can't believe what I'm hearing. Even though I'm skeptical of his words, when Luke grips my hand a bit tighter, I respond in kind. I lose everything and everyone around us.

I whisper to him, "Luke, I don't know what to say."

"Don't say anything." He leans back in his chair, pulling his hand back as he does, giving me a shy grin. "How about we eat something? I know hospital food isn't five star, but I could eat my right arm right now."

I nod in agreement and take a quick drink of my soda, quenching my incredibly dry mouth. Luke picks up his utensils and tears into his food. I give a sideways glance at the nurses and one of them gives me a slight nod. I laugh a little.

"What?" Luke asks.

"I think your elves are happy," I say with a tilt of my head toward his helpers, which makes Luke snort.

"Yeah ... they were totally into this. They set up the lunch and everything.

I'm glad that so far, it's worked out … at least I think it has. We wouldn't want to disappoint them now, would we?"

"No, we wouldn't," I say with a smirk. "That's one team I want on my side."

Luke nods at me with a laugh.

We eat quietly until I realize that I've got to bring up my parents' offer. I have no idea how Luke will take this. I don't want it to come across like he's a charity case or anything like that.

"Luke, there is something I need to mention and it's not exactly coming from me, but from my parents." There's a pause as he looks at me expectantly while I take a deep breath, getting up my nerve. "It's about your mom … and about you, I guess."

Luke stops eating, giving me his full attention.

"Knowing that your mom may need some help, you know, with rehab and things like that, Mom and Dad would like for you both to come and stay at our guest house." I'm watching his face and so far, I'm not reading anything in those dark eyes or the line of his jaw, so I keep going. "It's a ranch style … I pointed it out one day, and you'd have help or whatever you both need."

Luke's quiet and looks out a nearby window. He nods his head a bit and then runs his hands down his jeans. That's the first sign of stress I've noticed from him today. Uh-oh.

After a few moments, he fully looks back at me. He's not mad, I can tell that, but he looks defeated. "Let me think about it, Aria. That is a great and kind offer, and it may be what Mom really needs. But once we're at that point, I'll need to check with her." It's what he adds that makes me think we've crossed a line, "We do have insurance, you know; I've made sure that Mom has coverage and she has benefits from my dad's military service. So, we do have help."

My eyes dart up and down with embarrassment. "Of course … of course. I knew you'd have everything covered. Mom and Dad, and me too, we don't want you to worry about anything. They always want to help, Luke," I add with a nervous chuckle, and he gives a half-hearted smile with my words, but part of me knows we hurt his feelings. Luke's clearly been the man of the house ever since his father died, and my family's offer is probably viewed as charity. I try to change the subject and not spoil what's been an amazing afternoon, at least for me.

"Speaking of your mom, how is she today? She must be doing better if you went to all this trouble on our spread and the flowers." I give him a huge smile, and his face lights back up.

"She is better today. She'll move out of ICU and into a regular room tomorrow. She really wants to see you, Aria. I thought we'd head in there after we're done."

"Of course! I can't wait to see her."

As if sensing we're finished, someone from the cafeteria arrives and swoops up our dishes as we stand to walk over to Janet's room. I start to grab my flowers, but Luke is a step ahead of me and takes them to the nurses station, where a vase with water is already waiting. He takes my hand, and we walk inside Janet's room together. I swear a nurse sighs behind me, and I have to laugh out loud.

Chapter 70 – Raine

I'm finishing some work on the guest house with Jacob when my phone rings. It's Aria. We sent her to the store to pick up last-minute items.

"Yes, Reez."

"Dad, I have no idea what to get for them! You should have asked for specifics. What you gave me is not a list!"

"Just get the essentials to get Luke and Janet started. If they need something else, we'll send Luke to the store. Don't worry about it, it'll be okay."

Then there's a loud, "UGH. I'll see you later."

I look at my phone and smirk. Julia said that Aria would be a wreck about Janet and Luke's arrival, and that's an understatement. My daughter has never been so freaked out before. Julia had to clearly explain it to me like I'm a five-year-old, which made me second-guess my offer. Now Aria and Luke are back to liking each other and not just friends, which makes this awkward for Aria. I probably need to watch Luke like a hawk. But in the back of my mind, I know I won't have to. Luke's a great kid; I don't worry about him at all. But my daughter, she's another matter. She's lovesick and stressed out. This is not going to be fun.

Luke told me Janet will be in a rehab program for about a month. She has lost the feeling in her left side, and they think it's because she had a minor stroke, so she'll have people coming here to help her regain her strength and walk. We lined up a full-time nurse for the first week to make sure everything goes well, but I haven't told Luke that yet. Janet will have physical therapy a few times a week, so we've arranged transportation for that. Aria and Luke only have a week left before they go back to their classes. One week of managing two love-struck teenagers. Awesome.

Tonight is Christmas Eve and Julia's frantically getting both houses decorated. Jacob and I are tasked with putting up lights on the guest house, and then we should be good to go.

When we're done, a large van slowly enters the drive, making its way up. Luke's truck follows behind. Jacob lets me know he'll finish up and I race down the pathway toward our main house. Luckily, this walkway is smooth and straight, so they won't have a tough time getting Janet up here. The only challenging section is the slope up to the main house.

I meet Julia in the kitchen, and we both head out the front door to meet the waiting vehicles. We told Luke to pull up out front and then we'd take Janet around the side of the house and up to the guest house. As Luke gets out, he scans for Aria's truck, then he quickly finds us and walks toward us as two men get out of the van and open the side doors to get his mother out.

When Luke reaches us, he shakes my hand. He seems uncomfortable. Julia immediately tries putting him at ease.

"Luke, we're so happy you both are here. We have everything ready up at the house for you both, and Aria went to the store to grab a couple of more things for the fridge."

Luke nods and mumbles thanks, but we're all distracted as they unload Janet from the van. Sitting in a wheelchair, she looks incredibly small and weak. We all rush to help, although the two men seem to have it covered. A nurse, who was traveling in the back, steps out with a bag of items. Then they get her on the ground and ready to go. Julia rushes to her side as we surround the small group. Since it's December, they have her wrapped up tight, but you can see everyone's breath.

"Janet, so good to have you here," Julia says, taking one of her hands. "Let's get her inside immediately." Julia nods to me and I lead toward the side of the house and the walkway that wraps around to the guest house. As I mentioned, it's a bit of an incline, but one of the men steers her with ease.

Our small group reaches the house. Thank goodness we don't have to maneuver any steps. The house overlooks one of the pastures. There is a small doorstop that we get the chair over, but it's no trouble to get inside. To make things easier, we set up the hospital bed in what was a dining room that has a large picture window. Janet will have a lot of sunlight and scenery. As her team gets her set up, I give Luke a glance and lead him down the hall to the main bedroom in this house. He's carrying a couple of bags, which he proceeds to toss on the king-size bed.

While we have a moment, I make sure he's okay with everything. "Luke, I know this probably seems strange, but seriously, you and your mom are like family to us." I continue with a chuckle, "And my wife, she's a mother hen. She wants to make sure you both are taken care of. She'll go overboard ... so if it's too much, just let me know. We know you've got things covered."

Luke seems to perk up at my words. "Thanks, Mr. Wagner ... really, this is great and I'm sure it puts my mom's mind at ease. She's been so excited since I mentioned that we'd be staying with you all. It's all she talked about with the nurses."

Luke seems to want to say more but catches himself, so I continue. "Well, anything you need, you let me know. And tonight, Julia has dinner all planned for Christmas Eve. Not sure if your mom is up for it or not. If she can come down, great, or we can even come up here to her."

"I'll ask her a little bit later."

We both stop as the front door pounds open. Aria's struggling with several bags in her arms, trying to get in.

"Well, here you all are!" Her face is red from the exertion. Luke rushes to her side, grabbing a couple of bags while I watch in amusement.

Aria gives me a frustrated look. "Gee, thanks, Dad!"

"Luke's got it, sweetheart." I give Luke a wink and I swear his faces turns a deep shade of red.

Aria spins toward the kitchen and Luke follows along. He looks back, giving me a look that makes me laugh out loud. That boy is long gone in love.

I head into the dining room area where they have Janet all set up. We put a large-screen television in the room, and she also has an emergency button near the bed that rings directly to Luke, and one to us if needed.

Janet seems overwhelmed, "You all didn't need to go to so much trouble."

Julia quickly replies, "Of course we did! Now how about we all clear out of here and let Janet rest. Except your nurse is going to stay for a little while until our person arrives." The nurse nods and Julia proceeds to show her around the house before she leaves.

The two drivers make their way to the front door, and I follow them out, giving each of them a handshake and a large tip, which I'm not sure is allowed but I do it anyway.

I walk back into Janet's room to say goodbye and as I'm leaving, Luke and Aria head her way. Aria is obviously staying up here with him.

"I'll be down in a while to help Mom with dinner, Dad."

"I hope so ... you know she can't really cook, Reez."

Luke looks shocked as we both laugh knowingly.

Aria chimes in, "Don't worry, Luke. Mom usually buys Christmas dinner and acts like she made it, or Dad helps. It'll be fine."

But Luke doesn't seem convinced, which makes me chuckle as I head out the door. I glance back and Luke's taken Aria's hand firmly in his. This may end up being a long month. A heavy sigh escapes my lips as I search for my beautiful wife.

Chapter 71 – Julia

I'm glad that Raine took over our Christmas Eve dinner prep. With everything we've had going on, I dropped that ball. We had a nice, relaxing dinner of baked ham with all the fixings and pumpkin and apple pies. Store bought, of course. Janet was tired after her long day, so Luke ran a plate up to her and he plans on staying with her for the rest of the night. A look of disappointment flashed across Aria's face, but she quickly hid it by offering to help Luke in the morning.

I'm clearing up the last of our dishes and tidying up the kitchen when I feel Aria coming up behind me.

Aria looks at me sheepishly. "Mom … are you planning on going to Jonah's grave site tomorrow like you do every year?"

I give her a reassuring smile, "I am. We talked about having you join me. Do you still want to go?"

"I do. Will Dad come too, or will it just be us?" she asks, shifting her feet.

I need to make her feel that this is okay. "Your dad has driven me a few times, but he's gonna stay here tomorrow. I'll go early. I know you're planning on helping Luke. Will that work?"

Aria's eyes light up when I mention Luke's name. "Sure. I'll let him know I won't make it up there until a little later." There is a slight pause before she continues, "Are you sure you're okay with this, Mom? I know this is around the time that Jonah died. I don't want to get in your way."

I instantly want to wrap my arms around my girl, so I reach out and pull her to my side, "Reez, you can go anywhere with me and I'm glad you want to come and share this." I pull her in tight and then give her my serious mom look, "It will be cold though, so warm clothes. Don't worry about fashion."

She gives a loud guffaw before she walks out the door, replying with clear sarcasm, "Like I really care about fashion. Seriously, Mom, you know me better than that."

I laugh as she walks out the door, pulling her phone out, no doubt to text Luke. I've talked to Raine at length about having the two of them in such close quarters, and I worked hard to put his mind at ease. Watching them both today was convincing. There has been a little hand holding, but that doesn't bother me in the slightest. They're going to be just fine.

Thinking of my husband ... I wonder where he went. I finish what I'm doing and then stroll down toward his studio. The door is wide open, and Raine's on his phone as I catch part of his conversation.

"That's great, Wayne. I figured you'd get everything in on time and I'm sure we'll get good news in January. Okay ... I'll mention it to her. Talk to you later."

"Mention what to me?" I ask, startling my husband, but an enormous grin quickly covers his face as he sets his phone down, motioning for me to come closer. I take a seat in his lap as he enfolds me against him. This is by far the best part of my day.

"Wayne finished the submission of 'He'll Stay' for Song of the Year, and they already called and asked him to perform the song on the show, and he wants you to sing harmony. He also mentioned having you join him out on the road next year. That's what I'm supposed to ask you."

"Hmm ... performing on the show ... what if we all perform with him? I think that would be a better musical event. As for touring with him, let me think about it. But I'm sure you already have the band members and merch picked out," I say with a mumbled laugh against his chest.

Raine leans down and kisses the top of my head before answering, "You know me too well." He's quiet for a moment before continuing, "Both are good opportunities, Jules. Aria will of course agree to sing with you on the awards show, and you know I will. And you know my vote about touring."

"Yes, I do. Like I said, I'll think about it."

Raine pushes back so he's looking at me. "It is Christmas Eve ... we forgot to open gifts as a family. We always do one gift together."

"With Luke and Janet here, I didn't want that to be awkward, so I thought we'd wait until tomorrow."

And then Raine surprises me by reaching behind his back and pulling out a small, wrapped box, which clearly screams jewelry.

"How in the world! When did you have time to do this?"

"To be honest, I didn't. Tracy helped," he says sheepishly, and I smirk at him knowing how the two schemed.

I take the box from his hands. It only has a bow around it, which I quickly tear off, and he gives me a sly grin as I open the lid to take out the small container. I give him a side-eye as I have no idea what he could have gotten me. I have everything I need.

I gasp as I open the box and find a ring that is very similar to my engagement ring but has two small birthstones for Aria and Jonah around it.

He pulls the ring out for me and places it on my right ring finger. It fits perfectly. I grasp my husband's face with both hands and give him a long, lingering kiss. His hands wrap around my waist as he pulls me tight against his frame. Finally, we pull apart and he gives me a look I know well.

"Race you!"

Raine laughs as I jump up and out the door with him just steps behind me. I sprint up the stairs with him hot on my tail as we quietly hit the landing, trying not to disturb our daughter down the hall, and then we quickly move to our room.

Raine takes the time to close the door, but I'm already half undressed and waiting for him at the end of our bed. He takes long strides to the bathroom, while I continue to strip down to nothing. I hear water running and then he steps out with his shirt off. He leaves the door open with the light on and he's by my side in moments, pulling me to him and down on our bed. Then Raine and I have one of the most fun and blessed Christmas Eves we've had in years until the sun comes up on Christmas morning.

Chapter 72 – Aria

I put on my warmest clothes and grab my black knee-high down coat. I'm surprised that when I reach the kitchen, both Dad and Mom are there waiting with a mug of coffee for me.

"Hey sweetie, are you ready? Dad has the car warmed up for us."

I grasp the oversized thermal mug. "Wow, you both must have gotten up at sunrise."

A knowing look passes between them before Mom continues. "It's Christmas morning … we had to see what Santa dropped off at our house."

I laugh at that one. I guess I should be curious to see the presents under the tree, but I've been much more focused on my gorgeous boyfriend who's literally steps away.

"That might have worked years ago," I tease back. "Did I get a new pony? Maybe a sports car?"

Dad chimes in, "Better … I think I've talked your mom into going on tour next year."

This is surprising. Mom jokingly gives Dad an elbow to the ribs.

"I haven't decided yet, dear, but yes, Aria, it's on the table." She's quick to change the subject. "Let's go, Reez, so we're back before breakfast, which gives you your assignment, my dear. We expect our meal to be ready."

"Yes, ma'am." Dad gives her a mock salute and a huge grin as Mom rolls her eyes at him.

Dad walks us to the door, but before we walk out, Mom turns and gives him a long and tender hug. This is not easy on her.

"I'll be here waiting, love … for you both," and he gives me a tender look.

We load into Mom's warm car and make the short trip to the cemetery. I've been here before, but it's been a while. As we pull in, I glance at Mom's face, and she seems a little tense but there's a peacefulness there. She goes right to the exact location.

Dad put a small bouquet of white roses in the back seat and as we get out, Mom grabs them before closing the door. She waits for me and I take her hand as we walk to Jonah's tombstone. When we get there, Mom gingerly moves debris from the front out of the way and places the roses in front of the stone. Then she steps back to my side, taking my hand as we both silently stand there. Mom's eyes are closed. It's then that I notice a couple of tears rolls down her face, which makes me grasp her hand tight.

Mom opens her eyes and I ask, "Do you need me to give you a few minutes alone, Mom?"

She looks at me. "No, sweetie, I'm good. I like having you here. I was just saying a prayer, and then I talk to him," she says, gesturing to Jonah's stone. "I tell him about our lives … and about you, and that's what I'm going to do. I'll just do it in my head if you don't mind?"

"Of course not." I stand with her for several more minutes, staring at the stone, watching our breath in the wind, and saying my own silent prayer for Mom, Dad, and the brother that I never got to know.

Moments later, Mom lets go of my hand and then she bends down to rearrange the bundle of roses. I lean down to help. She leans against my arm, and I instinctively wrap my arm around her shoulder. Mom looks at me and smiles.

She whispers, "Do you know how happy and blessed we are to have you in our lives?" I nod as tears form on my lashes.

We both stand and Mom kisses the tip of her gloved fingers and touches the top of the stone. Then she lets me know she's ready to go.

As we're driving back home, I get up the nerve to ask a question I've always been too scared to ask. "Mom, will you tell me one day how you lost Jonah? I don't know what happened."

"I can tell you right now if you like. It helps to talk about it."

"Okay."

"Let's drive around for a while I'll tell you about that night."

For the next half hour, Mom relays the full story of how she miscarried, how it felt, and how she and Dad struggled to recover. She gives me all the gory details. Now I understand and love her even more. I've never been prouder or more in awe of my mom, and my dad.

My phone buzzes. It's Dad and by now, he's worried. I let him know we're heading home. When we park, Mom gets out and I meet her at her door, giving her the biggest hug and thanking her for this morning. She smiles, giving me a knowing nod. We don't have to say anything more. As we get inside the front door, we're greeted by the wonderful aroma of bacon. My heart swells. This is going to be a fantastic Christmas.

Chapter 73 – Luke

This whole living in Aria's guest house is more than surreal. The Wagner family has treated us like family; too much so. We shared Christmas with them and a week later spent New Year's Eve playing games and listening to music until just after midnight. It was a relaxing evening, and a nice change from trying to seem like I'm having fun hanging out with the guys.

I have no idea how I'll ever pay them back for everything they've done. Me and mom haven't had to worry about anything. They've taken care of our food, Mom always has a full-time caregiver, their ranch hand Jacob has been a godsend, basically picking up Mom whenever we've needed an extra hand. The overwhelming guilt I'm carrying is enormous.

Then, everywhere I go, there's Aria. It's wonderful, of course, but on more than one occasion it's been painful. Physically painful. All I want to do is wrap her up in my arms, but I know her father and mother are around, and I have to control myself. Today is the last weekend before we go back to class. Aria wants me to help her feed the horses, and I jump at the chance for some alone time.

I finish dressing when there's a light knock on the door. I check on Mom and she's napping after a light physical therapy session. We've got a few good hours before we need to be back for dinner.

I open the door and my breath catches in my throat. It always does when I see Aria. She's in casual jeans and work boots, with a stocking cap on her head.

"Hey there," Aria smiles before teasing me. "I think you're going to need a coat and hat, big guy. It's like thirty degrees today."

"I wasn't quite ready," I tease back.

Aria walks in and lightly closes the door behind her as I gesture that Mom's in the other room sleeping. I grab my coat and a hat from where they're hanging on a hook.

We're several steps out the door before we start talking. I'm keeping my distance from her. She's got on a light perfume; it's sweet and sensual and it's making my head spin.

Aria breaks the silence. "We'll find out about our songs on Monday. What do you think will happen?"

"Honestly, I have no idea … we've got a chance though, Aria."

"I don't know, not if Dr. Smith has any say we probably don't. I caught her watching us one time in the parking lot, Luke. She doesn't like me at all."

"Wow … well, that's odd. I think she likes you okay, and she's only a consultant, so not sure if she can really impact the judges, but I never thought about it. I hope she can't."

I try not to react as Aria takes a step toward me and touches my arm as she exclaims, "Oh gosh! I forgot to mention … they've asked Mom to sing on the country music awards show in April, and Mom wants me and Dad to sing, too." There's a bit of a pause before she continues. "You and your mom should come with us!"

I reply hesitantly, "Oh, I don't know about that … maybe, if your dad thinks it's okay."

There's an awkward pause as we continue walking up the hill to the stables. They've closed the big double doors at the front of the barn, so we walk in a smaller door and once inside, I notice it's still chilly as part of the back door is open. It looks like all the horses are inside, each in their own stall.

"It's supposed to be cold for the next few days, so Jacob and Mom brought them all up. We need to muck out the stalls and make sure they're all fed. You game?"

"Of course! Sounds like a good time," I say with a cheerful grin and Aria rolls her eyes at me.

"There are some muck boots over there if you want to swap those for your cowboy boots ... I would," Aria looks down at my boots expectantly.

I nod, following her orders, which I proceed to do for the next few hours as one by one we take a horse out of a stall and tether them. Muck out the stall, which basically is me doing that, while Aria gets the horses' feed ready. Then Aria puts the horse back in the stall, and we give them the feed. By the time we're working on the final horse, I've got the hang of it.

"Jacob usually takes care of this, but Dad gave him the weekend off. So, if you're free, I could use the help again tomorrow?" Aria asks, giving me a pleading smile and there's no way I could or would want to say no.

"Your wish is my command."

Aria walks toward the open back barn door and gestures for me to follow her. When I reach her, she takes my hand, pulling me against her side as she does.

"My wish, huh? Is that a promise?" she asks, swiveling her body toward mine. We're just a few inches apart. This is one of the first times we've been alone like this.

"Anything you could ever want," I murmur.

"I want you to kiss me then. I mean, like really kiss me."

She doesn't need to persuade me. I drop her hand and face her fully. I take both of my hands and put them alongside her face, one thumb lightly stroking along her chin as I scan her eyes. The light, teasing grin on her lips flashes like fire. I lean down slowly and my lips graze hers. Her hands reach out and grip my hips as she pulls me against her frame, and a deep groan escapes me. The light kiss quickly turns deeper as I press my lips against hers, and her lips slightly part as my tongue lightly mixes with hers. One of my hands moves up into her hair and I pull her even tighter against me. Aria's arms grip my back, and she pulls me against her as we melt against one another. She sighs and our lips pull apart, but our bodies stay entwined as I rest my head against hers, then she rests her head against my shoulder.

Aria whispers against my chest, "That was a really good wish."

A deep chuckle escapes my throat as I hold her against me, one of her legs wraps around mine, and we stand there, staring out the barn door at the scenery in front of us. The sun's just starting to go down, giving the field a light golden glow. It couldn't be more perfect.

"You have no idea how long I've wanted to do that, but your dad always seems to be lurking around."

"I know ... honestly, I was waiting for him to appear out of nowhere and catch us, but he had several calls today and Wayne planned to stop by, so I figured he was too busy to check on us. But you know what, Luke, I think he'd be okay. He likes you and he trusts us. I can see it."

"I think so, too. He's watching us, but he seems different."

Aria pulls back, looking directly at me. "And I want him to trust me and you, Luke. So, we'll have to keep our relationship just like this ... at least for now." And she quickly leans back against my chest as a light blush covers her face.

My hand rubs the back of her neck as I reply, "I completely agree. I'm not about to mess up a good thing, Aria. I care about you. I told you ... I'm not going to lose you."

Aria looks back up at me and then she gives me the sweetest kiss on my lips before taking my hand. We head out the barn door, back to our reality.

Before we walk out, I can't help but add, "Same time tomorrow?"

Aria looks at me and laughs. "It's a date. Same time tomorrow."

Chapter 74 – Aria

Break is over and I'm driving my truck to school, following Luke. We already know we'll have an all-school announcement after our music theory class. We park our trucks next to each other, but we've agreed we won't let anyone know that we're dating. For one, it's no one's business, but two, we thought it would be odd with the song contest going on.

We walk together, but Luke is met by some of his friends, so he goes on his own way. I put my things in my locker before going to our first class. Everything goes as normally as possible until our music theory class later that afternoon. During the entire hour, I swear Dr. Smith keeps glaring at me, but I tell myself that it's all in my mind.

It's near the end of the day and time for the announcement. As the bell rings and we make our way along with the hundreds of other students to the auditorium, the whole building is buzzing.

I find Charlotte and she sits next to me, with Luke on my other side. Again, we pick seats on the side, closer to the front. There seems to be deference from some of the other students toward Luke. Most are aware of his talents and figure he's in the top ten.

Just like the announcement about the contest, our principal comes out and brings out the judges, including Trent Austin, and of course, Dr. Smith's there, too. Then the lights dim, and they start rolling out the winners one at a time. I look down at Luke's hand next to mine and I want to grip it for reassurance, but I hold back.

They announce the first five top contestants and songs and it's not us. Luke seems as calm as can be, but I'm starting to majorly glisten. They announce number six, and again it is not us ... or Luke, for that matter. Uh-oh. Finally, they get to the last three and they announce Luke's name for his solo song. Several of us stand as he makes his way to the stage to join the other contestants. Only two more songs left. They announce number nine and it's Stacia, from my theory class. My eyes go to the judges and to Dr. Smith, who's staring at me with such an evil look that I get chills.

They're about to announce the last song. I find Luke's face, and he smiles at me, like he's trying to give me strength. My mind is racing. Our song is the only one with two writers, so maybe that's why we didn't make it. They start to announce the final top ten song. The air is heavy around me, and everything is in slow motion.

Principal Fieldstone reads from his paper, "And the final song in the contest is a song called 'Color of Love.'" As soon as he says the song's title, my breath floods out as he continues, "Co-written by Luke Greyson and Aria Wagner."

Somehow my shaky legs make it to the stage, and I join the other contestants. As I reach the group, Luke moves to stand next to me, while the audience cheers for the ten of us standing together on stage.

I briefly catch Trent Austin's eye, and he gives me the slightest wink, but I can't miss Dr. Smith's scowl.

I promised Mom I'd text her the results. I'm sure to tell her I was the last one announced. She mentioned that happened to her on *Next Real Star*, and texts, "it just makes you stronger, honey."

I think they can take that strength and put it where the sun doesn't shine. Dr. Smith probably made them announce our song last on purpose, but who the heck knows. Luke, of course, tries to make me feel better by reminding me they saved the best for last, but I'm not convinced.

We'll perform for the entire school in just two weeks, and then they'll narrow it down to the top three songs. The top three will be performed for a larger public audience for the final vote and winner. I'm instantly nauseous. Yes, I've performed for all kinds of people, but I do have my mom's nerves.

At the end of the day, when Luke and I get back to my house and get inside, we're greeted by balloons, a cake, the whole shebang. Janet and Mom arranged everything. Luke soaks it all in, but all this attention brings home the reality that I'll have to perform my own song for a large crowd.

Mom peppers us with questions and Luke tells her all that we know. Dad catches the end of the conversation, grabbing a piece of cake as he listens.

"Well, you two better go practice," Dad offers in a serious tone, in between bites.

Luke nods, "Yes, sir. We've already discussed it."

Mom adds with a sweet smile, "You can always use my office, like before, honey."

A frustrated look crosses my face. My tone lets everyone know we're on it. "We've already talked about it, and we'll start tonight."

Janet gives Luke a look, letting him know she's ready to go back up to the guest house, which is a good break for me. All this performance talk and my skin is crawling like I'm breaking out in hives.

Luke looks at me questioningly. "Aria, I'll be back here at seven?"

I nod yes. "Perfect, Luke. I'll have the room ready."

Janet is well enough to maneuver her electric wheelchair out the door and Luke grabs her coat, draping it across her shoulders. I watch them head up the path to the guest house.

Dad takes me out of my trance, "Earth to Aria ... your mom said they'll cut it down to three songs and then those three performers will do a public show. So, we may get to hear your song?"

"You'll get to hear Luke's song, Dad, but I'm not sure the song I wrote with Luke will make it. We're the only co-written song, and I don't think it's sitting well with everyone involved in the contest." I don't want to elaborate that it's just one evil consultant who hates me.

"Huh. Well, co-writing is a big deal. At least it is in this town. I think that's short-sighted." He gives my mom a quick kiss as he places his cake plate down. "Got to head back down to the studio. If you and Luke need anything, let me know."

I nod as he leaves, but Mom stays. She clearly has something on her mind.

When Dad clears the room, she asks, "Sitting well with judges or one judge?"

Mom reads me too well. "Actually, one consultant. My music theory teacher. She hasn't liked me from the start when I mentioned the Nashville number system, Mom. Plus, I caught her watching me and Luke one day in the parking lot."

Mom's head tilts as her eyebrows rise.

"We weren't doing anything, Mom," I say, giving her a "c'mon" look and she chuckles. "It was a vibe. She was there staring at us ... it was kind of creepy. It's a gut feeling, Mom. She does not like me, not at all."

There's a pause as Mom's wheels turn. "You know, I've had my share of dealing with betrayal from people I've trusted. Your gut is always right, honey. If something feels off, it is."

I nod, "But there's really nothing I can do about it, is there?"

"Just continue to do your best and do the right thing. If there's deception, it usually has a way of getting exposed. In the end, everything will turn out the way it's supposed to."

I nod my head yes, but my mind is telling me it's not so sure.

Chapter 75 – Julia

The next few weeks fly on by. Luke and Aria practice every free moment they have, and between that, we moved Janet back into their home after some minor modifications to the house. Raine and Jacob built a ramp over their front steps, and they made a few other changes to the house, so it's much easier for her to maneuver around, all with Luke's approval, of course. The doctors hope she's out of the wheelchair and using a walker soon.

During our busy holidays, and having Janet and Luke as guests, I had a follow-up with Dr. North, who said everything looks good. I'll have another scan in a few months to make sure we're on the right track, and then I'll continue my regular visits with Dr. Henley. Since I got this news, I've tried to take it to heart, but it's still hard to believe sometimes. My mind is constantly waiting for some shoe to drop.

I tentatively agreed to some kind of tour, so Raine's thrown himself into that whole affair. It looks like I'll do a few dates with Wayne in the spring and even do a few shows with Bret. Every day I'm hitting the gym and watching what I eat so I can lose a few more pounds, but I think I'm going to have to live with the pudgier me, and I think that's okay.

I'm up at the barn feeding the horses when Raine crashes through the barn door. I catch Raine's eye and with one hand, remind him to shut the door behind him. It's lightly snowing and the cold winter air rolled in with him.

"What in tarnation?" But that's all I can get out before he reaches me, swinging me up in his arms in one big swoop.

"You did it!" Raine says, giving me a huge, sloppy kiss on the cheek.

He sets me on the ground quickly, his hands gripping my forearms. He looks at me like a five-year-old chasing the tar-nation man.

"I did what?" I manage to squeak out.

"Song of the Year! You're nominated. I KNEW IT! I just knew it!"

And again, I'm wrapped up in his arms as he twirls me around the huge space. Luckily, every horse is in its stall, or we'd have a stampede. The horses sense his excitement because Butter's whinnying along with Raine's commotion.

Raine sets me down again and I take a step back to catch my breath. "Well, I'm glad you did! I honestly had no idea."

"Jules, your song has been in the top ten for months since Wayne released it. And you'll win too. I just know it!"

"I don't know about that ... that would be icing, Raine." But my mind is now racing. Great ... a big awards show with even more on the line. I was already singing back-up with Aria and Raine. Now this. I instantly tug at my mid-length hair wondering how it will grow six inches by the April show air date. Raine grasps my insecurity.

"You look fabulous, Jules."

I give him a shy smile. He caught me in a moment of vain weakness. "I know, it will be fine, but I'll be damned if I show up with all this holiday weight." I'm instantly rethinking pudgier me; I don't want everyone to see that on national television.

Raine laughs as he takes my hand, pulling me up tight against his frame, looking down into my eyes, "Well, we need to celebrate. A nice, big dinner ... with dessert."

I groan as he laughs, sprinting away fast back out the door. "I've got to tell Tracy, and a few others. This is big, Julia, really big!"

A loud "UGH" escapes me as he looks back laughing before shutting the door up tight, leaving me alone with my tormented thoughts. Of course, I'm thrilled. This is the first major award I've been nominated for in years. I've won songwriting awards, but I've never been up for Song of the Year.

My phone starts to buzz. It's a message from Aria, and a message from Tracy, too. Damn, Raine works fast. I let Raine know I'm inviting Trace over for dinner too, and he tells me he mentioned it to Bret and his family. So, we're not really having dinner, but a party. I shake my head knowing my gorgeous husband is going to go all out. I ask Aria to invite Luke and Janet. Why not?

That night, I drag myself down the stairs. I don't know why I'm dreading this, but I really don't like being the center of attention. The noise from our guests greets me before I make it to our dining room area. As I round the door and people come into view, the Raine celebration train hits me. He went all out with balloons, streamers, and an enormous cake with lavender frosting sits in the center of the dining room table. It's like I just turned sixteen. He really shouldn't have done this.

There is a good-natured cheer when I enter. I don't think I've ever been this embarrassed. Tracy gives me a look that says, "I'm so sorry; I couldn't stop him," which makes me laugh at her. I give her a look back letting her know it's okay. We'll let Raine have this moment. Raine expects me to say something, and I note in the back of my brain to strangle him later.

The room quiets down and more than ten pairs of eyes are on me.

"Wow ... Raine, everyone ... this is great. Truly. You didn't need to go to all this trouble, but I'm deeply humbled that you'd throw a party like this."

Raine jumps in, "That's a good start to your acceptance speech, sweetheart." And everyone in the room laughs, except for Tracy and Aria, sensing my discomfort. But then I have a moment of reflection, realizing I should laugh too. This is a wonderful moment for me, especially after everything lately. I need to lighten my ass up.

"You know, Raine ... you're damn straight. That is a good start!" I grab what looks like apple juice in a champagne glass, and I make a toast. "To songs that lead to new beginnings, good friends that take time out of their busy lives to be here, and to winning." Then I down my glass with a flourish, which makes many in the room toast and take drinks from their own glasses.

Raine looks so proud. He embraces me hard while whispering in my ear, "Where'd that come from?" He pulls back with the funniest smirk spread across that gorgeous, chiseled face.

"Love, I've beaten cancer and a second scare. I'm done being a chickenshit."

Raine's head goes back in a deep-hearted laugh, and he pulls me against him hard. Then he turns to the group. "All right gang, the food's in the kitchen ... let's eat!"

As everyone heads toward the other room, where I can smell some kind of barbecue, Raine says, "I don't think I've ever loved you more."

I reply, "Well, that's good, 'cause you're stuck with my old, sorry ass."

And then Raine lays a big kiss on my lips, hard and deep, like we don't have a care in the world and guests in the other room. This is exactly why I love him like I do.

Chapter 76 – Aria

I think we're ready for the performance tomorrow, but you never know. They told us the order today and thank God, Luke and I perform first. He'll perform his solo song last, which I think is fitting. They're saving the best for last.

I've been in my room for hours trying to put together a performance outfit. Clothes are all over my bed. I've sent several pictures of me wearing different options to Savannah and even a couple to Charlotte, but no one can give me a definitive answer. Luke's wearing black jeans and boots, and he mentioned a purple shirt. I've been trying to find something to match, but I'm not having much luck. I'm about to bring in the big guns and ask Mom when she knocks on my bedroom door, asking to come in.

Mom opens the door holding a bowl of soup in her hand. I could smell it cooking downstairs, but I've been too distracted by my clothes dilemma to eat. "I brought something up for you since you didn't come down."

Exasperation spills out with my words. "I have no idea what to wear tomorrow. Luke's going to wear black and purple. My good color is green."

Mom sets the soup down on my dresser. I can see the wheels churning in her head as she looks at all the clothes on my bed. "Hmm ... I might have something you can borrow." She whips out of the room.

I should have asked her earlier, but I didn't want her to see how freaked out I really am. I walk back over to my closet, staring numbly at the clothes hanging there when Mom quietly walks back in. I thought she'd be holding some kind of garment or dress, but she's holding a small box.

Mom takes a step toward me as she says, "Here, this should go with whatever you choose."

I'm sure I have an odd look on my face as I take the box from her outstretched hand. She just smiles at me serenely. I open it up and it's her amethyst necklace, the really big, breathtaking one she only wears on special occasions.

"Mom ... I can't! This is from Dad. What if I lose it or something?"

She smiles while saying, "You won't. You said Luke's wearing black and purple. Well, wear something beautiful in black to match and this. It'll look great."

She's right, of course. This necklace is stunning. I do have this flowing black dress that will highlight the stones perfectly. I pull the dress out and hold it up as Mom nods yes. She walks to my closet and pulls out some tall black boots that I've worn with the dress, and it's settled.

Mom reaches up and starts messing with my hair. "You could pull the sides of your hair back in braids ... maybe with the back down?"

"I love it. Could you help me fix it?"

"Of course."

She proceeds to help me clean up my clothing nightmare, and then I sit in front of her on the floor as she braids the sides of my hair, like she did when I was younger. We're quiet and it makes me wonder, so I have to ask.

"Why'd dad give you that necklace, Mom?"

"For Jonah. It's his birthstone."

"I thought so."

"Did he give you a birthstone necklace for my birthday?"

"Well, your father bought me a new necklace, ring, and a new Jaguar for your birthday, honey. He went all out." Mom gives a hearty laugh, and I can't help chuckling along with her, picturing Dad's extravagance. "I drove that car for years ... and I wear the necklace and ring all the time." A few moments pass and Mom adds, "You know, with all that was going on with my test and Luke's mom, we didn't have a very good birthday for you this year. We should have done more."

"The trip was it, Mom. That was plenty."

"Well, I'll talk to your dad about that."

When she's finished with my hair, I go to a nearby full-length mirror. I have two French braids running down the sides of my hair and it looks great. Plus, it will keep the hair out of my eyes when I'm playing.

"Just like when you were little," Mom says sighing. And now we've let your soup get cold. I can run and get you some more?"

"I'm good. Let me try everything on and then I'll run down and heat it up." She doesn't look convinced. "Seriously, I'm good, Mom. Thanks," I say, giving her my best "I'll take care of it" smile.

Mom nods and makes her way to the door, but my words stop her.

"Thanks for the necklace, Mom. It means a lot and I'll be really careful with it."

She looks at me from the doorframe. "I know you will. This is your big day to shine, just like I've had mine. Break a leg, honey." Then she slips out the door.

I quickly strip out of my sweats and throw on the dress and boots, and then gingerly put on the necklace that costs more than my truck. Wow. It shimmers in these lights. Imagine how it will look on stage. I send quick texts to Savannah and Charlotte letting them know I've got my duds all picked out. I don't send a picture; it'll be a surprise.

The next day, I can't stop squirming. We're performing over the lunch hour, so I've got to get through a few classes before we get out early to get ready. I've got my outfit in a garment bag that will fit in my locker, but I'm not taking any chance with Mom's necklace; it's staying with me in my purse. This morning, Mom assured me that it's insured, but I'm terrified I'll lose it.

By the time third period finally rolls around, and we're let out to prepare, my shirt is drenched with sweat. I don't want Luke to see me like this. After grabbing my clothes and my guitar, I'm supposed to go to the choir changing rooms. When I get there, a couple of other competitors are already there. I get into a room and quickly strip out of my clothes and into my dress and boots, with a heavy dose of antiperspirant. I pull Mom's necklace out with care. I get it on and take a final gaze into a full-length mirror. This will more than do. I grab my makeup bag to touch up my eyes, dab a bit of blush on my cheeks, and, lastly, some nude color lipstick. I'm taking my purse with me, but they said the room will have security, so I leave my other stuff here. I grab my guitar and head toward the back of the stage.

As I open the door and walk in, Luke's chatting with one of the sound guys. Since we're first up, I figured he'd be here. There's a chair to the side of the stage and I head over there to put my things down. When I stand back up, Luke's not more than two feet away and he's staring at me, a look of amazement filling his face.

I look back, my guitar in one hand as I self-consciously use the other to smooth down my dress. "Never seen a girl in a dress before?" I ask with amusement. But the look on his face stays, and it's a good look, like he's seeing me for the first time.

"Um, yeah. But wow … you are stunning, Aria. Truly stunning."

That's what I was going for, exactly that, I think to myself. "You look great, too, Luke. Purple's a good color for you."

A light blush crosses his cheeks as Luke's eyes drop slightly above my chest, then his eyes reach mine. "That necklace. Wow. It's gorgeous."

"When you said you were wearing purple, my mom wanted me to have something to match. So, she loaned me this." I place my hand on the stone.

He smiles broadly, saying quietly, "It's perfect."

"Should we tune up together?" This wakes him up to our task at hand. He grabs his guitar and we get down to business. We've only got about ten minutes and then we're on. Soon the murmur from the audience grows louder as more people fill up the auditorium. We run through a few lines of harmony to warm up.

Luke gives me a wink. "This will be a piece of cake, Aria."

"I hope so." I drop an honest moment. "Seriously, Luke, I swear I'm about to vomit. Happens every time."

Luke gives me a grimace, "Is there anything that helps?"

"Just distract me … tell me a joke or something. Anything to keep my mind off the fact that I could mess up in front of thousands of people."

Luke looks at me strangely and finally says, shrugging his shoulders, "I got nothing, Aria." And then he grins sheepishly, which makes us both laugh.

"That works … that works. At least it's a distraction."

Just then, our principal announces today's show, and moments later they're announcing our names to walk out to perform. Here. We. Go.

Chapter 77 – Luke

The dress. Wow. Mixed with her hair and that necklace and I don't think Aria's ever looked more beautiful. I should have said that the moment she faced me, but I stood there staring at her like a big dope.

We walked out to the large, enthusiastic audience and did extremely well. The group of judges sitting at the table in front, along with the crowd, was intimidating; I won't lie. But I don't think we've ever sung our song any better, and Aria's voice was as strong as ever. When we finished the crowd stood, clapping and cheering.

We walked back to the side of the stage, and I wrapped Aria in a side hug, holding her there for several minutes. I didn't care if anyone was watching. I know we're keeping our relationship a secret, but I love this girl.

Since I still have to perform my solo song at the end of the ten songs, I decide not to listen to any of the other performers. It's better this way. Aria went back to the choir room to drop off her stuff and then she's gonna go sit in the audience. I don't think having her out there will affect my nerves, but who knows? So far, I'm keeping everything in check, but as it gets closer, I start to pace around backstage. It's weird having a song with Aria and wanting to win with that song, but also really wanting to win with my own song.

When they finally call my name and I walk out, since I'm familiar with the setup, that doesn't get me. But the room is quiet, too quiet. I boldly plug in my guitar and start playing.

Throughout the song, the audience is breathtakingly silent. With the heat of the lights, beads of sweat start rolling down my face. I've performed for this school and this crowd before, but this is pressure I've never experienced from this audience. By the time I get to the bridge, the last verse, and chorus, I gather strength from inside and let the words pour out of me through my vocals, and the music through my fingers. I'm pulling the energy from the crowd to push through and finish this song with everything I have, not only for me, but for my mom, and for my dad.

When the last chord rings out, silence greets me for several seconds, and then there's this rush all at once from the crowd as they stand in unison, with loud cheers hitting me in full force. I drop my guitar to my side in exhaustion as I scan the crowd for Aria. I think I see her standing by the back doors of the auditorium because of her glittering jeweled necklace, but then she's gone. I look back at the audience and smile before I unplug my guitar and walk off the stage in complete satisfaction. That was the best performance of my life.

Chapter 78 – Aria

I've never watched anyone perform better than what I just experienced from Luke. He had the crowd from the moment he walked on stage, until the very last note and even after that. He knows exactly what he's doing; he's completely natural and that song is even more amazing hearing it up front with the audience than backstage.

While I'm thrilled for him, inside I'm devastated. Our co-written song won't win. Maybe I'm more sad for my parents than I am for me. I live in a family of strong songwriters and winners, and I won't win this. Not this time. I think I'll be okay, but I can't stand seeing Mom and Dad's faces. If we make it to the top three and then they hear the difference between the song we wrote, and what I just heard, it'll be obvious. Dad will sign Luke to a deal at that very moment.

I don't want Luke to see me right now. I'm oozing disappointment, and I can't shake it. Not yet. I rush to the choir room to grab my things and then I'm gonna leave for the day. I haven't skipped any classes before, so what's a couple? I'll have Mom say that I'm sick or something.

I'm gathering up my things and stepping out the door when I hear Luke's voice.

"I found you!"

I spin around to see him lightly sprinting my way, his face flushed from excitement. My face grows hot. I have no idea what I'm going to say to him.

"Yeah. You did," I reply, standing awkwardly with my guitar haphazardly slung over my back, and the rest of my things overflowing out of my backpack that's only halfway zipped up. There's an awkward silence, as if he's waiting for me to say more. But I decide to stay the course, so I start walking toward the main school doors as fast as my legs will carry me. It's not easy though with all my stuff, and I'm still wearing my dress.

Luke settles in right next to me, step for step. "Where are you going? I thought we could grab a quick bite in the cafeteria. They held over some lunch for us performers."

"No ... I'm going to go home. I'll have my mom call in or something. Not really feeling so hot."

Luke's steps slow and he looks worried. "Oh ... okay. Is it the stress of the show?"

My voice stiffens. "Yeah ... maybe that's it."

"Can I help you get this stuff out to your truck?" he asks as he leans over to help with my guitar. I'm walking fast trying to make my getaway and it won't stay securely on my shoulder.

I stop. "NO! I mean ... I'm fine, Luke. I've got this, really." Then I start walking again.

But Luke's not buying it. He stops in the middle of the large school foyer and says with conviction, "Aria Marie Wagner, what is wrong with you?"

There are a few students milling around and they stop and stare at us.

I give him a look and gesture for him to follow me outside. There, I let him take my guitar and we silently walk to my truck. When we get there, Luke speaks.

"Aria, I've been around you enough to know when something is up."

I open my truck door and put my guitar and backpack inside, then I turn back around to face him. I sigh heavily, looking away, and then I finally look at him.

"Luke, your song was amazing, it truly was. I don't see any way that you won't win." Luke starts to interrupt but I put my hand up and he stops as I continue. "I listened to all the other songs and your song is different. It clearly stands out above all the others ... but it's not just that. You have *it*. I've heard my dad say that before, and I know exactly what he means. You have what he's always looking for, which is why you intrigued him, and when he sees you perform, it's over."

Luke's embarrassed, looking down at the ground. Finally, he replies, "Okay, that's great that you think this and all, but why are you running out so upset?"

And here's my moment of truth, when I'll have to be completely vulnerable. My voice shakes as I reply, "I love that your song is great, Luke. It's facing my parents and the disappointment I'll cause them because I won't win. Does that make sense? Sure, I want to win for me, but I want to prove that I have what it takes to be a hit songwriter … and maybe I don't."

Something flashes across Luke's face that makes me feel worse. It's like he feels sorry for me, and I hate that.

I start to climb into my truck. I mumble toward him, "I shouldn't have said anything. Forget it."

"No, Aria, wait," Luke says, grabbing my arm as he steps closer to me, pulling me close to him until suddenly, I'm wrapped up in his arms. I'm breathing him in and it's a mix of his musky cologne and sweat. He pulls me in tight and I tilt my head up to look at him.

"Aria, win or lose this thing, no one will think any less of you, especially your parents. I know for a fact they are extremely proud of you. We're in the top ten and contrary to what you think, we wrote a damn good song. So, please, stop losing this thing before we have a chance to win it. And second, you in that dress with that necklace—you look like royalty. I was the goofball standing up there next to you. You are WAY out of my league, girl; do you know that?"

A loud guffaw escapes my lips at that last part, but I can't say anything else because Luke lays a big kiss on my lips, one hand wrapped up in the back of my hair as he presses me against his lithe frame.

When we pull apart, he smirks down at me, "Now how about you grab your regular clothes, we go back inside and change, get something to eat and finish the rest of our day so you don't have to play hooky?"

I nod, as a huge smile takes over my lips. I walk over to my truck and pull out what I'll need for the rest of the day before I lock the door. I spin back around and as I do, Luke takes my hand before we walk back inside.

"What about keeping 'this,' I say gesturing toward our enclosed hands, between us?"

"Over it. Everyone figured it out anyway. My friends all call you my 'girlfriend.'"

"And how in the heck did you know my middle name? I've never told you that."

"I was at your house for a month, remember? I heard your mom say that like a thousand times," he says with the biggest smirk.

He glances down at my neck, "I do think you should wear that necklace all day though. It suits you."

I look at him and laugh. "Royalty, huh? Then I guess you can refer to me as 'Your Highness.'"

"Yes, my liege."

"That's a good start. A very good start."

Luke shakes his head at me as we walk back into the school, hand in hand.

Chapter 79 – Julia

I didn't get much from Aria when she got home. The performance went well; the judges are deliberating; and they'll find out by the end of the week. That's it. The look on her face gave more away than her words. It's what she's not telling me. She's worried. Clearly worried. I don't want to pry, but it's taking all that I have not to ask her more questions. Maybe Raine can get more out of her, but right now, Raine's consumed with my upcoming tour, shows, and the awards show. I'm his new project. *Great.*

Aria gave me my necklace safe and sound, letting me know it was a hit, especially with Luke. I knew he'd like it. I like that kid, and even though they're both entirely too young for anything serious, they're good for each other, that's easy to see.

Raine's footsteps echo down the hall as I linger in the kitchen. I'm sure he has more plans that I need to approve, and that makes my stomach churn.

He pops his head in, "How about doing a couple local television shows when you're out with Wayne?" He sees my initial expression and adds, "Trace thinks it's a good idea."

I look at him and cross my arms while sighing loudly. "Oh, I guess so. Not a full-fledged media tour though, Raine. And I don't want to be out for entire weeks, just weekends. Just like we discussed."

He nods at me with that gorgeous grin. "I know, honey. Wayne said that's fine. He'll fill in the opening act slot with other artists, and then you can join him on the Friday and Saturday gigs with a few Sundays thrown in."

"When do we start?"

"Your first date is the beginning of March. You'll have a month of shows before the country music awards. I thought that would be good practice before that show. For the music awards, you'll do promos leading up to the main show … I thought you'd be okay with that?"

I look down my nose at him like, "Do I have a choice?" It's probably a done deal. "Well, at least you'll be with me. And what about Aria?"

"We can fly her out for some of the shows if she wants to. Did Aria say anything more about her contest?"

I shake my head. "Nope. But something happened, Raine. Maybe you can get something out of her. She's not budging with me."

He pauses, mulling over my words before replying, "She's not going to tell me anything she won't tell you, but I can try."

As he abruptly spins out of the door to leave, I blow him a quick kiss. This is all I get right now. He's preoccupied that we, mainly me, will be back out there performing. He's lined up the best players, transportation, and everything. Spending my weekends riding on a bus does not sound thrilling to me, but Raine loves it.

I have to confirm who will take care of the ranch, so I grab my coat and rush out the back door, the dogs at my heels, to make arrangements with Jacob.

Chapter 80 – Raine

Aria's upstairs and rather than wait until later, I decide to run up and do my own digging. I'm dying to know how their performance went, and hope that she'll tell me more about Luke's solo performance. I reach the landing in front of her closed door and give it a good knock. It takes a few moments, but she cracks the door open and peers through.

She blinks at me. "Hey, Dad."

"Can you open the door? Haven't seen you all day … I want to talk to you."

There's a slight groan and then the door swings wide. Aria's wearing heavy sweats, and her hair is up in a towel. The one thing that's clear is that she looks exhausted, and her eyes are extremely sad … like she lost something she loved.

A concerned tone takes over my voice. "Alright. What's going on? Something's wrong. Your mom's worried sick and now I am too."

Aria replies, softly, "Nothing, Dad, really. Just a long day with the show and all."

With the look on her face, I'm not buying it. "Did your performance go okay?"

Her words don't match her eyes, "It went great, Dad, really."

"Then what is it?"

There's a pause for what seems like years, so I go ahead and take a chair as Aria sits down on her bed. She takes the towel off her head and sets it down next to her. I can picture my eight-year-old little girl in this same room. My, how the time has flown. Finally, she breaks the silence.

"It's Luke … and his song, Dad."

"Okay … what about his song?"

She gives me her sad-filled eyes, "He was exceptional … like superstar good, Dad. He'll totally win this thing and I won't." Then the truth of what's bothering her tumbles out of her mouth, "And then you and Mom will be disappointed, you know, 'cause you guys are so talented and Mom is this amazing songwriter, and I doubt I'll even make it to the top three, especially with Dr. Smith, who clearly hates me … so we don't have a chance and my career is ruined, while you'll sign Luke and he'll be this big star and I'll be a nobody."

I've been listening to the entire spiel with my head resting in my hand, taking it all in. Aria thinks we aren't proud of her, and if she doesn't win, she'll be a failure in our eyes. That's it.

"Aria, honey. First, your mom and I would never, ever be disappointed in you. It doesn't matter if you wanted to be a dentist, we'd be all for it and want to see your work." She gives a hint of a smile with that one, before I continue. "Second, I'm sure the song you wrote with Luke is good, and no matter if anyone likes it or not, it's yours. Last, it doesn't matter what I've done or what your mom has done. You are your own person, and we don't expect you to be anything other than yourself." I've got her nodding along with me now. "But who is Dr. Smith and why does she hate you?"

"She's my music theory instructor and she's a consultant with the contest … it's a vibe. She clearly doesn't like me, Dad."

Now I'm intrigued. "Well, that's odd, but I don't want to talk about that now. I do want to say something about Luke. Luke's an amazing talent, I'll give you that, and if the song he wrote is that good and he wins, then we'll cross that bridge later. But first, you know your mother and I want you to be happy. Do you like writing songs?"

Her face lights up. "I love it."

"Okay then. Continue working at it. No one expects you to write song of the year on the first try. Your mother is in her fifties, and this is her first nomination. Heck, sometimes people are older than that before they get any recognition. It takes work, Aria, a lot of hard work."

I get up off the chair and make my way to her door. Aria runs over and gives me a quick hug, and inside I melt. She'll always be my little girl.

"Thanks, Dad. I really needed this."

"Sure, honey. I'm just glad this wasn't a boy thing … I would've had to call your mom for that."

Aria shakes her head laughing as I walk away.

Thank God it wasn't some romance thing with Luke. I like that kid, but she is my daughter. I head back down the stairs to relay some of our conversation to my wife. We've put too much pressure on Aria to be a performer. At the very least, we've got to make sure she understands we don't expect perfection.

Chapter 81 – Aria

I'll find out if I'm a failure today. Seriously though, no matter what happens, I'll be okay with it. Sure, if our song doesn't make it, I'll be devastated inside, but it won't be the end of the world.

Since I talked with Dad, they've eased up on asking me about the contest. They don't even know that today is the day we'll find out if we made it to the top three. My gut's mixed on this; part of me thinks we've made it, but then I picture Dr. Smith sneering at me, and my hope dies.

I make my way into the school when a familiar hand grasps mine. I'm thrilled we're telling our little world about us, although it wasn't a surprise to anyone.

"Nervous?"

Of course, I know what he's talking about.

"It's out of our hands, Luke. And really, in the grand scheme of things, it's one opportunity. There will be more."

He pulls back with a look like "Where did this 'Aria' come from?" and it makes me giggle.

"Seriously, Luke. It's okay if we're not in the top three."

He nods like he believes me or at least believes that I believe what I said. And I do believe it, although I know my pride will be crushed. Luckily, we don't have to wait long. They're making the announcement first thing this morning. We make our way into the auditorium. I asked Charlotte to save us seats near the front where we like to sit, and she didn't disappoint. The air is electric. Within minutes of sitting down, the lights dim and Principal Fieldstone steps out.

"Alright, alright. I'm not going to hold this up as you all are waiting anxiously for the final three. I do want to let you know that the finalists will perform on March twenty-third, downtown Nashville at the Bridgestone Arena."

Luke's grip tightens and a shiver runs down my spine. His face is bright with excitement. I'm sure mine is ashy.

Principal Fieldstone continues, "Without further ado, I'll announce the top three finalist songs and writers in no particular order. I'd like for the writers to come up and join me on stage. The first song continuing in the contest is 'Coming Home,' written by Luke Greyson."

Luke pauses to look at me and smiles as he drops my hand and moves to walk up on stage, but before he does, he gives me a quick wink. I knew they'd name him, but now I'm left all alone. Suddenly, the air around me grows icy.

Principal Fieldstone continues, "The second song selected to compete in our songwriting competition is 'At First Glance,' written by Stacia Cooper." I watch Stacia from across the room stand and join Luke on stage. I start to think 'it doesn't matter' over and over, remembering my mom struggled too. She didn't have success right away, so it's okay if our song doesn't make it. Time slows as the seconds tick like hours. The air around me is thick and sounds are amplified, like I'm in a tube. Finally, he gets to the last song.

Principal Fieldstone leans into the microphone, "And lastly, the third song moving on in our competition is 'Color of Love,' co-written by Luke Greyson and Aria Wagner."

I'm sitting there dumbfounded when Charlotte nudges me out of my seat. The only person I search for is Luke and he's all teeth from the stage, like he never doubted it. I thought I'd completely lost and convinced myself of that result.

It feels surreal as I join the other two contestants on stage. I wonder if this is what my mom felt on *Next Real Star*. Although this is not in the same league, standing here as the warmth of the crowd comes over you … it's an out of body experience. I get why people get totally addicted to it.

We walk off to the stage and are instantly greeted by the movie's production staff. This has become serious, arena production serious. A couple of public relations staff hand out a list of dos and don'ts on how to manage our social media accounts. I hadn't even thought about that. Then they walk us through a list of expected public appearances. Another aspect that hadn't crossed my mind. Luke and Stacia seem unfazed.

When we finally get a moment to ask questions, we stand there with blank looks until I ask about the sessions with Trent Austin. Trent's going to meet with us before our final show to walk through any tweaks we can make—not to our song, but any improvements on arrangement and performance. We'll have the opportunity to perform the song any way we want. With full bands, string sections, you name it, so this is our chance to work on the production with Trent. This is the most exciting part for me.

When we're finally free, it's difficult to go back to our regular classes, but I head off to class walking on air. I send Mom a quick text letting her know that we're in the top three. She sends a big thumbs-up and a heart. I get why Mom and Dad have pulled back, but I'd hoped for a little more than a couple of emojis.

The emojis were covering for the party my parents were already planning. Janet and of course Luke are here, and so are Tracy, Wayne, Bret, and his entire family, and my friends Savannah and Charlotte, and it's cool that they finally get to meet.

They didn't go over the top, but it's a fun-filled night that Luke really enjoys. Me, not so much. I don't really enjoy all the attention. Luke manages all the fame and everything that goes with it much better than me. We're both inundated with questions about next steps. We relay what we can, but we've already signed a non-disclosure agreement, and we can't talk about the live show other than where it will be and when.

After everyone leaves, I'm helping Mom clean up the kitchen.

Mom asks, "You mentioned promo. Does that start right away?"

"The next few weeks. I thought I'd call up Tracy if there's anything I need while you and Dad are away on tour?"

Mom's eyes light up. "Of course, she'll take care of anything like that.

She'd be thrilled."

I continue, "We have to be very careful with our social media, too, so I'm not sure what we can do."

"Again, check with Tracy if you have questions about posts. If you or Luke need help with anything for promo, let her help. That's her job."

My voice takes on this odd, high pitch, "This is freaking me out, Mom. I don't know if I'm up for this."

Mom stops cleaning and gives me her full-on mom look. "Aria Marie ... you're my daughter and you've got this. Okay? No matter what happens or what people will say, and believe me, you'll get some ugly comments, blow it off. That's not real. What's real is what you have here, and what you have with Luke. Remember that, okay?"

"Yep. I will." I walk over and give her a quick hug, and as I do I say, "You remember that too, okay?"

Mom laughs knowing exactly what I mean. She's about to go back out there in front of thousands of fans, and I know she's terrified inside.

"You got it, my sweet girl. Now help me finish this up so we can both get some beauty sleep ... at least one of us really needs it."

I smile as I continue helping Mom, lost in the thought that deep down, yes, I got what I want and am moving on, but what am I getting into?

Chapter 82 – Julia

I'm watching Raine throw our bags underneath the tour bus as I pull my body up the stairs to find the most comfortable seat I can, then I fling my body down hard. Finally, we're headed home after the third weekend of being back on the road. Granted, it's been a wonderful experience being out there performing again, and my band members are some of the best in town, which makes my job so easy. But this has been much harder than I remember. The lack of sleep as we travel overnight, bad coffee and not so great food, when I'm doing my best to stay as healthy as possible, has taken a toll. All this while trying to keep up with our daughter's crazed life back home.

For the past few weeks, Aria's done four public appearances promoting the contest with the other contestants. Most live promos have been local, but they did travel to Atlanta for an appearance. Thank God for Tracy, who's been with her while we've been gone, and of course she's had Luke. We've also relied on Bret to help them both.

Aria's show is this Wednesday, so I'll have a few days of downtime, then we have one more weekend with Wayne. Then we all leave for the music awards. I'm exhausted thinking about it.

Raine joins me on the bus, which thankfully we share alone as the band has their own. He can't miss the darts I'm throwing with my eyes. He grabs a drink from the small fridge and takes a seat across from me.

He answers, "I know. I don't remember it being like this, but a few more weeks and then you'll get a break. Then, luckily, Bret's tour is short."

I instantly soften seeing that he looks more tired than I do. "It's not your fault. I seriously don't remember it being like this." Then I catch myself, giving him a snide laugh before continuing. "Oh poor 'woe-is-me,'" I add, my hand going to my forehead with flourish, "I've got to sing on a few tour dates."

This makes Raine smile, but a dark look crosses his face. "That's funny, but I should have thought more about your health, Julia. Not smart on my part."

"Honey, I'm fine. And you're fine. We're just worried about our girl out there managing her new career on her own. That's not helping."

Raine relaxes against the back of his seat. "True, but she's got Tracy, and we'll be back this week to help."

"Wish we would have been there for the Atlanta thing … some of the comments on her social media pages about what she was wearing were terrible."

Raine's tone gets serious, "Please quit paying attention to that crap. It'll all blow over soon enough."

I tease, "But did you catch what they're saying about our show? It's been mostly good, so when it's good, it's not crap. Just crap when they say something negative about our daughter?"

Raine rolls his eyes. "Okay. Okay. I get it. I'll check in and let her know we'll be home early in the morning."

I lean against the pillows and close my eyes. Thank God we're headed home and I can go take care of my baby girl.

Chapter 83 – Aria

This crap has been hard, harder than I ever imagined. But Trent has been a blessing. Right now, we're finishing up our staging with him. We've changed our song up a bit. We're going to sit center stage, and we'll have a small string trio that'll join us on the second verse and will build up to the bridge section. We've added another acoustic guitar player, which takes some of the pressure off our live performance, at least for me.

Tomorrow's the big day. Everyone can feel the tension building with all the promo we've done. Tracy's been a huge help, but having Bret along has been a game changer. I've learned a lot from my parents, but Bret has major star power, and he's tutored us on answering media questions. I mentioned it to Mom, but it was a great idea to have him help us, and Stacia too.

We just ran through the lighting with our wardrobe. There's a ton of fringe on my jacket and pants, and we're both wearing cowboy hats. I just hope we're comfortable on stage. It'll show if we're not. We're wearing a light tan suede mixed with dark brown and black. Trent says the lighting glows gold and works with the title of our song, "Color of Love." They'll run a constant stream of love scenes behind us. I trust Trent at this point.

We're about to leave for the day when Luke gets a call. He steps aside to take it. He's unusually quiet as we walk out to our vehicles.

I try to get him to talk. "Hon, what's up?"

Luke gives me an unconvincing grin with his reply, "It's nothing really. Just thinking about tomorrow's show."

"Are you good with what Trent's done with your song?"

He hesitates before he replies, "Oh yeah, he's been great … I wish I could tell you about it."

Of course he can't. He's been working on that song alone with Trent, and I have no idea what they'll do with it.

I continue to pry, "Is there something going on with your mom? Is that it?"

Luke shakes his head at me and tries to convince me with his words, "Really, Reez, everything's fine. Just a lot on my mind." He pulls me against him, kissing the side of my head. "Just like you, I get a little nervous too," he says with a teasing smirk.

"Yeah, but you never fear losing your lunch."

"True … I'm not a vomiter."

I give him a lighthearted punch on the arm. We reach our vehicles and he gets me loaded up before he leans up, giving me the sweetest kiss goodbye.

"Try to get some rest … I'm sure you won't, but please do try."

"I will. I'll text you later."

Luke nods and shuts my door before he heads over to his truck. When he loads up he gives me a wave before I pull out and onto the road. I'm still not convinced. He's unsettled from that call and trying his best to hide it.

A dark thought crosses my mind that something is seriously wrong and he's not telling me the truth. With everything that's happened with my mom and the thought of losing her, and now not knowing what's going on with Luke, I want to crawl into a room and hide for a while. Will anything ever be good and normal? Why do things always seem to be going off a cliff?

Chapter 84 – Luke

Thrown for a loop is an understatement. When I heard Principal Fieldstone's voice on the line, asking to speak with me, I knew it was about the show and something serious, but what is it? There's no way I was going to tell Aria. No. Way. I pull out heading toward the school. I'm sure there will only be a few people left by the time I get there. This really isn't good.

I think about punching the wall as I leave this little impromptu meeting, but rationality takes over and I don't want to hurt my hand. It was just me and Principal Fieldstone. He told me they've had an anonymous complaint about letting me perform two songs. It's too late to pick another writer and song. He says the judges will let me perform both songs tomorrow, but I'll have to withdraw one song, and they'll make an announcement tomorrow at the end of the show. If I withdraw my song with Aria, that eliminates us both as she can't submit the song on her own. So, I have to withdraw my solo song, which means the world to me.

I run my hands through my hair as I lean my forearms against my steering wheel, staring toward the school. Why would someone wait until now to complain? I want to talk to someone about this, but I don't want Aria or her parents to find out, especially her dad, even though he'd be the best person to talk to. Then I think about Bret. Although I don't know him that well, I can trust him with this.

I find Bret's number in my phone, and he picks up right away. I explain that I need to talk to someone about a business decision, and we decide to meet at a diner near his house. I call Mom, letting her know I won't make it for dinner with a little white lie that rehearsals are going late. Then I head to the location Bret gave me. I hope I'm making the right decision. If I drop my song with Aria, she'll never forgive me, like ever. This sucks. I wanted a fair competition, and this isn't it.

Bret's truck is at the diner when I pull up. When I step inside, he's at a booth in the back.

"What's up, man?" he says, standing to shake my hand. Even though I'm a tall guy, Bret's taller. I'm always intimidated around him. He oozes country music star.

I reply, "Thanks for meeting me on such a short notice." Bret nods as a server interrupts us. I order a soft drink and fries. Bret orders a burger and fries to go with his soda.

Bret cut to the chase, "I'd expect that you'd go to Raine with anything to do with business, so this tells me you can't talk to him or Aria about this?"

I nod, then pause before spilling it. "Exactly. Well ... someone filed a complaint about me having two songs in the contest. So, I have to pick one. I can sing both tomorrow, since they don't want to mess up the show's production, but afterward, I've got to withdraw as a writer from one."

Bret's incredulous. "Seriously? Who would complain about such a thing? And why now?"

"I have no idea, but the whole thing doesn't seem fair. Not at all." Bret nods in agreement as I continue, "But it seems there's nothing I can do about it. So, I know I've got to drop my solo song and stay in the contest with Aria. It's the right thing to do."

Bret nods along before he replies, "But how would Aria feel if you did that? That you dropped your solo song for the one you wrote together. Aria told me how great your song is, Luke."

"I didn't think about that ... I think she'd get it. Plus, it's not like I couldn't do something else with it. I can't let Aria down, Bret. There's no way I could do that."

"I think you have your answer."

Our food arrives. I'm eyeing Bret's hamburger and he laughs. He motions to the server, "I think this young man is second guessing his choice."

I give an embarrassing nod. "Yeah, I think I'll take one of those," I say pointing at Bret's plate.

As we continue our meal making small talk, I'm good with what I'll do, but there's a lingering tightness in my chest. Something about this whole situation doesn't sit right with me. Not at all. Who in the world would call to complain about me singing two songs, and why?

Chapter 85 – Raine

As students who are performing today, Aria and Luke get the day off from school. A makeup team was at the house earlier, along with Tracy, and now we're pulling up into the basement parking at the arena. Luke and his mom are following us, and Tracy, Bret, and Wayne are also driving behind us, our own small entourage.

Aria, of course, is like a deer in headlights, but now that we're here for the show, she's starting to snap out of it. Luke's been unusually quiet. He's always a bit jubilant, but he's unusually subdued. Aria said I'm going to be blown away by his performance, so I'm betting it's a case of nerves.

The producers put each of the three contestants in their own greenrooms. Wayne and Bret are hanging out in the main backstage area but pop their heads into Luke and Aria's rooms from time to time, after Aria changes, of course. Trent also stops by with some encouraging words.

The order of performances will be Luke and Aria's song, then Stacia's song, followed by Luke at the end. When it's time for us to take our seats, I give our baby girl a quick hug, trying not to mess up her face, and step outside to give her a moment with her mother, then we make a quick stop by Luke's room to wish him luck. He gives us both an encouraging smile, but it doesn't reach his eyes. Maybe it is nerves, but now I'm leaning toward something being wrong.

They've seated us in the front row, with Julia on the end near the main aisle, for the cameras. Janet, and people I assume are Stacia's family, are sitting in the same row. Bret and Wayne and their families are sitting directly behind us. Tracy stayed behind in the greenroom with Reezie.

When the lights go down, I take Julia's hand and give it a tight squeeze. The arena is full. I didn't know what to expect for a show for a bunch of unknown songwriters, but they've done an excellent job of promoting it. As the stage lights go up, I'm surprised when an old friend of ours, and former *Next Real Star* host, Katy Reynolds, walks out to do hosting duties. Except for a few lines of gray in her jet-black hair, Katy looks as amazing as she did all those years ago. The show is taped live to air later this week, so there will be breaks and stops between performances. They tape Katy's opening segment and then they take a brief break to prep for the judges' opening.

This will be a long morning. I told Aria and Luke not to expect a real live show. Aria rolled her eyes at me and reminded me that the production team walked them through the entire day. Reez also let me know that the judges will deliberate, and then they'll tape it as they announce a winner at the very end.

The lights come back up, and the taping begins again with announcing each judge, beginning with Trent Austin, followed by the other two judges, and then finally Dr. Smith is named as the consultant. *Interesting.* So, this is the evil Dr. Smith. I look at my wife, and we exchange a knowing glance. It's odd that she's a consultant and not an actual judge. I hope this works out in our favor. They film the judges taking their seats and then continue through a brief segment of what each judge expects from the winning song and how it should fit with the movie. Then it's time for another break.

Julia's hand in mine is slightly wet, so I pull our hands apart and wipe mine off as she winces.

I give her an encouraging smile, "They're first, so we'll get this out of the way, honey."

Julia nods at me, "And I'm thankful ... for her and for me. It sucks being on this end."

Just then I feel a slap on my back from Bret as he leans forward and murmurs in my ear. "She's up next, big guy."

I give Bret a scowl, "Yeah, no shit. Wait until it's your daughter doing something like this and then you'll know exactly how this feels."

Bret sits back in his chair with a mischievous grin at our noticeable misery.

Then the lights flash in warning that we're getting ready to go again.

Katy walks back out to a small side stage. They've covered the center stage with a flowing curtain, but there's movement behind it. I wrap my arm around Julia's shoulder as she leans in. I look into her eyes and they're glistening. We're both so proud of our daughter. Terrified and proud.

It's a blur as they announce Luke and Aria's names and the curtain swoops up to a glowing set. They're seated center stage, slightly facing each other with a small string trio of a violin, cello, and stand-up bass off to their side. The setting is intimate, but homey. When they start playing "Color of Love" with the background images playing behind them, it fits together perfectly. Trent really is good at this. When the strings join in through to the end of the song, my heart soars. Aria's voice mixed with Luke's is perfection—like they're meant to sing together. People are listening intently. I glance at the judges. They've heard the song before too, but they're listening with rapt attention. As the song builds to the end, the strings stop, and then it's just Luke singing with Aria joining in, basically singing a cappella with one acoustic guitar to the end. It's simply perfection.

They stop and the crowd roars their appreciation. Julia and I, along with our small group, all stand immediately. Janet nudges Julia, who helps her stand. "Well done, baby girl," I mutter under my breath as they both stand with their guitars in hand taking in the applause. Then the curtain drops. We won't get any words from the judges until the very end.

After a short break, next up is Stacia Overton with her song "At First Glance." Stacia steps out between a break in the curtains center stage in a flowing purple gown singing with a full band behind her. Her set is equally as well produced as Aria's was and her song is well written. She's also an exceptionally good singer. She'll be tough to beat. Julia squeezes my hand when she's finished, thinking the same things I am. This will not be easy.

Then the last break. They take a bit more time as they tear down Stacia's set and we have a bit more time to stretch our legs. Finally, the lights dim and we're ready for Luke's solo song. All I know is the title, which Luke told me a few days ago.

After he's announced, the lights dim, and a solo spot appears center stage on Luke. He's standing alone with his guitar. There's no fancy production and it doesn't seem like he's going to have any other players. Before he begins, Luke says, "This is for my mom … and for my dad."

Then he begins, opening with simple chords, but it's the way that he holds himself and sings … and those lyrics. I've never heard this song before; he didn't play it for me and by far, it's the best work he's ever done. His voice is strong and true, and he's holding the crowd in his hands—just him and his guitar. There are few people who can do this and do it well. I completely get why Aria said he has "it," and she's right.

During the song's bridge, we get to see his guitar playing as he skillfully runs through some licks that elicit a nudge in my back from Bret. I glance back at him and Wayne, and you can tell that they're both impressed. When he gets to the last chorus, his voice rings out strong to the end with the last strum of the guitar. He's holding the entire room in his hands. The crowd's reaction is instant and in unison. He's clearly the winner; his song and performance are outstanding. Now I completely understand what Aria meant. She could see it.

Of course, we're all standing, and I run over to Janet to help her up as we all give Luke the honor he deserves. He takes it all in as sweat runs off his face and he smiles and waves, but there's still something off about his reaction. Like he doesn't believe it or something.

Now we'll have to wait for the results. The judges walk up the stairs and off the stage. I scowl at Dr. Smith as she trails behind. Julia's watching her too.

"Something's not right about her, I can feel it," Julia says, and I nod at her.

I reply, "Yeah, Aria told me about her. I hope it doesn't impact these results."

Julia looks up at me and replies, "We shall see … we shall see."

Our little group makes small talk. We're all fretting about our kids backstage, wondering how they're doing, as we wait to find out who will win. But no matter what, win or lose, they were all amazing.

Chapter 86 – Aria

I don't remember a thing. Seriously. One minute we're sitting on the stage and the next, it was all over and we're standing up to applause. I should have tried to capture every moment in my brain, but it seemed so out of body, like I was outside of myself. Maybe it was adrenaline. Who knows, but at least it's over.

After Stacia and Luke have performed, we're all waiting in the back for the judges to deliberate on their decision. They pulled Luke aside for a moment and a knowing glance passed between me and Stacia like "yeah, he won, he was amazing." When Luke came back and joined us, he had an odd look on his face to match his unusual quietness.

I reach out and tenderly take his hand. "I know you can't tell us anything, but we know, everyone knows, Luke." But Luke's not biting, at least not in the way I thought he would.

"I don't know what you're talking about."

That's all I get, and it's the way he says it, like he's furious or something. I'm totally confused. Didn't they tell him he's won?

I speak softly, looking directly at him. "Luke, what is it? Did something happen?"

He looks at me, shakes his head, and then walks away to his greenroom muttering something about wanting to leave. Stubborn me follows.

He opens the door, and my hands go up to stop it before it has a chance to close it on me.

"Seriously, Luke. What happened in there?"

He walks over to his things but pauses and looks at me. His eyes are fierce, not angry, but frustrated. "I can't say anything, Aria. I'll tell you later … after …I can't. It will be explained soon enough."

Just then a stagehand reaches us, telling us we're about to go back to taping and we need to be ready by the side of the stage. All three of us will go out on the stage when they announce the winner.

I wait for Luke as he walks back to me, but his gorgeous brown eyes won't meet mine. He does take my hand though and we head over to the side of the stage just as the judges walk out of their room. My eyes catch Trent's, and he gives me a serious look that I can't decipher. What has happened?

The lights come back up, and they announce Katy. She starts to read from the teleprompter as one by one we're invited back out onto the stage.

The words that come out of the mouth of the show's host stop the room. They've eliminated one song due to a formal complaint of having one writer with two songs and it was deemed by the majority of judges as not compliant. My mind is reeling. What in the? My eyes dart to Luke and he's staring straight ahead as they announce that the only two songs eligible are Stacia's song and our co-written song. They eliminated Luke's solo song. There's a loud, angry reaction from the crowd, boos echoing throughout the arena. Luke's the obvious winner and it's not fair for the judges to remove his song. My eyes immediately scan to Dr. Smith. You can see her smirk for miles. Of course. She must have something to do with this.

I search the crowd for my family and Janet, but I can't find them. When the boos finally die down, they proceed to announce the winner: Stacia's song "At First Glance."

The crowd reacts to Stacia's win with polite applause, but they clearly aren't over Luke getting the shaft. Then it hits me hard. Our song came in last.

Chapter 87 – Julia

I swear steam is coming out of my ears. I've been through some shady crap, but this takes the cake. Our group stands stunned, like what the heck just happened? I almost walked over to Trent during the live taping and pulled him out of his chair.

When the little lights on the video cameras go black, I scamper up and make my way over to Trent. Of course, Raine's a step behind me. We're standing in front of Trent before he knows what hit him.

"What the hell, Trent? You don't eliminate a song like that ... at the end of a show after the performances?" Trent's sitting there staring at us in silence as his security team takes a step toward the table. Trent waves them off.

"Julia, Raine, let's go in the back and I'll explain what happened."

Raine's booming voice breaks in, "No, you owe us an explanation, right here and now, in front of everyone."

From the corner of my eye, I catch the other two judges trying to sneak away from the table, but Raine won't have it.

Raine bellows, "Stop! You two. Stop right there! You can't snake your way out of this. This was shady as heck, and now it's going to be on national television. This is not cool. Not cool at all!"

By now, our little entourage has encircled the table with several angry faces staring at them. They'll have to do something.

One of the other judges shrugs his shoulders as if to say they didn't have a choice. "Please, can we take this in back and talk about it? Let's not do this here."

He proceeds to walk toward the back, and we all follow, and I mean all of us, follow along. I don't think the producers realize what they've done. When we get in the back, Aria's standing off to the side looking as stunned as we are, while Luke's head is down, not looking our way. But they see all of us with the show's judges and Aria's eyes grow wide.

We walk into their deliberation room, which is barely big enough for four people let alone the swarm filling up the small space. When I see Dr. Smith start to join us, I react.

"NO! Not you. We need to meet with the judges and you're some kind of consultant. Principal Fieldstone is okay, but not YOU!" Dr. Smith gives me a pissed off scowl, but I don't care. My gut says this is on her. I don't know why or how, but I'd bet money that she has something to do with this.

When we get inside, I slam the door and take over. "Okay, tell us what happened. Who filed a complaint and how did you make this decision?"

All eyes go to Principal Fieldstone. At first, we get hems and haws, before Raine makes him spit out exactly what happened. He got an anonymous call at the school, which was a complaint that Luke had two songs in the final, and the caller didn't think it was fair. He brought the complaint up with the show's consultant, Dr. Smith, who agreed. She suggested they ask Luke to choose one song. When asked, he chose the song he'd written with Aria. When presented with the situation, the judges agreed that they'd let all three songs air on the show, and then they would make the decision about the winner at the end, without Luke's solo song being eligible to win. They didn't think it was fair to remove any song from the performance.

Raine spits out, "Do you know how utterly unprofessional this is? Trent, seriously, I expect more from you!"

"I'm sorry, Raine and Julia, and to you, too, Janet," he says, gesturing toward Luke's mom, sitting in a chair in the crowded room. "I didn't want this at all. I didn't want to remove any song, for any reason. It was a majority vote and I voted against this. In fact, because of how this went down, I've withdrawn from this project. I was contractually obligated to finish the show, but I won't have anything further to do with this movie. I resigned today."

I'm sickened by all of it. Some anonymous call removed Luke's song and the whole thing stinks to high heaven. Now that we've heard all three songs, Luke's solo song is clearly a standout. This entire contest is one big sham. But now that I know Trent's resigning from the project, it's better that Luke and Aria didn't win, not with unscrupulous producers like these. I don't have to say anything because Raine's reading my mind.

"Well, it's a good thing Luke didn't win, and Aria, too. We don't want them affiliated with this project after this show." Raine looks at Principal Fieldstone, "First, I'm launching an investigation into your anonymous caller. We'll find them. Almost no one uses a landline these days and cell phones are traceable. Second, if Stacia wants to leave the project too, I'll offer her a song deal. I'm offering one to all the contestants and their songs. Hopefully, no one will want to work on your movie after this. What a joke."

He looks at our group, and we all move to leave together, but Raine stops and speaks to Trent. "Trent, are you in or out?"

"In with you, of course."

"Good."

Then we all hightail it out of the room, leaving the two judges and Principal Fieldstone stunned. As I walk past Dr. Smith, the look on my face lets her know that she's done. For the first time, the smirk has disappeared from her face, and she looks terrified.

I gesture to Luke and Aria, "Get your things. We're out of here."

Raine walks over to Stacia's greenroom door and gives it a rap before she calls out to enter. He opens the door wide. She's inside celebrating with friends and family. Raine walks in and obviously stuns the small group with his words. A huge grin overtakes Stacia's face as she nods at him.

He walks out as I ask, "What did she say?"

"She'll think about it, but she wants to call me tomorrow. Who knows, we may end up with our own record label after this, Jules. It's about time I did that anyway."

A broad smile fills my face as I gaze at my husband. God, how I love this man.

Chapter 88 – Luke

There's a small crowd filling up the Wagners' kitchen. We've ordered pizza and everyone is relaxing after what was one of the strangest days ever. I've been trying to cheer up Aria for hours. Having our song lose to Stacia was a gut punch for her. I've been trying to convince her that Stacia's song was better suited for the movie and that's why it won, and I've almost got her convinced. Luckily, her mom is saying the same thing, that it wasn't the strength of the song or our performance, but what was right for the project.

When Raine mentioned a song deal for "Coming Home," I was over the moon. I'll run everything by a lawyer first, but when he mentioned starting his own label, my head starting spinning. I'm still in high school. I've been standing at the kitchen bar, picking Bret's brain on what I should do and thanking him for keeping our conversation about my song decision a secret. Of course, Bret completely trusts Raine and has known him for years, but he's also objective. He mentioned that after the show airs, I'll get other offers and I may want to wait. But would I trust anyone else the way I trust the Wagner family? I doubt it.

When the conversation turns to the family's upcoming awards appearance, that's when the night really gets weird.

Raine asks me, "You know, Luke, you need to join us on the awards show coming up. We're going to join Wayne singing harmony, but what do you say, Wayne? Need another guitar player?"

Before I can object, Wayne responds with a nod, "Sounds good, and you can sing, too, so sounds like a plan."

My mom beams, while it's my turn to vomit. Playing guitar and singing background for Wayne Carson was not on my bingo card. My head spins to Aria, who's sitting at the table with Tracy, and she's laughing at me, like "welcome to my world."

The madness continues as Raine says enthusiastically, "You know, Luke, we're out with Wayne this weekend, why don't you come along for that, too, and you can get some practice in. Heck, we'll all go! We have room on our bus."

Julia chimes in, "Of course! It'd be great for you and Aria to come along; we could use the company."

I can't get any words in before my mom answers for me. "That's a great idea, Luke!"

I just shrug my shoulders, and Aria laughs as she adds dryly, "It's decided. One big, happy family band. Just what Dad always wanted."

We leave that Friday and drive all night to get to the venue in Florida. Now, this is alright. Two sun-filled days in warmer weather, playing guitar, and singing some back-up for one of the biggest stars in country music, and I get to hang out with Aria. This was the first time I've traveled all night on a tour bus. I didn't sleep, of course, but they said I'll get the hang of it. We're doing a show near Orlando Saturday night, then we have one outside of Tampa on Sunday. Then we'll head back to Nashville, driving all night. I've been frantically listening to Wayne's songs trying to learn all the acoustic guitar parts.

Next week is the real fun. Mom has already cleared it with school to get me out on Wednesday through Friday for the awards show in Texas. We were going to fly, but now we're going to take the bus and Mom's going to come too. Since the whole song contest debacle, Principal Fieldstone's walking on eggshells around the Wagner family and me too. Raine did have investigators go to the school and they have a lead on the anonymous caller. We'll see what happens with that.

After the show aired last week, I got a few calls from labels in Nashville, and I did meet with two of them. Bret offered to go with me, so they didn't treat me like a novice. It was good for me to meet with them and hear what they thought. One offered me a development deal, and another made me a publishing offer. After that, I talked everything over with Raine, and he exceeded everything out there. I'll be his first flagship artist on his new label, Reezie Records, named after Aria, of course.

Right now, I really can't believe my life. After the show aired and they eliminated my song, the show dealt with a brutal response. I gained at least five hundred thousand followers on one social media platform alone. I don't post much, but Tracy helps me with a schedule and content, and once the contract is officially signed, I'll do more.

We're heading back to Nashville late Sunday when I finally have a moment with Aria. Her parents are sleeping in the back and we're up front watching television. Lute and Lyre came along too, and they're sleeping at our feet.

Aria's leaning against me, her head resting against my chest as we're stretched out with some mindless movie playing.

I get up the nerve to ask her, "So, are you sure you're okay with me signing a deal with your dad? You said you can't date his artists."

She responds but doesn't look at me. "Sure, I'm okay with it. But I'll break up with you the moment the contract is signed. Just so we're clear."

Aria says it so matter of fact, my breath catches. She peers back at me and laughs. "No, silly, I won't break up with you. I wanted to see your face and it's priceless."

I squeeze her tight and since she's between my arms, I tickle her while she's captive.

"Stop it!" she squeals. "You're … going … to wake … them up!"

"Good! I hope you get in trouble." I stop, smirking at her. This girl is going to drive me crazy in the best way possible. She's such a smart ass and I love it.

She looks at me, "Seriously though, if Dad is okay with it, then I'm not going to worry about it. He's making an offer to *my* boyfriend."

I smile. "Ah … I get it. It's all his fault."

"Exactly. Did he mention when you'll start recording your stuff?"

I shake my head. "No, not yet, but he mentioned that he's recording our song. That's one of the first songs he wants to do."

"Hmm ... well that's good, since I'm such a loser and all." A flicker of disappointment crosses her face, but she looks like she's kidding.

"Oh my gosh! Just stop it. You are not. That makes me a loser too, and I am not a loser."

Aria rolls around so she's facing me, lying across my midsection, and the lower part of my body starts to stir. She smiles and crawls up so that her face is near mine, laying her body fully on top of me as I wrap my arms around her tight.

I look at her with all seriousness, "If your parents walk out right now, I'm a dead man."

She leans in to kiss me and says, "I don't care."

And then she gives me the sweetest kiss that quickly turns into something deep and filled with so much lust that I must push her up and away from me fast. This girl drives me crazy.

"Dang it, Aria. We're seriously going to get into trouble." She looks disappointed, so I sit up and pull her down into my lap as my hand goes up to her face. And then I go there. "You know that I love you, right?"

Those gorgeous green eyes of hers meld with mine as she nods, and I lean in to give her a tender kiss. I do love this girl, more than I love anything on this earth. She's my light and everything I've ever wanted, but if right now she gets me killed by her father, I'll never forgive her.

She slides down and rests her head in the crook of my neck and sighs, and then she softly says, "I love you too, Luke. I fell in love with you that first day I slammed into you at the library. Who knew you were such a klutz."

I can't help it, but a chuckle starts deep in my throat and soon we're both laughing as I try to convince her that she's the klutzy one. Moments later, her mom's voice comes from the back room.

"Do we have to separate you two?" she says sternly but there's a lightness to her voice.

I quickly reply, "No, ma'am."

"Good. I think it's time for you two to go to bed."

Yes, ma'am."

"And please call me Julia."

"Yes, ma'am."

"Oh, good night!" her mom says with exasperation.

We both laugh and then we get ready for bed and climb into our respective bunks as quietly as possible, but Aria drops her hand over the edge of her bunk above me. I grasp it as we fall asleep holding hands.

Chapter 89 – Julia

As we're walking on the red carpet, I look at my tall, handsomely dressed husband and smile. Of course, when asked, he won't have a clue what designer he's wearing. He never does. So, I help him out. I'm wearing one of my favorite designers, Mitchell Clark, along with some major bling Raine purchased for the occasion. He got a glimpse of the outfit I picked, and he went out and bought a necklace and earrings to match. I tried to convince him that I could borrow something from a designer and credit them, but he wouldn't have it. Today is different though, we have Aria and Luke in tow and they're getting just as much, if not more attention, and I'm glad for the diversion.

Aria is wearing a shorter green dress and matching knee-high boots. Luke is wearing black with a hint of green to match, and they look adorable. I wish Raine would coordinate with me like that, but still, he looks dashing in a black suit with a black matching tie and a red handkerchief. The spot of color works. I opted for a black pantsuit with brown fringe to match the highlights in my hair.

We make our way down the carpet, and of course they ask about my song, but Raine gets hammered about his new label, signing Luke, and about working with the kids on their songs. Stacia continued working with the movie project like she agreed, but she's kept in touch with Raine, so who knows what will happen down the road? Trent's agreed to join us on projects; not exclusively, but when people found out he quit the movie, everyone knew something was amiss.

Wayne will perform "He'll Stay" about a third of the way through the show and then they'll announce the Song of the Year winner. We all head to our seats. We're seated a good four rows from the front, and not in direct view of cameras tonight, thank goodness. After the show opens and they get through a couple of performances, we make our way to the back to change. For the performance with Wayne, we'll all wear black to match his band.

When they announce Wayne and that we're all singing with him, the air in the arena becomes even more electric. It's been years since we've performed in front of our peers and the warmth is palpable. Aria and I stand to the side of Wayne to sing back-up. Luke and Raine join the band behind us, both playing guitar. Raine takes the guitar solo on the bridge and when the song ends, we get a standing ovation from the crowd. Wayne gestures my way and I give a small bow acknowledging the response.

We walk off stage and wait. They announce one of the biggest country duos, who will announce the winner of Song of the Year. I'm standing on the side of the stage, holding Raine's hand. Aria and Luke are right behind me. When they get to my song, "He'll Stay," a camera pans in front of us and I give a small wave as I try to hold it together.

They announce, "And the winner is ..."

I'm holding my breath; Raine's hand on my shoulder tightens.

"Well, it's not a surprise to anyone in this room, or at home for that matter, the winner is Julia Tate, for 'He'll Stay.'"

My knees buckle as I'm engulfed in Raine's arms, and Aria and Luke swarm me in an impromptu group hug. They finally let me go and I lean up to Raine for a quick kiss as I whisper, "More than anything on this earth." A camera captures it all.

I head out onto the stage where they're waiting for me. Wayne walks out and joins me on stage. I ask him to say a few words first.

"When Raine called me about this song and I heard it, I knew I'd won the lottery. I can't thank them both enough for thinking of me, and Julia for writing such an amazing song—it's your best work yet, truly," he says and then moves away from the microphone. Now it's my turn. Uh-oh.

My hands visibly shake as I hold the award. I finally speak, "I've often thought about a moment like this, and then when it hits you, you realize, I got nothing." I hold up the award, "First, this thing weighs a ton!" There's a slight chuckle from the crowd. "Seriously though ... to everyone out there who sees this and wants to do this, this took me about thirty years. It's not easy. But I'm glad it wasn't easy, because writing songs and this work makes you stronger, and it's led me to some of the best moments in my life, from meeting and working with my amazingly gorgeous and generous husband, to having a daughter who makes me proud to be a mama and fills my days with so much joy, to being able to bring hope and love to people who may need those words when they're going through something. Music brings people together and I've been blessed by songs. To the artists who've recorded my songs and made them better, I thank you. And to anyone out there who's listened and liked a song, thank you from the bottom of my heart. That's the biggest compliment in the world, and it means everything. Thank you, and God bless."

END

Epilogue

Aria

I'm standing here trying to keep the light breakfast I ate from spraying all over the wood floor of the barn. There are more than two hundred guests waiting outside and it would not be amusing if I vomited all over my gown. Dad would never let me live it down.

My hands are not just trembling; they're visibly, violently shaking as I hold the bouquet of purple tulips in my hand. As I look down at the flowers in my hand, I pause. Instantly a sense of calm overwhelms me as I think about how my mom loves purple tulips. The music starts to play and soon it will be my turn to take long, scary steps out the door and down the long aisle to where I see my dad standing at the very end.

I glance back behind me, just in time to see my mom walk out of the small office we were using in the barn for our dressing room. She gives me one of her gorgeous grins, looking as calm and cool as ever, like this is no big deal to her. She places a shaky hand to her chest and takes a deep breath, letting me know she's as terrified as I am, and I let out a light laugh.

When Mom and Dad told me they wanted to renew their vows, I was ecstatic, but then Mom said she wanted me to be her maid of honor, and I truly didn't think about what that meant. Sure, now I can walk out and sing on any stage, but this is different. I might easily trip and fall in front of hundreds of people, and that will make it on everyone's social media. This seriously sucks.

It's my turn to start walking and I notice the grayish sky above. It's a cool spring day and there's a chance of rain. I take that as a good sign. With our family, you never know what you're gonna get. I lock my eyes on my dad's, and it helps as I slowly take leaden step after step. The blistering heat from all the eyes is on me, but I make it to the end of the narrow aisle, and spin around to catch my mother making her way toward us. I shift my eyes up to Dad and he's locked on her, a lone tear streaming down his face. It's all I can do not to lose it.

When her whole cancer nightmare began, I wasn't sure we'd be here. Mom still has her regular checkups and each time we hold our breath, but she's been cancer free and there have not been any other spots on her lungs or anywhere. Every day we count our blessings.

My eyes scan the crowd, and I catch Luke sitting in the second row with Janet, behind my Aunt Jody and other family, and of course Bret's family, Wayne Carson, and all the other celebrities are in attendance. Luke gives me a wink, and I send him a slight wink in return. Today will be a glorious day.

Luke and I finished high school, and now he's getting ready for his first big-time tour opening for Wayne Carson, after releasing his song "Coming Home" to country radio. We're still serious but taking it slowly, both deciding to save ourselves for marriage, and that's harder than it seems. I'm writing a ton and have even been working with Trent Austin, who decided to stay in Nashville for the time being. Trent's dating my former teacher Dr. Grace, and I'm sure that has a lot more to do with why he's still here in Nashville. He's not a total full-fledged partner with dad in Reezie Records, but they're almost there. I'm also continuing to study music production at a prestigious school in town.

A new artist on another label recorded the song I wrote with Luke, "Color of Love." Dad thought it was cool, and if he's good with it, then so are we. We've done a ton of promo to help support it and it almost broke the top twenty country charts. I'll take that as a good start. One of the best parts though is now that Luke is a signed performer with a hit song, he's been able to do more for Janet. So that part is wonderful; he can now help his mom just like he wanted.

I should mention, Dad finally found out who the anonymous caller was to Principal Fieldstone. It wasn't Dr. Smith, but her sister, so like we all suspected, Dr. Smith was involved. The school suspended Dr. Smith pending an investigation. During the investigation, somehow they found out Dr. Smith was an aspiring songwriter who had been submitting songs to publishers for years. She also had hundreds of searches of my parents, specifically my mom, and other songwriters on her computer, so this likely had a whole lot to do with jealousy that stemmed from her lack of a successful songwriting career. That jealousy was transposed onto me, and subsequently Luke. They got it out of her that she didn't want us to have the success that she didn't have. They eventually terminated her. Stacia published her song with the movie, but then the movie flopped. She's still writing, and Dad helps to get her songs out there. He's got a softer heart than people realize. Mom was right, things all happen the way they're supposed to, I guess.

I look down at Dad's feet and there's Lute and Lyre dressed up in bow ties, curled up on the ground. How in the world he got those things to stay on the dogs is a mystery. We all watch Mom make her way toward us, when it hits me how oddly amazing our family is. Even though it's been a wild and often turbulent ride, we're so blessed. I can't wait to see where music continues to take us.

He'll Stay

He'll Stay

Verse 1

Can you imagine
Six young kids and a stack of bills reaching to the sky
What's a man to do? No one to turn to
It's a brand-new game, struggling by himself
Does he walk away, or try to run?
Is it all too hard?
But a good man

Chorus

He didn't walk away, or try to run
With his back against the wall, he didn't fall or falter
Stood strong as stone
He could have left; it was oh so hard
But a good man ... he'll stay

Verse 2

Can you imagine
Sitting by her side, each and every night, is she gonna make it?
Such an endless fight, so many tests and scans
It's a heavy load he carries by himself
Does he walk away, or try to run
Is it all too hard?
But a good man

Verse 3

Can you imagine
Carrying a heavy cross for all of us, up the steepest slope
What's a son to do?
He was asked to give the greatest gift for all our souls to save
He could have walked away, or tried to run
It was oh so hard
But not this man

Chorus

He didn't walk away, or try to run
With his back against the wall, although he may have faltered
Stood strong as stone
He could have left it was oh so hard
But this man, he stayed
Cause a good man
He'll stay

Free to Roam

Free to Roam

© J. D. Williams/Benji Kushner 2000/2002

Verse

I'm starting to climb walls, baby, gasping breath and falling down
Running hands all over the ground, I can't seem to get it all
I'm trying desperately to pick up everything
Collect my soul scattered on the ground
Never know if it will be found, I can't seem to get it all

Pre-chorus

Sometimes you feel the good-hearted, oh honey, they have the most to fear
Constantly climbing upward scrape
Broken nails, broken everything

Chorus

I've been picking up pieces of my heart, that were gathering dust
I'm trying to tell you something, you're free to roam
Gather up your pretty promises, put them where they belong
I'm trying to tell you something, you're free to roam

Pre-chorus

Sometimes you feel the good-hearted, oh honey, they have the most to fear
Constantly climbing upward scrape

Broken nails, broken everything

Chorus

I've been picking up pieces of my heart, that were gathering dust
I'm trying to tell you something, you're free to roam
Gather up your pretty promises, put them where they belong
I'm trying to tell you something, you're free to roam

Tag

Free to, free to, free to roam

Pre-chorus

I'm letting you out the gate, I'm letting you out the gate
Got all the room you need
You're free to run and chase down everything
You're free to run and chase down everything
You can have it all, you can have it all

Chorus

I've been picking up pieces of my heart, that were gathering dust
I'm trying to tell you something, you're free to roam
Gather up your pretty promises, put them where they belong
I'm trying to tell you something, you're free to roam

Tag

Free to, free to, free to roam
Free to, free to, free to roam

Resources

Treatment for breast cancer, to include the stage, type, size, and location of a tumor results in complex treatments and options. For Julia's diagnosis and treatment in this book, I read through numerous articles and resources. I realize the path for each person is different and personal. I tried to relay this experience the best way that I could using these resources and from experiences shared with me from others. A resource list is included along with the grief resources I relied on in book two, *Born by Song*.

As I mentioned in the author's note and acknowledgment sections, breast cancer has likely touched everyone in some way. I tried to take care with this disease, and those directly impacted. My heart is with you. God bless.

Breast Cancer Diagnosis and Treatment

Molly Adams. "HER2 positive breast cancer: What it is, diagnosis and treatment." The University of Texas MD Anderson Cancer Center. Her2-positive-breast-cancer—what-it-is—diagnosis-and-treatment

Timothy Huzar. Medically reviewed by Faith Selnick, DNP, AOCNP. "Stage 3 breast cancer: Life expectancy and survival rates." Medical News Today online. June 11, 2024. Stage 3 breast cancer: Life expectancy and survival rates (medicalnewstoday.com)

"Chemotherapy Treatment Side Effects." The University of Texas MD Anderson Cancer Center. Chemotherapy Treatment Side Effects | MD Anderson Cancer Center

"Immunotherapy." The University of Texas MD Anderson Cancer Center. What is Immunotherapy? Know Before Treatment | MD Anderson Cancer Center

"HER-2 Positive Breast Cancer: Symptoms & Treatment." Medically reviewed. Last updated 08.28.23. Cleveland Clinic. HER2-Positive Breast Cancer: Symptoms & Treatment

Mayo Clinic Staff. "Breast cancer types: What your type means. Not all breast cancers are the same. Find out how healthcare professionals decide the breast cancer type and what it means." Oct. 31, 2024. 1998-2026 Mayo Foundation for Medical Education and Research (MFMER). Breast cancer types: What your type means - Mayo Clinic

Kendall K. Morgan. Medically reviewed by Melinda Ratini, MS, DO, on April 21, 2024. "HER-2 Negative Breast Cancer." WebMD online. What Is HER2-Negative Breast Cancer?

Mayo Clinic Staff. "Mastectomy." Dec. 23, 2025. Mastectomy - Mayo Clinic .

"Treatments for Locally Advanced Breast Cancer." Canadian Cancer Society. Last medical review: March 2024. Treatments for locally advanced breast cancer | Canadian Cancer Society

Colleen de Bellefonds. Medically Reviewed by Paul Boyce, MD on April 5, 2024. "What to Expect from a Lung Biopsy." WebMD online. Lung Biopsy: Types, Purpose, Procedure, Risks, and What To Expect

Julie Scott, MSN, ANP-BC, AOCNP. Learn more about where breast cancer could metastasize, to prepare you for conversations with your doctor. People magazine online. February 28, 2025. Where Does Breast Cancer Most Commonly Spread?

"HER2-Targeted Therapies for Early Breast Cancer." Susan G. Komen. 2026. Targeted Therapies for HER2-Positive Early Breast Cancer | Susan G. Komen®

Emotional Health Resources

Mayo Clinic Staff. "Cancer survivors: Managing your emotions after cancer treatment. Get to know the emotions that are common for cancer survivors and how to manage your feelings. Find out what's typical and what indicates you should consider getting help." Dec. 24, 2025. Cancer survivors: Managing your emotions after cancer treatment - Mayo Clinic

Angela Morrow, RN. "The Four Phases and Tasks of Grief." Updated on May 24, 2022. Medically reviewed by Isaac O. Opole, MD, PhD. Fact checked by Elaine Hinzey, RD. verywellhealth. https://www.verywellhealth.com/the-four-phases-and-tasks-of-grief-1132550

About J. D. Williams

After graduating from the University of NE – Lincoln, J. D. Williams toured with a pop cover band and as a songwriter and performer, worked with some of the most talented writers, producers, and managers in the music industry. She has been involved in movie and video production, and artist management. She is an award-winning writer and has had work printed in national publications.

Now living in Nashville, Tenn., she continues to write music, and her songs are featured in the Julia Tate Song Series of books.

For more information, go to **www.jdwilliamsbooks.com**

Follow on Facebook @jdwilliamsmusic

Follow on Instagram @jdwilliamsbooksofficial

Follow on Instagram @jdwilliamsmusicofficial

www.ingramcontent.com/pod-product-compliance
Lightning Source LLC
LaVergne TN
LVHW090551110826
845146LV00001B/99

* 9 7 9 8 9 9 4 8 8 5 9 0 1 *